KU-478-858

Game for Anything

Fee could see William's hand stroking Beatrice's bottom: long, smooth strokes intended to arouse, and arouse quickly. They fell on to the carpet and he discarded the rest of his clothes. Fee couldn't tear her eyes away. It was clear that Beatrice didn't have sex all that often and, as a result, she seemed torn between wanting it very badly and not wanting to seem a pushover. William's touch began to get rougher; Fee saw a red line appear where he drew his thumbnail across Beatrice's shoulder. She yelped. 'We'll have none of that,' said William. 'Fortunately, I know of a way to silence you. It's a favourite little number of mine. Sixty-nine.'

Other titles by the same author:

INTENSE BLUE

Game for Anything

LYN WOOD

BLACK
lace

Black Lace novels contain sexual fantasies.
In real life, make sure you practise safe sex.

First published in 2001 by
Black Lace
Thames Wharf Studios,
Rainville Road, London W6 9HA

Copyright © Lyn Wood 2001

The right of Lyn Wood to be identified as the Author of
this Work has been asserted by her in accordance with
the Copyright, Designs and Patents Act 1988.

Typeset by SetSystems Ltd, Saffron Walden, Essex
Printed and bound by Mackays of Chatham PLC

ISBN 0 352 33639 0

*All characters in this publication are fictitious and any
resemblance to real persons, living or dead, is purely
coincidental.*

This book is sold subject to the condition that it shall
not, by way of trade or otherwise, be lent, resold, hired
out or otherwise circulated without the publisher's
prior written consent in any form of binding or cover
other than that in which it is published and without a
similar condition including this condition being
imposed on the subsequent purchaser.

Chapter One

'Shh.' Fee put her hand over David's mouth, slid on top of him and fucked him slowly and deliberately, watching his face. The high cheekbones, the Grecian nose; her own private version of Michelangelo's *David*. She started to speed up, feeling the hardness of him inside her. His face tensed and his breathing became more irregular. I can play you like a flute, thought Fee, first one register, then another, hold this note, tongue that one . . . She slowed down again, and he made a little noise of frustration. Fee moved her hips in a circle, teasing him. He opened his mouth to say something, and she shook her head. 'Hush, David. You're not allowed to speak. Say anything and I'll stop.' He made a faint strangled sound in his throat, but otherwise he remained silent.

Why do you always let me take the initiative? thought Fee. Are you just lazy, or don't you have an imagination? How about a bit of real daring, dressing up and acting something out, or doing it in the garden with the trains passing by? But I'd have to spell it out in words of one syllable and then it wouldn't be your idea, it would be mine, and consequently pointless. Oh well. Seize the moment, and enjoy it for what it is.

She speeded up again, the mechanical action of his cock against her clit having the inevitable effect. After a minute

1

or two they both came, more or less together, although they weren't exactly setting the world on fire, thought Fee.

'Wow,' said David. 'That was nearly as good as Saturday's match.'

He made a joke. Things are looking up.

'That goal in injury time,' he went on, 'did you *see* it? The sweetest back-heel ever. Fucking magic.'

'You're serious, aren't you?' said Fee. 'You really do think football's better than sex.'

'But Arsenal won,' he said, as though that explained everything.

'*Men,*' said Fee's friend Rachel. 'It makes you want to give them up altogether.'

'It's more a question of finding the right one,' said Fee. 'One with an imagination.'

Rachel snorted, twiddled a lock of fiery Pre-Raphaelite hair round her finger, and poured herself another gin and tonic. 'And a healthy bank balance,' she said. Then she made a face. 'There aren't any right ones. Look what Oliver's just done to me.'

'What?'

'Left me in the lurch over this holiday.'

'What holiday?'

'A week-long house-party in some exclusive residence in Oxfordshire. Feather beds, candlelit dinners. *Bastard.*'

'Why don't you go on your own?'

Rachel made a face, her freckles bunching together for solidarity. 'I don't know anyone. They're some group Oliver meets up with from time to time.' Then she tilted her head and looked at Fee, and a thoughtful expression came into her grey eyes. 'David's history, isn't he? So why don't *you* come instead?'

'Can't afford it.'

'Paid for.'

'I don't know if I could get time off at the florist's. When is it?'

2

'A week on Sunday. Lots of new people. Lots of new *men*.'

'I'll ask.'

And now here they were, taking their bags out of the boot of Rachel's car and staring wide-eyed at the building in front of them. It was set in extensive grounds, with little box hedges and statues scattered around. There was a swimming pool as well.

'Seventeenth century, some of it,' said Rachel. 'Charles II met one of his mistresses here, apparently.'

A tall man dressed in black opened the front door.

'Rachel Carpenter,' said Rachel assertively. She could play the pushy redhead to perfection.

The man looked at Fee. 'And you must be Taurus.'

'Gemini,' said Fee, slightly taken aback.

'Your pseudonym. Taurus.'

'Taurus is *Oliver's* pseudonym,' said Rachel. She smiled winningly. 'My boyfriend Oliver couldn't make it, so Fee's come instead.'

'Fiona Ferris,' interjected Fee.

'Fee's *your* pseudonym?'

What was this, a Dungeons and Dragons Week?

'I don't think I've ever seen one of yours,' said the man.

'One of my what?' asked Fee, with some trepidation.

'Crosswords.'

'We seem to be talking at cross-purposes here,' said Rachel. 'Oliver – Taurus to you – Oliver and I were booked on a week's holiday.'

'That's right. The word-games week.'

'*Word games?*'

'Scrabble, crosswords, quizzes, treasure hunt.'

Rachel gave Fee an old-fashioned look and said, 'I knew a week's unbridled luxury was too good to be true.' She turned back to the man. 'I thought it was going to be crystal glasses and champagne and roast venison and quails' eggs.'

He smiled. 'It is. Drinks at six and dinner at seven. Oh,

3

-and you need to surrender any mobile phones or laptops. Not allowed outside help.'

Rachel handed him her phone and he gave her a receipt. 'And you are?'

'Gavin Smythe, the master of ceremonies. And I must say what a delight it is to welcome two such beautiful young ladies to our gathering.' There was a mischievous glint in his eye that made Fee wonder what youth and beauty had to do with crosswords.

'I couldn't do a cryptic crossword to save my life,' said Fee, hanging her favourite dress in the cavernous wardrobe.

'I've never even tried,' said Rachel. 'Oh well. It's a fabulous place though, isn't it? Let's go and mingle.'

'I'm not at all sure about this.' Fee smoothed her straight black bob into place, and felt like a fraud. She had a heart-shaped face with a turned-up nose that gave her a pixie-ish look if she wasn't careful. The slanting amber eyes didn't help either.

Rachel smiled encouragingly. 'You look great.'

They made their way down the oak-panelled staircase and into one of the reception rooms. There were Persian rugs on the floor and chandeliers hanging from the ornate plaster ceiling. A maid was handing out glasses of champagne from a silver tray. 'I don't think it's going to be *too* tortuous,' said Rachel, tossing back her mass of auburn hair and taking a canapé. There were about forty people in the room all told – a surprisingly varied mix of men and women, from a girl with a diamond nose-stud and a tattoo of a snake on her shoulder to an elderly man with a handlebar moustache.

'Oh, look,' said Rachel under her breath. 'Over there, by the window.'

Fee looked. Two men: one of them tall and dark, with a mouth like a Cupid's bow and finely arched eyebrows. The other was shorter and more rugged: vigorous brown hair that refused to lie flat, craggy features and bright blue eyes that really sparkled when he smiled. Hang on, he was smiling at *her*. Fee returned the smile briefly, feeling as though she'd been caught out somehow.

'Not such a washout on the man front after all,' said Rachel.

'I bet they don't talk about football all the time, either.'

They sauntered into the dining room arm in arm, and found themselves seated next to a bald lexicographer and a man who said very little.

'Is this your first word-games week?' asked the lexicographer.

Fee nodded.

'I'm terribly prosopolethic,' he added. 'Never remember faces. You could have been at the last three and I'd never have remembered. Peverall Danby.'

He really was totally bald, not a hair anywhere on his head. I wonder if what they say is true, thought Fee, and bald men really are more virile. 'Peverall?' she queried.

'It's not a pseudonym, alas,' said Peverall. 'It's my real name. You're not phalacrespic, are you? Just tell me now, and get it over with.'

'No,' said Fee. Was he asking her if she was gay?

'That's a relief,' said Peverall. 'So what do you do?'

'I'm a florist.'

'How unusual.'

'Not especially,' said Fee, feeling she was missing something.

'Well, it is unusual here,' said Peverall. 'Most people have more letters after their names than they have letters *in* them.'

'I'm a translator,' said Rachel, coming to the rescue.

'Anything interesting? Mandinka or Potawatomi or Estonian?'

'French and Spanish.'

'Oh.' He looked disappointed.

Rachel turned to the other man. 'I didn't catch *your* name,' she said, popping an after-dinner mint into her mouth.

'Probably because I didn't give it,' said the man. He

was very unassuming; forty-ish, maybe, brown hair, hazel eyes. 'Swallow.'

'Is that a suggestion or a surname?' asked Rachel sweetly, rolling the mint from one side of her mouth to the other.

'Neither. It's a pseudonym.'

'You're another compiler then?'

'That's right.'

'I'm a solver,' said Peverall to Fee, running a hand across his bare shiny head. 'Analytical, not creative. I'm really looking forward to the treasure hunt. Two to a team: wouldn't it be felicitous if we were paired together?'

'Peverall!' called the girl with the tattoo. 'Graham here says an ecdysiast is a stripper, and I say it's an insect shedding its skin.' The man to her right smiled faintly. He had chips of ice for eyes and very short steel-grey hair, although he couldn't have been more than thirty-five.

Peverall excused himself and turned to the girl. 'You're both right, Scarab,' he said, and started an animated conversation about etymology and entomology.

Fee looked at Swallow. 'How do they pair people off?'

'The men get to choose the women,' said Swallow offhandedly. Fee felt righteous indignation rise within her, but before she could think of something suitably cutting to say Swallow added, 'And of course, now you've said you're not phalacrespic, you're Peverall's number one choice.'

'The majority of women aren't phalacrespic,' said Fee desperately.

'That's reassuring,' said Swallow, 'if somewhat surprising. I'm getting a little thin on top myself.'

Fee's brows furrowed in confusion.

'I think I'd better put you out of your misery,' said Swallow. 'Phalacrespia is an aversion to bald-headed men, not men in general.'

At the far end of the neighbouring table Gavin Smythe got to his feet and raised his hand for silence. 'Welcome to another word-games week,' he said. 'The treasure hunt is a little special this time. Not only do we have a more valuable prize than usual – donated by the late Alfred Hicks – but we also have a set of clues designed to tax the best of you, compiled by Hicks himself. Many of you will remember Alfred, who died last November, aged eighty-two. He was a setter of considerable skill, albeit with a somewhat idiosyncratic personality.'

There was a ripple of knowing laughter from one corner of the room.

'I don't know the exact location of the treasure,' Gavin went on. 'Nobody does. The secret died with Alfred – unless someone solves his puzzle. He left instructions with his solicitor, and the first batch of clues will arrive tomorrow. So, apart from wishing you all a pleasant evening's Scrabble, there's only one thing left on the agenda – sorting out the treasure hunt teams. I am going to pass round a hat. Take a slip of paper. You will be paired with the person who picks the same number as you. However, we'd like the couples to be mixed doubles, so there will be two rounds. Ladies first, of course.'

Fee glared at Swallow. He ignored her. You bastard, thought Fee, letting me think I was saddled with Peverall. I still could be, I suppose, but the odds are against it.

Gavin picked up a top hat and shook it. Then he walked between the rows of seats, and each woman took a slip of paper. Fee saw the craggy face with the bright blue eyes glance in her direction and smile. He held up his hand: the fingers were crossed. Rachel took a number out of the hat. 'Five,' she said.

Fee unfolded her slip of paper. 'Twenty.'

'Twelve.' Scarab, the girl with the tattoo.

When the hat was empty, Gavin refilled it and went round the men.

'Eight.' The man with the handlebar moustache.

'Sixteen.' Graham, the man with the gun-metal hair and the icy blue eyes.

Fee watched twinkly-smile undo his number. He

glanced at her, made a mock-tragic face and said sadly, 'Fifteen.'

A woman with a severe haircut and spectacles looked pleased. *Bugger*, thought Fee.

The man with the Cupid's bow mouth. 'Five.'

'*Five?*' Rachel was ecstatic.

He's just her sort, thought Fee. Tall, dark and a wee bit supercilious.

Peverall opened his slip, and his face flushed with disappointment. 'Twelve.'

Thank God, thought Fee. Scarab screwed her scrap of paper into a little ball of annoyance and threw it on the floor.

'Twenty,' said Swallow.

Fee stared at the two and the zero in her lap. She was going to be paired up with the second most unpleasant person she'd met.

'The name's Eric,' said Swallow. 'Eric Summers. I quite like treasure hunts as well, so you won't have to worry too much about the clues.'

Fee felt her anger bubble up like hot tar, the way it always did when she felt that someone was putting her down. 'That's an extremely arrogant thing to say.'

'I merely indicated that I would be happy to do the donkey-work. Your inference was an assumption. Scrabble?' He got to his feet. Rachel and her dishy partner did likewise and left the room together.

'No thanks,' said Fee icily. 'I'll see you in the morning.'

She went outside. There was a full moon, and somewhere in the distance an owl hooted softly. A whole week of word nerds, thought Fee. I don't think I can take it. I feel stupid and uneducated and left out already. It's all right for Rachel, she's got a degree; I hated exams.

She sat on the low brick wall, remembering her French oral. They'd been primed to prepare something on current affairs and they'd boned up on the vocabulary. And then the examiner asked Fee to describe her house. Everything went downhill after that.

Rachel had simply smiled sweetly and given a perfunctory description of her bedroom. Then she told the examiner how she liked to sit in her room and think about current affairs. She expanded on this at some length, and got an A.

'Scrabble not your cup of tea either?'

She turned round. Twinkly-smile was standing there, smiling that gorgeous smile.

'I haven't really played it very often.'

'Angus Macdonald.'

'Fee.'

'Felicity or Fiona?'

'Fiona. Fiona Ferris.'

He sat down next to her. 'My partner's called Beatrice. She doesn't appear to be capable of using words with less than three syllables, and she's got a sneer like a garrotte. I feel a bit of an impostor, to be honest.' He looked a bit sheepish. 'I only came along to keep William company.'

Fee giggled. 'I only came to keep Rachel company. I don't know my downs from my acrosses.'

There was a burst of laughter from the Scrabble room, and someone shouted 'Callipygian!'

Angus made a face. 'That was the formidable Beatrice. There are some very high-powered people here – your partner, for instance. Eric Summers.'

'What do you know about him?'

'He's one of the favourites to solve the treasure hunt. Don't be deceived by the laid-back indifference. They're all as competitive as hell under their well-mannered exteriors.'

'And Peverall?'

'Oh, he's good too – words are his career – but he's not as good as Summers.'

'What do *you* do?'

'I'm an antiques dealer. You?'

'Florist.'

'How delightfully down-to-earth.'

Fee looked at him to see if he was being sarcastic, but he wasn't. He was smiling at her again. The smile wasn't patronising or condescending; it was slightly conspiratorial – we're two of a kind, we are. She felt approved of, and it warmed her right the way through.

'You can have a brain without a PhD,' he said. 'And you can have a doctorate and be remarkably stupid. How many of that lot could restore a pew, or take a fuchsia cutting?'

There was another explosion of laughter from the Scrabble room. 'Angus,' said Fee, 'do you have any idea why some people sniggered when Gavin said that the treasure hunt setter had an idiosyncratic personality?'

'He was a bit of a lad, was Alfred Hicks,' said Angus. 'Or so William tells me. Had some very athletic pastimes for someone of his age.'

Fee raised an eyebrow.

'It could be quite an interesting treasure hunt,' said Angus. 'Particularly if Hicks wanted to get his own back on some of the stuffier members of the group. We get the clues tomorrow, at breakfast. Then we ferret around like stink until dinner at seven o'clock, and no one's allowed to leave the house after that.'

'Why not?'

'Because you'd have people gallivanting round the countryside at three in the morning, trying to solve things. They're all obsessives. And the only way to stop obsessives is to lock them in and hide the key. It'll be crosswords after dinner tomorrow evening. If you want to give it a miss, I could keep you company.'

'I might just take you up on that.'

Footsteps, and a dry little cough. Beatrice. 'So this is where you're hiding,' she said to Angus, ignoring Fee. 'Shouldn't you be brushing up your cruciverbal skills in the Scrabble room?'

'Oh do talk English, Beatrice,' said Angus.

'I was,' said Beatrice.

'I don't know what cruciverbal means either,' said Fee.

Beatrice gave Fee a sharp look. Then she laughed. It sounded like the rattle of a diamondback. 'I see Eric's drawn the short straw then,' she said.

Bitch, thought Fee.

Beatrice smiled. 'Come along, Angus, I want to see how many reference books we have between us.'

Angus made a wry face, stood up, and said goodnight. Fee reciprocated, and Beatrice merely nodded. Fee watched them walk back to the house. Beatrice was brisk and no-nonsense, but Angus moved with a loose, easy grace that Fee found very attractive. There was an understated sexual charge to him that made her wonder what would happen if she lit the touch-paper. He had a nice body – muscled arms, but not too muscled – and a stocky solidity that suggested a businesslike approach to anything physical. On the other hand, she wasn't convinced that he fancied her. He may simply have seen her as a kindred spirit in a depressingly cerebral setting.

Fee went back to her room. Rachel hadn't returned. For just a moment Fee felt a sense of déjà vu – Rachel was whooping it up somewhere, and Fee was stuck at home. Then she told herself not to be silly: the feeling of inferiority at dinner that had settled like dry ice in the pit of her stomach had almost gone, thanks to Angus – but not quite.

Her mother had never expected her to be any good at anything, and her father – well, he had been a nice man, a kind man, but never her champion. He seemed to have given up on life when Fee was quite small. He had died the previous year, and she missed his quiet acceptance of her. Fee had been his companion in under-achievement, a buffer against two high-powered sons and a domineering wife. She had followed his example from a sense of loyalty: don't put yourself in a position where you'll be tested, then you'll never be disappointed. And here she was, on a word-games week of all things, facing certain humiliation. She curled up in the big feather bed, and dreamed of dictionaries with teeth snapping at her heels and drawing blood.

Rachel must have come back at some point during the night, for she was there the next morning. 'Wake up,' said Fee, 'it's breakfast time.'

Rachel groaned and pulled the pillow over her head.

'Get up,' insisted Fee, 'it's important,' and she yanked the quilt off the bed.

'You're very keen on this treasure hunt all of a sudden,' said Rachel grumpily.

'Boring evening?'

'No, actually,' said Rachel, crawling out of bed as though standing upright was too demanding.

'You got pissed.'

'Only a tiddly bit. I played Scrabble with William.'

Fee snorted.

'Laugh all you like. It was wicked. We kept using the naughtiest words we could think of, and cheating like mad. There's one hell of a buzz about playing *real* word games with a man.'

Fee examined herself in the mirror, and wished her eyes didn't tilt upwards quite so much. The pixie-look was predominating this morning. She tried to negate it with some eye-liner, but it only made matters worse. She washed it off again. Her days as a Brownie were two decades behind her, but they would insist on returning to haunt her.

'He turned my *bra* into a *vibrator*,' said Rachel fondly, 'and I turned his *semen* to *chastisement*.'

'And after that?'

'I went back to his room for a nightcap.'

'Aha.'

Rachel sighed theatrically. She'd had dramatic ambitions as a teenager but had only got as far as a sixth form Snow White. 'Angus turned up,' she said tragically, 'and told William he ought to be nice and fresh for the morning. I like men who are nice and fresh in the morning, of course, but Angus made sure I didn't get a chance to find out. What did you do?'

'Talked to Angus.'

Rachel raised an eyebrow.

'Beatrice dragged him away.'

'What a pity,' said Rachel.

* * *

The seating arrangements at breakfast were different from the night before. The members of each pair were now sitting opposite one another. Fee toyed with toast and coffee, while Eric Summers disposed of devilled kidneys, hot chocolate and waffles. Rachel and William exchanged smouldering looks and ate their croissants as though they were tackling one another's anatomy. Angus twinkled into a smile the moment he saw her. Beatrice turned her head to identify the recipient, saw Fee, and bristled. Peverall was arguing with Scarab about something called tmesis. Fee realised that the tattoo wasn't a snake at all: it was a bookworm.

'What's tmesis?' Fee asked Summers.

'The insertion of some-ruddy-thing in the middle of something else,' said Summers dryly.

'Look,' said Fee, 'I know you're stuck with me, and I'm not going to be much help. But we could at least try to get on.'

'I wasn't aware that we weren't,' said Summers.

Gavin Smythe got to his feet. There was a pile of envelopes in front of him. He surveyed the gathering and said, 'I'm going to hand out the first set of clues, and when I say *go* you can open them.'

There was an expectant hush as he dished out one envelope to each couple. Then he glanced at his watch, held up a hand, and waited a few seconds. Peverall was turning his envelope this way and that, feeling the thickness, estimating how many sheets of paper were inside.

'*Go*,' said Gavin.

There was a flurry of feverish activity. Summers leaned back in his chair and closed his eyes. The envelope lay on the white tablecloth, between them. 'Aren't you going to open it?' asked Fee.

'After you,' said Summers, without opening his eyes.

Fee slit open the envelope. Inside were three sheets of paper. The first one was a detailed map of the surrounding countryside, and underneath it was written: *All clues will be found within this area.* Most of the buildings were named, and even a few of the shops in the market town.

There was one called Anita's – a clothes shop? A chapel, a railway station, something called the Maitland Clinic. There was a box in one corner with a plan of the house itself. All the room numbers were there, as well as odd little symbols that didn't seem to mean anything – a Tudor rose in the library, a miniature pyramid in the passageway between the kitchen and the games room. Fee passed the map to Summers and opened the second sheet of paper. This had only one sentence printed on it, which read:

Anne's china plates got broken in the home of the patroness of housewives (5, 5, 6).

She shrugged and passed that over as well. The third sheet read:

Stingy, this chap? Thin rope, but it will support standing choirboys! (10).

The elderly man with the handlebar moustache got hurriedly to his feet and said, 'Thought as much. The dissolute old sod. Come on, Elsie, let's be off.'

Fee watched them go, feeling slightly perplexed. Dissolute? Surely that meant morally lax?

Angus caught Fee's eye and made a gesture of defeat. Rachel and William were scribbling things on the sheet of paper. The other couples left in dribs and drabs, whispering to one another. She overheard Scarab say, 'Seriously graphic in the genital department . . .'

'Easy ones to start with then,' said Summers.

'*Easy* ones?'

He sighed. 'They're crossword clues.'

'I can see that,' said Fee.

'Haven't you ever done a cryptic crossword?'

'No,' said Fee shortly.

'Well why on earth are you here then?'

'I came to keep a friend company.'

He didn't actually raise his eyes to heaven, but he

might as well have done. 'One half of the clue is a definition,' he said, 'and the other half a coded version of the same answer. If you had to break the sentence, where would you do it?'

Fee thought for a moment. 'Between *broken* and *in*.'

'Mm hm. Now look for an anagram indicator.'

'What the hell's that?'

'Something that tells you a word or words have been mixed up. Mixed, muddled, re-arranged, confused . . . get the idea?'

'*Got broken*, then.'

'And how many letters does *Anne's china plates* have?'

'Five, five, six. Oh, I see.'

'Now look at the definition.'

'*In the home of the patroness of housewives.*'

'The saint responsible for housewives is Saint Anne. What's left?'

'C, H, P, L, A, E.' The panic started to rise. She couldn't untangle it. Her mother's voice made an unwelcome intrusion. *C minus again, Fiona? You're no Einstein, are you?*

'Chapel,' said Summers. 'Saint Anne's Chapel. Now look at the map.'

And there it was, up in the left-hand corner. Saint Anne's Chapel.

'Wow,' said Fee.

'Wow indeed,' said Summers dryly. 'The second clue will refer to something *at* the chapel, and half the contestants will be swarming over the building like flies, hoping for the best. Better we solve it before we leave, then we can be in and out of there without anyone being any the wiser. It *is* more difficult than the first one.'

'You've solved it already?'

He smiled slightly.

She looked at the sheet of paper, and re-read the clue. *Stingy, this chap? Thin rope, but it will support standing choirboys! (10).* 'I can't see anything that looks like an anagram indicator,' she said eventually.

'That's because there isn't an anagram this time. And it's rather an obscure word: you probably don't know it.'

15

Fee felt ignorant and uneducated and cross.

'Misericord,' he said. '*Stingy* stands for *miser*. *This chap* stands for the setter himself, so it's *I*. *Thin rope* stands for *cord*.'

'What does it mean?'

'It's a shelving projection on the underside of a choir stall.'

'Oh,' said Fee sarcastically, 'just one of those everyday words that's part and parcel of a normal vocabulary.'

'This isn't a treasure hunt *for* normal people,' said Summers.

'Damn right,' said Fee. Her mind drifted back to the remark she'd overheard from the man with the handlebar moustache. *Thought as much. The dissolute old sod.* Was that a reference to Alfred Hicks, the setter? And Scarab's comment . . . *Seriously graphic in the genital department.* Something obscene in a *chapel*?

'Come on,' said Summers, 'or we won't get to the church on time. Your car or mine?'

'I don't have one.'

Eric Summers had a Saab. It was unprepossessing on the outside, a sort of dull grey, but inside the seats were leather and the stereo was expensive. The car purred into life like a big cat, and moved just as smoothly.

When they reached the chapel Summers was very fussy about how he parked the Saab, lining it up so that it was exactly parallel to and equidistant from the vehicles to either side. 'That's Arnold's,' he said, indicating a BMW.

'Arnold?'

'The guy with the moustache. He's good. Very good, actually.'

They walked up to the door, and met Arnold and his partner Elsie on their way out.

'Hello, Arnold,' said Summers. 'Who else is in there?'

'Thaul Thlick.'

Summers looked momentarily at a loss.

'Saul Slick. Tall fellow; forty-something, mad hair, lisp. Balliol.'

'Oh,' said Summers, '*him*.'

'Unusual theme,' said Arnold mysteriously. 'But then, Hicks always was a bit of a devil.' He gave a dirty laugh, and went off whistling.

The chapel was cool and dark inside, although the choir stalls were lit by a stained-glass window. Fee could see the man who was presumably Saul Slick ferreting through some hymn books.

'We don't want to look as though we know what we're after,' said Summers quietly. He walked towards the stained-glass window and stood beneath it, ostensibly deep in thought. Then he beckoned to Fee, turned into the choir stall, and ducked down so that he was out of sight. Fee did likewise. Very carefully, Summers lifted the first seat. Fee saw the intricately carved wooden support beneath, and stifled a gasp of surprise. It was quite beautiful – two farm-workers in medieval clothes, depicted in considerable detail, one on either side of a perpendicular strut.

Summers lowered it so gently that it made no sound settling back into position. He moved on to the next. This time the figures were both female – and naked. Fee looked a little closer. One of the women definitely had her hand on the other's breast, and the nipple was conspicuously erect. She glanced at Summers. He replaced the seat.

The third one revealed a man with a huge erection, and a woman who had tied a length of rope around it and was leading him like a dog. Behind the strut, almost out of sight, was a piece of plastic. Summers prised it loose, but it would only travel so far – it was fastened to the misericord by a slim chain like an identity tag. Summers fiddled in his jacket pocket and pulled out a notepad and a fountain pen. Then he started to copy down what was written behind the laminate. Fee peeked round the corner of the choir stall, and saw that Saul Slick had gone. 'There's no one here any more,' she said, and stood up. Summers carried on writing. Fee lifted another of the seats. This misericord depicted a devil buggering a man. The devil had little horns on his head, and a leer that meant the same thing whatever century you hailed from.

17

The woodcarver had taken a lot of trouble with the genitals. She put the seat down again and lifted the next. This one looked a bit like an incomplete jigsaw – two men, one on either side of the central strut. She could see their legs, their balls and the base of their penises clearly enough – but the top halves of their bodies seemed to be missing. Then she realised that the men were bent over, performing auto-fellatio.

You'd have to be a contortionist to do that, thought Fee. Easier for a man than a woman, though. But supposing you *could* flex your spine that far? What would it be like, licking yourself off? I wonder if dogs do it? They've got the right sort of anatomy, and they always have that soppy grin after they've finished washing themselves. She imagined her own tongue circling her clit, applying just the right pressure, sliding between the folds, finding all the best places, doing everything at exactly the right pace. Then she wondered if Angus was any good at it – and after that she shivered, just thinking about it.

After a moment or two she had to force herself back into the present. She still had the rest of day to get through, before she saw Angus in the evening. She gently replaced the seat and moved on. How strange these carvings were, and whoever would have expected to find them in a church? The next one was of two women, their dresses in disarray, playing with themselves. Maybe they were cautionary tales – this is what you're *not* allowed to do. A kind of instruction manual on sin.

The last misericord showed Leda being raped by the swan. It was a very sensual piece of work: deliberately erotic, rather than instructive. Summers put away his notebook and leaned over her to have a look. She felt his jacket brush her face.

He gave a dry little laugh. 'She looks as though she's enjoying it, doesn't she?'

Fee imagined the weight of a giant swan on her body. Imagined the soft feathery quilting over the powerful muscles, the cool grip of a beak, the webbed feet on her thighs. There would be little claws on his feet, sharp claws. His wings would hold her prisoner as he penetrated her, and it would be divine. He was, after all, Zeus in disguise. Oh for a man who would act *that* one out. She found herself daydreaming about Angus again.

After a while she realised that Summers was looking at her a little oddly. 'We can go now,' he said. 'Unless you have an overpowering urge to see the misericords on the other side.'

She shook her head, and they walked down the aisle.

'Alfred Hicks always had a theme to his treasure hunts,' said Summers, opening the door for her. 'I've worked out the second part of the next clue, and I'm getting an idea of what the theme might be.'

'Churches?'

'No,' said Summers. 'Sex.'

Chapter Two

'Saint Anne's Chapel,' announced William, screwing up the pieces of paper he'd been working on.

'Jolly good,' said Rachel, trying to sound enthusiastic. William looked so enticing, with his dark hair flopping across his forehead, his grey eyes narrowed with concentration. The ascetic type, with fine bone structure and the pale indoor skin of a poet. He wasn't effeminate, however; there were muscles in that elegant jaw, and although he was tall and slim, he wasn't weedy.

He stood up, jerked on his leather jacket and made for the door. 'Come on,' he said, rather more sharply than Rachel would have liked. 'The prize is worth a lot of money.'

They got into his Range Rover and drove to the chapel. William pursed his lips and strode into the building as though he were about to wage war. Rachel followed him inside; several other couples were there already, some of them looking furtive, others reading the information board. She glanced at it: playgroup leaflets, Sunday school classes, a brief history of the building. William was examining the lectern. She joined him.

'We need to be in the choir stall,' he said, *sotto voce*, 'I'm just waiting until no one else is watching.'

'No sign of Angus and – what's her name? The snooty one with the glasses.'

'Beatrice. It could take Angus a while,' said William. 'I don't think crosswords are his thing. On the other hand, Fee has probably been and gone.'

'*Fee?*' said Rachel, surprised. 'Fee has no more idea of how to solve crosswords than I have. I can't see her even trying, to be honest. She used to throw up before spelling tests.'

'She's paired with Eric Summers.'

Rachel grinned. 'She was well pissed off. He was so *boring*. She likes a laugh, not mental gymnastics.'

'Most people here would give their biggest dictionary to be in Fee's shoes, Rachel.' He glanced round. 'Stand in front of me, so that no one can see what I'm doing.' He slid into the choir stall and knelt down.

'And what *are* you doing?' asked Rachel.

'Lifting seats,' said William unexpectedly. Then, '*Christ.*'

'What?'

'Look.'

Rachel looked. Then she looked at the next one. And the next.

William was scribbling something down on a piece of paper, and after that his mood changed abruptly and his irritability evaporated.

When Rachel got to Leda and the swan, she had to lean right over so that she could see better, and then she overbalanced. William caught her and they knelt there together for a moment, looking at the carving. She was very aware of his proximity, and the pressure of his arm against hers. 'Feathers,' said Rachel wistfully. 'I bet she enjoyed it.'

'Women like that sort of thing, don't they?' said William, still looking at the carving. 'The lepidoptera effect.'

'Butterflies?'

'Or moths.' He ran the tip of his finger very lightly across the back of her hand. 'This sort of thing.' Then he brought his other fingers into play and ran them up her arm, across her shoulder and round to the nape of her neck. It was the first time he'd deliberately touched her. She leaned towards him slightly. He moved into the wild forest of her hair, skittering about in unpredictable directions. She shivered at the thrill of it: he hadn't looked at her once, and she rather liked the lack of eye contact. It focused the mind wonderfully on the here and now of the tactile.

He stopped what he was doing far too soon and stood up. 'Men, on the other hand, like the canine approach,' he said. 'Much more direct, and preferably with plenty of licking.'

'There isn't enough room here,' said Rachel, 'quite apart from it being a chapel.' She knew she was being disgracefully easy – but she had always gone for what she wanted in the past, and she saw no reason to make an exception this time.

'I wasn't suggesting it,' he said. 'I was merely drawing your attention to the difference in male and female foreplay. This isn't going to be just any old treasure hunt. I suspect that an encyclopaedic knowledge of sex is going to be a major asset.'

Rachel felt snubbed. He'd made her put her cards on the table, without showing any of his. They went back to the car and sat inside, looking at what he'd copied down. The butterfly moment in the chapel might never have happened.

This time, only the first bit was a crossword clue: the other was a riddle.

Rachel read the first part aloud. '*A knot takes in edited author. Four letters, then eight.*' She was trying very hard to sound cool and detached.

'*Knot*, and *edited*. *Two* possible anagram indicators.'

'Twelve letters. Twelve letters in *edited author*.' It was an effort to sustain it.

'What Christian names can we make with four of those letters? Rita, Theo, Edie . . .'

'Dora, Rudi, Rhea . . . there are loads.' *Sod the man.*

'Tricky,' said William. 'I tend to think better when I'm relaxed.'

Was he playing games with her? If he was, there was something very erotic about being used so blatantly. She took a deep breath and risked it. 'And how do you relax, William?'

'I find myself a bitch.'

Rachel felt her whole body tense with fury – then she remembered the canine allusion. There was a wicked little smile on his face, and she was glad she hadn't risen to the bait and snapped at him. 'One with whom you can revise your encyclopaedic knowledge of sex?'

'*In situ*, if necessary.'

She glanced round the Range Rover and licked her lips. 'Big car. Lots of space in the back.'

'To hell with the back,' he said. 'You can suck me off here.'

The sudden shift to the utterly explicit was like a shot of neat aphrodisiac. 'Here? In the front seat? In the chapel car park, where anyone could see?'

'That's right.'

'Sounds a bit one-sided.' But deliciously exciting.

'You'll get your lepidoptera later.'

He unzipped his flies. Rachel slipped her hand inside his boxer shorts, and pulled out his cock. It was warm and hard, and just the feel of it made her squirm a little in her seat. A cock as stiff as this was a very direct compliment. William put a sheaf of papers on the steering wheel and got out a pen. To all intents and purposes he was working on the clue – and if he looked a bit dreamy from time to time, he could simply be thinking.

Rachel started to stroke him, feeling the silky warmth of him beneath her fingertips. She ran her palm down the thick straight shaft: then she licked her finger, ran it back up to the head and trailed it lightly across the underside, concentrating on the sensitive part. He was sitting very still, his hands grasping the steering wheel, staring into space. She circled the head with her thumb, then she took hold of him properly and moved his foreskin up and down a couple of times. His cock jerked in her hand, and she started to squeeze him gently and rhythmically. He took a deep breath and looked down at the mess of papers in front of him.

Someone's coming, thought Rachel, and it isn't William. Not just yet. Her heart beat a little faster with the threat of imminent discovery. She saw Peverall walking towards them, but instead of stopping what she was doing she speeded up. Two could play the manipulation game. William made no attempt to stop her, and when Peverall came level with the window he simply moved the papers so that they obscured his lap.

'You got *misericord* then?' said Peverall.

William inclined his head. Rachel felt the tip of his cock moisten. Then she saw Scarab, standing a little way off, grinning.

'Lovely word, that,' said Peverall. 'Nearly as good as mallemaroking. But not quite.'

'Not now, Peverall,' said William. 'I'm thinking.'

Rachel fought the urge to giggle. Peverall nodded in an understanding way, and went. Scarab followed him, still grinning.

'I think it's time you got your head down,' said William.

Rachel moved her head down to his lap and breathed in the lovely musky smell of him. He casually rearranged his papers as camouflage. She ran her tongue up and down his shaft a few times until he was good and wet, and then she took him in her mouth. She felt him tense slightly. This won't take long, she thought, he got very excited when Peverall was talking to him. He liked feeling superior to him. She sucked him for a few moments, then she started to circle the head with her tongue, vibrating it every time she got to the most sensitive part, then skirting away again. His whole body was tense now. She sucked him again. He arched his back. She started to fuck him with her mouth, up and down, up and down, and after a couple of seconds there was a warm jet. She swallowed it, and the rest, and then she licked him clean in an extravagantly canine way.

'Well done, good girl,' he said, zipping up his flies. 'Now then. About this clue . . .'

There was the dull crunch of two vehicles colliding in the distance.

'Someone just hit a parked car,' said Rachel.

'Excellent. With any luck, it'll slow the owner down.'

Fee and Summers were back at the house, drinking coffee in the library. It was the most sensible place to work, as there were a lot of reference books available.

'The answer to the second bit is *Greek urn*,' Summers told her. 'There are some very explicit sex scenes on Greek vases, so it ties in with my theory about Alfred's theme. The first part of the clue will give the location.'

'You haven't solved it yet then?'

'Not quite,' he said, with a sidelong glance at her. It was a cautious look that said, just give me a moment, I didn't realise I was on display. He smoothed out the sheet of paper and straightened a folded corner. 'Let's see. *A knot takes in edited author. Edited* is the anagram indicator, despite the red herring of *knot*. *Author* is the definition. What four-letter Christian names can we find in *A knot takes in*?'

'Anne. Nina.'

'Toni . . . Toni Morrison. Pity it doesn't fit. Kate . . .'

Fee felt a sudden rush of euphoria. 'Kate Atkinson. She wrote a book called *Behind the Scenes at the Museum*!'

'Shh.' But he was smiling as he took the map out of his pocket and laid it in front of her. 'Bottom of the page.'

She looked. And there was a little black square, marked *Museum*. She felt a surge of pure pleasure.

'I think we're ahead of everyone, with the possible exception of Arnold and Elsie. And they're civilised: they'll be taking a lunch break as well as us.'

She followed him into the dining room. She had consommé; Summers, who said he didn't see the point of soup, had brie. They followed it with lobster salad and pecan pie, and talked about music. She told him that she used to play the flute.

'Used to?'

'Well, I left the orchestra when I left school. I still play on my own occasionally – when I'm sure no one's listening. When I'm cross, to be honest.'

He smiled. 'I put on some Mahler and turn up the volume.'

'I like Mahler too.' Fee's musical tastes were very varied, from grunge to Gregorian chants. She sipped her coffee. 'Do you compile crosswords for a living?'

'No. I'm the editor of *Better Mousetraps*.'

Fee's mouth dropped open.

'It's a magazine about inventions. I'm a logician.'

'Oh.' It sounded monumentally boring. They finished their coffee, gathered their papers together, went out to the car and drove to the museum.

It was a small stone building, situated at a crossroads. Summers parked the car in the tiny car park – which was empty – placing it very precisely between the demarcation lines as though it were a chess piece. They went inside. A woman was sitting behind a desk, working at a computer. 'There's no charge,' she announced, without raising her eyes.

'I'm awfully sorry to trouble you,' said Summers, 'but I believe you have a Grecian urn in the store that I would particularly like to see.'

The woman looked up. 'The treasure hunt,' she said in a resigned voice, and got to her feet. 'Follow me, please. And don't touch anything else.' They followed her into a room marked PRIVATE. It was lined with shelves, and cluttered beyond belief. 'I would never have agreed to it,' the woman said, 'if we didn't need every donation we could get to keep the place open. Be extremely careful, please. The vase is over there, on the bench.'

It had a rounded body and two curving handles; there was a lip at the top and a base at the bottom, and the whole thing was perfectly proportioned. The background glaze was black and it was decorated with a frieze of ochre-coloured figures. Summers walked over and stood beside her as she slowly rotated the pot. The whole scene was a continuous narrative, although you could start anywhere. She began with a naked woman, standing above a seated one. The seated one was fondling the other: Fee could even see the position of her fingers, the way they were opening the lips and tickling the clit at the same time. Next to them a man was buggering another man, who was lying on his side on a bench. The man on the bench was sucking off a third man. After that came a man with a black beard, who was fucking a woman from behind; she in turn was jerking off another man. And then it was back to the beginning.

'You were right about the theme,' said Fee dryly. 'Where's the clue, though?'

'Underneath, I'd imagine,' said Summers. He lifted the pot and moved it to one side. There was a sheet of plastic screwed to the bench beneath.

Fee read the clue as Summers copied it down. *Box clever, in the view of the Marquis of Queensberry.* And beneath it: *Ring-a-Ring o' Roses. Price up three of our services correctly: lick the opposition, and get a straight result.*

'There aren't any numbers in brackets,' she said. 'No word-lengths.'

'Then they aren't crossword clues this time.' He put his notepad back in his pocket, and the cap back on his pen. 'Let's go back and think about it.'

As they were leaving the museum, Summers asked whether there had been any other couples from the treasure hunt in before them.

'Two.'

'Tall man with a handlebar moustache?'

'Yes.'

'Who else?'

The woman behind the desk looked irritated. 'I can't remember.'

They drove back through the winding country lanes. 'The Marquis of Queensberry invented the rules of boxing, didn't he?' said Fee.

'Yes.' Summers didn't seem inclined to talk, so they travelled the rest of the way in silence. He drove very correctly, always indicating in plenty of time and never taking risks. When they got back to the house they went into the library, and Summers settled himself down on one of the chesterfields, put his hands behind his head and closed his eyes.

Fee felt superfluous.

'I think I'll take a shower,' she said.

'Fine.'

She went upstairs to her room. Rachel had beaten her to the shower – the bathroom door was ajar and she could hear the water gushing out. Steam was drifting through the doorway in a lethargic sort of way. Rachel wasn't the tidiest of people and her clothes were strewn across the floor. Fee started to pick them up – the cashmere sweater, the sequinned top, the black lacy bra, the boxer shorts . . . boxer shorts?

She glanced towards the shower, and saw the outline of *two* figures. Oh shit, she thought, William's in there with her. What do I do? Wait until they've finished? Finished what, though? Maybe I just ought to go back downstairs. Hang on, though – if I can't have a shower, I can have a swim. She took her swimsuit and a spare towel out of the wardrobe as quietly as she could and headed off to the pool.

William pressed Rachel against the cold tiled wall of the shower and began to soap her all over. She warmed up rapidly, although she wasn't sure whether it was sheer anticipation or the warm water.

'I'm cheating and letting the shower do the butterflies,' he explained. 'It's got more outlets than I have fingers.'

And it really was the most exquisite feeling; the warm pattering of the spray on her face, like a hundred moths tiptoeing in unison. The rhythmic movements of his hands over her body provided a delicious contrast – and it was impossible to concentrate on both sensations at the same time, it had to be either one or the other. She

28

switched her mind back and forth, immersing herself in sheer physical pleasure. He started innocuously enough, with her shoulders and her arms, then he moved down to her hands. He washed each finger individually, and she was mildly surprised to realise that the fingertip wasn't the most sensitive place at all, it was the space in between, where the fingers joined the hand. He ran his nails lightly across her palm; that was equally as effective, especially the section between the head line and the heart line. The mount of Venus, at the base of her thumb, didn't live up to its name. The inside of her wrist, on the other hand – literally as well as figuratively – was far more erotic, and she was almost disappointed when he moved further up her arm. He seemed to be progressing in the general direction of her breasts, which seemed like a good thing – but at the last moment he veered off and started to concentrate on her neck.

It was heavenly. The more he kneaded and massaged, the more sensitive the area became. She was as loose as a rag doll, and just as helpless. When he let up on the pressure and opted for the thistledown approach her knees started to give way, and she had to cling on to him for support.

'I think maybe you're good and ready now,' he said, and suddenly his finger was inside her. He hadn't touched her below the waist other than to wash her legs, and the surprise factor contributed in no small part to the instant escalation of sheer lust. 'I said you'd get your reward,' he murmured, 'and get it you shall.' Then he fucked her so expertly with his fingers that she could do nothing except take it. He twisted his knuckles every so often, catching her where it mattered, rubbing where it had greatest effect; the feeling built and built until it could build no more, and she climaxed with a surprising ferocity.

He turned off the shower and handed her a towel. Then he said, 'Let's have another crack at that clue.'

* * *

Fee did three lengths of the pool and then floated on her back for a while. The sun came out and she closed her eyes and let the water support her. With her head right back and her ears underwater, she didn't hear anything until she felt something touch her leg – then she flipped up like a jack-in-the-box and heard Angus laughing.

'Hi,' he said, tossing the water out of his hair. 'Not chasing clues then? Or are you leaving it up to Summers?'

'I could ask you the same thing.'

'I'd be only too delighted to leave it to Summers,' said Angus. 'But unfortunately, he isn't my partner.'

She felt a twinge of disappointment. She'd much rather he'd wished *she* was his partner.

He glanced at the stretch of lawn beside the pool. 'I've got a couple of freshly mixed Margaritas over there. This may not be Mexico, but we could pretend. Señorita?'

They climbed out of the pool, sat cross-legged on the grass and clinked glasses. Revealed in swimming trunks, his body was even better than she'd imagined. Perhaps he was thinking the same about her – his eyes certainly strayed away from her face now and again. She tucked her hair behind her ears to stop it dripping into her drink.

'That's it,' he said suddenly, 'that's what you remind me of.'

'What?'

'A pixie.'

She uncrossed her legs as quickly as she could and shook her hair loose again.

'Said the wrong thing, didn't I? Let's have another go. Such a beautiful señorita to be on holiday with just a girlfriend. There is no man in her life?'

'Not at the moment.' He'd used quite a passable Spanish accent; she could forgive him the pixie remark. 'Such a presentable young man to be on holiday with no woman,' she returned. 'Is there one at home?'

'Not at the moment. Is the señorita free this evening?'

'*Sí.*' Crosswords were absolutely no competition for an evening with Angus.

'You have been to Central America before?'

'I haven't been anywhere much.'

'*Caramba!*' exclaimed Angus. 'You have never smelt the ginger growing on the banks of the river, had humming birds buzzing round your head, seen the fire in the crater of a volcano?'

'And you have?'

'*Si.*'

'Tell me about it.'

He told her how he'd had a brush with a crocodile, swimming in the Nile at Luxor, and how he'd been chased by a black mamba in India. He spread his hands to show her the size of a morpho butterfly, and landed them on her arm to demonstrate what it felt like. She shivered. 'The lepidoptera effect,' he said. 'Men tend to brush them off, but women like it.'

Damn right, thought Fee, but before she could pursue this interesting topic of conversation any further, Rachel and William appeared.

They sat down on the grass next to Angus and Fee. '*Thousands of drachma an hour,*' said William. 'It's a bugger, isn't it?' He looked at Angus. 'Where's your partner?'

'Beatrice? In her room.'

'She doesn't look like the type to give up that easily.'

'She hasn't given up,' said Angus. 'She's mucking about with anagrams.'

'Thousands of drachma an hour,' repeated William, tapping his fingers impatiently on the ground.

'I bet *you* know the answer,' said Rachel to Fee.

Fee smiled and said nothing.

'Oh come on, be a sport.'

Fee felt in a very difficult position. On the one hand, she wasn't taking the treasure hunt as seriously as the men, and she rather fancied flashing her new-found problem-solving ability at Angus – after all, she *had* known the name of Kate Atkinson's book. No doubt Summers would have found it in the library – but she had beaten him to it, and the feeling had been very pleasant indeed. On the other hand, she felt a curious sense of loyalty

31

towards the man, boring as he was, and she wanted to impress him further.

'It sounds like the answer to something,' said Rachel. 'Something stupid, like *what's a Greek earn?*'

Something in Fee's face must have given her away, because William said, 'That's it, isn't it? A Greek urn. I bet there's a clue hidden in a book somewhere in the library.'

'Oh good,' said Angus. 'I'll enjoy telling that po-faced Beatrice the answer.'

I'm going to have to be careful from now on, thought Fee.

She and Angus got dressed, and then they all made their way to the library. Summers was still there. He stood up as they entered and gave Fee a calculating look. William had his arm round Rachel. Fee realised that she'd thrown her clothes on any old how, her hair was a mess and there was still a damp patch on her skirt.

'Stuck?' queried Angus cheerfully.

Summers made some non-committal movement of his head. Then he looked at Fee, and she knew he'd solved the clue.

'Beatrice is going great guns,' said Angus. 'Good job you're not paired up with *her*, Eric, or you'd have finished by now.'

It took a moment for what Angus had actually said to filter through: he clearly didn't think Fee was a patch on Beatrice in the brains department. She felt the anger boil up the way it always had at school, when her maths teacher told her she was being stupid. Her face went tight and she dug her nails into the palms of her hands. She knew her reaction was over the top, but she couldn't help it.

'Beatrice is very good, certainly,' said Summers. 'Her crosswords are very sound. But two crossword buffs aren't necessarily the best combination for this sort of thing; it can merely be a duplication of strengths. I'm quite happy with Fee. She's been pulling her weight.'

Angus looked surprised.

William laughed. 'So has Rachel.' It was perfectly obvious that he didn't mean she'd been pulling her weight in the treasure hunt. Rachel smirked and tossed back her frizzy red hair. There was a love bite on her neck.

Summers glanced at his watch.

'Gotta go,' said Fee.

'See you later,' said Angus – and then, to cap it all, he winked at her.

Fee hated men winking at her. It always seemed so patronising; it didn't really mean anything, and she was still seething from his previous remark. 'Maybe,' she said. 'And maybe I'll join in the crossword session this evening.'

Angus looked astonished, then irritated. 'Who's rattled your cage?'

'A maths teacher,' said Fee.

She followed Summers out of the library and they went outside to his car. 'So,' he said, 'your maths teacher used to make you feel stupid, did she?'

'He.' She was surprised at his perspicacity.

'Were you scared of him?'

'Terrified.' A horrible, paralysing fear that made her tongue stick to the roof of her mouth. And then that evil moment of silence, before he turned on the sarcasm.

'Pity,' said Summers. 'You've got a logical mind; you should have been good at maths.' They got in and he started the engine. 'The Marquis of Queensberry is a pub in the town. I looked it up in the telephone directory. Time for a quick drink before dinner.'

They drove for a while in silence. 'Look,' said Fee eventually, 'about Angus –'

'None of my business,' said Summers. 'As long as you don't go telling him any of the answers, of course.'

They lapsed into silence again, and Fee felt just a little bit guilty. Eventually she felt she had to say something, so she muttered, 'We talked about his travels, actually. He's been all over the world. He had a close encounter with a crocodile at Luxor, and he got chased by a black mamba in India.'

'There are no crocodiles below the Aswan dam,' said Summers. 'And the black mamba comes from Africa.'

The Marquis of Queensberry was at the end of a little parade of shops. One of the shops had wooden shutters over the windows: the name of the shop was *Adults Only*. Fee smiled. They reached the pub and went inside. Summers bought the drinks, up-ended a charity box on the bar, and peered underneath it. 'Oy!' said the barman.

'Sorry,' said Summers, putting it back and posting some coins through the slit. 'Not that sort of *box clever* then,' he said to Fee.

Arnold and Elsie were sitting at one of the tables. Elsie was finishing a gin and tonic and Arnold's beer glass was nearly empty. His moustache was tipped with froth.

'Eric!' Arnold called to Summers. 'We're still ahead of you then. Probably won't last. Bit of a rum do, eh, these clues?'

'I think they're rather amusing,' said Summers.

'Well you won't for long,' said Elsie darkly. She was a pleasant-looking woman with snow-white hair and grey eyes.

'You knew Hicks, didn't you?'

'Not as well as he'd have liked,' said Elsie.

'I think we'll amble back,' said Arnold hurriedly. 'Best of luck, Eric.' Elsie followed him.

'We've found the pub,' said Fee, 'what now?'

'In the *view* of the Marquis of Queensberry,' said Summers. 'It's going to be something outside, I think.'

'Something to do with roses?'

'Might be right up your street,' said Summers, 'being a florist.'

She was surprised he had remembered. They finished their drinks and went outside.

'Right,' said Summers, 'what can we see from here that has something to do with boxing? Or boxes?'

'Box office. There's a theatre over there.'

'Too much to hope they're doing *The Rose and the Ring*, I suppose?'

'It's *Much Ado About Nothing*,' said Fee.

He laughed.

He's got rather a nice face, thought Fee suddenly. Nothing that stands out – but that's because his features are so regular: straight nose, straight mouth, even teeth. Those hazel eyes turn neither up nor down; everything about him is as straight as can be.

'Phone boxes,' he said. 'You can see three of them from here.'

They went into the nearest one. The back wall was covered with postcards, advertising different services. French lessons, water sports, massage, correction: every sort of gym-slip, every sort of habit. One of the cards read: *Genuine gypsy rose: your future is in her hands.*

'There,' said Fee.

'Here's another,' said Summers. '*This Rose has enough thorns to satisfy any naughty boy.*'

They looked at each other.

'We'll have to ring them both,' he said. 'The clue asks us to *price up three services.*'

'*Which* three services, though?'

He looked at the clue again. 'The answer has to be here,' he said. 'Hicks was always sound.'

She leaned across and looked as well. *Ring-a-Ring o' Roses. Price up three of our services correctly: lick the opposition, and get a straight result.* 'Lick,' she said. 'A blow-job.'

'That's one. *Correctly* is another – the basic Miss Whiplash deal, I'd imagine. What's the third?'

They studied the piece of paper. She glanced sideways at him. His face was calm and serene; he was thinking. There was no embarrassment, none at all. It was just another puzzle. She wondered whether anything ever ruffled his calm. She couldn't imagine him in bed with anyone – after you, no after *you*.

'We could play it by ear,' she suggested.

'Off you go then.'

She stared at him, aghast. '*Me*? I can't ring her, it has to be you.'

'Why?'

'Because you're a man.'

'That's not a proper reason.'

'Of course it is. You're posing as a client. It *has* to be you.'

'No it doesn't. Tell her why you're calling straight away, tell her the truth. She has to be in on it, whoever she is, like the woman in the museum.'

'You're chicken.'

'Damn right,' he said.

Not so unembarrassable after all, thought Fee, but goading him isn't going to work; he's the obstinate type. I need to employ reason. 'If I do the first one,' she said, 'you should do the second.'

'Fair enough.'

She picked up the receiver and punched in the first number.

'Rose,' said a rather abrasive woman's voice.

'Hello,' said Fee hesitantly.

'I don't do women,' said the voice.

'No,' said Fee, 'that's not exactly –'

'Or three in a bed.'

'No, that's not . . . I'm calling about a treasure hunt.'

There was a snort at the other end. 'And whatever *that* is, darling, I don't do it either.' The phone went dead.

Fee looked at Summers. 'Your turn.'

He took a deep breath and rang the second number. Fee put her ear to the other side of the receiver. Summers tried to turn away, but the cord wouldn't stretch any further. He glared at her.

'Fair dos,' hissed Fee. 'You listened to mine.'

'Rose here,' said a woman's voice. This voice was softer, more welcoming.

'Hello,' said Summers. Then he hesitated.

'You haven't done this before, have you, darling?' said Rose. 'Don't worry, you'll have such a stiffie by the end of this little chat that by the time we meet you'll be like a stallion. Now then, any particular requests? French maid? Fellatio? A straight fuck? Funny how they all begin with F, isn't it? Or are you into games?'

'Treasure hunts,' said Summers.

'I see. In that case, you'd better come over straight away. I'm just round the corner: 14B Mount Pleasant Road. Do you want to know what I'm wearing? I'll tell you. A pair of sheer silk stockings –'

'I'm afraid I can't this evening,' said Summers, glancing at his watch. 'I was really just after a price list.'

'I'm very reasonable,' said Rose. 'And I always throw in a little extra something for a first-timer.'

'How much is a blow job?' asked Summers desperately.

'Twenty-seven pounds,' said Rose. 'Are you a virgin, dear?'

He scribbled down the figure in his notepad. 'And correction?'

'Seventy-five.'

'What else do you do?'

'I think you'd better come round and find out,' said Rose. 'How about ten o'clock tomorrow morning? You know you want to.'

'Straight sex?'

'Fifty. And no playing with yourself tonight.' She hung up.

Fee burst out laughing.

Summers looked put out. 'I thought I did rather well.'

'Not as well as you'll have to do tomorrow.'

His expression changed to one of alarm. Fee cracked up again. After a moment his mouth twitched, and then he was laughing as well. It was the sort of laughter that just won't go away; every time it faded a little they would catch one another's eye and have hysterics once more. When eventually they did stop, from sheer exhaustion, she felt the sort of glow she associated with the aftermath of a violently energetic sex session. There was the same togetherness about it as well. She wondered if a similar thought had crossed *his* mind. If he'd ever had a violently energetic sex session, that was.

'Six digits,' he said, still smiling. 'It's probably a phone number. Let's give it a go.' He handed her the receiver. 'Your turn.'

'Do I have to? You were much better than me at it.'

'Flattery will get you nowhere.'

'I was useless,' she said. 'Totally useless.'

'No you weren't.' But he took back the receiver and punched in the number.

'Sister Perpetua of the Bleeding Heart,' said a woman's voice.

Summers rolled his eyes. 'I'm phoning in connection with the treasure hunt.'

'You're the second one today. I'm afraid I don't know what you're talking about.'

'I was under the impression that you would furnish us with the next clue.'

'I think you've made a mistake somewhere.'

'Does that mean I should ask you something in code? A code I haven't yet worked out?'

'What did you say your name was?'

'I didn't,' said Summers, 'but since you ask, it's Eric Summers.'

'Never heard of you.'

'Alias Swallow,' tried Summers.

'Swallow? Not the crossword setter?'

'Yes.'

'Oh, this *is* an honour,' said Sister Perpetua. 'I loved your last one, the PD clues were very clever. When's the next one due out?'

'Not for another three months,' said Summers.

'I really wish I could have been of assistance,' said Sister Perpetua.

'No, *I'm* sorry to have bothered *you*,' said Summers gallantly.

'Not at all – oh, and while we're at it – stasivalent. Only capable of having sexual intercourse standing up. Am I right? It's not in any of the dictionaries we have here.'

'Absolutely.'

'Oh good. That's three across solved. Goodbye, Mr Summers. It's been *so* nice speaking to you.'

Summers put down the phone. Then they looked side-long at one another, and burst out laughing again. Once more, it was the rib-aching laughter that takes a while to subside. Eventually Summers said, 'We *have* made a mistake somewhere. But we don't have time to do anything about it now. If we're not back for dinner, we'll be disqualified.'

Fee's post-hysterical glow lasted all the way back to the house.

Chapter Three

*A*t dinner, Fee found herself seated between Beatrice and Saul Slick. Saul Slick talked mainly about his teenage sons, who he suspected of continually having a better time of it than he was. He wrote storylines for a soap; he had a cultured voice that was softened with a slight lisp, and hair that seemed to have a life of its own. His car had been dented in the car park of Saint Anne's Chapel, and he hadn't seen who had done it. No one had owned up, either.

Beatrice was in her mid-thirties; the severe haircut and glasses gave a fairly accurate impression of her personality – sharp and intense. She had very dark eyes, set a little too closely together, and a pointed chin. She gave Fee the cold shoulder from the moment they sat down, so Fee just sat and listened to Saul telling wickedly surreal stories about his sons' exploits. Despite Beatrice's dry interjections, a faint trace of spice began to creep into everything. The sons' girlfriends became endowed with pneumatic breasts as well as high IQs, and Beatrice started to absently fondle the salt cellar. Sex was on everyone's mind, and the conversation kept looping back to it like a tune that won't go away. They all took their coffee into the games room.

Angus sat down next to Fee before anyone else could,

and looked soulfully into her eyes. 'I have some sangria in my room, if the señorita would care to sample some.'

Fee glowered and didn't answer.

'Your cage is still rattling,' he said, dropping the Spanish accent. 'And I don't for the life of me know why.'

'Don't you? You said it was a good job Summers wasn't paired up with Beatrice, or they'd have finished by now.'

'Beatrice Webb, alias the Black Widow. She's a famous compiler. Of *course* she's going to be better than you at this.'

'You don't get it, do you? You just don't *say* things like that to people.'

'How many clues have *you* solved then?'

'I've helped with a couple.'

'Sure.'

'I *have*,' said Fee, incensed. 'I knew the Kate Atkinson book.'

'That's just one.'

'And I got the blow-job.' She suddenly remembered thinking that she should be careful about what she said from now on, and felt wrong-footed.

'I apologise,' he said. 'You're hot stuff, Fee. Let's go upstairs. Then I can beg your humble forgiveness properly.'

She sniffed.

'The señorita needs to relax after hard day's work. Mañuel here, he a whiz at massage. Learned it in India.'

'Where you were chased by a black mamba?'

He grinned. 'You've looked it up, haven't you? No black mambas in India?'

'No.'

'It was a good story, though, wasn't it?'

'Not quite as good as the crocodile at Luxor.'

'My school report always said I had more imagination than was good for me.'

He was looking at her in a way that suggested she should take this thought a little further. She did.

'I wasn't fibbing about the massage. I did a course.' He rubbed his hands together and flexed his fingers.

They were nice hands. He took hold of her wrist, pulled her gently to her feet, and then let go. A bracelet of coolness lingered for a moment, where the moisture on their skins had mingled.

'I didn't bring any scented oils with me, but I do have talc.'

No, she couldn't resist this. It was too enticing. 'All right then.'

They made their way to the door. As they left the room, Fee glanced back and saw Summers regarding her with something akin to disappointment.

Fee had been introduced to massage by her first boy-friend, Mark. Mark had been five years older, and Jamaican. She had never taken him home – her parents would probably have embarrassed themselves.

Mark had taught her to value her own body, and to appreciate his. He took her virginity with care and consideration and not a little skill, and the world of sex had opened up like an exotic flower. The relationship had come to an end when Mark got a job in America. Fee had never felt quite the same way about anyone else since. One lover had been equally good at cunnilingus; another had been just as athletic; others had matched his interesting positions and unusual sex toys. But no other person had been in possession of *all* of Mark's skills.

It was a warm evening. Angus put on a tape of some quietly evocative pan-pipes, and they got through the sangria rather quickly.

'I like Spain,' said Angus. 'There was this little town where they spent all the revenue from parking tickets on fireworks, and every weekend they had a really spectacular display.'

Fee gave him a sceptical look.

'Straight up this time,' he said. 'I was only trying to impress you with the snake. Let me impress you with something I really *am* good at.'

He spread a towel on the bed. She wondered how many clothes she should take off, so she started with just her skirt and blouse. He raised an eyebrow. She took off

42

her bra. He glanced down, then politely turned his back and took off his shirt. This was going to be a serious massage. She removed her panties as quickly as she could and lay down on her stomach. She heard him move over to her and flip open the top of a container. She could feel the towel, rough beneath her, and the cool draught of the air-conditioning on her back. The next thing she felt was the butterfly touch of talcum powder as he sprinkled it over her.

He started to knead her neck and shoulders. It was clear that he really had done this sort of thing before. She felt her body relax, bit by bit, as his hands worked their magic. Time went AWOL. He matched his movements to the breathy rhythm of the music and she felt herself swoop and rise with it, like a bird. She lay there, transported, as he worked his way down her body, carefully avoiding the erogenous zones and arriving at her feet. Fee had always had a thing about feet. Tackled in the right way, feet could be a serious turn-on, and take her to the edge of orgasm. He massaged them all over with little circular movements of his thumbs; then he started to concentrate on her toes, one by one. Every time he slipped his finger between them it was a metaphor for penetration, with just the right crescendo and diminuendo of pressure. She heard herself moan, and the moan sounded as though it had been wrenched from the depths of her subconscious, the place where sensation retained its dominance over language.

'Roll over.'

She rolled over, glancing at the bedside clock in passing. He'd been working on her for three-quarters of an hour.

Once again he sprinkled her with talc. Her skin was more receptive this time, and she felt as though she were being seduced by a shower of snowflakes. He started with her shoulders as before and worked his way down, avoiding her nipples and her cunt. After a while she began to wish he'd get round to them; a slow insidious arousal was creeping through her, and making her want more direct action. He arrived at her feet again, and she couldn't stop herself writhing with pleasure. Down the instep, all along the little cavity between her toes and the ball of her foot, back up under the arch to her heel, then down the instep once more. A musical refrain, repeated over and over until the tune blotted out everything else.

Eventually he stopped what he was doing and moved back up the bed. He laid his hands on her breasts with the quiet deliberation of a faith healer, and stroked them for a while in a frustratingly non-sexual way. After that he began some gentle kneading movements, finally allowing each sequence to complete its movement at her nipple. They both came erect very quickly, and started to transmit their excitement to her clit. Suddenly he ran his tongue over her. She felt her body jerk in response. He didn't do it again for several minutes, by which point she was desperate for it. Then he started in earnest, varying the length of time he devoted to each nipple so that she couldn't predict what she'd feel from one moment to the next. It was getting almost impossible to keep still.

'Hot work,' he said after a while.

She realised that it was only the second time he'd spoken in over an hour. 'I'd take the rest of my clothes off if I were you,' she said. Her voice sounded throaty and alien.

'If I do, it will become quite apparent what effect this is having on me.'

'Good,' she said.

He unzipped his trousers and took them off. Then he removed his underpants, and his erection sprang free. Neither of them commented on it.

'Turn over again.'

She turned over. He applied more talc. Then he sat astride her, his balls nestling in the relevant crease, and turned his attention to her backside. He ran his fingernails across her, so gently that she shivered with delight, tracing a line from the underside of her thigh to her waist and back again. It was bliss. Gradually the movements got closer to her buttocks, and he shifted his position down to her thighs. She was more than ready now.

He started to tickle her arsehole, very, very lightly; round and round in a figure of eight, never quite entering her, but threatening to. She was getting very wet. His thumb found her clit, and the two-pronged attack on her anatomy drove her to the edge of orgasm. All she needed now was the big finish.

He changed position, so that his hand could perform further acrobatics. Then she had it all; one finger moving in and out of her pussy, another finger up her arse, and his thumb rubbing her clit. Her body couldn't take it for long, and she came with a violence that left her breathless.

He kissed her on the tip of her turned-up nose and popped a Belgian chocolate into her mouth.

'Full marks,' said Fee.

'Am I forgiven now?'

'Oh yes.' She glanced at his erection. 'I think we ought to do something about that.'

'I'd like to fuck you.'

'Then go ahead.'

He rolled on top of her and entered her immediately. She was still very wet from the orgasm, and his thrusts quickly increased in tempo. No gentle preliminaries this time, just a good hard screw.

'Wow,' said Fee, 'definitely con brio.' Then she was racing back up the switchback of arousal, and she couldn't have said anything further if she'd tried. She heard his quick intake of breath and knew that he was about to come. The very idea of it shot her over the top of her fairground ride, and they both climaxed together. It was the best sex she'd had for quite a while.

'We'll try your idea next time,' he said. 'It all got a bit urgent.'

'What idea?'

'Licking cheese off each other.'

'Sorry?'

'Con brie, or something.'

Fee kept a straight face with difficulty. 'Con brio,' she said. 'It means with spirit. It's a musical term.'

'With spirit, eh.' He got up, fetched a bottle of vodka,

and poured them both a measure. It was good vodka, and they followed it with another, and then another. Before long, Fee was feeling very tipsy.

'It's good fun, this treasure hunt,' said Angus.

'I'm enjoying it much more that I expected,' said Fee.

'What was that blow-job one you solved?'

'Lick the opposition,' said Fee. It was getting difficult to string sentences together. 'And the basic Miss Whippy.'

'That's ice-cream.'

'Ice-cream's not correct,' she said, and laughed uproariously at her own joke. When he looked blank she added, 'Correct. Discipline. You know.'

'So where did you slope off to with Summers this afternoon?'

'Smashing little pub,' said Fee expansively. Then the room tilted rather alarmingly and she had to lie down.

'What pub?'

But she couldn't remember. Perhaps if she closed her eyes the room would stop spinning.

When Fee woke up it was morning, and her head was splitting. She had no idea how she'd got back to her own room. Rachel was still asleep.

She walked very slowly down to the dining room and sat at the table in the corner. After two glasses of orange juice and some toast she felt a little better, and she looked round to see who else was there. No sign of Angus or William. Beatrice was having a very strange conversation with Saul Slick.

'He forced me,' Fee heard her say, in her brittle cut-glass voice.

'Were you vulnerable?'

Beatrice nodded, taking off her glasses and cleaning them.

Fee was so engrossed in her eavesdropping that she gave a little start when Summers said, 'Good morning. Sleep well?'

Beatrice said something inaudible.

'Nothing like a strong spade in that situation,' agreed

Saul Slick. Fee had a sudden flashback to Mark, carrying her on his shoulders across the shingle at Brighton, the tight black wool of his hair studded with water droplets.

'I asked if you slept well,' repeated Summers, sitting down next to her and helping himself to some toast.

Fee blinked. 'Oh. Yes thanks.'

'Rubber?' queried Saul.

Fee nearly choked on her coffee.

Summers started to laugh.

'What?' said Fee.

'They're talking about a game of bridge.'

Fee felt very silly. Then Angus made an appearance. He didn't see Fee sitting in the corner, as she was shielded by Summers. He walked over to Beatrice and whispered something in her ear. Beatrice smiled, pushed her plate away and stood up. 'See you later Saul,' she said. She and Angus left the dining room together, talking animatedly in low voices.

Summers looked at Fee. 'What have you said?'

'What do you mean?' Her heart did a quick tattoo as she remembered boasting about her prowess the previous night in general terms, though she couldn't recall the exact words.

'You know what I mean.'

'I didn't say anything,' she lied.

'If I find evidence to the contrary, I'll finish this treasure hunt on my own, thank you.'

Oh shit, thought Fee. I was beginning to enjoy it as well – I haven't laughed the way I did yesterday for ages. She changed the subject and said, 'We'd better get started if we're going to make your ten o'clock appointment with Rose.'

'Yes, OK,' he said, with a marked lack of enthusiasm.

They drove into town. He never accelerated through an amber light and always used the handbrake when he stopped. 14B Mount Pleasant Road was a maisonette, and they were early. They sat outside in the Saab and looked at the clue again. *Ring-a-Ring o' Roses. Price up three of our services correctly: lick the opposition, and get a straight result.*

'We're fairly sure we've got the right Rose,' said Summers, 'although we can't be certain. Maybe we haven't asked her for the right services. Maybe there's a red herring in there somewhere.'

'Maybe it isn't a phone number.'

'I'm sure it is. Ring-a-*ring* o' roses. More than one rose.'

'Did you copy it down exactly as it was written?'

'Of course I did,' snapped Summers, obviously annoyed that an inaccuracy on his part had even crossed her mind. Then his thinking face replaced the irritated one, and the hazel eyes focused somewhere in the middle distance. 'We've ignored the punctuation.'

'One apostrophe, two full stops, a colon and a comma.'

'Exactly.'

'You've cracked it? What is it?'

But he wouldn't tell her. He doesn't trust me any more, thought Fee. And I don't blame him, either.

Suddenly the door to 14B opened, and a man came out. The handlebar moustache was unmistakable: Arnold. He didn't notice the Saab as he walked past, which Fee suspected was out of character. He didn't seem to be able to decide whether to smile or whistle, so he alternated between the two. It took several snatches for Fee to identify the tune.

'He's solved it,' said Summers.

The tune turned out to be 'She'll Be Coming Round The Mountain When She Comes.'

'Not necessarily,' said Fee.

'Rachel. Wake up.' William was banging at the door. 'Come *on*, we've got a museum to visit.'

'Oh bloody hell,' Rachel called out. 'Can't you forget all that and climb in here with me?'

'Either you're dressed and downstairs in two minutes or I go without you.'

Ten minutes later they were at the museum – William had exceeded every single speed limit. The woman at the desk was operating a queue system, and William and

Rachel had to wait their turn. William tapped his fingers against his leg impatiently.

'I don't know why you were in such a rush,' said Rachel. 'We're never going to win the thing; there are far too many people ahead of us.'

William gave an odd little smile. Once they had the clue and were outside in the car again, he astonished her by solving it instantly. 'The Marquis of Queensberry is a pub in the town,' he said, and ten minutes later they were there – although it took them half an hour to make the phone box connection.

'Rose is a hooker,' said William, running his finger down the cards on the back wall of the booth. 'We need the price for a blow-job, a correction session and straight sex.'

'Wow,' said Rachel, 'you're on good form today.'

The number was engaged. They tried every phone box they saw on the way back to the house, but without success. To Rachel's delight they went straight up to her room, but instead of leaping on her William started to pace the floor.

'Oh for goodness' sake,' said Rachel. 'Come here. You're all tense.'

He stopped pacing. 'Don't patronise me.'

'I wasn't.'

'Yes you were. It's not as though you're the brains of this partnership.'

'You arrogant bastard,' said Rachel.

'I thought you liked being my bit of rough,' retorted William.

'I've got an honours in Modern Languages,' said Rachel 'I am not *anyone's* bit of rough.'

'Oh yes you are,' he said, and he started to take off his clothes.

Rachel's eyes glinted with excitement. He hadn't meant any of it, it was all a game. She was to be his tart from the Victorian East End, he was to be her aristocratic patron.

'How would sir like me?' she asked.

'Naked, bitch, and bent over the chair.'

'Doggie style?'

'Just get on with it,' said William, pulling off his trousers. His erection was immediately evident.

Rachel stripped. Then she bent over the way he'd asked, and presented him with her posterior. He entered her from behind, with no foreplay at all, and at first it hurt. Then the combination of physical friction and mental roleplay wove its moistening spell, and she began to enjoy it. He was pounding into her as though he really had paid for it, and he was going to get his money's worth. The chair was digging into her but she didn't care, his lack of concern for her comfort was all part of the scenario. She let the fantasy take over. Each thrust with its teetering edge of pain took her a little further out of herself, then she'd slip back a fraction and he'd slam into her again.

'Oh wow,' she said, 'this is –'

'Shut up.'

He came very quickly, with a series of grunts, and Rachel was left high and dry and close to screaming point. Before she could complain, the phone rang. William picked it up. 'Angus,' he said. Then he listened for a while. 'Right.' He hung up and got dressed.

'Where are you going?' asked Rachel, making no attempt to hide her anger.

'Out.'

'Are you and Angus collaborating?'

'Don't be ridiculous. I'm out of Angus's league; how would consulting *him* benefit *me*?'

'By picking Beatrice's brains *through* Angus. That's how you solved those clues so quickly.'

'Well thank you for your confidence in me,' he snapped, and he slammed the door as he went out.

Rachel lay there, feeling very angry. She didn't take that sort of treatment from men – when a man pissed her off, she moved on to the next. And there always was a next – she was a natural redhead with a sexy face and a terrific body, and she knew it. 'Don't settle for second best,' her mother had always advised. 'Get an education, make the most of your looks and play the field. Oh, and never fake an orgasm. *Tell* a man what you want.' And Rachel had done just that.

She wondered whether to finish herself off with a wank, but she didn't feel like making the effort. Her vibrator would have solved the problem but she'd forgotten to buy new batteries, and the ones in her torch were the wrong size.

Fee sat in the car, waiting for Summers. She couldn't work out how to operate the stereo and the only books in the car were on game theory. The covers looked interesting, but they were full of mathematical symbols. She ate two of his peppermints but couldn't find anywhere to put the sweet-papers. The ashtray was as spotlessly clean as the rest of the car. After five minutes she decided to get some fresh air. It wouldn't do to go too far though, so she strolled down the road and then back again. Summers didn't reappear. There was a narrow alley down the side of 14B and at the far end of it she could see a dustbin. She decided to get rid of the sweet-papers. Halfway down the alley there was a window. Although a net curtain had been put there for privacy it had caught on something, and there was a patch of bare windowpane. The windowpane had a small hole in one corner and several cracks radiating away from it, as though someone had thrown a stone at it. She stepped up close and peered through.

A large blonde woman was standing in the middle of the room, wearing a red brassiere with holes for the nipples. Bra seemed too slight a term for a construction such as this, designed to support breasts most men would have called magnificent, and most women a liability. Beneath the bosom, several rolls of flesh struggled for supremacy. Beneath those, a matching red suspender belt attempted to contain the rest of her – without any notable success. Summers was standing there, shaking his head and saying something. Fee pressed her ear to the little hole in the windowpane and listened.

'It's not the fifty quid that's the problem . . .'

'You don't fool me, Mr Summers, I know cold feet when I see them.'

'Feel them,' said Summers automatically.

'I think what you really want to feel are these,' she said, unhooking the red rigging underpinning her bosoms and letting the garment fall to the ground. Two enormous breasts settled comfortably into their new positions. She took a pace towards him, seized his hand and placed it over her nipple. 'There,' she said. 'Isn't that nice?'

'Rose,' said Summers, 'it's the anal sex I'm interested in.'

On the other side of the window, Fee's eyes widened with surprise.

'Your first time, and you want the backdoor?'

'Oh, for God's sake, all I'm trying to do is find out how much you charge for anal sex. I don't actually *want* it.'

Rose picked up the brassiere, laughed, and put it back on. 'Just my bit of fun,' she said. 'The colon after *correctly* did refer to anal sex. The numbers you want are seventy-five, forty-three, and twenty-seven.'

'Thank you.'

'I had such a laugh with the first gentleman,' said Rose. 'He got quite annoyed with me by the end of it.' She smiled at the memory.

'He didn't *sound* particularly upset,' said Summers. 'He was whistling.'

'Oh, that was the second gentleman. You're the third.'

'The *third*?'

'The second one was a lovely man. Did some amazing things with that wonderful moustache of his. Gave me a very nice tip as well.'

'Who was the first?'

'Oh, I don't think I'm allowed to tell you that. I only spoke about Arnold because I know you saw him leave. I have to obey the rules. I don't get the second half of my money until the treasure hunt's over.' They moved towards the door.

Fee scuttled back to the car. After a minute Summers appeared, and got in.

'Where are we going now?' she asked brightly.

'Back to the house. To make another phone call.'

'It's a shame we're not allowed mobiles.'

'No it's not,' he said, as though his was the only opinion that mattered. 'I can't bear the things.'

When they got back, he rang the number. 'This is a recorded message,' said an elderly man's voice. 'Murines! They're not the best thing in the world. Re-interpret location appropriately, and enter wondrous portal. That was the fourth clue.'

'That was Alfred Hicks himself,' said Summers, writing down the clue in his notepad with his fountain pen. 'It looks as though he was planning this treasure hunt for a long time.'

'What does *murines* mean?'

'Mice or rats.'

Wondrous portal had been ringing a bell at the back of Fee's mind from the moment she heard it. 'Rats!' she recited. 'They fought the dogs, and killed the cats ... tum-te-tum-te-tum ... lo, as they reach'd the mountain's side, a wondrous portal open'd wide. *The Pied Piper of Hamelin*.'

'Your English teacher was more congenial than your maths teacher, presumably.'

'My English teacher was lovely. That and music were the only subjects I got an A for. So how do we re-interpret a mountainside?'

'It need not be the mountainside. The rats drowned in the river, remember?'

'Oh yes.'

'This needs some thought.'

Rachel turned on the shower, but there was no hot water. She pulled on her satin robe and went out into the corridor. Either it was just *her* shower, or nobody had any hot water. She met Saul Slick coming the other way. He looked at her rather revealing attire with surprise.

'No hot water,' explained Rachel.

'There is in my room.'

There was a moment's uncomfortable silence. Then they both spoke at once.

Rachel said, 'I'd better find the caretaker.'

Saul said, 'You're more than welcome to use my shower, if you want.'

They laughed.

'Thanks,' said Rachel. She collected her sponge bag, then went back to his room and had her shower. As she turned off the water, she realised that she'd forgotten a towel. Oh well. 'Saul,' she called out, 'I've been a bit of a prat. No towel.'

'No problem.'

A moment later his tall figure appeared through the steam, carrying a large expanse of pale-cream fluffiness. He had his eyes shut.

Rachel laughed. 'You'll bash your head on the door if you don't watch out.'

He turned his head sharply, without opening his eyes, and hit it smartly on the towel rail. That *did* make him open his eyes. He put a hand to his head and said, 'Bugger.'

'Never mind,' said Rachel, stepping out of the shower naked and taking the towel from him. She was still feeling horny, so she decided to be provocative and moved in close without wrapping the towel round her. 'Let me see,' she said, lifting his chin with her fingers and feeling through the frizzle of hair for a lump.

He submitted to her examination, though his eyes didn't meet hers.

'Hm,' she said, 'I don't think you've done any great damage.'

'That's a relief.' He wasn't an unattractive man, despite the faint lisp.

'Talking of relief . . .' said Rachel.

He stepped backwards so quickly that he bashed his elbow on the door handle.

'Oh dear,' said Rachel, tossing her wet hair back from

her face, and knowing that her breasts would jiggle as a result. They were full and freckled, with rosy nipples, and they usually dispelled any lingering doubts in the male mind.

'I'm married,' said Saul Slick hoarsely, and he turned and fled.

Christ Almighty, thought Rachel, two let-downs in the space of half an hour. I'm losing my touch.

Fee was leafing through a copy of *The Pied Piper* in the library. Summers was sitting on one of the chesterfields, his eyes shut, the tips of his fingers together, his face composed in its customary serenity as he pursued his favourite activity: thinking. At least, Fee assumed that was his favourite activity. Peverall was taking books out of the art history section, flicking through the entries on Greek vases and putting them back again.

Rachel appeared in the doorway, her hair dampened to deep auburn.

'Hi,' said Fee. 'Where's William?'

Rachel shrugged.

Hm, thought Fee, he won't last long if he carries on treating her like that.

'Peverall,' said Rachel winsomely, 'what's a drachma?'

Peverall snapped shut the book he was looking at and turned to her. 'It's a Greek coin,' he said. 'It's in the dictionary.'

'You're a dictionary all on your own,' said Rachel, with wonderful sincerity.

Peverall looked pleased. 'I collect books of intriguing words,' he said.

'I wish I was paired up with you, and not William.'

'I don't know whether William's an aristophren or not,' said Peverall. 'He hasn't been to one of these house parties before.'

Rachel looked surprised. 'He hasn't?'

'No.' He looked thoughtful. 'Scarab's decided to work solo,' he said. 'She's the independent sort. So I've been doing it on my own as well. If you really wanted to switch partners, I could ask Gavin Smythe to okay it.'

And it would serve William right if I did, thought Rachel. Then she remembered how good the sex in the shower had been. After that she remembered how he'd walked out and left her a semi-quaver short of the final note. She still wanted to finish the tune. Perhaps she ought to find out how well Peverall played the fiddle before she made any irrevocable decisions. He wasn't bad looking, apart from his bald head and his rather prominent Adam's apple. Comes from swallowing dictionaries whole, she thought. She found his dress sense execrable; the concept of things going together had, obviously, never entered his head. He had a very good body, however, wide shoulders and powerful arms, and he was far too gentlemanly to leave her unsatisfied. 'Peverall,' she said, 'what does stasivalent mean?'

He flushed.

'All William would say was that it is one of those things you need to demonstrate in order to explain it properly.'

Fee saw Summers smile. He still had his eyes shut.

'It's a bit difficult,' said Peverall.

'To explain it without demonstrating it? I know,' said Rachel, seizing him by the hand. 'Why don't we do it in your room, then you can show me some of those books of intriguing words you mentioned.' She led him out of the library.

'She'll eat him alive,' murmured Summers, his eyes still shut.

Fee felt embarrassed at Rachel's transparency, though she couldn't quite believe Rachel would actually go through with it. Not with *Peverall*.

'Hamelin's a red herring,' announced Summers. He handed Fee his notebook. 'Look at the clue again.'

Fee looked at his neat black handwriting. *Murines! They're not the best thing in the world. Re-interpret location appropriately, and enter wondrous portal.*

'Where were rats the *worst* thing in the world?'

Fee shook her head. The answer was there, somewhere, but the harder she tried to summon it up, the more slippery it became.

'Room 101,' said Summers. 'Orwell's *Nineteen Eighty-Four*.'

She nodded, feeling really angry with herself – she *had* known the answer, but she'd panicked again. She glanced at the map. 'The room numbers only go up to fifty-something.'

He thought for a moment. 'What if it's in binary?'

'101?'

'Mm.'

'No idea.'

'The answer's 5. Room 5 is our next destination, I think.'

He seemed to be trusting her again.

Room 5 was on the ground floor, at the back of the house. Summers opened the door and they went inside. The only furniture was a desk and two chairs. On the desk was a computer and some other apparatus, linked together by a cable.

'Lie-detector,' said Summers. 'Curious.'

He pressed *enter* on the keyboard, and the screen was filled with a Japanese print. Initially, Fee noticed the swirls of patterned fabrics; then she identified the back of a man's head, and the partially obscured face of a woman. Shortly after that, she realised that the woman was holding her sex wide open, so that her pussy resembled a flower.

'Utamaro,' said Summers.

'Sorry?'

'The artist.'

After a moment or two, the picture was overlaid with the following words:

Welcome to Alfred Hicks's Treasure Hunt. If you have found this room by accident you won't know the passwords. If you are here legitimately, please proceed.

'What passwords?' asked Fee.

Summers typed in something so quickly that Fee couldn't see what it was. So much for the resumption of mutual trust.

The new screen that appeared read as follows:

This is a questionnaire about your sexual history. Absolute honesty is required, hence the polygraph. Fibs will score zero. Lie-detectors aren't foolproof, but they're good enough in this instance. Follow the instructions on the machine; both members of each team must be hooked up, as the questions are designed to be answered first by one, then the other. Ladies first, naturally. The higher your scores at the end, the faster you will get the next clue.

Oh my God, thought Fee. I'm going to have to sit here and admit to all sorts of things in front of Summers. This isn't funny. She glanced across at him, and saw him looking at her. For the first time, he dropped his eyes before she did. Oh ho, she thought, he's as apprehensive as me. Is that because he's going to score bugger-all?

They both got wired up, as instructed. He had to help her, and she had to help him. Their hands touched accidentally a couple of times, and on each occasion they said 'Sorry' in unison. Then Fee pressed *continue*, and the first set of questions flashed on to the screen.

Her heart sank. It was becoming clear that the further they progressed with the treasure hunt, the more outrageous it was going to get.

Chapter Four

'Whoops, sorry,' said Rachel, deliberately tripping over something, knocking Peverall against the wall and pressing the length of her body against him. He caught her by the elbow and steadied her. She noticed that he was wearing cuff-links and an antiquated gold watch.

'How old are you?' Rachel asked him.

'Thirty.'

'Good God. You're younger than me. I thought you were at least ten years older.'

Peverall didn't seem to know whether he should be flattered or insulted. In the end Rachel kissed him on the mouth. His first reaction was to try to pull away, but he had his back to the wall and he couldn't. Then he seemed to change his mind. He's not very experienced, thought Rachel, as they bumped noses. Oh well, never mind. I like urgency as much as expertise, and urgency certainly matches my mood at the moment. That feels like a kingsize cock as well. She unzipped him and felt around. It was the business all right.

'Rachel,' said Peverall, 'I haven't . . . I mean . . . I'm not ready.'

'You feel ready enough to me,' said Rachel, pulling off her T-shirt.

'No, I meant . . .'

'Oh, it's all right, I've got some,' said Rachel, unfastening her bra as she went over to her bag. She pulled out a selection of condoms. 'Lemon, chocolate, ribbed, peppermint, Union Jack . . . What?'

Peverall was looking at her like a rabbit transfixed by a car's headlights.

Rachel glanced down at herself. Her breasts looked just the same as ever, round and freckled and pink-tipped. 'What?' she repeated.

'Fernytickles,' said Peverall.

She stared at him.

'Freckles,' he said lamely. 'Fernytickles. Fabulous word, always wanted to use it in an ordinary conversation.'

'This isn't an ordinary conversation, Peverall,' said Rachel. 'I'm as horny as a toad.'

'A curious expression,' said Peverall. 'I imagine it stems from the fact that when batrachians mate, their amplexus can last for several days . . .'

'Will you stop behaving like a nerd and just fuck me?'

'All right,' he said, 'I will.'

And with that, he stripped off the ghastly mustard shirt, the spotted bow tie and the brown trousers and stood there in his briefs, with his prick peeping over the waistband.

'And them,' said Rachel, taking off her pants.

He did as he was told. Without any clothes, he was a much more exciting proposition. His body was beautifully proportioned, long-legged and slim-hipped. He had muscles. Suddenly the bald head looked virile, not middle-aged.

'Do you work out?'

'I fence.'

For a moment Rachel visualised him with a hammer and nails; then she realised he meant foils. She pictured him on guard, with a sword in his hand. Nice.

'You'll have to show me what to do,' he said.

Rachel's eyes widened. 'You're a virgin?'

He nodded.

'Ground rules then,' said Rachel hurriedly. 'This is just sex. You are not to fall in love with me, nor are you to feel guilty about any of it. I am going to enjoy it just as much as you are. It may only happen the once and you are not to gripe if that's the way it turns out. Agreed?'

'Agreed.'

'Then come here,' said Rachel, and she pulled him on to the bed.

She started to guide his hands over her body, sensing his excitement, and getting very aroused by it. Being wanted – *really* wanted – was one of the biggest turn-ons there was. The ultimate compliment.

She ran her hand up his muscled thigh and over the flat athletic stomach; then she slid it lower, through the only hair he seemed to have on his entire body, and grasped his cock. Her fingers were only just able to close around it. She heard him take an uneven breath, so she coasted her hand up the shaft and started to move his foreskin up and down – only the tiniest of movements to begin with, but gradually getting more and more pronounced. His body stiffened. You're going to come if I'm not careful, thought Rachel, and she let go.

'We're going to take this slowly,' she said. 'It's more fun. I want you to explore me. I'm going to lie on the end of the bed, so that you can see everything there is to see. Then I want you to separate out all the different folds, very gently, and try out different things. Stroking, rubbing, tickling; putting your finger inside me, moving it around, vibrating it . . . Find out what gives me pleasure.'

He was an able student. Once he got over his initial fear of hurting her, he brought both hands into play. He realised very quickly that switching techniques around was more effective than doing the same thing all the time. He made his fingers behave like feathers; he also used them to excellent effect inside her, twisting and thrusting and pressing in turn. He listened to the sounds she made and used them as cues for how effective he was being, continuing, desisting or intensifying as required. Rachel felt her logical thought processes start to slip away as the sensations took over, layer after layer of finely judged contacts. Suddenly he stopped what he was doing. She felt unfairly deprived and opened her eyes. Peverall was in the process of kneeling down on the floor at the foot of the bed. This looked promising. She closed her eyes again and waited with bated breath – then she felt his hands on her ankles. He pulled her down the bed until her thighs were hanging over the end of it, then he opened her legs wide. His tongue was flickering against her clit, and she knew she was going to come if he carried on doing it like that. He was catching every signal and choreographing his responses accordingly; a bird that was learning to fly, and making a pretty good job of it. She could just let go and let nature take its course. The pleasure heightened and heightened until every muscle in her body was tensed with anticipation and the melting ache in her abdomen was almost more than she could bear. When she did climax it felt incredible, like launching herself off a mountainside; she'd been so wound up with frustration that the release was prolonged and intense. She let out her breath, wiped the perspiration from her eyelids with the back of her hand, and managed a smile. It had been more powerful than she'd expected.

Peverall looked astonished with himself. There was a little smile on his face that made her want to pat him on the head.

'That was fantastic, Peverall,' said Rachel, rolling on to her side and looking at him with new respect. She couldn't recall ever reaching that peak of perfection with someone at first try before. His unselfishness had been remarkable, considering the stakes. She kissed him full on the lips and said, 'I think it's your turn now.' Then she showed him how to roll on the condom and added, 'Slip your cock inside me and go at it hell for leather.'

He pushed it in, very slowly and carefully.

'Cunts are pretty tough,' said Rachel. 'You can get a baby down one, after all.'

Peverall didn't manage more than half a dozen thrusts before he came, his eyes screwed tight shut, his breath finally escaping in one long sigh. After a moment or two he shivered like a dog, then apologised profusely for his lack of self-control.

'Don't be daft,' said Rachel, kissing him on his bald head, 'you did brilliantly.'

'Does that mean I might get another crack at it?'

Rachel grinned. She had an ace word up her sleeve. 'Yes,' she said. 'As long as you don't use too many sesquipedalians.'

An expression of sheer delight crossed his face. 'Deal.'

He started to stroke her as tenderly as he might have stroked a kitten. She nestled against him, sinking into an affectionate tactile world that was as comforting as chocolate.

'The answers are just yes, no, or a number,' said Summers to Fee. 'No sesquipedalians.'

'What the hell are sesquipedalians?'

'Many-syllabled words.'

'Oh.' She turned her attention to the screen.

Are you a virgin?

She typed in *No*.

He typed in *No*.

Have you ever masturbated?

Yes, and *Yes*.

How old were you when you first had penetrative sex?

17.

He glanced at her, then typed in *24*.

Hm, thought Fee, a late starter. I suspect my score is going be an awful lot higher than his. The questions carried on, getting slightly more risqué every time. After they'd answered ten, the screen said:

Your honesty is commendable. You are going to get to know one another even better from now on.

The next ten questions appeared.

Have you ever paid for sex?

No from both of them.

63

Have you ever used a vibrator?
Yes from Fee, *No* from Summers.
Have you ever had sex with someone of a different colour?
Yes from Fee, *No* from Summers.
Have you had sex under the influence of illicit drugs?
Yes from Fee, *No* from Summers.
Have you had any sexual experiences with members of the same sex?
She hesitated. Did teenage experimentation count? She typed in *Yes*.
'I went to boarding school,' said Summers shortly, also typing in *Yes*.
Have you had oral sex?
Yes from both of them.
Have you ever experimented with bondage?
Yes from Fee, and, to her surprise, *Yes* from Summers.
How many sexual partners have you had?
Fee couldn't remember. She typed in *9*, wondering whether Summers would think she was a slut. *Liar! Zero Score!* flashed on to the screen. She blushed.
Summers typed in *21*. 'I'm older than you,' he said irritably, as though Fee's *9* hadn't been challenged.
'How old *are* you?'
'Thirty-nine.'
'That's only eight years older than me.'
'A lot can happen in eight years. Get on with the next question, we're losing time.'
Have you ever had sex with more than one partner?
No from Fee, *Yes* from Summers.
Have you ever seen a live sex show?
No from Fee, *Yes* from Summers.
Fee managed to contain her astonishment, but it wasn't easy. The screen changed and a new message read:

Well done. Not a bad score. And now for the final ten questions.

Have you ever played strip poker, dressed up to act out a

fantasy or *had sex in a public place?* got a *Yes* each time from both of them.

Have you ever had sex with a close relative, or with an animal or indulged in Water Sports? got Nos.

Have you ever had anal sex?

Fee suddenly felt really embarrassed and typed in *No*.

Liar! Zero Score! appeared on the screen once more. Fee felt her face go crimson again.

A hesitation, then *Yes* from Summers.

Have you ever used, or had used on you, a cockring?

No from Fee, *Yes* from Summers.

Have you ever used Chinese Love Beads?

No from Fee, *Yes* from Summers.

How extraordinary, thought Fee. He doesn't look the type at all.

Do you find your partner in the treasure hunt attractive?

This, the very last question, took Fee completely by surprise. After a moment or two, she typed in *No*.

Liar! Zero Score! lit up the screen.

She stared at it in disbelief. *No way do I fancy him*, she thought. The bloody machine's fucked up. She sat there, slowly shaking her head.

Summers typed in *No* as well.

Liar! Zero Score! flashed up once more.

'Polygraphs are notoriously unreliable,' said Summers dryly. 'And there's always the possibility that Alfred Hicks decided to make mischief and give a zero score to everyone who typed *No*.'

A new message appeared.

Well done. You have scored average to high on the questionnaire, and the next clue will be made available to you on this screen in two hours' time if you use the passwords *Railway Arch*.

'I think I could do with a drink after that,' said Summers.

'And lunch,' said Fee. 'That should kill two hours.'

They drove to a pub and ordered some food.

'I don't really know anything about you,' said Fee, deciding to make a bit more of an effort to get on with him.

Summers laughed.

'Well, apart from all that questionnaire stuff. Tell me about yourself.'

'Only child, public school, Oxford. I wanted to be an inventor, but I ended up testing other people's inventions instead.'

'Married?'

'Not now.'

'Kids?'

'No. What about you?'

'No. I lived with someone for three years, but it didn't work out.'

'Family?'

'My father died last year. I've got a brother in Australia and another one in the States.'

'You haven't mentioned your mother.'

'No. We ... er ... don't get on too well.'

'Why?'

'Oh, I don't know. We just don't.'

'Describe her.'

'Oh God ... grey hair, brown eyes. Slim. Energetic. She's got this penetrating voice ... she doesn't shout, but her voice carries. She pronounces every consonant and you can always hear her, wherever you are ... If there's a hell and that's where I go, the first voice I hear will be hers.'

'Saying?'

'Trust you to end up here.'

'I see,' he said. 'She's ashamed of you. Why?'

How strange, thought Fee. This feels far more personal than the questionnaire. 'Both my brothers went to university,' she told him. 'I'm just a florist.'

'Are you good at it?'

'Yes,' said Fee. 'I'm very good, actually.' Then she heard her mother's voice in her mind saying, *Your instru-*

ment is not the trumpet, Fiona, it's the flute. She added hastily, 'Well, fairly good.'

'What did your mother say to you, just then?' asked Summers.

Fee's mouth dropped open. Then she simply told him.

'How far did you get with the flute?'

'Grade eight.'

'And you never thought about going to music college?'

'You need maths for that.'

And there was the voice again. *Forget it, Fiona, you've failed maths twice. There's a job going in the florist's . . .*

This time he simply raised his eyebrows, and she told him.

'Suits me,' said William, settling himself on Rachel's settee. 'You weren't much help anyway.'

This guy's a shit, thought Rachel; I'm much better off with Peverall.

William took off his sweater. 'Who are you going to team up with now, then?'

'Peverall.'

He looked annoyed. 'He was one of the top solvers last year.'

'Mm,' said Rachel, 'I know.'

'Oh well,' said William, 'you know what they say. Don't mix business with pleasure.' He moved himself closer to her and started to fondle her neck.

Rachel moved away slightly.

'What's the matter? You're always up for it.'

'Not this time,' said Rachel, remembering Peverall's tongue.

'Oh for God's sake,' said Beatrice irritably to Angus, her dark eyes flashing. 'It is *not* a misspelling. It's got nothing to do with marines. Murines are mice or rats.'

'It's the beginning of that poem then,' said Angus, looking smug. '*The Pied Piper.*'

'*Orwell's* rats, not Browning's,' said Beatrice, with some asperity, her little pointed chin lifting and adding emphasis to her words. 'The location is Room 101, from *Nineteen Eighty-Four* – the place that holds the worst thing in the world. So we re-interpret 101 – and that's 5, in binary.'

'And what are we going to find in Room 5?' asked Angus sarcastically.

'A computer, into which we will enter the passwords *wondrous portal*.'

'Enter wondrous portal,' said Angus. 'Yes. Very clever.'

They found Room 5 and opened the door. Fee and Summers were sitting in front of a computer screen. They turned round to look and Summers said, 'We won't be a minute; this is our second visit here and it'll be brief.'

Beatrice and Angus went outside again. Angus tried to peer through the crack in the door and Beatrice hit him on the arm. 'That's cheating,' she said.

'I want to win,' said Angus. 'Don't you? That prize is worth thousands.'

'Nobody knows how much it's worth,' said Beatrice, her eyes narrowing very slightly. 'Not even Gavin Smythe. Alfred Hicks hid it himself.'

'Gavin said it was valuable.'

'He didn't say it was worth thousands.'

'Alfred Hicks was wealthy. Very wealthy.'

'You're using a very shaky reasoning process,' said Beatrice. 'And not for the first time, either.'

The door opened and Fee and Summers came out. 'All yours,' said Summers.

Angus patted Fee possessively on the backside. 'We're right behind you,' he said. Then he stepped up close to her and added, 'Breathing down your neck, even.'

'You're on good form, Beatrice,' said Summers.

'It was *me* who got the Marquis of Queensberry,' said Angus.

Summers looked sharply at Fee. Fee felt sick. Angus and Beatrice went into the computer room and shut the door.

'I got a bit tight,' said Fee. 'It won't happen again.'

'No,' said Summers coldly, 'it won't.'

'What do you mean?'

The sudden frost was more of a shock than being found out. He copied down the last clue on to a second sheet of paper in his notebook and gave it to her. 'You're on your own from now on.'

Fee felt as though she'd been thumped in the stomach. 'Oh for crying out loud,' she said. 'You're over-reacting.'

'I don't think I am.'

'And your opinion is the only one worth having, is it?'

'Naturally.'

She couldn't think of a single thing to say.

'I didn't come here to assist that moron Angus,' he said levelly. 'You obviously can't keep your mouth shut in bed, which is no doubt a double bonus for him.'

She still couldn't think of anything to say.

He walked off down the corridor, leaving her standing there. To her annoyance, she felt a tear trickle down her nose. She wiped it away so forcefully that she scratched herself – and then felt even more pathetic, for there was no one to blame for her predicament except herself.

'How far had you and William got?' Peverall asked Rachel.

'We phoned this Rose person. But the numbers she gave us didn't make sense.'

'I've got beyond Rose,' said Peverall, and he showed her the clue.

'Murines?' queried Rachel.

'Rats.'

'*The Pied Piper!*'

Peverall shook his head.

'Not the best thing in the world,' mused Rachel. 'The worst then? How about Room 101?'

'*Re-interpret location* – 101 is binary for 5 – Room 5 then. Could be something computery – *enter* wondrous portal. Passwords, maybe. Come on.'

They sprinted down the corridor and flung open the door to Room 5. Angus and Beatrice were sitting in front of a computer, wired up to some apparatus or other.

Beatrice looked upset. Angus looked amused. He glanced round. 'You'll have to wait your turn,' he said.

Rachel and Peverall went outside again and sat at the foot of the staircase.

'What's this evening's entertainment?' asked Rachel, fiddling with her hair.

'Translating a poem from a foreign language.'

'I might have a go at that,' said Rachel. 'It's rather more up my street, being a translator. What languages will they be in?'

'Oh, Wolof, Basque, Vietnamese, Xhosa . . .' He pronounced the last one with a click at the side of his mouth.

She stared at him.

'That's how it's said. Xhosa.' He did it again.

'There are people here who speak all those languages?'

'Of course not. That's the point.'

Rachel shook her head in bewilderment.

'It's guesswork for everyone,' said Peverall. 'We look for words that are repeated – and capitals, because they head names – and punctuation. Then we all extrapolate like mad, and end up with poems about everything under the sun.'

The door to Room 5 opened and Angus and Beatrice emerged. Beatrice looked shell-shocked.

'I wouldn't mind betting everyone gets a zero score for that last question if they type in *No*,' Angus was saying.

Beatrice was shaking her head as if to clear it. Then she said, 'We've got to wait five hours for the answer. I think I'll go and lie down.'

'See you at dinner then,' said Angus.

Rachel and Peverall input the passwords, wired themselves up and looked at the first screen of questions.

Are you a virgin?

Rachel typed in *No*.

Peverall smiled at her as *he* typed in *No*.

Have you ever masturbated?

Yes, and *Yes*.

How old were you when you first had penetrative sex?

16.

70

They both laughed. Rachel put a hand on Peverall's muscular thigh. Peverall put his arm round her shoulders. The time passed pleasantly and amusingly, with Peverall getting more and more wide-eyed at the things Rachel was answering *Yes* to. When it got to the last question they both answered *Yes,* and Peverall put an exclamation mark after it. He started to kiss her, and it was only when the screen flashed up a different colour that they broke off to read the message.

'*Five hours,*' said Peverall. 'That's a long time to wait.'

'No it isn't,' said Rachel, and she unzipped his flies.

'Here?'

Rachel went over to the door and locked it. Then she took off her shirt. Peverall removed his trousers. Rachel slipped off her skirt. One by one they shed their garments until they were both standing there naked. And once again Rachel was struck by how beautiful his body was; how neatly his muscles overlapped, how clearly they were delineated. He was staring rather fixedly at her breasts – then he noticed her looking, and blushed.

She smiled and ran her finger up his erection. He took a quick little breath. She took a condom out of her bag and smoothed it on, then she lay down on the carpet and said, 'Long and slow, Peverall, with a bit of sound and fury at the end.'

His fingers tiptoed down her body until they were between her legs. Then he licked his finger and gently massaged her clit. She stretched out on the floor, totally relaxed in the knowledge that he was as intelligent in his lovemaking as he was at other things. A far more sensitive man than she'd initially expected. He had one finger inside her now, and the others over her mound, massaging her and finger-fucking her in the most inflammatory of ways. His tongue was flicking lightly over her nipple, and his other hand was stroking her buttock. She could feel his prick hot and hard against her leg. He's learned me already, thought Rachel; he never misses a trick. He can tell from the way I press back whether he's got it right, he listens for changes in my breathing, watches my face: he wants me to enjoy it even more than he does. His timing is perfect. And then, as though to prove it, he slid inside her and gradually built to long, easy strokes, as rhythmical as a drumbeat. She closed her eyes and let the sensations ebb and flow. The moth-wing touches of his lips on hers, then on her cheek, her forehead, her eyelid, her earlobe. The stiffness of his prick, the long slick of pleasure as he withdrew, stopped, moved in again, pressed her *there*. A slow, hypnotic arousal that became harder and harder to contain, and then – the sound of someone trying the doorhandle.

Peverall's eyes widened with alarm.

A voice from outside. 'Is anyone in there?'

'It's Saul Slick,' whispered Rachel, stifling a giggle.

'Hello? Is anyone in there?'

'We'll be a little while longer!' called Peverall.

'Oh. OK.'

They heard Saul Slick's footsteps recede.

'That was very cool,' said Rachel.

'I think we'd better draw this to a conclusion,' said Peverall. 'He'll be back.'

The first thrust of the new session moved her across the carpet, and the burn of it across her back was wickedly erotic. She clung on to him, and he slammed into her again. She wasn't going to be able to take much of this: each time he did it she climbed another rung of arousal, and the only way down was orgasmic. He was watching her face intently, holding himself back, trying to gauge when to really speed up and let go. She squeezed her legs together and he took care to rub his cock on her clit each time he rammed into her greasy pussy. His consideration and control at such an early stage of his sex life augured well for the future; there were so many things to try together. And then he must have seen something in her face for he speeded up – and she wasn't thinking any more, she was coming, and so was he.

* * *

Fee went into the library and sat there, looking at the clue. One moment she was concentrating on it, the next she was reliving the split with Eric Summers and feeling both angry with herself and sorry for herself at the same time. She jerked her eyes back to the sheet of paper and read the clue again. *Danny Archer's with an East End accent.* And suddenly she had it. *Down the arches.* She'd heard the phrase over and over again in a TV soap. Arches. What arches? She looked for the map; then she remembered that Summers had it, and she cursed under her breath. Railway arches? There was a station in the town. But she didn't have a car. Then she remembered Summers saying *solve it before you leave* – and she looked at the second part of the clue. It read:

Initially, these flowers don't make sense – you need to be a linguist. Magnolia, rosemary, jasmine, columbine, forget-me-not, daisy, quince and foxglove.

The language of flowers. She couldn't believe her luck. 'Magnolia is grief,' she said – under her breath, for in the corner of the library she could see Arnold's handlebar moustache over the top of the local newspaper. I bet he had a longer time penalty than we did, thought Fee: he's still waiting for this clue. I'm ahead of him. Wow. The thought fizzed around like champagne.

She started to whisper to herself again: 'Rosemary – remembrance; jasmine – amiability. That's g, r, a . . . then columbine – folly. Forget-me-not – fidelity. G, r, a, f, f? Daisy – innocence – Oh! *Graffiti.* Quince is temptation and foxglove is insincerity.' She glanced across at Arnold. He was still reading his newspaper. There was a big advertisement for a store that covered half the back page, with a map of how to get there. Fee walked towards him, on the pretext of looking for a book. She bent down, ostensibly to get to a lower shelf, and looked at the map. Yes, there was the railway line . . . and a viaduct symbol . . .

The newspaper suddenly turned back to front, and Fee was confronted by the headline: INSURANCE COMPANY

SUES SECURITY FIRM OVER ART THEFT. Next to that was a picture of a donkey and a piece about harvest festival. A very local newspaper. She smiled, stood up and walked over to the noticeboard. There was a bus timetable there; she ought to be able to get into town and back again before dinner.

She found the arches without difficulty, but there were a lot of them; dark grimy holes in the landscape, some of them half-filled with rubble, others just empty. Fee walked along the weed-choked path that ran alongside them, peering into each as she passed. There was a burnt-out car under one of them, a collection of supermarket trolleys in the next. Litter everywhere: hamburger cartons, discarded syringes, used condoms. It would be getting dark soon, and it wasn't a very nice place to be. But then, she wasn't meant to be on her own, was she? A smell of rotting leaves and cat's piss – and there, beneath the second-to-last arch, a sudden riot of colour. The whole wall was covered in graffiti.

I was right, thought Fee: *I was right.*

She picked her way across an old mattress, and found herself on the relatively clean sandy floor beneath the arch. The graffiti was spectacular. There were names, jokes, drawings, patterns. A dog with wings, a cartoon pig, a clenched fist. There were many different styles, and presumably many different artists. Fee started to search the text for clues, working from left to right and jotting down anything that might, just conceivably, be relevant. The light was fading and she castigated herself silently; she'd left her torch beside her bed. She wouldn't make that mistake again. She was into this now, hell for leather – she felt as though her mind had undertaken a bodybuilding course and was developing new muscles with the exercise.

Something rustled in the foliage outside. She turned and peered into the gloom. Cat, probably. She resumed her task. Three quarters of the way along the first wall now, and still two more to do. She glanced at her watch. The numbers glowed pale green, telling her that she'd only fifteen minutes before the bus left. She'd have to come back the next day. But that would mean she could lose the advantage she had over Arnold and Elsie – there was bound to be a book on the language of flowers in the library. Yes, of course there would be – that little Tudor rose symbol on the map they'd all been given.

This looked more promising. A drawing of an erect penis, and a poem inscribed within it:

If you take the I from chilli.
That's your third, then I from taxi –
That's your sixth, and make an earl from that word
ear . . .

That sounded like a riddle.

The scrape of a shoe, surely? Fee spun round, the adrenaline coursing through her body as though someone had fired a starting pistol. For a moment everything looked just as it had – then she realised that there *was* a difference. There was a silhouette of a man in the entrance, his hands in his pockets, his face in shadow. He was quite motionless. Neither of them said anything, and he just carried on standing there. Oh shit, thought Fee, no one else is going to come, I'm ahead of the field, I'm on my own. And the longer this silence goes on, the harder it's going to be to break. A cold trickle of sweat ran down the side of her breast.

'Fee, isn't it?' said the silhouette finally.

Fee didn't recognise the voice. 'Who are you?' she asked.

'Graham. Graham Steel. From the word-games group.'

Graham, thought Fee. Oh yes, I remember, the guy with the gun-metal razor-cut and the ice-chip eyes. Relief flooded through her.

He switched on a torch and the cavity beneath the arch was flooded with light. 'That should help matters no end,' he said. 'We're obviously here for the same thing. I have to admit I'm surprised – I've been in the lead from the start and I didn't think anyone else was that close behind me. On the other hand, you're Eric Summers's partner, aren't you?'

'Not any longer,' said Fee. 'We're working separately – and I think I might be ahead of him.' She felt a sharp twinge of delight as she realised it was almost certainly true.

'A not inconsiderable achievement, if you are,' he said. 'Who's your partner?'

'Grace. But she's getting on; she leaves most of the off-the-premises stuff to me.'

Fee glanced at her watch. 'I've missed my bus,' she said.

'Well, we can be civilised about this. Let's look for the clue together and I'll give you a lift back to the house in my car.'

'Thank you,' said Fee. 'But I think I've found it.'

He shone his torch where she pointed and they both copied down the words. Then they put their notebooks away and walked back along the path to his car. He held a bramble twig out of the way for her, so that it didn't slap her in the face. 'Enjoyed the week so far?' he asked, as he held the car door open for her.

'Yes,' said Fee, 'on the whole.'

'Doing the questionnaire with Eric must have been interesting.'

Fee laughed. 'Surprising, actually.'

'I won't ask,' he said, 'much as I'd like to.' Then he added, 'What are you going to do if this clue requires a partner?'

Fee bit her lip. 'I don't know,' she said, 'I hadn't thought. See if anyone else has lost a partner, I suppose.'

'I could moonlight.'

'Wouldn't Grace mind?'

'No. It's solving the clues she's interested in, not winning.'

'Thanks,' said Fee. 'I might take you up on it, if the occasion arises.'

They drove back to the house and arrived in the dining room with thirty seconds to spare. Fee went and sat next to Angus, as he'd saved a place for her and it was the only spare seat she could see. William was talking to

Beatrice, and Rachel was snuggled against Peverall. Fee stared. She hadn't expected the Peverall episode to be a success.

'Good day?' asked Angus, flashing his infectious smile at her and squeezing her arm.

'Yes and no,' said Fee, tearing her eyes away from Rachel. Rachel and Peverall. *Peverall*, of all people. 'I've split up with Summers,' she said.

Angus looked devastated. The reaction seemed to be quite out of proportion to the announcement.

Fee wondered why he was so upset about it. 'But I'm doing even better on my own,' she added.

Angus looked sceptical. 'He's probably ahead of you, and you don't realise.'

'I don't think so. I met someone at the last ... place ... and *he* thought *he* was in the lead. Graham Steel.' She turned round to show Angus who she meant, and saw Graham's ice-blue eyes looking straight at her. The eyes flicked to Angus, then he looked away.

Angus shook his head. 'You're actually joint leader?' he said. 'On your own?'

'I think so.'

'This calls for a celebration. Let's take some bubbly upstairs after the meal.'

'What's up with William and Rachel?'

'They've broken up. Rachel's with Peverall now, and William's trying to poach Beatrice off me ... Hang on. Why don't we let him, and then you and I could be a team?'

Fee hesitated. It was what she'd wanted, right at the start. But now she wasn't so sure.

'Gavin was OK about Rachel and Peverall.'

'I'm enjoying doing it on my own,' she said obstinately.

'Getting a bit overconfident, aren't we?' said Angus.

Fee wanted to hit him – then he turned on the smile. But she was still sufficiently annoyed to say, 'I think I might go to the poetry translation thing this evening. It sounds like fun.'

Chapter Five

*T*he poetry translation *was* fun, once Fee got into it. The recreation room had all sorts of board games available, most of which she'd never heard of before. Graham Steel and Grace were playing Scrabble, although for some reason they hadn't started in the middle.

Fee looked at the photocopied poem Gavin had handed out. She had no idea what language it was in; there were funny accents and strange letter combinations. The word at the end of the first line began with a capital letter. Basia. A name, then, or a place. She tried to sound the poem out in her head, and realised that there was a rhythm to it that seemed familiar. It's a limerick, she thought – the rhymes are in all the right places. Hey, that makes it a whole lot easier. She started to really get into it and the time flew. She could hear Peverall and Rachel giggling every so often, as they showed one another their efforts. William and Beatrice were taking it more seriously, and Fee suspected that Beatrice really had dumped Angus for William. Angus wasn't there. She could see Summers sitting next to Saul Slick; he leaned across and said something and she heard Saul Slick laugh out loud.

'Time's up,' said Gavin Smythe eventually. A couple of people looked frustrated, and others looked smug. They started to read out their translations, working from left to right round the room. There were a few worthy attempts at serious poems, but most people had opted for the light but lewd approach. Arnold got a general groan for translating Basia correctly – it turned out to be Barbara, in Polish.

Rachel's wasn't bad.

Peverall's was incomprehensible. Half the room erupted with mirth, and the other half looked totally blank.

Fee took a deep breath and read out hers.

> There was a young woman named Basia,
> Who wanted a stud who would thrash her;
> After that she'd be putty,
> For ravishing, but he
> Got out his cock just to flash her.

She got a round of applause and she felt great. She had been accepted here, she didn't feel as though she were taking part under false pretences any more. The last one to go was Summers. He won; deservedly so, to her annoyance.

Everybody milled about, refilling glasses and talking. Fee saw William and Beatrice slip away. I wonder if Beatrice has just solved something, thought Fee. She is the Black Widow, after all. The room had become very hot and Fee decided to go and change into something cooler. As she walked down the corridor she noticed that the door to Room 6 was slightly ajar; this was unusual, as Gavin locked them all at curfew. I'll just check that there's a computer with Internet access in there, thought Fee. She opened the door and went inside. This room was far more cluttered than the previous one had been; eventually she found the machine, hidden behind a cupboard. She switched it on, checked it out and turned it off again – and then she heard the door open. Pure instinct took over, and she hid.

Eavesdropping is cheating, Fiona, said her mother's voice inside her head.

Sod you, thought Fee, why do you always expect the worst from me? But at the same time she knew that if she heard something important, she would use it.

'So you can pick locks,' said Beatrice. 'Well, well. Incidentally, someone's taken the book on the language of flowers out of the library.'

'Me,' said William, switching on the computer.

'That's not fair,' said Beatrice.

'I'll put it back when we've finished.'

'I'm not sure we even need it,' said Beatrice. 'And switch that computer off – we only wanted to ascertain its existence. We're in here to talk, not break the rules.'

William switched it off.

'Now then,' Beatrice went on, 'I know some of these . . . magnolia is grief. Rosemary's remembrance. So we have g, r . . . the next letter has to be a vowel. Forget-me-not could be . . . oh, I don't know. Constancy? Fidelity? And daisy is innocence . . .'

Fee made herself comfortable as silently as she could, and peered through a gap in the metal shelving. It didn't look as though her integrity would be put to the test – she was ahead of them. But it already felt far too late to reveal her presence.

'Why don't we go back to my room and look it up?' suggested William.

'Because I want to work it out on my own,' snapped Beatrice.

'Do you do everything on your own, Beatrice?'

Beatrice's sallow complexion coloured, and the little pointed chin moved upwards a fraction.

William lifted her glasses off her nose and ran his fingers through her short dark hair. 'You don't make the best of yourself.'

'I don't pay much heed to appearances. They're not important.' But she didn't move away.

'How old are you, Beatrice?'

'Thirty-four. And I don't think age is of much importance, either.'

He laughed. Then he kissed her, and after a moment or two she started to kiss him back. Then she broke away and looked dubious.

'What's the matter?'

'I didn't get a score for *sex in a public place* for the perfectly good reason that it doesn't turn me on.'

'Easily solved,' said William, and he walked across to the door and locked it.

Oh shit, thought Fee. But she still watched.

'Strip,' said William, sitting down on a chair and folding his arms.

Beatrice undid a single button and then stopped, looking undecided.

'Keep going, teacher lady,' said William. He unfolded his arms, made his right hand into a fist and pointed two fingers at her. His hand became a gun. Fee could see that Beatrice got the reference to *Butch Cassidy and the Sundance Kid* immediately. She slipped effortlessly and convincingly into the part, taking off her shoes and tights first, then unbuttoning her blouse with the fumbling helplessness Etta had shown when Sundance did the same thing to her, and stopping coyly halfway down.

He made a slight movement with his revolver.

Beatrice finished unbuttoning the blouse and let it fall to the floor. Then she unzipped her skirt and let that fall on the floor too. She was wearing very plain white underwear, which fitted the part rather well.

'S'OK, don't mind me, keep on going.'

Beatrice undid her bra and slid the shoulder straps slowly down her arms. Then she took it off and held it demurely in front of her.

'Ruffle your hair,' said William.

She did it, one-handed, and oh so slowly.

'Shake your head.'

She shook it. He looked at her appreciatively for a moment or two, then he waved the gun at her. She didn't move. He cocked it with his thumb. Beatrice let the bra

81

she was holding in front of her drop. Her breasts were small but shapely, and the nipples were erect. She brushed her hair back from her face and Fee could see that her lip was wobbling. Beatrice was quite an actress.

A slightly more assertive wave of the weapon. Beatrice slipped her hands inside the waistband of her knickers and slid them down her thighs. They crumpled at her feet, and then she was completely naked.

William unbuckled his belt, stood up and walked over to her. His put his hand on her hip.

'You know what I wish?' said Beatrice in a faultless American accent.

'What?'

'That just once you'd get here on time!' She was word-perfect. She flung her arms round him and they kissed. Fee could see William's hand stroking Beatrice's bottom; long smooth strokes intended to arouse, and arouse quickly. They fell on to the carpet and he discarded the rest of his clothes.

Fee couldn't tear her eyes away. It was clear that the Black Widow didn't have sex all that often, and as a result she seemed torn between wanting it very badly and not wishing to seem a pushover. William's touch began to get rougher; Fee saw a red line appear where he drew his thumbnail across Beatrice's shoulder.

Beatrice yelped, although she sounded more surprised than hurt.

'We'll have none of that,' said William. 'Fortunately, I know of a way to silence you.'

'Oh yes?' said Beatrice dangerously.

'It's a favourite little number of mine. Sixty-nine.'

'Don't know the tune.'

'I'll teach you.'

William swivelled round, so that they were head-to-tail. He was now facing Fee; Beatrice's back was towards her. She saw him bury his head between Beatrice's legs and heard Beatrice's little gasp of surprise. After a moment or two he surfaced and said, 'You're meant to suck my cock, Beatrice.'

'I know,' said Beatrice. 'I just haven't done it before.'

'One thing at a time then,' said William. 'I'll do it to you, then you can do it to me, and then we'll fuck.'

'OK,' said Beatrice in a small voice.

William opened her legs wide and settled down to do the job properly. He opened her lips gently with his fingers, then he started to lick her, darting here and there, surprising her. She made some funny little noises in her throat and ground her hips against the carpet. William changed tactics and slowed to long, deliberate strokes. Beatrice's breathing became uneven and her hand clenched and unclenched a couple of times. When he put his finger into Beatrice's pussy and started to fuck her with it, she groaned, tried to stifle it, and failed abysmally. He carried on licking her at the same time, and her body writhed as she fought to keep her hips in the right place.

Fee could almost feel the sexual tension in the air, hot and heavy; she was getting turned on by it – there was an ache in her belly that wouldn't go away. She decided she would go and find Angus the moment she was free to leave. Sex with Angus was definitely better than no sex at all.

Beatrice moaned again, an unearthly double-register sound; her leg muscles tensed, then her arms. After that her whole body went into spasm, her face contorted in naughty indulgence, and she came. She lay there for a minute, her eyes closed. When she'd got her breath back she sat up, looking mildly astonished.

'Now me,' said William.

He lay back, his cock fully erect. Beatrice looked at it for a while, then she dipped her head over his body and took it in her mouth. William sighed with pleasure. Fee watched as Beatrice's head bobbed up and down and William's tension increased. He kept on holding his breath and letting it out again in little shuddering bursts. He can't last much longer, thought Fee; she's going to have to stop unless she wants a mouthful of spunk and no shag.

William raised Beatrice's head with his hands. 'That

took a supreme effort of will,' he said. 'But I want to see that grimace when you come a second time.'

He took a condom out of his trouser pocket and put it on. Then he rolled her on to her back and entered her. 'Long and slow, or fast and hard?'

'Fast and hard,' said Beatrice.

William obliged, with a vengeance. Fee watched as the violence increased. She caught fleeting glimpses of Beatrice's face: her eyes were alight with excitement, her jaw clenched, her mouth set. She raked her nails across William's back; William seized her wrists and jerked her arms above her head. Beatrice struggled, and William subdued her with his size and weight. They thrashed and fought their way towards orgasm, and afterwards they both seemed to collapse like rag dolls.

Beatrice sat up rather suddenly after a few seconds and said, 'Graffiti.'

'What?'

'The answer to the clue. Graffiti.' She looked pleased with herself.

Hurry up and go now, thought Fee. But it was another ten minutes before they did.

She made her way back to her room. Rachel wasn't there. She changed out of her hot clothes, got out the clue and looked at it.

If you take the I from chilli,
That's your third, then I from taxi –
That's your sixth, and make an earl from that word
    ear –
Make your blank the fifth, be nifty –
You can score an extra fifty,
For the seven you relinquish; put them here.

No idea, thought Fee. Then she remembered seeing Graham Steel and Grace bent over the Scrabble board. *Make your blank the fifth* ... A blank tile wouldn't score anything, but get rid of all seven and you'd have an extra fifty. Scrabble.

Two reds, six greens, a powder blue,
The total score I'll give to you,
Three hundred, plus another ninety-six;

It *is* Scrabble, she thought. The colours are the squares;
that means there are nine letters in the word. And the
word scored three hundred and ninety-six. Blimey. But
then, it covered two triple word scores.

A questionable answer,
Cue the first, and you the chaser,
See the third to last. Now read the appendix.

Appendix:
Room 6: http://xxx.answer.co.uk

Hang on, she thought: *Cue* could be Q, *you* – U; and *See*
– C. And I could be the third and the sixth letter. So . . .
Q, U, I, –, –, I, C, –, –. *Quizzical*. A questionable answer
indeed – and she could check it.

She ran downstairs. Graham Steel and Grace had gone,
and the Scrabble board was neatly packed away. Fee got
it out and experimented with a few arrangements. If she
started in the top right-hand corner, she could score three
hundred and ninety-two. She added it up again, then she
remembered that she hadn't counted *earl* as a new word,
which gave her four more points. She'd cracked it. She
felt euphoric. It was almost better than sex.

Sex. She'd intended to find Angus and get something
out of her system. But she had to try the Internet address
first. She went back to Room 6, but the door was now
locked.

She went off to look for Angus. She had no luck in the
bar, so she tried the library. No joy. She heard Saul Slick
say, 'But there is a book on the language of flowers in the
catalogue. It ought to be here.' Maybe Angus was in his
room. And with any luck, William would be in Beatrice's.
She went back upstairs and found the door ajar.

'Angus?' she queried, sticking her head round the

doorjamb. No reply. She went inside. He wasn't there. He's bound to be back in a minute, thought Fee, leaving the door open like that. She started to flick through a magazine. Then she noticed a briefcase, open on the table. Overcome with curiosity, she went across and looked. Papers, to do with antiques. A couple of computer discs, a calculator . . . something metal, under a dictionary . . .

'Fee. Just the person I most wanted to see.'

Fee turned round. Angus put his little boy smile on display, letting it light up his rugged face, and she felt a tug in her stomach.

'Nosing around?' He was quite offhand about it, although he flipped shut the lid of the briefcase.

'Not really,' said Fee. 'I was bored. Where were you?'

'Removing a spider from Elsie's washbasin. Anything I can do about the boredom?'

'Hm,' said Fee, remembering William and Beatrice and the Sundance scenario. 'How are you at acting out things?'

'I'm game for anything, Fee. Successful day?'

'Very.'

'Care to elaborate?'

'No.' She wasn't going to get caught again. She was beginning to feel quite possessive about the information she had.

'Tell you what I've always fancied,' he said. 'Teacher and schoolgirl.'

'Haven't got the gear.'

'Don't be too sure.' He went to the wardrobe and pulled out a white shirt and a tie. Then he found a pair of navy blue shorts with an elasticated waist. He added a pair of white sports socks and threw them at her. 'This'll work,' he said. 'Go and wash off your make-up.'

Fee did as she was told. Then she took off the dress and put on the clothes. She looked at herself in the mirror. Her eyelashes and eyebrows were as dark as her hair, so the absence of mascara wasn't terribly apparent. But the lack of eye shadow and lipstick did make her look younger; she could have walked in straight off a hockey pitch.

Angus was now sitting in an armchair, wearing a tweed jacket. 'Now then, Fiona,' he said, 'what were you doing in the games hut?'

'Nothing,' said Fee truculently.

'You know it's out of bounds. I think you were waiting for someone. I think you were waiting for the gardener.'

Fee shook her head, but without real conviction.

'You're a dirty girl, Fiona. I know what you get up to. You let the gardener feel you up for a small cash consideration. I saw you through the window of the hut.'

Fee looked alarmed. 'You won't tell, will you?'

'On one condition, Fiona.'

'What?'

'You allow me to do the same.'

He moved her closer to him and slid his hand up her leg. She felt his fingers go underneath the fabric of the shorts, then feel around the elastic of her knickers. He wormed his way beneath them and began to explore her crevices in a rather maddening, teasing way.

'Naughty girls like you enjoy this sort of thing,' he said. 'I can tell, because you're all wet.' He slipped his finger inside her and moved it in and out a few times. 'Look,' he said, showing it to her, glistening. 'You did that. Now come and sit on my lap and let me explain what the gardener feels when he does that to you.'

Fee sat on his lap. She could feel his erection through his trousers, right between her legs.

'When you let a man do that, his cock goes very hard. That's so that he can push it inside you and move it in and out, just the way I did with my finger. Do you ever play with yourself, Fiona?'

'Don't know what you mean.'

'Do you ever get a nice warm feeling, between your legs?'

'I get a funny feeling when I try and climb the rope in gym,' she said. 'I can only go a little way up, and then I have to stop.'

'Have you ever seen a man's cock, when it's ready for action?'

'I saw a flasher once.'

'I'm going to let you see mine,' he said. 'You can touch it if you like.'

He moved her to one side, unzipped his fly and pulled out his cock.

Fee tentatively put out a finger and ran it experimentally up and down the shaft. Then she took hold of it and squeezed it a little, and it jerked in her palm.

'If you sit on it properly, you'll get that nice warm feeling you had when you tried to climb the ropes.'

Fee turned round so that she was facing him, pulled her knickers and shorts to one side and lowered herself on to him. She just sat there for a moment, making him wait; then she began to move up and down, and he closed his eyes. She watched his face for a while, noticing little things about him, the way his eyebrows grew, the six o'clock shadow that was turning to stubble, the slightly crooked angle of his nose. A rough diamond to look at, but a sexy one. She kept the rhythm slow and tantalising. He leaned towards her, took her nipple in his mouth and moved his hand to between her legs. The combination of gentle sucking and expert rubbing made her shiver, and after a while she didn't want his fingers there any more, she just wanted his cock. She moved his hand away and repositioned herself so that the pressure was just right. Then she slowly increased the tempo in time with her own arousal. His face tightened, and his hand slid round to her bottom, pushing her harder against him. She speeded up. The tingling started in her belly, spread everywhere, then concentrated in just one place as the climax overtook her.

She stopped fucking him, breathing hard.

'Don't stop now, you stupid girl,' he said, and he seized her by the hips and started to pound her from beneath. After a moment or two he shot his load; then he leaned back against the chair, his eyes closed.

Fee climbed off and got dressed. She felt confused. The

schoolgirl persona wouldn't quite leave her, and Angus calling her stupid had only intensified it. She felt sixteen again, and no good at anything. How could he have done that to her, with just one word? It was all wrong, because sex was the one thing that *did* make her feel good about herself. It had been her own personal discovery, because it was a topic her mother had never discussed. She had developed no preconceptions about being bad at it. All the men she'd ever slept with had reinforced this self-image. In bed she was desirable, uninhibited, experimental, fun.

'You know about flowers,' said Angus. 'What does magnolia represent?'

'Secrecy,' lied Fee.

'And columbine?'

'Victory.' Pulling the wool over his eyes was easy; the stupid, helpless feeling suddenly left her, and she felt in control again.

'Oh.' He looked disappointed. 'Fee, I think I've got the others wrong. Why don't you team up with me?'

'Because you'd hold me back,' she said, and walked out.

She went to bed and lay there for a while, being seventeen again, the age when she'd left Fiona behind and re-Christened herself Fee. Rachel had lent her some books: *The Perfumed Garden*, and *The Joy of Sex*. She remembered trying things out with the handle of a hairbrush, and then vowing to try them for real. She'd started to buy sexy clothes, but she always left them at Rachel's house – and her mother never even knew they existed. Every Friday she'd go to Rachel's and change, then the two of them would totter off to a disco, sparkling with glitter and unbridled lust. Fee's face and figure became her passport to another world, one where she did everything right for a change, and the rewards were immediate. Immediate but disappointingly ephemeral, like a rainbow that dissolves as you watch.

* * *

Fee awoke with a delicious sense of anticipation – a feeling none too different from the one she'd have felt if there had been a gorgeous man beside her, stiff with morning rapture. She had solved the Internet address on her own, and as soon as Room 6 was unlocked she would be in there, copying down the next clue. Rachel was curled up like a cat, her red hair spread out on the pillow. Fee made a sound like an alarm clock and Rachel opened her eyes.

'Peverall,' said Fee. 'I can hardly believe it.'

Rachel smiled. 'Neither can I.'

'He's not your type.'

'I don't have a type,' said Rachel.

'Yes you do. Tall, dark and dangerous. Peverall's such a prat.'

'No he's not,' said Rachel, her eyes narrowing. '*You're* the one who goes for stereotypes. Try looking below the surface for once, Fee, and you might find something a bit more worthwhile.'

Fee felt taken aback; this wasn't like Rachel at all. 'You're having a proper relationship with him?'

'Very improper, actually,' said Rachel.

An expression of disbelief crossed Fee's face.

'Stop looking at the packaging, Fee,' said Rachel. 'Angus is probably just as much of a shit as William.'

'At least I could run my fingers through his hair,' retorted Fee, before she could stop herself.

Rachel gave her an icy look and disappeared beneath the bedclothes.

Fee got dressed and went down to the dining room. She'd fallen out with both Summers and Rachel in the space of a few hours, and she was feeling hard done by. Someone was leafing through a book on Greek urns, and someone else was reading a book on the history of boxing. Fee brightened a little – there were still people struggling with the early clues. There are only half a dozen of us at the sharp end of the hunt, she thought. Graham Steel and Grace, me, Arnold and Elsie, William and Beatrice . . . Angus isn't too far behind. Nor is Summers, presumably.

She finished her coffee and scuttled along the corridor. It was three minutes to nine. Saul Slick and his partner were also standing in the corridor, trying to look as though they were terribly interested in one of the paintings hanging on the wall. At one minute to nine Gavin Smythe appeared, carrying a bunch of keys. He unlocked the room containing the computerised questionnaire and the other two went inside. Then he unlocked Rooms 6, 7 and 8, put the keys back on his belt, and walked away whistling.

Ah ha, thought Fee, there are clues in both those rooms that come later on. She was about to nip into Room 7 and have a look, when Graham Steel turned the corner. She stood there in the corridor, undecided about her next move.

'Good morning,' he said. Then, before she could reply, he opened the door to Room 6 and went inside.

'Hang on,' said Fee, following him, 'I was about to use this room.'

'I got here first,' he said pleasantly.

'No you didn't. I just hadn't . . .' She trailed off.

'I'd have expected you to have teamed up with Angus by now,' he said.

Fee shook her head.

He looked sceptical.

'I've gone off him. Will that do you?'

He still looked sceptical. It suited him, in a way, with his wire-wool hair and his light-blue eyes. The sensitive mouth was very expressive; just a lift at one corner of it was enough to suggest informed doubt. He looked like someone from the less burly end of the SAS, someone who could take care of himself. There was an attractive body under the expensive casual clothes. He certainly had more of an idea about how to dress than most of the men in the hunt.

'Look,' said Fee, 'you once offered to partner me for the bits that might need it. Let's do this Internet thing together.'

He thought for a moment. Then he said, 'All right.

There's no point me asking you not to tell Angus. If you're going to, you will. But Angus is bad news.'

'I didn't know you knew him.'

'I don't. I know *of* him. He spent last year inside.'

'*What*? What for?'

'Fencing.'

For a moment Fee visualised Angus with a hammer and nails; then she realised Graham meant passing on stolen goods. 'How do you know that?' she asked him.

'Mugshot in the paper,' said Graham. 'I'm pretty sure it was him. Handling stolen antiques.'

He could be mistaken, thought Fee. But the antique angle is a bit of a coincidence.

Graham sat down in front of the computer, and hesitated. Then he turned to look at her.

He's thinking the same as me, thought Fee, that either of us could be bluffing and waiting for the other to enter the correct address.

'Alternate letter each,' said Graham.

Fee grinned and tapped in Q. Graham did U, and when the two of them had completed the word they watched what followed:

Welcome to Alfred Hicks's Treasure Hunt Website. There is a video feed, which will run as soon as you enter the first one-word answer you solved. This is just an extra precaution against unwelcome visitors. Have fun!

'That's clever,' said Graham. 'If you find a later clue by accident, so you're able to miss some out, you may end up stuck.' He typed in *Misericord*, and a message appeared:

By now, I expect, you're wondering what the treasure actually *is*. No doubt there have been rumours, and speculations as to how it relates to the theme of the hunt. It certainly is appropriate; in fact, it was the prize that gave me the idea for the whole thing. I have had a lot of pleasure constructing this; I've always thought you were a straight-laced lot. I have a heart condition and it is unlikely that I will be around next year to hear you give vent to your fury. But my mind's eye has furnished me with much amusement, which is ample recompense for the labour involved in setting up this enterprise. Rest assured, the prize is worth the effort.

You need to find the common denominator in each of the following shorts. When you have done so, you will find what you are looking for in the grounds of the house.

The screen went dark. Then the first film started. A kitchen maid was sitting in a Victorian kitchen, peeling a cucumber. She was in her early twenties, blonde and buxom, with a full red mouth and a pert nose. After a moment or two she glanced towards the door. Then, having established that she was alone, she lifted her skirts – revealing that she was not in possession of any underwear. She moved her legs apart slightly and settled herself more comfortably on the stool. Then she started to slide the cucumber back and forth, quite slowly and sensually. After a little while she shut her eyes and began to breathe more deeply.

Graham was taking notes every so often. Fee felt she ought to be doing something similar – but she didn't know what to write, apart from *cucumber*.

The camera cut to the kitchen door. The cook was standing there, her massive arms folded across her equally substantial bosom. There was an expression of disapproval on her face. She marched into the kitchen, and seized a flat wooden spatula hanging on the wall. For a moment she considered a copper frying pan, but put it back in its place as it was too heavy to wield with much vigour.

The girl heard her, turned to look, dropped the cucumber and clapped a hand to her mouth in fright.

'It won't do, Hettie,' said the cook. 'Bend over.'

The kitchen maid stood up, bent over the table and lifted her petticoats out of the way. Fee could see the girl's cheeks, round and white, and the dark hair in the crease between them. The cook stood to one side and whacked her with the spatula. Hettie shrieked, and a pinkness began to flush through the white. The cook hit her once again, her lips curling slightly with pleasure. At the end of each stroke she trailed the tip of the implement between her own legs.

Fee glanced at Graham. His eyes were glued to the screen.

Another blow, and the cook's eyes were fairly twinkling with delight. Hettie moaned, and the camera went into close-up. The moan was a moan of pleasure, not pain. The camera cut to the doorway again. A youth was standing there this time, dressed in riding breeches and boots. The young master, presumably. He unbuttoned his fly and took out his cock. It was as stiff as the spatula. He started to masturbate with some urgency as the cook carried on paddling the girl. As soon as he came, the clip finished.

Fee looked at Graham. Graham shrugged, but he looked slightly uncomfortable. *Uncomfortable because he's watching it with me,* wondered Fee, *or uncomfortable because he got turned on by it? I wonder what he's like in bed. Pretty businesslike, I reckon.*

The second short had been filmed in what looked like a wood. A dark-haired girl was carrying a basket and picking mushrooms. She was dressed in a simple white dress and her hair was pinned up in a Grecian or Roman style. The bushes behind her started to rustle and she looked up. A figure emerged. Half man and half goat, the creature had little horns on its head and a lecherous leer. It also had a big erection.

The girl gasped and let go of the basket. Chanterelles and truffles tumbled out – along with a scroll, which unravelled to reveal illustrations of different sorts of mushrooms, interspersed with blocks of text and lists. It looked like the Roman equivalent of a cookery book. The goat-man moved forward, seized her by the shoulders, ripped the dress off her, threw her on to her back and ran his hands all over her body.

The camera moved in close, and Fee realised that the girl was the same one who had been in the previous film. The goat-man licked his hand, wiped it over his cock and entered her. He started to fuck her energetically, and she thrashed and moaned and beat her fists against his hairy body. It was violent and exciting – although it was all artifice, it was easy to suspend disbelief and imagine it was real. Fee was feeling the first stirrings of arousal between her legs, and she was slightly shocked at her own reaction. She did like to be controlled by a man now and again, and this was control *par excellence*.

The girl stopped struggling; she was obviously starting to enjoy it. The fucking was real enough – the camera zoomed in, and Fee could see the man's cock sliding in and out of the girl's cunt. His eventual orgasm was real enough as well. Then the screen went dark again.

The next scene opened with a lengthy shot that panned from left to right along a beach. The beach was deserted, except for two couples, lying a long way apart from one another. Palm trees fringed the sand and a signpost read: RAROTONGA, with an arrow pointing inland.

'Got the answer,' said Graham Steel.

'I haven't,' said Fee.

'Oh well,' said Graham. He got to his feet. 'There's no point me staying for the next one. See you.' And with that, he left. Fee felt as though she'd been stood up all of a sudden.

Chapter Six

'What do you reckon the treasure is?' Rachel asked Peverall, wondering for the umpteenth time how she could find someone so bald so strangely attractive.

'Could be any number of things,' replied Peverall, shining his torch on the railway arch wall. 'But knowing Alfred Hicks, I would expect it to be in keeping with the theme of the hunt.'

'A silver vibrator? A weekend in Amsterdam? A year's subscription to a porn site?'

Peverall laughed. 'Something classier.'

'An erotic painting?'

'Maybe,' said Peverall. 'He *did* collect. Though I'd expect there to be two of whatever it is. Hicks was always fair, though he wasn't always an easy man to get along with.'

'Did you know him?'

'Yes, I did. He had a wicked sense of humour, but he could be a little sadistic as well. Bit cagey about his love life, but we all knew he had one. Even at eighty. No doubt he loved compiling this.'

'What sort of paintings did he collect?'

'Oh, it wasn't just paintings. He had a real gallimaufry.'

'Gallimaufry? Was he a sculptor?'

'No, darling,' said Peverall, kissing her on the tip of her

nose. 'It means a miscellany. A total hotchpotch. Masks, sculptures, vases. Erotic jade figures, Tibetan gilded bronzes . . .'

'A good burglar alarm as well, no doubt.'

'Funny you should say that . . . oh, hang on. Look. Here. *If you take the I from chilli . . .*' He read the rest of it out loud as he copied it down.

'Red, green and powder blue,' said Rachel. 'That rings a bell somewhere.'

'Scrabble,' said Peverall. 'Come on.'

Fee watched the camera come to halt, and focus on a couple lying naked in the sand. With a jolt of surprise, she realised it was two women. The one with long red hair was lying on her back, with her legs spread wide. The other woman was the same one who had been in the previous two clips, and she was blonde once more. She was stroking the redhead's breasts and rubbing herself against the girl's leg at the same time. Both of them seemed to be enjoying themselves. After a moment or two, the blonde woman reached behind her and picked up a vibrator. She switched it on and started the tickle the other woman with it.

Fee knew the feeling only too well – you had to have something on the occasions when you got bored with fingers. She remembered the sudden rush of arousal when the vibrator first made contact with her own clit, and the feel of the cold hard plastic against sensitised skin, the mad gallop towards orgasm. She shivered. The redhead didn't last very long either – she came with a series of shrieks and shudders, and the camera moved away, right the way back along the beach to the other couple.

This couple was male, but either the timing or the editing was at fault and they were nearly at the end of a slinky laid-back fuck. Fee watched the man's hips as he moved, and it was almost as exciting as watching a man's hips moving over her, in a mirror. The bunching of the muscles, the play of light on exposed flesh: naked desire scripted by a master and danced in style – with two male leads. Then both of them seemed to tense all over, after which one of them ejaculated with a loud groan.

The screen darkened again. Fee thought back through the previous clip, and remembered the signpost. Where was Rarotonga? At least it was something she would be able to look up.

The screen brightened once more, and this time a girl with flowers in her hair was walking along a rocky path, driving a goose before her. There was ethereal music in the background, pan-pipes or something – pan-pipes! That was the link! Pan. The frying pan in the first clip; Pan, the god of the forest in the second; a pan-shot from a video camera in the third, and pan-pipes. I just need to explore the grounds, she thought, and find something that relates to Pan. Has to be one of those statues, surely.

She went outside. It was a beautiful day, one of those early September jewels with a deep-blue sky and a faint smell of wood-smoke; someone somewhere was burning the detritus of the summer. The swimming pool was as flat as a sheet of turquoise glass, and the speckles of dew on the lawn were evaporating in the sunshine. Fee felt quite light-hearted as she checked out the statues around the building. A sphinx, a griffin, Nelson, Captain Cook, a phoenix ... there was a mythological flavour to quite a few of them. When she'd exhausted the material around the house, she set off across the vast expanse of lawn in the direction of the woodland garden. Here, little pathways wound between banks of rhododendrons. She turned a corner and found herself confronted by a small lake, dotted with water-lilies. There was a statue of a mermaid in the middle, but that was all. She carried on walking. She found a stone elf, sitting cross-legged on a tree-stump. A unicorn, one foreleg raised as though it had just stopped to think about something; white, ghostly. A cluster of fly agaric toadstools under some birch trees, real ones, their cream-spotted scarlet caps almost too fairytale to be genuine. This was something else her mother hadn't spoilt for her, this buzz she could get from nature. She couldn't recall her mother ever identifying anything. Toadstools were toadstools, not ink caps or amethyst deceivers, and birds were just birds. Names like willow-warblers and velvet scoters were affectations. It was her father who'd given her a field guide to wildflowers and enabled her to tell the difference between a speedwell and a forget-me-not. She turned another corner. A rather delightful statue of a fairy, then one of Peter Pan . . .

Peter Pan! She could have danced for joy. He was playing his pipe cross-legged on a tussock of stone grass, but although Fee went all round the statue she couldn't see anything that looked like a clue. She pushed it and pulled at it – but nothing moved, so she prodded it all over. Eventually she gave up, feeling stupid. Why couldn't she spot whatever it was? Surely this was the right statue? She examined it more closely, in case there was some tiny writing somewhere. Nothing. After a while she decided it was silly just sitting there, stumped. She might as well explore the rest of the grounds, just in case.

When she turned the next corner she saw a folly in the distance. It was a small building, but it had proper Corinthian columns. When she was closer to it, she realised that someone else had got there before her. There was a small seating area inside, and two alcoves, both occupied by statues. A man was standing in front of one of them, and she could see neither him nor the statue clearly. Then she recognised the gun-metal hair and the wiry body. Graham Steel. He looked up as she approached; she saw that the statue he was examining was the god of the woodland. *Pan.*

'Hi,' he said. 'I didn't think you'd be long.'

'Got the clue?'

'No, I haven't.'

Fee surveyed the statue. It was life-sized and made of grey stone. It didn't look weathered at all; perhaps it was well protected from the elements where it stood in its alcove, or maybe it was a recent acquisition. The statue's torso was powerful and muscular; hairy from the waist down, the feet cloven-hoofed. He was playing his pipes, his big square fingers covering some of the holes. His face was coarse, almost ugly – thick lips and heavy eyebrows, and slanting lecherous eyes. The grey locks were wild and unkempt and two sharp little horns projected through them, dik-dik style. Fee moved round so that she could see him from the side. A goat's tail and a ridge of hair down his spine. The fur on his rump was thick and curling, quite a lot of detail, nooks and crannies everywhere, though none of them very large. A dead ringer for the satyr in the film clip.

'I've searched it from top to bottom,' said Graham. 'Nothing.'

'Did you see the Peter Pan statue?'

'No,' he said, surprised, 'I didn't.'

'Nothing there either,' said Fee. She looked more closely at the pedestal. There was a faint inscription: *Ecce homo ad libitum*. She glanced at Graham.

'Latin,' he said. 'Behold the man . . . *ad libitum*. Literally, at pleasure.'

They grinned at one another.

'Genital inspection,' said Graham.

Fee raised her eyebrows.

'The statue, not you.'

Almost without thinking, Fee made a gesture of mock disappointment.

They both peered into the tangle of stone hair. Pan's penis was there all right, nestled comfortably against his balls. Both scrotum and prick were somewhat larger than standard issue, even in flaccid mode; this wasn't immediately apparent due to the surrounding ornamentation.

Fee looked closer. 'There's a line here,' she said. 'It's as though his wedding tackle has been carved from a different piece of stone.'

Graham squinted at it. 'Maybe the whole thing lifts out,' he said.

'Try it.'

'After you. I'm not used to handling other men's willies.'

Fee bridled. 'Are you making out I'm a tart? Just because I slept with Angus?'

He shook his head, surprised. 'No, of course not. I just meant I'm not interested in men.' There was a moment of uncomfortable silence. Then he said, 'Are you going to give this statue the time of its life, or not?'

Fee swallowed, took hold of the stone cock and pulled. Nothing. She twisted. Nothing. What was she going to have to do, wank it? She tried pushing instead. There was a sudden grinding sound, as though some ancient mechanism was being activated, and the penis swung up and out, clearing the scrotum and standing proud. It was now much longer, and there was a plastic card attached to the underside.

'Congratulations,' said Graham. 'The woman capable of arousing a man made of stone.'

She looked into his flinty blue eyes and thought – what about you, then?

'I'm just made of flesh and blood,' he said. 'I'm a pushover.'

'Really?'

'Really.'

She stretched out her hand and pushed. He collapsed theatrically to the ground, catching hold of her wrist and pulling her down with him. She landed on top of him and he held her there, his hands gripping her arms, looking into her eyes. She didn't look away, and nor did he.

'What about Angus?' he said.

'History.'

He slid his hands up her arms, across her shoulders and down her spine to her waist. 'You'd better get your clothes off then.'

'What, here?'

'Don't tell me you didn't score for sex in a public place.'

She glanced out of the folly, down the long stretch of grass. Deserted. They were on their own. Was this what she wanted, a quick screw with someone to say *sod you* to Angus? She had instigated it, after all. He moved his hand up to her throat, brushing her breast lightly in passing, and undid the top button of her blouse. It resisted for a moment, mirroring her mood; then it gave way, and so did she. What the hell. He was an attractive man, and she liked attractive men.

He unfastened the next button, and the next. She sat astride him, feeling the silk lapels of her blouse part company. He slipped the blouse off her shoulders and continued the movement in one easy sweep to unhook her bra. A blackbird sounded its alarm call. He ran the tip of his finger across her nipple and she shivered. Then he lifted her off him; they stripped and made a sort of mattress of their clothes on the stone seat beside the statue. Naked, with only the folly as a backdrop, Fee felt as though they were figures from a painting by Poussin.

'This is all very pastoral,' he said, catching her train of thought.

They lay down on the bench. He kissed surprisingly well – not forcing himself on her, just trying out different things, seeing what produced a response, remembering it, elaborating, using his tongue so delicately that she was the one who eventually encouraged it to a more passionate level. He carried on kissing her, stroking her all the while, getting lower and lower. Down the middle of her spine to the small of her back, across the top of her hipbones, down to where they joined her thighs, over her buttocks and back around to the front until – at last – his hand brushed her between the legs. She pushed against him; it was almost a reflex action, and he began to do wonderful things with his fingers, sliding them from orifice to orifice until she didn't know where she wanted him. She could feel the breeze on her skin, like angel feathers – there was something so sensual about doing it outdoors; she felt so alive, part of a natural world where inhibitions didn't exist. Her body was beginning to react without her brain intervening, and it was heady stuff.

She felt for his cock, twisted round and licked it everywhere. It wasn't the biggest one she'd ever seen, but it was as hard as a diamond-cutter and the tip tasted faintly of come – the sort of come that tickles the tongue like sherbet. She sucked away the dewdrop, circled the head a little lower down, then moved back up for the next minute leakage. He made no sound, but she could feel the tension in his body increasing. The next time, she took all of him into her mouth and squeezed the base of his prick at the same time. After a little while he lifted her head and said, 'Much as I'd like you to continue, I think a proper fuck is what's needed.'

She glanced back down the stretch of grass one last time. And there, right in the distance, were two people, walking in their direction. '*Company*,' she hissed.

He looked where she had. 'We can finish this before they get here.'

'You're confident.'

He answered this by sliding his cock inside her and moving in a way that made her catch her breath. She then found herself swept away by it all. She lifted her legs and rested them against his flanks, so that he could get more leverage. The change in angle heightened things even more, and the sensations intensified until she felt she was going to turn inside out. He held back until she took a great gasp of air and held her breath, and then he let go, and exploded inside her. They lay there for a moment, panting, but by the time Saul Slick and his partner Joan had reached them they were dressed again, the clue copied down and their notebooks put away.

'Hello,' said Saul, 'taking a break? It's such a lovely day, Joan and I thought we'd take advantage of it.' His eyes strayed to Fee's cleavage. Fee realised she'd done her buttons up wrongly, and far more was visible than usual. She didn't know whether to turn away and attend to it, or brazen it out. She brazened it out. Then she realised that Graham hadn't done up his flies. And after that, she realised that Saul and Joan weren't there chasing a clue; they didn't know there was a clue there. They were quite simply doing what they'd said they were doing, taking a walk. She moved in front of the statue, trying to hide the evidence, until she could feel the tip of the stone penis pressing against her bottom.

'I need a little sit down,' said Joan, making her way over to the stone bench. The used condom nestled in the far corner.

Suddenly the grinding sound started up again, and Fee felt Pan's organ retract.

Joan jumped, quite visibly, gave a little gasp and looked round.

'What in God's name was that?' asked Saul Slick.

Graham and Fee looked at one another, shrugged, said goodbye and walked away. When they were halfway down the stretch of grass, Joan's voice floated back to them, faint and distant – but saying, with horrible clarity, 'They might have cleared up after them.'

Fee studied the clue over lunch. Graham and Grace were doing likewise at the next table. She was very aware of him sitting there, the square shape of him, the tilt of his head, the knowledge of what he felt like under the fabric of his shirt. This wouldn't do at all. Concentrate.

Lost in bothersome Chelmsford? Park under the trees. (3, 4).

Well, that's definitely a crossword clue, thought Fee, though I can't see an anagram indicator. I wonder which bit's the definition? But she couldn't decide, so she looked at the next part.

Sounds like two for tea, by the back gate. Dating Diana should result in her E-mail address. Then – Room 8.

What back gate? There must be one in the grounds somewhere. Maybe it would be clearer after she'd solved the first bit.

Summers walked into the dining room and went and sat by the window. She watched him get out his notebook. He angled it so that he could read it, and studied it carefully as he ate; then he opened out the map and spread it on the table.

Surely he's got beyond the railway arch, thought Fee. Then she remembered Saul Slick saying that the relevant flower book was missing. If Summers couldn't solve the language of flowers clue, he wouldn't have got as far as the graffiti. If he *had* got beyond the graffiti, he'd have no trouble with the Scrabble. But she hadn't bumped into him anywhere, they hadn't been chasing clues at the same time.

She looked at her own clue again. *Lost in bothersome Chelmsford.* Did *lost in* mean the answer was hidden in the words that followed? *Park under the trees.* The name of a park, maybe, rather than a command to put your car in the shade. She needed the map. She glanced across to Summers's table, but he'd gone.

Gavin Smythe came in. Fee went over to him and asked him for a spare. Then she said, 'What do you know about the prize, Gavin?'

'Nothing. The favourite theory seems to be an antique of some sort – well, two antiques. However, Alfred Hicks was burgled a few months before he died, lost practically everything. Got a whacking insurance pay-out, but I don't think there was much left. Your guess is as good as mine.'

Fee went to the library, curled herself up in one of the big leather armchairs and looked at her new map. Then she started to wonder what she would do if she won – something that hadn't occurred to her before. She had to be in with a chance. Supposing the prize *was* worth a lot of money? An exotic holiday? A deposit on a flower shop? Or further education? *That* would render her mother speechless.

After a moment or two William came in. He didn't see her. He went over to the bookshelves, took a book out of a carrier bag and put it back on the shelf. Then he left. Fee got up, and went over to look. *The Complete Language of Flowers.* You creep, thought Fee, deliberately holding other people up.

She went back to the armchair and studied the map again. Eventually her patience was rewarded in the form of a building at the end of a long drive, surrounded by a lot of land. *The Elms.* You could find *The Elms* in bothersome Che*lms*ford, and maybe even park under them. Excellent. Now then.

Sounds like two for tea, by the back gate. Go in by the back gate, maybe? *Dating Diana should result in her E-mail address. Then – Room 8.* Then find someone called Diana, and ask her for a date.

Yup. She would try it. *The Elms* was only about half a mile away; it was a beautiful day – she could walk it.

There were two big wrought-iron gates that were very definitely shut, and an entryphone to one side of them. She pressed the button.

'Hello?' crackled a woman's voice.

'Is that Diana?'

'No, it's Laura. Who is this, please?'

Fee didn't know what to say.

'There's no Diana here. Sorry.' The crackling stopped as the connection was broken.

Bugger, thought Fee. Then she remembered the bit about the back gate. There was a footpath off to one side, and it looked as though it ran the length of the property. She started to walk along it. To her right, there was a high wall blocking her view of both *The Elms* and its grounds, with broken glass cemented on to the top of it. To her left, a field of sheep. She carried on walking. Every so often she saw the tops of trees on the other side of the wall, and eventually a building. It looked like quite a grand house, grey stone and Virginia creeper. She kept walking. A little bit further on she heard voices and the thwack of a tennis ball. Then splashing and laughter, suggesting a pool. The sounds were too distant for Fee to make out any words, and she left them behind. The wall started to curve round, and a rabbit bounded out of her way. She walked for another few minutes, then she saw a hefty wooden gate, set back in the wall. There was a number pad next to it. She had to key in a code to be able to enter. What code, for goodness' sake? And how many digits? What *was* this place? A leisure centre for MI5? She considered keying numbers in at random, then remembered the way cash machines withdrew cards. Would an alarm sound after a certain number of unsuccessful attempts? She sat down on the grass and pulled out the clue again.

Two for tea, by the back gate. *Two for tea*, not *tea for two*. She started to sing the song in her head, and then she stopped. *Sounds like* two for tea. *Two forty*. She jumped up and keyed in the numbers. The gate clicked open. She'd solved it, and once again she felt a surge of pure joy. Maybe she'd just never given herself the opportunity to feel like this before. Followed her father's example only too well: don't try, then you won't fail.

Fee cautiously widened the gap, a little at a time. All she could see was foliage of some sort. When there was enough room she slipped through, and found herself in an ornamental garden. She shut the gate carefully behind her and followed a little path through some flower beds and out to a lawn. It was surrounded by trees and quite secluded. There were two white loungers on the grass and a little low table with nothing on it. She slipped through the trees to another glade, also furnished the same way. Beyond that was a rose garden, with some unusual floribunda varieties and a little fishpond. There was a deep cloying perfume everywhere and the faint buzzing of bees. The atmosphere was soothing yet secretive, as though the place was some sort of retreat. The tennis court was next. The match had been abandoned and two racquets and a number of balls were lying scattered on the asphalt. Beyond that was the pool. Fee stopped. There was someone swimming in it – a man, probably, if his close-cropped hair was anything to go by. Beyond the pool was a long lawn, with a fountain in the middle of it. The lawn sloped up to the back of the house, which had steps leading up to the doors. As she looked, the doors opened and a large group of people came out.

Every single one of them was stark naked.

Fee's mouth dropped open. She'd only ever seen bare flesh in that quantity on television, in documentaries. She heard laughter and saw that some of them were carrying croquet hoops and mallets. Others had newspapers and towels, or cups of coffee. It's a naturist club, she thought. No wonder the security was so strict. They look as though they've all come out of a meeting of some sort, or afternoon tea. And there are loads of them; I'm bound to be noticed.

And then she thought – well, there is one way to disguise myself. Have I got the nerve? Yes, dammit, I have. She retraced her steps until she reached the second glade, then she glanced round, stripped and hid her clothes under a bush. Carrying just her notebook and pen she headed back towards the house. She started to smile at people, for they smiled at her – and after a little while, it was just the same as taking a walk in the country and nodding at passers-by. The notebook and pen gave a bit of authenticity to her being on her own – she could be looking for a nice quiet spot to write a letter, or some poetry.

A man was standing by the pool, presumably preparing to dive in. The other one seemed to have gone. This man was middle-aged, with a bit of a beer belly, a beard and a lot of body hair. He wasn't tall, or good-looking, or athletic – but there was something about his figure that was a real turn-on, something very primitive about his all-over tan and his total lack of modern trappings. No clothes, no watch, no rings. No packaging. A thoroughly male body from a bygone age. After a moment or two he dived into the pool and swam off. Fee had a sudden flashback to the only holiday her family had ever taken abroad, when she'd been thirteen. They'd tramped for what seemed like hours across parched terrain to find a good picnic spot. Eventually they found a little inlet, which looked as though it was practically deserted, and they made themselves at home. Her mother had started to slice a sausage, while her father and her brothers tried to locate the cricket score on their little transistor radio. Fee had decided to explore. As she rounded the headland, she saw a man. He was middle-aged, with a bit of a beer belly, a beard and a lot of body hair – and he was completely naked. Fee had never seen a man without his clothes on before and she watched, fascinated. The sight stirred something inexplicable inside her. She wondered what the man's body felt like, under all that hair. And then her mother's voice, shrill, imperative. 'Fiona! *Fiona!*' She'd run back, to find her mother packing everything away. He brothers were sniggering behind their hands. 'We're leaving,' said her mother, but she wouldn't say why. Years later, she'd realised that they'd been picnicking on a nudist beach. 'I'm never coming to France again,' her mother had said as they trudged back across the baked earth under a midday sun. 'It's totally uncivilised.'

Diana. Was there a Diana here, even though the receptionist had said there wasn't? Taking a peek at the club register seemed like a good idea, if it was ever left unattended – but that meant going into the house. She took a deep breath, walked up the steps and into a large room. An elderly couple were sitting on a sofa, drinking coffee. Fee felt as though her eyes had suddenly become iron filings, and the couple were the magnet. All of a sudden she desperately wanted to look; she'd never seen the unclothed body of a really old person. Her mother had wrapped herself up like a Christmas present, from knee to throat, and the only time Fee had ever got close to seeing what was under the courtelle had been early one winter's morning, when she'd dashed downstairs to try and do the homework she hadn't done the night before. As she'd tried to open the kitchen door, her mother had slammed it back in her face and shouted, 'I'm having a wash next to the boiler, as it's the warmest place in the house! Don't come in; I'm all horrible and naked.'

The words *horrible and naked* had stayed with her like an albatross, a prediction as to what she'd look like herself in years to come. The couple on the sofa were talking, and paying Fee no attention at all. Fee let her eyes stray to their bodies. The woman's skin was very white, and the flesh was looser on her frame than on a younger person's. But Fee's imagination had been far worse than the reality; this woman didn't have the sagging rolls of fat Fee had expected, nor did she have varicose veins or liver spots or unidentifiable lumps and bumps. Fee turned her attention to the man. Here was another one with an all-over tan. He had a few operation scars and a bandage round his knee, but the hideous reality of what went on under pensioners' clothes wasn't so hideous after all. Then, just as Fee was finishing her stare, he looked up.

Christ, thought Fee, I've got to have something to say. 'Your name isn't Diana, by any chance, is it?' she asked the woman.

'Christine. Sorry. I'd ask at Reception if I were you; Laura's the only one who knows everybody. People come and go all the time, there are always a few new faces. Yours, for instance.'

'Yes, it's great here, isn't it?' gushed Fee, sidling towards the door. 'I'll definitely come again.'

'Well, you wouldn't fork out a fortune for membership if you only wanted to come the once, would you?'

Shit. Careful, now. 'Actually,' she said, 'I don't know how much it cost. It was a present. From my boyfriend.'

'Hang on to him then,' said Christine. 'He must have a generous nature.'

Fee gave her what she hoped wasn't too sickly a smile, and made her escape. The house was a rabbit warren of oak-panelled corridors and rooms. Some of them were labelled – sauna, gym, table-tennis room. Others doors just had numbers. Deep-pile carpet underfoot, paintings on the walls, a gilded mirror, a noticeboard ... Fee studied it. Advertisements for riding schools, osteopaths and herbalists. A chart of a table-tennis tournament. She looked at the names, but there weren't any Dianas.

A phone rang in the distance. She heard a woman's voice answer it – Laura's presumably. It was hard to tell without the crackles that had accompanied it at the wrought-iron gate. I bet that's Reception through there, thought Fee. She walked to the end of the corridor and peered through the little window in the door. A grey-haired woman was sitting at a desk, quite nude, talking on the phone. There was a thick ledger on the counter in front of her. Whoopee, thought Fee, I just have to wait until she leaves the desk for a bit.

She stood in the corridor, ostensibly looking at the paintings. A few people passed her, but she affected total engrossment and they didn't speak to her. She took another peep through the window. Laura had got to her feet, and to Fee's horror she started to make her way towards the door behind which Fee was standing. She looked up and down the corridor. There were plenty of doors leading off it, but she only had time to make the nearest one, which wasn't labelled. She opened it. Pitch dark, a cupboard of some sort. She felt for a light switch, but it wasn't in the obvious place and she didn't have time to investigate further. She nipped inside, closed the door behind her, and listened for Laura's footsteps. Then she thought, I'm not going to hear them, am I? That carpet would deaden a herd of elephants.

She felt around for a light switch again, but only encountered soft folds of material, stacked on latticed wooden shelves. Towels, blankets, something smoother – sheets, maybe. It's a linen store, she thought, still straining her ears for sounds outside. And yes, she could hear something . . . someone breathing, very softly . . . but it was someone *inside* the cupboard.

She froze. The other person must have seen her quite clearly as she came in. Why hadn't he or she said any-thing? More to the point, why was he or she sitting in here in the dark? Her heart began to beat faster and a little trickle of sweat made the back of her neck go unpleasantly clammy. The silence just went on and on; nerve-racking, horrible. She didn't know what to do. The other person must have realised he or she had been heard, for the breathing got a little louder as whoever it was stopped trying to conceal it. Maybe it was a cat and she was being really silly. Cats loved airing cupboards. But it didn't sound like a cat. It sounded as though someone was trying very hard not to laugh.

She went from fear to anger in the space of a couple of seconds. She had been really frightened – and whoever it was knew that, and found it highly amusing. She ran her hand back along the bit of wall by the door, before the shelving started – and at last she found it. Her finger hooked over the top of the light switch, ready to press – but she hesitated. Who would have to explain themselves: the unknown person, or her? The security was as tight as it was to deter peeping Toms, and this might be one. *She* would be able to take the high ground. She was now almost certain that the person was a man; the breathing sounded – well, masculine.

Fee took a deep breath and flicked the switch.

It was Eric Summers – and he didn't have a stitch on either.

Chapter Seven

'Where's Rarotonga?' asked Rachel, as she and Peverall sat in front of the computer screen.

'Capital of the Cook Islands,' said Peverall.

The screen darkened, then brightened once more; this time a girl with flowers in her hair was walking along a rocky path, driving a goose before her. There was faint music in the background.

'Got it,' said Peverall.

Rachel looked at him and smiled. 'Clever clogs,' she said. 'What is it, then?'

'Cook. The cook beating the girl with the spatula. The Cook Islands ... the girl in the woods could have been a cook.'

'And cooking your goose!'

'Or goosing your cook.'

'You're wonderful,' said Rachel. 'I love you to bits!' And she leaned over and kissed him passionately on the forehead.

'Do you?'

'Do I what?'

'Do you love me to bits?'

Oh shit, thought Rachel, he's moving much too fast here. 'Just a turn of phrase, Peverall,' she said. 'I don't even know what brand of toothpaste you use yet.'

He told her. Then he told her which soap, and which washing up liquid, and which scouring powder. 'But don't get alarmed,' he added, 'I can wait to find out what *you* use. If you decide you want to tell me, that is. I'm very patient.'

And very clever, thought Rachel. I wonder if anyone else has had a declaration of love in cleaning materials?

'I thought Peverall and Rachel would never leave,' said Beatrice, as she and William sat in front of the screen, watching the kitchen maid being beaten by the cook. She glanced sharply at him. 'Are you writing these down, or am I?'

'What?' William managed to tear his eyes away from the clip. 'I thought *you* were.'

'I *am*,' said Beatrice sourly. 'But you might get something I miss.'

William got out his pen, and at the end of the four films they compared notes.

'Cucumber, kitchen maid, cook, spatula,' offered William.

'And the youth,' added Beatrice. 'Right. Satyr, chanterelles, truffles – trees.'

'Hm,' said William. 'Sea, sand, vibrator, signpost . . .'

'Rarotonga,' said Beatrice. 'Capital of the Cook Islands.'

'Are you sure?'

'I'm a geographer,' said Beatrice.

'There's a statue of Captain Cook in the grounds,' said William.

Beatrice gave him one of the rare smiles that she usually reserved for particularly interesting wadis or especially elegant crossword clues. There wasn't a lot of call for smiles when you lived on your own, but Beatrice liked it like that. Solitude was comforting and familiar. She'd been an only child who divided her time between books and rock samples, and university hadn't really changed her at all. She got a first, did a doctorate, stayed in academia and allowed herself just the one hobby – word games. She liked being the Black Widow, for she liked the idea of an alter-ego. An alter-ego might be able to shed a few inhibitions, when the real Beatrice could not.

'Why do you reckon there's a statue of Captain Cook here?' asked Rachel, surveying the imposing figure with its eighteenth-century hairstyle – combed straight back flat and gathered into horizontal sausages either side of the head, just below the ears.

'There's a story that he brought a couple of Tahitian girls back from a voyage,' said Peverall, 'and kept them here, at the house. I don't think it's true, but that's why there's a statue.'

'There's something in his pocket,' said Rachel.

Peverall climbed on to the pedestal, and had a look. 'Eureka!' he cried. 'Pass me the notebook darling. We're in the home straight.'

Rachel couldn't decide whether she liked being called darling, or not. No one had ever done it before. She handed him the notebook, and he copied down the clue that was on the laminated sheet. It was attached to Captain Cook's wrist with another little chain, like the one round the misericord. Then he jumped down, seized hold of Rachel's hands and swung her round in a circle.

'Stop it,' said Rachel, laughing.

'Happiness,' said Peverall. 'A quark of an emotion. Observe it, and it's gone. But this knocks quantum mechanics for six. I am happy, I know I'm happy, and it doesn't go away when I say it.'

'Peverall,' said Rachel sternly, 'we'll all be going home at the end of the week.'

'Mm,' said Peverall. 'And if I play my cards right, you'll be coming with me.'

'You don't know anything about me,' said Rachel desperately. 'I leave hairs in the sink, and I forget to clean the bath.'

'And I'll be right there with the scouring powder,' said Peverall.

'You're impossible,' said Rachel, hitting him playfully on his lovely muscular chest. 'Let's see the clue then.'

115

Peverall glanced towards the house. 'Not here,' he said. William and Beatrice were walking towards them. 'In the car,' he said. 'And I've solved it.'

'Have we got time to go anywhere?' asked Rachel. 'Curfew in half an hour.'

'I think we might have won,' said Peverall. 'In which case, it doesn't matter.'

They waved gaily at the other couple and scampered off to where Peverall's Mercedes was parked. Peverall reversed out, while Rachel looked at the clue and read it out loud. 'Use a serious accent when asking for a lot of ale; then find a dead glass, and take steps to win gold.' Rachel looked at Peverall, her grey eyes shining. 'Win gold,' she repeated. 'Put your foot down, darling, we've got to get there before Beatrice and William do.'

Peverall was smiling as though they'd already won.

Bit premature, thought Rachel. Then she realised that wasn't why he was smiling. Oh shit, she berated herself, I just called him darling, didn't I?

'Graveyard,' said Beatrice. 'Grave accent, and a yard of ale. Then find a dead glass . . . someone with the surname Glass.'

'We've only got twenty minutes,' said William. 'Ten minutes to St Anne's Chapel, ten minutes back. Rachel and Peverall are just ahead of us. If the answer isn't immediately obvious and they don't solve it, they'll come back to the house for the curfew – and we're in with a chance.'

'But supposing we've fouled up somewhere? We get disqualified for being late back.'

'We can't have fouled up,' said William. 'But just in case – we could split up.'

'What do you mean?'

'I'll go to the graveyard, while you go back and make an appearance. Tell everyone I've got a headache and I'm lying down. There's a back gate in the grounds. Go and unbolt it at – what – nine o'clock? That gives me loads of time.'

'That's not strictly fair,' said Beatrice.

'Do you want me to get fairly strict about this?' asked William.

Beatrice's dark eyes narrowed. 'How strict?'

'I might have to tie you up.' And before she could answer he said, 'Look, I need to go *now*. Be at the back gate. Nine o'clock.'

He sprinted over to his car, and Beatrice couldn't have caught him if she'd tried. She watched him drive away, then she went back to her room and removed the cord from her dressing gown. After that, she found a belt. She was beginning to suspect that the Black Widow had rather unorthodox appetites.

'We're looking for something with steps,' said Peverall. 'One of the big memorials. There are quite a few of them, but they're scattered. You start at one end and I'll start at the other.'

They trotted between the tombs, reading the names, travelling in a circular fashion where the paths led, passing one another now and again. After a while the flowers and the headstones and the statues turned to a blur, with odd moments of clarity as they focused on the epitaphs.

'Here!' called Peverall, and Rachel ran over.

The grave was a proper crypt, the last resting place for members of the Glass family. Behind an ornate wrought-iron gate there were steps leading down.

Rachel looked at the padlock. 'Bugger,' she said.

Peverall pushed at it; the padlock fell apart and the gate swung open. He switched on his torch.

'We've only got fifteen minutes until the curfew,' said Rachel, as she followed him down the steps.

'Well, well,' said Eric Summers. He was sitting at the back of the linen cupboard on a cushion he'd made for himself from a pile of blankets.

'Scaring the shit out of people's a hobby of yours, is it?' said Fee.

'That was *your* imagination at work, not mine,' said Summers.

She didn't know where to look. Dropping her eyes was far too demure, and glancing away too rude. She decided to take a leaf out of his book; simply behave as though they were both clothed.

'Found Diana yet?' His eyes didn't stray below her chin.

'No.'

'Going to look in the ledger, were you?'

'Yes.'

'I'll save you the trouble,' he said. 'There's no Diana there.'

'Oh.' She did what she normally did when she was thinking – dropped her eyes and let them focus on nothing. Then she realised that she was looking straight at Summers's dick. It twitched slightly and showed signs of increasing its surface area.

'Any man stuck in a cupboard with a naked woman would get an erection,' he said irritably. 'It's a knee-jerk reaction, nothing more. Automatic. What's the time?'

'I don't know,' said Fee, feeling about as attractive as a washing machine. 'I left my watch under a bush.'

There was a long silence, as though he were silently castigating her for this lack of foresight. Eventually he said, 'I think we've been following a red herring.'

'What do you mean?'

'That Alfred Hicks gave some of the clues two interpretations.'

'What, deliberately?'

'Of course. There may be any number of blind alleys.'

'So where did we go wrong?'

'I don't know. I need to look at the last few clues again, but they're in my trouser pocket.'

'And that's where, exactly?'

'In my trousers,' he said.

Fee glared at him.

'Teamed up with Angus yet?'

'No. Graham Steel said he'd help me out if a clue needed two people.'

He laughed quietly. 'You do pick them, don't you?'

'And what's that supposed to mean?'

'Graham Steel's never been on a word-games week either.'

'He's jolly good, nonetheless.'

'No he isn't. He cheats.'

Fee stared at him. 'How?'

'Didn't surrender his mobile.'

'How do you know?'

'Heard it beep in the corridor. He was talking to Scarab at the time, but she didn't seem to notice. Odd, that. Scarab's a bright girl.'

Fee felt rather let down – if it were true. But why would Summers lie about it?

'And you didn't tell Gavin?'

'No.'

'Why not?'

He shrugged.

'You thought you could beat him anyway, didn't you?' she said. 'Mobile or no mobile. Are there no limits to your arrogance?'

His face tightened. 'Sleeping your way through the clues is morally superior, is it?'

'I didn't *get* any information out of Graham! That's not why I . . .' She trailed off.

'So you did sleep with him,' said Summers. 'I thought so.'

'Oh, I get it,' said Fee, her voice rising. 'You think there's no way I'd have got this far on my own, don't you? Well I *did*. I solved everything myself.'

'Shh.'

'Oh shut up,' said Fee.

'I think we'd better try and make our escape,' he said. 'Otherwise we won't be back before the curfew.'

They both headed for the door at the same time and ended up crushed together against it. Fee had a fleeting impression of warmth and hair and softness, so different to Graham Steel's tough been-there-done-it body. They both jerked back, bashed bits of themselves against the wall and apologised in unison. Summers held the door open for her, his face unreadable, and she went out into the corridor. Fortunately, it was deserted.

'What now?' she asked him.

'Bye,' he said.

No, she thought, I don't want to have to walk all that way back on my own. 'We'd look more convincing as a couple,' she said.

'I don't think we look the slightest bit convincing as a couple,' he retorted, 'but I shall pander to your insecurities if I must.'

'It wasn't a request,' she said, incensed, 'it was just a suggestion.'

'Fine,' he said, turning round and walking away.

Fee ran after him. 'All right,' she said, 'it was a request.'

'In that case,' he said sadistically, 'we'd better hold hands.'

She put her hand in his. It wasn't cold or clammy or fleshy, it was dry and slightly warmer than hers. His grip was neither too tight, nor too loose. It was a good, businesslike arrangement. They walked down the corridor and found the big room that led out on to the garden. The elderly couple were still sitting on the sofa. The woman noticed Fee and said, 'Did you find your Diana?'

'No,' said Fee. Then, anxious to bring the conversation to a quick close, she added, 'but it doesn't matter now.'

'I can see that,' said the woman, smiling at Summers.

'We're just good friends,' said Summers, and he yanked Fee by the wrist and propelled her out into the garden. The sun was getting low in the sky and people were coming back indoors. The lights in the fountain had been switched on and the statue in the middle of it was touched with gold.

'I bet membership of this place costs a fortune,' said Fee.

'*Chacun a son goût,*' said Summers.

* * *

Peverall shone his torch round the sepulchre. Rachel shivered. It was surprisingly cold down there – and so grey. Everything was grey – the flint walls, the half-light that filtered down the stone steps, the grey dust on the two coffins in the middle of the main chamber. The cobwebs.

'Mr and Mrs Edward Glass,' said Peverall. 'Victorian tradesfolk, I would guess, from the rather sickly sentiments about angels and worldly goods.'

'There's nothing in here – apart from whatever's in there.' Rachel pointed at the coffins.

'The seals haven't been broken,' said Peverall. 'There won't be anything in there, except more dust.'

Rachel felt relieved, and followed him into the next crypt. This had four smaller sarcophagi in it; children aged between eighteen months and three years. There was only one more chamber, off to one side. This housed the remains of the Glass's eldest son and his wife.

'And there the dynasty ended, by the look of it,' said Peverall.

'Look,' said Rachel. 'Over there.'

A small alcove was cut into the stone. It was angled, so that it couldn't be seen from the direction in which they'd come. They went over to it and there, in the recess, was a wooden chest the size of a smallish suitcase. Peverall lifted it out; it was obviously heavy. He opened the lid.

A mess of gold glinted in the torchlight: chunks of it, lumps of it, rough angular nuggets of it, reflecting on the inside of the lid and turning it yellow. Rachel gasped and put her hand to her mouth, thinking, theatrical or what? But that's the only way you *can* react to something like this: theatrically. It's so dramatic, down here in the gloom with all this death about.

'I think that's mine,' said William, from behind them.

Rachel spun round. She noticed in passing that Peverall was smiling. It registered as an odd reaction – but there wasn't time to consider it further, as William walked over to Peverall and took the box from him, one-handed. He kept his other hand in his pocket.

'Hang on,' said Rachel, appalled. 'You can't just let him *take* it.' How could Peverall be such a wimp?

'Oh, I think Peverall knows better than to try to stop me,' said William.

There was something in his tone that brought Rachel up short, a sort of chilly certainty that Peverall would, indeed, know better. William's armed, she thought. I don't know what with – a knife? A gun? And somehow or other, Peverall cottoned on right away.

William glanced down at the contents of the box for the first time, smiling. Then, so slowly that it was barely perceptible at first, the smile left his face. His dark brows furrowed and he looked up at Peverall.

'That's right,' said Peverall. 'They're iron pyrites. Fool's gold. Worthless.'

William lifted the box and upended it over Mrs Glass's coffin. There was a clattering, like someone tipping gravel, as the iron pyrites scattered across the oak. The last thing to leave the box, and the lightest, was a laminated piece of card. It fluttered down like a feather and landed on top of the biggest heap of golden nuggets. There was no writing on it. Instead, there was an illustration of a ruddy fish. A red herring.

'Come on,' said Fee, taking the steps two at a time, 'we're going to be late.'

'We *are* late,' said Summers. 'There was a clock in the corridor. Dinner was half an hour ago.' They walked across *The Elms*' lawn, although the temptation was to break into a run.

'Who's the statue in the middle of the fountain?' asked Fee as they passed.

Summers stopped dead in his tracks, then he turned round on the spot, quite slowly, and looked at the white marble figure with the bow and arrow. 'Artemis,' he said. 'Alias Diana. You take one side, I'll take the other.'

And, without thinking, they were working together again. 'Got it,' said Fee, and Summers came over. A little bronze plaque, with the date the statue had been put in place inscribed on it: 27.11.57. Fee wrote it down.

'Right,' said Summers, 'let's go.'

They walked across the lawn towards the tennis court. The light was failing quite badly now, and it was getting cold. Fee shivered.

'My clothes are right by the back gate,' said Summers.

'Mine are a bit closer,' said Fee, 'but not by much.'

Summers put his arm round her. She was so surprised that it was an effort just to keep walking.

'You *are* cold,' he said. There was no ulterior motive. He was just warming her up a bit.

By the time they reached her clothes, she was grateful for it. Her fingers were too cold to cope with buttons and zips, and Summers had to do it for her. 'Aren't *you* cold?' she asked him, her teeth chattering.

'I went to boarding school,' he said. 'Snow blowing over the counterpane from the open windows, icicles hanging from the lavatory cisterns, quick swim in the lake every morning before breakfast; you could hear the frost crackling under your feet as you sprinted down to the water . . .'

She looked at him. 'You're having me on.'

'Only partially.'

And there they were by the gate, and he was pulling on his clothes, and she had warmed up nicely. He lifted the latch, the gate swung open and they slipped outside.

'What are we going to do?' asked Fee, as they walked back along the footpath.

'Try and get in round the back,' said Summers.

'Isn't that cheating?'

He scowled at her. 'We were unavoidably detained. It wasn't as though we deliberately carried on clue-hunting beyond the curfew.'

'Yes, my conscience can handle that,' said Fee.

'You've really got into this treasure hunt, haven't you?'

'Yes.'

'I can see why you didn't want to team up with Angus,'

he said. 'He's a liability, not an asset. But Graham Steel . . .'

'He's got Grace,' said Fee. 'And besides, he hasn't asked me.'

'And if he does?'

'You mean, if Grace dropped out for some reason?' One fuck with Graham was nothing like sufficient; Fee had spent quite a few idle moments working out how she could engineer another one. Partnering him would certainly throw up some interesting opportunities. On the other hand, did she want to partner a cheat? If he *was* a cheat. It didn't seem to fit his personality, somehow. Could Summers have been mistaken about the phone?

'No,' she said eventually. 'I wouldn't partner him. I don't mix business and pleasure.'

Summers looked at her thoughtfully and said, 'I suppose you must have learned to keep your mouth shut to get this far on your own.' They reached the main road; his car was parked close by and he opened the door for her. 'Shall we team up again then?' He said it quite casually, but Fee felt a little stab of glee.

'OK,' she said, equally casually. It *was* more fun solving clues with someone else, and she did like working with Summers. It was a pity he was so . . . so what? She didn't quite know.

He parked the car as meticulously as ever and they walked round the perimeter of the grounds of the house. The gate wasn't too far away.

'I doubt they've forgotten to lock it,' said Summers. 'But we might as well try.' And to their surprise, the gate opened.

'At last,' said a voice. 'I was beginning to think you'd run out on me, William.'

The gate swung open to its full extent and Fee saw Beatrice get up from the tree-stump on which she was sitting, take a pace forward – and stop.

'Eric,' she said, lamely.

'Beatrice,' said Summers. 'I think I'm as surprised at you as you probably are at me.'

'Look,' said Beatrice, 'just forget you saw me, OK? And I'll forget I saw *you*.'

'Fair enough,' said Summers. For a moment he looked as though he were about to say something else, then he seemed to change his mind. He and Fee left Beatrice there and walked back to the house.

'What were you going to say to her?' Fee asked him.

'I was going to warn her off William. But there's no point; she's besotted.'

'She doesn't look terribly besotted to me,' said Fee.

'You don't know Beatrice. She'd have to be head over heels to break the rules like that for someone.' They went into the house by one of the garden doors, which remained open. 'We ought to join the puzzle evening now,' said Summers, 'make ourselves seen.'

Fee nodded. 'I'm starving though,' she said, as she trailed into the games room behind him.

'Go and have a rummage in the kitchen during the break,' he said. 'There's always bread and stuff available in case anyone wants to make toast.'

Fee settled down with the sheet of paper Gavin handed her and started trying to use the very obscure words that were written there to make sensible sentences. It was good fun and she got into it.

Rachel and Peverall had only been five minutes late, in the end, and Gavin had been lenient. They had dinner, excused themselves, and went up to Peverall's room.

'What did you make of William's behaviour in the crypt then?' asked Rachel.

'I don't think he came on this week because he enjoys solving puzzles. He came on it to get the prize, by whatever means. Maybe it *is* worth a fortune. And Angus is his sidekick.'

'We ought to tell Gavin.'

'Tell him what? There's nothing to tell, and William knows it. The only way we'd get him thrown out is to prove that he had a gun in his pocket – if he did. He certainly wanted me to think he did, and I wasn't going to argue, not once I'd realised the box was full of fool's gold.'

'You know,' said Rachel, 'I thought there was something odd about the last couple of clues.'

'What?'

'No sex in them. Captain Cook, and a graveyard. Quite unlike all the other clues.'

'I like sex,' said Peverall. 'It's nice.'

'Indeed it is,' said Rachel, going over to him and unbuttoning his shirt. 'I think an evening up here instead of downstairs would be an evening well spent. Anything you've ever fancied trying?'

He gave a her a sidelong look, then feigned shyness, lowering his eyes and glancing up at her now and again.

'What?'

'Have you ever heard of something called a body-body massage?'

Rachel grinned. 'Yes,' she said. 'Someone I was with once spent a lot of time in Thailand. And that's what you really really want?'

He nodded enthusiastically, bright-eyed and bushy-tailed, a small boy being offered the run of the sweet shop. He was rather good at the small boy impression – it made her want to fling her arms round him and cuddle him.

'Right,' she said. 'We need a tiled floor – the bathroom is perfect, the floor slopes in to the drain-hole for the shower. And we need some warm soapy water. And maybe some massage oil, for the last bit. I've got some, I can go and get it. But the big problem is getting hold of an air-bed.'

'I bet there's one in the hut by the pool. There are beach balls and floats in there, I've seen them.'

'I'll see what I can do,' said Rachel. She went back to her room and found the oil and a couple of joss-sticks. Then she ran downstairs, out into the grounds, and over to the hut by the pool. Sure enough, there were several air-beds there. She grabbed the one on the top of the pile, dashed out of the hut – and ran slap-bang into Saul Slick.

The little bottle of oil somersaulted into the air and landed at his feet. He picked it up.

'Good job the lid didn't come off,' he said, glancing at the label. Then he suddenly seemed to realise what it was for. He handed it back to her as though it were red hot and strode off, his hair taking a second or two to catch up.

Rachel hurried back upstairs and knocked on Peverall's door. When he opened it, she saw that both the bedroom and the bathroom had been transformed. In the space of five minutes he had lit some candles, switched off the lights, put on some oriental music and – somehow – produced an ice bucket, champagne and glasses.

'Welcome to Madam Sin's,' he said, closing the door and taking the joss sticks from her and lighting them. 'Pecattiphilia our speciality.' He opened the champagne and poured them both a glass.

As they clinked them together he said, 'To us. No, don't say anything. I am going to win you properly, Rachel – but if, after an intense campaign, I lose – I hereby promise not to sulk, or make things difficult for you. Is this acceptable?'

'Yes, darling,' said Rachel. One act of generosity deserved another. Peverall inflated the air-bed and took it into the bathroom.

After two glasses Rachel was thoroughly in the mood. She laid him on the bed, unlaced his sensible shoes and took them off. He was wearing odd socks – one black, one grey. She laughed; he twisted round to look and made a face. Rachel peeled off the socks and finished unbuttoning his shirt. She slid it off him, and marvelled once again at the beautiful naked torso in front of her. The smooth unblemished skin with its faint tan, the clear definition of the muscles beneath. She undid his belt, unzipped his flies and pulled off his trousers. His cock stood proud immediately, thick and long and straight, and she bent over and kissed it. It wasn't an erotic kiss; it was a kiss of pure affection. What on earth is happening to me, thought Rachel. I'm getting really fond of the guy.

He's inexperienced, he's a word-nerd, he's as bald as a coot – and he's a total poppet. He's rather well-off, too, said a little voice inside her head.

They went into the bathroom, rolled all the towels into sausages to soak up any excess water and placed them at the foot of the door. Rachel filled the washbasin with warm water and put a whole bar of soap in there, swishing it around until the water went milky and frothed. Then she undressed and sloshed the solution over the air-bed with a tooth-mug.

'Lie down and roll on to your stomach,' she said. 'This starts at the back and ends up at the front.'

The sweet smell of the joss sticks mingled with the perfume of the soap as she smothered them both with the contents of the washbasin; the music rose and fell suggestively in the background, and their images danced on the tiled wall like shadow puppets as the candles guttered. She still had the taste of champagne on her lips.

She lay down on top of him, head to head, her whole length against his. Then she gripped hold of the sides of the air-bed and started to slide herself down his body, her breasts pressing against first his shoulders, then his buttocks, then his thighs. He sighed. She slid all the way up again, a firm push to start, a brief increase of pressure, then a petering out. He closed his eyes. There was a little smile on his lips, dimpling the corners. She repeated the sequence over and over again, loving the feel of his skin against hers, the give of his flesh, the shape of him. She extended the movements so that she went right up to the crown of his bald head, then down to the tips of his toes.

She applied more soapy water and trailed her nipple into the crease between his buttocks. 'Squeeze,' she whispered. He squeezed, and she felt a thrill run through her. She could tell from the sound of his sharply indrawn breath that he was getting a kick out if it as well – for every clench of his buttocks there would be a corresponding surge of pleasure in his cock. He was beginning to get wriggly; she suspected his erection was shouting more urgent messages at him.

She changed tactics and moved her body at right angles to his; then she rotated it in semi-circles, massaging him properly for a while, his shoulders, his spine, the backs of his legs. She ran a bit more hot water into the sink, then doused both of them with it again; she'd got the proportion of soap and water just right, they were both as slippery as eels. Her abdomen slithered across his thighs; the contact pulled momentarily against her clitoris, then released it. She felt a stab of desire.

Normally she would have thought of herself at this stage – girl wants fuck, girl makes sure she gets it. But instead of giving in she kept at it; every so often there was that little tug at her clit, and every time it happened she got a little more aroused. She fought the urge to initiate an escalation of her own pleasure. This was Peverall's treat, and satisfying him was more of a turn-on than satisfying herself. She suppressed the craving to rub harder and rolled on to her back instead. Now they were buttock to buttock, spine to spine; she imagined herself polishing his skin, using her body as a shammy leather, burnishing his lust until it shone like brass. Up and down, up and down; there was something almost hypnotic about it, the smell of the incense, the softly plucked strings of the sitar, the touch of skin on skin.

'Turn over,' she said.

He turned over. His cock was rock-hard, huge. She repeated her actions front to front, feeling first her mound and then her breasts sliding down his chest, his abdomen, his cock, his thighs. Then up again, until her pussy pressed momentarily against his lips. He was fighting to control himself, and he was losing. She climbed off and dried him with the towel; then she dried herself. After that she unscrewed the lid of the oil, upending the bottle and making a little puddle of it in her palm. She waited until the oil had warmed through, then she smoothed it over his prick until it was gleaming. When she'd finished his cock she did her breasts, standing well within his field of vision and taking her time, lingering a little, making her nipples erect, preparing herself. He watched her, his head on one side, his eyes following her every move.

'Now we get more direct,' she said, taking hold of him and running her fingers up and down his shaft. He closed his eyes and held his breath. She started to wank him, her oily fingers sliding up and down, squeezing him just a little, and he let the breath out again. Careful, she thought, he's going to come. She let go. He opened his eyes, a pained expression on his face.

'All in good time,' she said, and she placed his cock between her breasts and started to massage it with them. 'You can come all over them if you like,' she added. But rubbing herself like that against him was an incredible turn-on; her nipples were becoming super-sensitive, and the friction seemed travel down her body in one long wave, culminating in that fizzy feeling between her legs. It's me who's going to come first at this rate, she thought. I don't think anyone's ever had an orgasm through breast contact alone – but, wow, that would be something!

But it wasn't just the friction alone that was doing it – it was the expression on his face, the wanting. She rubbed a little faster, and he took a great shuddering breath. Then he came with a strangled cry, shooting spunk out all over her. She clenched her buttocks and pushed herself against him, alternately rubbing her hands between her legs. And then she came as well, contraction after contraction. Not the most intense climax ever, but a long one . . . on and on, until she was quite drained.

'*Gradu diverso, via una*,' said Peverall.

'The same road, by different steps,' translated Rachel.

'And I intend to make sure it isn't a cul-de-sac,' said Peverall.

'Peverall,' said Rachel, '*please*. Don't rush me.'

He kissed her on her shoulder. 'OK. How many children do you want?'

Rachel looked at him, speechless.

He laughed. 'Just kidding.'

'Kidding is not on my current agenda,' said Rachel. 'I'm going to check all the condoms myself from now on.'

'I've always fancied Cheltenham Ladies' College for a girl,' he said. 'Then St Hilda's maybe. Boys are a bit trickier.'

'Boys are *extremely* tricky,' said Rachel. 'Especially when they don't *listen*.'

He smiled. 'Oh, I listen. I just don't necessarily agree.'

Chapter Eight

*S*ummers won the first game, and the next. Later on William appeared, followed by a tight-lipped Beatrice. There was no sign of either Rachel or Peverall. Graham Steel was sitting with Grace, as always, and Angus was talking to Scarab. At half time Fee went into the kitchen and made herself some cheese on toast. She was just finishing her second slice when Graham came into the kitchen as well. She felt her body react in a very physical way.

'Good day today?' he asked.

'Yes, in the end,' said Fee. 'Summers and I have settled our differences and teamed up again.'

'I'm pleased to hear it,' he said. And he really did look pleased.

Fee felt a little twinge of regret. She'd have preferred it if he'd been more disappointed – some comment about how much he'd have liked to work with her, if the opportunity had presented itself. Had once been enough for him? Surely not – he'd enjoyed it as much as she had. He was a cool customer, very cool, and she liked that. It was the sort of demeanour that made you want to crack it the way you'd crack a thin layer of ice, just to see what happened and hear the sound effect.

He glanced at his watch. 'I ought to play a few more

games with Grace,' he said. 'But after that ... free as a bird, should you wish to fly with me. Room 31.'

'I'll be there,' said Fee. They went back and played two more games. Saul Slick won the first one, and Summers the second. Fee couldn't concentrate, so she went back to her room and had a shower. As she was drying her hair, Rachel came in.

'I'm sorry,' said Fee, before Rachel had a chance to speak. 'I should never have made that remark about bald-headed men.'

Rachel shrugged.

'I'm back with Summers,' said Fee, anxious to get a conversation going.

Rachel looked surprised. 'I didn't know you'd split up.'

Fee didn't feel inclined to go into it in any detail, so she said, 'How's the hunt going?'

Rachel's face suddenly lit up with excitement. 'Oh boy, have I got news. Peverall and I thought we'd won, just for a moment.' She sat down on the bed and told Fee everything that had happened in the crypt. 'It's clear William thinks the prize is worth a lot of money,' she concluded. 'And he wants to win rather badly. He's a nasty piece of work.'

'You were right about Angus as well,' agreed Fee. 'He was always putting me down. I've switched to Graham Steel.'

To Fee's surprise, Rachel looked horrified. 'Graham Steel? The iceman himself? Oh for goodness' sake, Fee, don't you ever learn?'

'I thought you'd be pleased.'

'Yet another example of presentation over content.'

Fee bit her lip. 'I always imagine what people are thinking, I can't help it. *She must be crap if that's all she can pull.*'

'And that's what you think people are saying about *me*?'

'No,' said Fee desperately. 'Everyone here knows that Peverall's a nice guy.'

'But in the wide, wide world people are going to look at *him* and judge *me* accordingly. People. What people? People who count? I don't think so.'

Fee imagined taking Peverall home herself, and the not-so-quiet aside that would issue, sooner or later, from her mother. *Honestly, Fee, eggheads are all very well, but this is taking it to extremes.* People who count, Rachel said. How did you turn your mother into someone who *didn't* count? Stop caring? Or was there another way?

'Oh, run along and get your fuck,' said Rachel. 'It'll just be another Chinese takeaway. Tasty, but not very filling.'

'I thought we both liked trying out different cuisines?'

'I suspect your menu would give me indigestion,' said Rachel.

Fee made her way to Room 31.

Graham opened the door, wearing just a pair of jeans, and let her in. The casual look suited him; the bare feet, the bare chest, the muscular arms and the sinewy wrists – one of which sported a very expensive gold watch.

'Drink?' There was a bottle of chardonnay on the table, in a cooler.

'Mm, thanks.'

He uncorked the bottle and poured two glasses. Fee glanced round the room. A pile of reference books on the table and a mess of papers half-covering something that could have been either a briefcase – or a laptop. She reserved judgement. A classy leather jacket was thrown over the back of a chair. The bathroom door was open and she could see a very wet towel hanging from the towel rail. There was a faint smell of chlorine. He'd been in the pool then. She drank some of her wine. 'What do you do for a living, Graham?'

'I'm in salvage.'

This sounded as boring as lexicography, or being the editor of an inventions magazine. Was there no one here who did anything exciting for a living? She decided to take the bull by the horns so she said, 'Salvage needs a mobile phone, does it?'

'What?'

'Summers heard it beep in the corridor, when you were talking to Scarab.'

He laughed. 'Oh, that. I think you'll find the phone belongs to Scarab.'

Then he kissed her, and she began to remember how good he was at it. So gentle, at the outset, those little light touches that started the process of arousal so gradually you hardly realised it was happening. Top lip, bottom lip, the briefest touch with the tip of his tongue. She slid her arms round his body; he moved his round to her back, and unzipped her dress. Top lip, bottom lip again – then a slow lecherous penetration of the tongue to just inside her mouth. She felt her bra go the same way as her dress. She fumbled with the button on his jeans, unzipped them, slid them down as far as they would go. He wriggled out of them. He wasn't wearing any underpants.

He laid her down on the bed and opened her legs. Then he knelt on the floor and delicately explored her with his fingers. The intention to lick her pussy was obvious, but he didn't rush it. When he did bring his tongue into play it was to lick the inside of her thighs, gradually working higher and higher. She lay there, eyes closed, loving every second of it. She could feel the soft bristle of his close-cut hair. Further up, further up, just a little bit at a time, like herring-bone stitch . . . and then he was licking between her legs, long soft strokes with a relaxed tongue, back and forth, back and forth. She wanted to wriggle, but she didn't want to make him change what he was doing either; it was too nice. And then his tongue stiffened, and went inside. When it was obvious she wanted something more intense, he pulled back and slid two fingers inside. She felt him make contact with her G-spot, caressing it skilfully, and the heightened sensations lifted her to a new plane of arousal. Another finger slid into her anus; she contracted around it, and heard herself gasp. Now his tongue was soft again, licking round her clit, still not hitting the spot, teasing, getting closer and closer by almost imperceptible degrees.

She wanted more intensity, her body was crying out for it. He started to nibble at her, not too hard, tenderly almost. She was surprised; no one had ever done that before. The sensations were sharp, but not at all unpleasant. A shot of whisky after a glass of mellow wine. The finger in her anus started to move in and out, very, very gently. She was holding her breath; she was very close to orgasm. When he finally touched her clit with his tongue she felt an immediate response. Her body seemed to gather itself as though it was about to do the high jump – then she came, with a wonderful primitive violence.

When she'd recovered her equilibrium, Fee started to suck him off. He was a responsive partner, letting her know with little sounds and movements when she was doing the right thing. She had intended to make him go to the limit, but at the last moment he put on a condom, and fucked her like there was no tomorrow. The sudden switch of mood was infectious, and Fee gave herself over completely to the action, loving the hard, pounding rhythm in her cunt. He went at it with enthusiasm and, after a few minutes, he shot his load, crying out his ecstasy before collapsing back on the bed next to Fee, thoroughly sated.

And then, in the middle of the rosy post-coital glow, the bedside phone rang. Graham leaned across her and picked it up. Fee wondered who it was – the only calls allowed in from outside were emergencies.

He listened for a moment. 'Mm hm.' Another pause. 'Right. Bye.' He hung up.

'Everything OK?' asked Fee.

He hesitated.

'Your wife, no doubt?'

She'd meant it as a jokey aside, but after another pause he said, 'Yes.'

Her mouth dropped open. She caught a glimpse of herself in the mirror, a fish out of water. She shut her mouth hurriedly.

'You didn't ask me, and I didn't say,' he said. '*You* could be married, for all I know.'

Fee waved her ringless left hand at him.

'Doesn't necessarily signify, these days.'

'Kids?'

'Two.'

'Names?'

'John. And Sandra.'

He's lying, thought Fee. I wonder who was really on the phone.

'Sandra's grade three flute results,' he said. 'I told my wife to call me if she got a distinction.'

'That's an emergency?'

'Yes,' he said glumly. 'I'll have to get a present to take back.'

'Oh well,' said Fee. 'It's been a pleasant evening.'

'Look,' he said, 'you seemed to enjoy it as much as I did. There's no reason we shouldn't carry on until the end of the week, is there?'

Fee said something non-committal. She wanted to think about this. She'd always avoided married men like the plague, especially ones with children. *If* he was married. She still suspected he was lying. She got dressed and made for the door.

'I'll see you in the morning,' she said. And then, as an apparent afterthought, '*I* play the flute. Does Jack play anything?'

'No,' said Graham. 'He's only five.'

Got you, thought Fee. Jack was John a couple of minutes ago. But she didn't let on.

Fee and Summers were waiting by the door to Room 8 when Gavin unlocked it. There were quite a few other people waiting in that particular corridor now, queuing for Rooms 5 and 6. They all smiled at one another, commented on the beautiful weather, the choice at breakfast and the games the previous evening. Not a single remark was passed about the treasure hunt itself.

'You were on good form, Eric,' said Saul Slick. 'I liked your one about the arctoid angekokk.'

Room 8 was exactly like Room 5 – just a computer on a desk and two chairs. Summers typed in the E-mail address, then wrote: Diana gave us your number, and we now feel we're entitled to the next clue. He opened a chat window, sent the message and, after a moment or two, the reply came:

Who are you?

Summers tapped in: Eric Summers.

A brief pause. Then: *Nice to speak to you again, darling. I do have a little clue for you, but you're going to have to earn it.*

Summers typed in: So who are *you*?

Rose, sweetie. You're the one who was interested in the anal sex, am I right or am I right?

Only the price, wrote Summers. How do I go about earning my clue then?

Talk dirty. If you can turn me on, you get the next clue.

Summers raised his eyes to the ceiling and sighed. 'Just what I needed, right after breakfast. Oh well. Here goes.' He wrote: Would chastising me for my shortcomings give you pleasure?

Not necessarily. I want you to tell me the things you'd like to do to me. Start with my tits.

Summers thought for a moment. Then he wrote: I'd like to run my hands all over them, feel the fullness of them give under my fingers. Then I'd take your nipple in my mouth and suck it quite slowly like a firm juicy grape.

Fruity, but far too restrained. Move down to my privates, poppet.

Summers glanced at Fee. 'There's absolutely no reason why you shouldn't be doing this,' he said sourly. 'She can't identify who's on the other end of the keyboard.'

'I couldn't possibly,' said Fee. 'Buxom women don't turn me on at all. My prose would lack that ring of authenticity.'

He glared at her. 'Rose doesn't turn *me* on either.'

'You must have a good imagination then. That tit stuff was OK.'

'I just imagine it's someone else,' said Summers. He turned back to the screen.

There was now a message saying: *Hurry up. You're losing any advantage you gained with my tits.*

He scowled, then his thinking expression took over his face, and he started to type: I'd like to explore your body and learn the shape of you. The swell of your breasts, the curve of your back, the angle of your hip bone.

Rose doesn't *have* any visible hip-bones, thought Fee. He's going to have to be careful here.

I would slip my hand between your legs, wrote Summers, and brush your lips gently with my finger in passing. Then I would stroke you a little more and repeat the action, decreasing the space of time between each touch. I would trace patterns in the most sensitive places and run my nail lightly between the folds until I felt you begin to respond. I would circle your arsehole with my fingertip until it contracted with pleasure. Only then would I move to your clit, and touch it with feather-like stabs that barely reach their target. I would slip my middle finger inside your cunt, loving the warm wetness I would find there, and I would fuck you with as many fingers as you could take until I felt you seize me with your orgasm.

Not bad, thought Fee.

The next message read: *A stylish performance, Eric. You have earned the next clue. It goes as follows: Aunt Dolly's befuddled; in this shop the remedy's UTC (6, 4).*

Summers wrote it down in his notebook. The screen went blank again after a bit. Summers waved the page around to dry the ink, put it back in his pocket, and they left the room.

They went and sat in the library. '*Aunt Dolly's* is an anagram,' said Fee.

'Well done. How about the definition?'

'What's UTC?'

'OTC is over the counter, so UTC could be under the counter. Let's look at the anagram again.'

'Aunt Dolly's ... Lloyd's aunt? Untold lays? Lady no slut?'

'Adults Only,' said Summers. 'It's that sex shop in the town.'

'Oh yes,' said Fee, remembering the shuttered shopfront. 'What do we do when we get there?'

'Ask for something under the counter, I suppose. And it's *your* turn.'

'I suppose that's fair,' said Fee. 'Seeing as you put so much of yourself into the last clue.'

He gave her an old-fashioned look.

They went out to his car. Arnold and Elsie were just getting out of theirs. Fee watched Arnold twiddle the end of his moustache; then she heard him say, 'You only have to be my guest the once, Elsie. I'm now a fully paid-up member. There are lots of people there our age; you're a fine figure of a woman, you've nothing to be self-conscious about. And I'll buy you a box of Suchard.'

Fee grinned. Arnold didn't intend to go in by the back gate of The Elms at all; he was going for the full-frontal attack.

'Just the once then,' said Elsie. 'Never could resist a man who knew his chocolate.'

Summers demanded a civilised lunch before Adults Only, so they found a little restaurant and ordered a seafood salad each and a bottle of wine. They talked about their jobs for a while and then their early lives. Summers's upbringing sounded bleak – an only child, his father had died when he was seven. His mother had taken a long time to get over it, and he had been sent away to school. He talked warmly of an aunt with whom he had frequently stayed, but it looked as though he had had to become self-reliant very early on. University had been a let-down, socially. He'd never mixed with girls, they were as strange to him as Martians, and after a couple of failed attempts he threw himself into his studies instead. He left with a first, as inexperienced and as full of unrequited lust as when he'd arrived.

'You said you were married once,' said Fee. Three glasses of wine had made her brave.

'Did I?' He looked surprised. 'Yes, I was. For five years.'

'What happened?'

'She squeezed the toothpaste in the middle of the tube, and decorated the bathroom tangerine. We split up quite amicably. What happened to your three-year stint?'

She was surprised he had remembered. 'I chose the wrong sort again. I'm good at that.'

'What sort's that then?'

'The quick thrill, I suppose.' The wine was making her disturbingly honest. She viewed what she'd said with some surprise. It was true, she was nearly always the one to call a halt to a relationship. Neither she nor Rachel had wanted permanence – it was one of the main things they had in common. They'd gone from man to man, comparing notes, having a laugh. It was only over the last couple of days that the pattern had started to break up, like a televised news report where you had to guess the words and the images that were missing.

'The flash of tanned biceps and the sheer lust in a pair of piercing blue eyes?'

Fee laughed. 'Something like that.'

'What's so scary about wanting more than that?'

'I just don't want more. No, that's not quite true. I don't want *him* to want more, whoever he may be at the time. Oh, I don't know.' Fee suddenly realised that Summers had only had one glass – he was, after all, driving; she must have drunk the rest. The bottle was empty.

He smiled. 'Dutch courage, for when you ask for that little something under the counter. But back to the previous topic. What is it you don't want Mr X to find out? How worthless you think you are, at rock bottom? Leave him, before he leaves you?'

Fee suddenly found that her eyes had filled with tears. *Nobody's going to want to take you to the altar*; her mother's voice again. And Fee's reply, which had taken great daring: *I'll just have to alter myself then, won't I?* Followed by the furious response, *Don't you try and play word games with me, my girl. You haven't got what it takes.* A tear left each eye simultaneously and slid down her cheek. It was most inconvenient, they shouldn't be there, she'd have to get a tissue.

'I'm sorry,' said Summers, laying a hand on her arm. 'That was really insensitive of me.'

That made it even worse. She blubbed into her tissue for a little while, then she said, 'I'm all right,' and put it away.

Summers signalled for the bill. 'The best thing we can do,' he said, 'is to win this treasure hunt. *That* ought to do your ego a power of good.'

'You come back an hour later than you said you'd be,' said Beatrice, the little pointed chin rising, 'you stay for the rest of the evening in the games room so that we don't get a chance to talk, then you say, see you in the morning. And now it's afternoon, and here in my room is the first time we've been alone together.'

'Are you hassling me?'

'Bloody right,' snapped Beatrice. 'So what happened? I take it we're not stinking rich?'

'It was a red herring,' said William. 'A casket full of fool's gold. I got there at the same time as Rachel and Peverall, and we had a good laugh about it.'

A good laugh? thought Beatrice. I doubt it. William's far too competitive to find a blunder *fun*. I wonder what really happened. Their eyes locked for a moment, and she knew he was concealing something. But rather than irritating her, it made him more attractive. She liked secrets herself, and she liked the sort of people who could keep them. When she allowed herself a fantasy, it usually involved someone from the SAS or MI5 or the KGB.

'It's not just falling behind in the hunt that's bugging me,' she said icily, 'it's the fact that you reneged on your promise.' She took off her glasses and rubbed her eyes.

'What promise?' asked William suspiciously.

Beatrice's eyes flicked across to the corner of the room. There was a little pile of cords and belts on the dressing table.

'Oh,' said William, brightening, 'that one.'

In two strides he had crossed the room. He seized her by the wrists and threw her on to the bed. Then he tore her clothes off her, pulling a button off her blouse in the process. After that he picked up the dressing gown cord and lashed her wrists to the bedpost. The wonderful rough-edged feeling of being restrained washed through her whole body until she felt quite weak with it. He took her left ankle and tied it to one of the corner posts at the end of the bed. Then her took her right ankle and tied it to the other post. Her legs were now spread wide, and she was completely helpless. He took off his own clothes with a grim deliberation, throwing them viciously across the room. One of his shoes hit the bedside telephone, knocking the receiver from its cradle. When he took off his belt, he ran the leather between his fingers in a very sensuous way and placed it carefully on the pillow next to her. The excitement was almost unbearable. She had never felt so naked.

He stood and looked at her for a moment, and her skin prickled with anticipation. The Black Widow was caught in her own web, helpless. He could do anything to her. When he made no move to touch her she began to wonder if he would just leave her there to teach her a lesson – those who ask don't get. Should she plead? It wasn't something that came naturally to her. She tried to read his face, work out what he was going to do, but it was impossible. He was looking at her as though she were an object, a newly acquired possession, one that could be returned if found wanting. And she did want him, painfully, desperately; she had never wanted to be touched so badly in her entire life. When he finally chose to make contact, he ran hands over her body as though he were assessing a piece of meat. Impersonal, no emotion. She quivered beneath his fingers. He pushed his thumb inside her, moved it around, and withdrew it. She shuddered. Then he rubbed his cock against her breasts, smiling his coldest smile, and wet her nipples with the leakage of his spunk. She tried to move her hips, but all she could do was wriggle a tiny little way to either side. The cord cut into her wrists if she moved any further, and although the burn was pleasant in its mild form, she didn't want it to go too far.

He stepped back from the bed suddenly and took his cock in his right hand. Then he started to masturbate, slowly and sensuously. Beatrice writhed as best she could; the deprivation of skin-to-skin sensation was sudden and unwelcome.

'I want you to fuck me,' she growled.

'I know you do,' he replied, his hand moving his foreskin inexorably back and forth.

'Please,' said Beatrice, the word catching uncomfortably in her throat.

'No,' he said. 'I'm going to come all over your body.'

'That's not fair,' whined Beatrice.

'I know,' said William. Their eyes locked.

Beatrice overcame her antipathy towards pleading and started to beg properly. He smiled, but the hand carried on its relentless personal massage.

'I want you,' implored Beatrice, slightly shocked at the submissive tone in her voice. 'I want you to fuck me. I want you to fuck me like there's no tomorrow.'

'Do you?' The hand kept moving. 'Do you like banana?'

'What?'

He stopped wanking, went to the bedside cabinet, put on a banana flavoured condom and moved up to her face. 'Suck,' he instructed. She sucked. 'Run your tongue round and round – yes, that's it. Tease me.'

Beatrice did as she was told. Then, quite suddenly, he pulled away and slid down the bed. She felt his cock between her legs, and then it was inside her, and she almost howled with relief. He fucked her the way a soldier might fuck a girl he knew he would never see again. Carelessly, for his own pleasure, selfish in his drive towards release. The belts tugged at her ankles, the cord tugged at her wrists, and the feeling inside got more and more intense until she saw the other-worldliness come over his face. His joy in coming was a picture of rude indulgence. It was too much for her to see this display of male lust and animal drive. It tipped her over the edge and she felt the restraints jerk at her with every contraction.

Before he untied her William said, 'We're going to win this together, aren't we? Because you want more of this, don't you, and you'll do whatever I say. And we'll do whatever it takes. *Whatever*.'

Beatrice nodded her head. Post-coital practicalities were her scene too, not chocolates and cuddles. He loosened the cord, then removed it; after that he unbuckled the belts round her ankles. And then, gambling heavily, Beatrice said, 'I know you know what the treasure is. And it *is* something gold. You said that, just for a moment, you thought you'd hit the jackpot. When you saw the iron pyrites.'

'They're figures,' he said. 'Solid gold figures of Indian gods having sex with their consorts. They're worth a lot of money.'

'How do you know?'

'They disappeared at the right time,' he said. 'I can't snitch on my informant, but I'm certain they were hidden this way to beat an insurance claim.'

'Are you really a policeman then?' asked Beatrice, astonished.

'No. I deal in salvage – for insurance companies.'

'Oh,' said Beatrice.

'I may not be the only one here under false pretences,' said William.

'Who else?'

'The original thief. The one who stole the loot and found out that the statues in the safe were fakes. Whoever it was wants another crack at it. Look, I don't know any more than that, it was just a whisper from my informant. So be on your guard.'

Beatrice was torn between her innate instinct for fair

play and the sheer physical buzz she got from being under William's control. William won. 'We'd better get a move on then,' she said. 'Back to the film clips, and look for a different link.'

'Don't boss me about too much,' said William, 'or I might have to assert my authority.'

Beatrice's knees did something strange at the sheer thought of it.

Fee and Summers stood outside Adults Only. Fee was wondering why anyone would paint the wooden shuttering in such a revolting shade of brown; then Summers opened the door for her, and she had to step inside.

It was an Aladdin's cave of sexual possibilities. Condoms hanging like party balloons from a rack, bottles of massage oil, jars of chocolate body paint, vibrators of every shape and colour imaginable. A book section, from the Kama Sutra to French flagellation; masks, whips, boots; feathery things, rubber things, things for which she couldn't even imagine a use. Videos, CDs, computer programs. Red satin sheets and pillow slips; maids' outfits, nurses' outfits, codpieces, basques. She and Summers weren't the only customers either. There were men on their own – though none of them were sporting dirty raincoats. A few couples, both heterosexual and gay, talking quietly to one another and laughing now and again. A man with a weird and wonderful collection of tattoos was talking to the man behind the counter. She heard the phrases 'body piercing' and 'increasing frenulum sensation'.

'Well?' said Summers.

'I'm just going to wait until he's free,' said Fee. She had no urge to interrupt the conversation going on over the counter – she'd never been able to face having even her ears pierced, and the thought of deliberately doing it elsewhere . . . no.

'OK.' Summers started to investigate the book section. After a while he seemed to get very interested in one particular book. Fee sidled over, trying to see what it was.

He noticed her and lifted it up so that she could see. It was dictionary of obscure erotic terms. Typical.

After a while the man with the tattoos left. Fee took a deep breath and went up to the shop assistant. 'I've been told to ask for something under the counter,' she said.

He looked slightly surprised. Then he bent down, retrieved a brown paper package and gave it to her. 'That'll be eighty pounds.'

Fee's eyes widened. 'What?'

'Eighty quid,' said the man. 'You don't get photographs like that for peanuts.'

'Photographs?' Fee looked at the package. It was sealed.

'Hang on,' said the man, 'we are talking about the same thing, aren't we? Sheep, pigs, donkeys, hamsters –'

'*Hamsters?*'

He snatched the package back from her. 'We're talking at cross-purposes,' he said.

'I'm doing this treasure hunt,' said Fee miserably. Things weren't working out too well here.

'Oh shit,' said the man, 'I *am* sorry. I'd forgotten about that. As far as I know, you're the first ones that have been in – though Freddy was on duty earlier.' He bent down behind the counter again, and this time he came up a with a small brown envelope. 'This is what you're after,' he said.

Fee opened it immediately. As soon as she saw the name Alfred Hicks she heaved a sigh of relief. She didn't read the rest of it; it was neither the time nor the place. She slipped the clue back in the envelope and turned to Summers.

'Hang on,' he said, getting a credit card out of his pocket. Then he bought the dictionary he'd been looking at and they left the shop. He read it all the way back to the car, avoiding two lamp-posts at the last possible moment.

They went back to the house and sat in a corner of the library; Summers got out the clue. Graham and Grace were sitting in another corner. Suddenly, Graham didn't seem quite so attractive any more; his lips were pressed hard together in a thin line, bisecting his face in an unpleasant geometric way. Grace looked upset. They had something spread out on the table in front of them, and she saw Grace push it away. 'I can't take this,' Fee heard her say. 'Everything else has been a bit of fun. Risqué, certainly, but not offensive. I didn't think Hicks was this sick. And I can't for the life of me see what the next clue is. How much did you say you paid for this?'

'Eighty quid.'

Fee and Summers looked at one another. 'We're in the lead,' said Summers quietly.

'Not by much.'

'Curfew in half an hour. They're going to be hard pushed to get back to Adults Only and get the right clue.'

'They might do a William and Beatrice. Have Grace waiting by the back gate to let Graham in after hours.'

'William may be that rash, but I don't think Graham Steel is,' said Summers.

'I really thought we'd got to The Elms before him . . . *oh*.'

'Oh what?'

'When I . . . last night . . . when we . . .'

'When you were at it like rabbits – yes. Go on.'

And he'd made it so easy for her. She laughed. 'OK, I did sleep with him.'

'The flash of the tanned biceps and the piercing blue eyes?'

'Uh huh. Anyway, there was a wet towel hanging on the towel rail, and a definite whiff of chlorine. I thought he'd been in the pool *here* – but now I come to think of it, I saw a man in the swimming pool at The Elms, a man with very close-cropped hair.'

'Neat way of concealing yourself,' said Summers. 'Just wait in the pool until the coast's clear, preserving your modesty at the same time. Though he doesn't strike me as the modest type, to be honest – but you'd know more about that than me. Any idea what he does for a living?'

'He said he was in salvage.'

'That covers a multitude of sins.'

'I tackled him about the mobile, but he said it was Scarab's.'

Summers looked sceptical.

'The bedside phone rang while I was there. He told me it was his wife, but I don't think it was. I caught him out by deliberately using the wrong name for one of his kids. Jack, instead of John.'

'Jack's often interchangeable.'

'Then why didn't he ask how I knew they called him Jack?'

'Just being pedantic,' said Summers. 'It's a hobby of mine.'

'What man lies about being married? It's usually the other way round.'

Summers didn't say anything.

'Yeah, OK,' said Fee. 'The sort of man who wants a fling but doesn't want to get involved.'

'Just your sort.'

'I don't go with married men,' said Fee shortly.

'So what are you going to do?'

'I don't think he *is* married,' said Fee. 'The phone conversation sounded all wrong. Too short. Too brusque. He didn't ask any questions.'

'Maybe they hate each other's guts.'

'I still think I'm right,' said Fee obstinately.

'I think you are too,' he said. 'Well done, Fee. You're developing a bit of faith in your own reasoning process.'

Fee stared at him. 'You think I'm right?'

'I'd bet on it. There's something very odd about this word-games week. I've been to lots of them, and this one's weird. It's not just the sex angle – it's the fact that there are so many new faces. You always get a few, but not this many. William, Angus, Graham, Heather, Patrick . . .' He went on to name a few more.

Summers had obviously mixed far more than Fee had, for she didn't know half the people he mentioned.

'It's making me wonder what the treasure actually is,' he said. 'I'm getting the impression that some people have a rather better idea than I do – but as Hicks died, this is the only way of getting at it.'

'Valuable, you mean.'

'Mm.' He smoothed out the clue they'd got from Adults Only, and they both studied it.

Chapter Nine

'So how are you doing?' William asked Angus.

'OK,' said Angus. Scarab had taken a little persuading to team up with him, but the collaborative nature of the questionnaire had clinched it. Angus had had no objections to doing it a second time, and Scarab's answers had been far more entertaining than Beatrice's.

'Pity you fell out with your other source of information,' said William.

'Fee, you mean?'

'She's back with Summers.'

'Is she? Do you want me to rekindle the hotline?'

'Might be a bit difficult. She's sleeping with Steel now.'

Angus looked slightly miffed.

William said quietly, 'I think Steel's the one to worry about.'

'Know anything about him?'

William shook his head. 'But I bet Fee does.'

'I'll see what I can do,' said Angus.

'The first line's a crossword clue,' said Fee, looking at the sheet of paper on the coffee table in front of her. It read:

Bam! Thud! Splattered in runny clay! (3, 4).

Then it said:

Ask for the above and at the following exalted location – Dearest Cornelia; Peace, Prosperity, Orangeade and Summer Sunshine Pour toi.

Summers shut his eyes, and his face smoothed over the way it did when he was thinking.

The library door opened and Scarab came in. She was wearing a very tight leather skirt and there was a bulge in the right-hand pocket. She went over to one of the shelves and ran her finger along the spines of the books. Fee concentrated on Scarab's black leather bottom, trying to ascertain the precise shape of whatever it was she had in her pocket. Scarab picked out a book – then suddenly she stiffened, turned and made for the door. Fee's eyes strayed one more time to the pocket. It was jiggling slightly. The door swung shut and Fee nudged Summers. He opened his eyes.

'Scarab does have a phone,' said Fee. 'I saw it vibrating.'

Summers shook his head as if to say, *whatever next*, as though the phone doubled as a sex aid. Fee turned her attention back to the clue.

Peace. Orangeade. A bubble of glee rose in her throat. 'I've got the second part,' she said.

Summers looked surprised. 'I've done the first bit,' he said, 'but after that I can't find any patterns. No similarities, nothing – though the capitalisation's interesting.' Then he just looked at her, waiting, a faint glimmer of amusement in his hazel eyes.

'They're all names,' said Fee.

'That much I've realised. But apart from wondering if Orangeade is somewhere near Sugarloaf Candy Mountain, I'm stumped.'

'They're the names of roses. Dearest – that's a rose. Cornelia, Peace, Prosperity, Orangeade – they're all roses too. *And* Summer Sunshine, and even Pour toi.'

'Brilliant,' said Summers. 'So we go to Rose's to locate whatever the crossword answer is. Finish it off then.'

She blinked. 'What?'

'Finish it off.'

He *expects* me to be able to do it, thought Fee. How very strange. No one's ever expected anything like that of me before. Here goes then. '*Splattered* is the anagram indicator, *bam* and *thud* have seven letters between them . . . runny clay . . . mud . . . *mud bath*.'

'Well done.'

Fee felt a warm glow envelope her. Praise was unfamiliar and seductive, it embarrassed her with one hand, and wrapped her up and cuddled her with the other. Excruciating and delicious at the same time.

'I think we'd better ring Rose and make an appointment,' he said. 'There isn't enough time to get there today.'

They went out to the payphone in the hall and Summers rang the number. 'Hello, Rose,' he said. 'It's Eric Summers. I think you've got a mud bath in which I'm rather interested.'

'My,' said Rose, 'you are making good progress, aren't you? Tomorrow at eleven suit?'

'Admirably,' said Summers.

'I have to be absolutely fair about this,' said Rose, 'it's in my contract. I take people strictly in the order in which they contact me, and everyone's visits are meticulously recorded. You are still working with a partner, aren't you?'

'Yes.'

'Good, because you'll get the answer faster tomorrow if there's two of you. I've got my money on you to win, Eric Summers. You don't try to cheat, and you did a lovely job on my tits yesterday.'

'How do the others cheat?'

'Oh, they try to ring after hours – I've got a nice little number I do on them if they try that. Or they send me an E-mail from their laptops, because it's too late in the day to use the computer in Room 8. That's *very* naughty and is punished accordingly. Anyway, must dash, lashings to do. See you tomorrow. Bye.'

Summers hung up, a smile on his face. 'I like Rose,' he said. 'I wonder how much she's getting paid for all this?'

'Presumably it's better than her standard rate.'

'Hm,' said Summers. 'I don't think Rose is just any old hooker. She's too smart; she thinks fast and she's got a great sense of humour. I think she's probably an ageing porn starlet – one of the better ones. She can act.'

'Well, at least finding Diana was quick,' said William to Beatrice, as they made for Room 8.

'We've only got a few minutes,' said Beatrice. She opened the door and they went inside. William sent the message: Send next treasure hunt clue.

Say please, came the reply.

Please, typed in William.

Do it properly. Please may I have . . .

William gritted his teeth and tapped in: Please may I have the next clue.

So who are you?

Before William could type in anything further, the door opened. Gavin Smythe stood there for a moment, a set of keys in his hand. Then he said, 'Sorry. Time out for tonight.'

William's face flushed with anger. 'Can't you just give me another couple of minutes?'

'Sorry,' repeated Gavin. He walked over to the computer and switched it off.

William got to his feet so quickly it looked like a reflex action, his lips thin with fury; Beatrice could see that his knuckles were clenched. Then his face relaxed, as he got a hold on himself. 'Fair enough,' he said. 'Come on, Beatrice.'

Beatrice followed him outside. They walked down the corridor; then William said, 'We need someone with a laptop and a mobile phone.'

'Everyone surrendered their mobiles.'

'Scarab didn't,' said William. 'Nor did Graham Steel. I

think he's got a laptop, as well. I'm going to go through his room during dinner.'

'How are you going to manage that?'

'Balcony,' said William.

'I'm coming too,' said Beatrice.

'OK. But I'll do the gymnastic bit and let you in once I've managed it.'

It didn't take him long, and Beatrice was impressed. She was being impressed with all sorts of unexpected things these days – it was as though the uninhibited sex with William had made her free to break other rules as well, rules she'd obeyed from childhood.

And sure enough, Graham had both a laptop and mobile phone. William fiddled around for a while until he managed to by-pass the password, and then he sent the following: Sorry we were cut off earlier. Please may I have the next clue now?

Who are you?

William Dacre. Who are *you*?

Rose, darling.

There was a pause. Please may I have the next clue? repeated William.

I'm not sure you deserve it, came the reply. *You'll have to work for it.*

Of course, wrote William.

I think I'm going to have to spank you.

William gave Beatrice a look that said, the woman's mad. His fingers started to tap the computer table impatiently.

And you're going to tell me how it feels.

OK, wrote William.

Is your partner with you?

Yes.

If you decide to act this out, you'll find the inspiration for the words you want much faster. But it's up to you. If this is going to be interactive, take down your trousers now.

William just sat there.

'If it speeds things up,' said Beatrice, 'I think we should do it.'

William stiffened slightly.

Lie across the chair, with your backside sticking up, leaving your right arm free to operate the keyboard.

'Bloody well do it,' said Beatrice, unfastening William's belt and yanking it off.

William stood up.

Beatrice unzipped him and pulled his trousers down to his knees.

'Hang on,' said William.

'You'll write like the muse has descended and taken hold of your wits,' said Beatrice. 'I promise you.' She pushed him so that he fell back across the chair. 'Turn over.'

He turned over, albeit reluctantly.

Slap him on his right buttock.

Beatrice slapped him.

Harder.

Beatrice did it harder. A faint pink mark appeared.

How does it feel, William?

Warm, wrote William.

Pathetic. Let's have a bit of passion in it. Beatrice, slap him on the left one now.

Beatrice slapped him on the left one. It was a satisfying feeling. She was enjoying the give of his flesh when the palm of her hand made contact. His skin had been cooler than hers at the outset; now it was warming up.

Just keep going now, until he's ready to write something good.

Beatrice kept going. William bit his lip; then he said sharply, 'OK, OK, enough.'

He repositioned himself conventionally at the keyboard and wrote: I felt as though someone was stroking me with a fiery rag, burning me just a little more every time. To start with, the blows merely stung slightly; a tingling that died away and then returned with the next slap. I felt helpless, yet strangely excited. The anticipation before each strike was exquisite, an ebb and flow of desire and fulfilment. The pain became inseparable from the

156

pleasure. I wanted it to stop, and yet I never wanted it to end.

William glanced at Beatrice with raised eyebrows. She nodded, and he sent the section.

That'll do, came the reply. *Surprisingly poetic, actually. Did you plagiarise it? You've been very naughty in another way as well, haven't you? You're doing this after hours, from a laptop. I'm afraid that means you don't get the next clue until tomorrow afternoon. There are time penalties for that sort of thing, you see. Goodbye.*

For just a moment Beatrice thought William was going to throw the laptop across the room. *'Bitch,'* he said finally.

'I quite enjoyed it,' said Beatrice, liking the idea of winding him up a bit.

'Oh you did, did you?' said William. 'Let's see if you like it the other way round.'

He kicked off his shoes and trousers, grabbed hold of the hem of Beatrice's skirt and pulled it up to her waist. Then he knocked her over the chair and took down her knickers. She was now sideways across the seat, her head hanging over one side, her bum supported by the opposite edge. Her legs were more or less straight out behind her and she could hold on to the chair-legs to steady herself.

He slapped her exactly as many times as she'd slapped him, with exactly the same amount of force. His words to Rose were echoing in her head – *I felt as though someone was stroking me with a fiery rag, burning me just a little more every time.* And yes, she did feel helpless and yet strangely excited, and the anticipation *was* exquisite. She had surrendered control, and it had liberated her. She was on a helter-skelter into the unknown, travelling faster and faster, hitting the sides, hurting, loving it. The thrill caught in her chest and stayed there; she had never felt so alive, or so aware of her body. For the first time in her life, anything seemed possible. She had found something that couldn't be measured, or weighed, or mapped.

'I think you're enjoying this just a little too much,' said

William. He landed the final blow with an expert flick of his wrist. It stung briefly like salt water on a graze; then he slipped his hard cock between her legs and rubbed it back and forth.

Beatrice heard herself sigh with pleasure. The tingle in her buttocks was like a backing track for the main tune; the main tune was the feeling she was getting from each thrust of his cock. He seized hold of her breasts, his fingers massaging the silk of her blouse against her nipples. It was rough handling; a man who knew what he wanted, and to hell with what the woman thought about it. She was his plaything – to chastise, fuck or restrain, whatever he wished. He could treat her like dirt, and she'd beg for more.

He broke contact. She turned her head to see what he was doing. He gave her a sardonic smile, then he spat in the palms of his hands and wiped them over his cock. He spat a second time, but this was for her. She felt his finger moisten her anus. This he did gently – so gently that she shuddered with anticipation. Round and round the outside of it, then inside the tiniest bit. Then further up.

'Relax,' he said. 'Coming like this is meant to be spectacular.'

Beatrice forced herself to relax. She began to enjoy the feeling of his finger inside her, and to enjoy the idea of how wicked she was being, liking it. Then the finger was replaced by his cock. He pushed it in very slowly and carefully, then he moved his hand round to her clit, and started to rub it. The double sensation was exquisite. Beatrice felt him begin to move, and after a little while he started to synchronise the movement of his hand with that of his cock. Beatrice relaxed naturally; the feelings strengthened, and she knew this was going to be quick – for both of them. His breathing became more spasmodic, and then they both tipped over the edge together. It must have been intense for him, too, because he roared out loud when he came. Beatrice felt her own climax go right the way through her body; the initially localised pleasure spread out in wave after wave.

William withdrew, and Beatrice stood up – and that was when they heard Graham Steel's key in the lock.

Beatrice grabbed her knickers and wriggled them back on. Her skirt fell obediently back to her knees; she was dishevelled, but decent. William hadn't made any attempt to get dressed – he had gone straight to the laptop and shut it down. By the time Graham had seen them, William was well away from the table. The laptop was in exactly the same position it had been in when Beatrice had first entered the room. William's trousers however, were on the floor.

'What the hell?' said Graham Steel.

'Oh shit,' said William miserably, 'I'm sorry.' He looked convincingly sheepish. 'Angus is trying to pull Scarab in the room we share, and Beatrice's room-mate is in residence in *her* room. I thought we'd be out before you'd finished dinner, and you'd be none the wiser. We haven't left any mess.'

'How did you get in?'

'You hadn't shut the door properly.'

Beatrice could see that Graham was pretty sure he *had* shut the door. He glanced round the room; his eyes came to rest on the table, and lingered. He was looking at the laptop as though he couldn't make up his mind about something.

William pulled on his trousers, and laced up his shoes. 'You know how it is,' he said, in a man-to-man voice. 'Us married men have to make hay while the sun shines.'

Beatrice looked affronted, but she didn't say anything.

'Who said I was married?' snapped Graham.

'No one,' said William. 'You are though, aren't you? And you've been fucking Fee.'

'Did *she* say anything?'

'No. But you're not exactly hooked on her, are you? I've seen the way you look at her – the way a cat looks at a mouse.'

'Get out,' said Graham. 'I'm going to report you.'

'I don't think you are,' said William. 'Not if you want

to keep your mobile.' He ushered Beatrice through the door and they walked off down the corridor.

'So you're married,' said Beatrice.

William laughed. 'I was just playing a part. I'm not the marrying type.'

'Neither am I,' said Beatrice. And she wasn't. Sex was one thing – commitment something else entirely.

That evening, Gavin announced that all the teams had got past the fourth clue, so they were free to talk about their experiences up to that point. Several people had rung Sister Perpetua instead of the recorded message. She had entered into the spirit of the thing with genuine enthusiasm and had taken to answering the phone with the following riddle: What ruby jewellery of hers was found disordered on the fish counter?

Some of the callers had got the answer straight away – red, her ring – *red herring*; others had taken a little longer.

Fee was enjoying herself; she no longer felt at a major disadvantage in the word games – she didn't have the vocabulary, true, but a lot of the activities allowed dictionaries. They had to see how many words they could make, taking four or more letters from *sesquipedalian*. Summers and Saul Slick were still going when Gavin called, 'Time ladies and gentlemen, please.'

Rachel seemed different somehow – more laid back, and she laughed a lot. Peverall was on sparkling form and had everyone in stitches with his description of his session with Rose. They only stayed for a couple of the games, making their excuses and leaving disgracefully early. It was quite obvious from the expression on Peverall's face that they weren't going to be tackling lexicographical niceties upstairs.

'I don't think I've ever seen Peverall so happy,' said Summers to Fee. 'Not even when he won the Crack Cracker's Crystal Crock. I hope your friend lets him down gently, if that's what she decides to do.'

'I'm not sure I've ever seen Rachel quite so involved with anyone either,' said Fee. 'I'm still finding it quite hard to believe. He's just not her type. She likes the tall dark brooding sort – William was just the most recent in a long line of them.'

Peverall and Rachel ran up the stairs two at a time, dashed into Peverall's room and subsided on the bed. 'It's my turn to do something to you,' said Peverall, when he found a spare moment between kisses.

'Well you can't do a body-body massage on *me*,' said Rachel. 'You're too heavy.'

'Ever fancied a bit of podophilia?'

'What's that?'

'Foot massage, with some toe-sucking thrown in.'

Rachel liked having her feet rubbed. She went into the bathroom, washed and dried her feet and smothered them in talcum powder. Peverall removed the rest of her clothes and laid her down on the bed. He put on some music, lit the candles and switched off the light. Then he positioned himself at the end of the bed and got started.

To begin with, he simply ran the palms of his hands all over her feet. This got rid of the excess talcum powder, and brought his skin up to the same temperature as hers. He commenced his more detailed approach on her left heel, stroking it rhythmically, then pressing his fingers a little harder until he was almost kneading it, moving round it in a circular fashion. It was probably the least erotic part of her foot – but as the massage progressed it became more sensitive. She lay back against the pillow, totally relaxed, feeling the pleasure percolate through her. Then he began to stroke her ankle, concentrating on the sensitive areas just beneath the bone, letting his fingers drift down now and again towards the arch. The arch was much more susceptible to a sexual subtext, and Rachel shivered each time he glanced off it in passing. After a while he moved down to the arch properly, his fingers smoothing her sole from front to back, over and over again; she felt the first sympathetic twinge of arousal between her legs. From there he moved on to the ball of her foot, alternating between feather-light touches of his fingers to deep delicious massage. This was someone she could trust to do the job properly, and he'd take as long over it as she wanted him to.

'This is fantastic,' said Rachel, her eyes closed, her red hair spread out in a Pre-Raphaelite halo around her head.

'I read up on it when you were in the shower this morning,' said Peverall. 'Now stop talking, if you want your little piggies seen to.'

He slipped his finger between her big toe and the next one and slid it back and forth, hooking first the underneath of one, then the other. Between the second and third toes now, and the feeling in her crotch was building to something that needed contact. She wriggled.

Peverall put his hand on her hip to still her. 'I've still got the other foot to do,' he said. He finished the left one and moved across to the right. This one seemed to have become just as responsive all on its own, by some mysterious process of osmosis. He tackled it as he had the other, and by the time he got to her toes she was squirming uncontrollably. He separated them out with his fingers and caressed each one individually. Then the spaces between, and she was hard pressed to decide which was the more erogenous zone. Her whole foot felt capable of orgasm.

He bent down and licked her big toe. It was as though someone had put an electrode on it; Rachel heard herself give an involuntary gasp. Peverall placed his lips on the tip of it, where the nail ended, then he slid his mouth slowly over it and down, and Rachel wondered fleetingly how close the feeling was to the one he got when he slipped his cock inside her. Warm soft wetness, with the suggestion of a muscularity to come. The sensations were so acute that she tensed her foot slightly. The pleasure began to turn to discomfort, and what he was doing began to feel like tickling. Relax, she told herself, and as she loosened up, the tickling feeling went away. It was replaced by a blissful ebbing feeling.

He slowly licked her big toe, running his tongue around it the way she ran her tongue round the head of his cock. Then he started to suck – gently at first, so that she was hardly aware he had started doing it, then a little harder.

Is this how it feels for him, wondered Rachel, this dissolving downwards, this falling sensation? Like the one you get at the top of a switchback, when the ride slows down before plummeting over the edge? I never wondered what a man might feel before; perhaps I never cared that much.

But she cared now. He was doing the most incredible things to her, and he was doing them because he wanted to. It wasn't a prelude to him getting his satisfaction, it was purely for her, no conditions, nothing. He was acknowledging her as person in a way no one had before. Even the thought of it was a turn-on, and she couldn't help writhing against the sheet. Part of it caught between her legs so she left it there, feeling it rub against her every time she wriggled. The sucking got faster and harder; he was wanking the other big toe with his left hand. Then she stopped thinking and let the experience take over. His ministrations brough her to the edge of an orgasm and now she was in need of his cock.

She leaned over and kissed him right on the top of his head. Then she placed him on the bed, so that he could see himself in the mirror, sat on his lap and fucked him with her back towards him so that she could watch as well. It was a position that did wonderful things to a man. When he came it lasted a long time. She grinned, and said, 'How was it for you?'

'I'm just a little bit shattered at the moment,' he replied. 'I might be available for comment in a moment or two.'

And when, a few moments later, he did speak, he caught her at a disadvantage.

'Why don't you move into my room?' he asked, not looking at her. 'I'm sure Fee would like a room to herself.'

Oh hell, thought Rachel. 'I hog the duvet.'

'I can manage without.'

'I'm a harridan until I've had a cup of coffee.'

'Costa Rican or Kenyan?'

She was having trouble keeping a straight face. 'I read *The Guardian*, dammit.'

'Good crossword.'

'And if it's the wrong time of the month I usually start throwing things.'

'They still talk about my magnificent diving catch at Trinity.'

'Oh, you're impossible,' said Rachel. And then she thought, why not? So she said, 'All right.'

Peverall just looked at her. Then, very slowly, a smile started at the corners of his mouth and gradually spread across his face. After a moment or two he said, 'You'd better tell Fee, and then go and get your things.'

Rachel got dressed and went out into the corridor. I'm mad, she thought, he isn't my type, what am I *doing*? But the thought of spending the nights with him wasn't unpleasant at all. There was something very protective about him; she would wake up with his arms round her, and he would make love to her in the slow lazy haze of the morning and tell her how wonderful she was.

As she turned the corner she saw William's door open. Beatrice stormed out and marched off the other way, without seeing her. Rachel stepped back round the corner, and peeped round it. After a moment or two William followed, slamming the door behind him. He slammed it so hard that it bounced against the lock and opened again, and came to rest slightly ajar.

Wouldn't it be cool to do a bit of detective work, thought Rachel. Go back to Peverall afterwards and tell him what I've found – if I find anything at all, of course. And the thought became the wish, and the wish became the deed. Rachel slipped into William's room and glanced round. She'd been in it before, of course – but her mind had been on other things.

She wasn't quite sure what she was looking for – a mobile phone, a computer? She saw neither. The cupboards were empty, the wardrobe just held clothes, and although there was a pile of papers on the table, none of them seemed to relate to the treasure hunt. The bathroom was equally unproductive. There was a tube of some sort of soothing cream on the side of the washstand, the lid left off, a white worm of it creeping across the tiles where it had been squeezed in the middle. It looked as though it had been used in a hurry. She tried the bedside locker. There was something in here – a book of some kind, large, stiff-backed, thick crinkly pages, some of which seemed to be stuck together. She opened it.

It was a home-made catalogue. Rachel opened it at random and thumbed through it. It was full of photographs and drawings of antiques, numbered and dated, with handwritten notes below each item. African masks, sculptures, vases. A collection of erotic jade figures, Tibetan gilded bronzes, Chinese porcelain bowls, paintings, engravings. She turned to the front page – and there was the name Alfred Hicks. Rachel stared at it, trying to put two and two together, and failing. She went through it more carefully, horribly aware that time was passing all too quickly for her liking. It had to be the catalogue of Hicks's private collection – and at least half of it was erotica. Very few of these pieces would ever have made it on to general display in a museum – there were goats and elephants and chickens, and on the vases there was every variety of group sex you could imagine. One page had had the corner turned down. There was a pen and ink drawing of two pairs of oriental figures, both pairs locked together in sexual intercourse, the woman's legs around the man's waist. The man had an awful lot of hands and arms and was using them to arouse every orifice the woman possessed. Underneath was written: Solid gold, acquired 16.4.1979 from Sanjay Patel.

Rachel heard a sound in the corridor. She slipped into the bathroom and held her breath. The footsteps passed. This is too risky, she thought, I'd better scram. She closed William's door properly behind her and scuttled back to Peverall's room.

He looked at her empty hands with only partially disguised disappointment. 'Changed your mind?'

Rachel was at a loss. 'Changed my mind about what?'

165

'Going and getting your things.'

'Oh.' She'd completely forgotten why she'd been any-where near William's room in the first place. 'No, no, I'll get them in a sec. I've just made a very intriguing discovery . . .'

She told Peverall all about it. When she'd finished Peverall said, 'I suspect you've just been looking at a drawing of the treasure. I ought to take you shopping in the town to celebrate.'

This sounded good. 'Wine and roses?'

'A deerstalker, a magnifying glass and a decent briar pipe. I think we'll omit the cocaine.'

Graham Steel intercepted Fee on their way out of the games room. He was wearing a classy pale-blue silk shirt, which matched his eyes, and he had rolled up the sleeves, revealing a pair of tanned biceps. Summers smiled and made himself scarce.

Graham put his arm round Fee's shoulders. 'Fancy a nightcap? I haven't seen anything of you today.'

'You're married,' said Fee. 'I don't do married men.'

'My wife doesn't understand me,' he complained mel-odramatically, running his fingers along the top of her shoulder blade to the nape of her neck.

Leave my neck alone, thought Fee, or I might waver. 'You've got kids,' she said, although it was difficult to get the right amount of authenticity into her voice.

He made a *that's the way the cookie crumbles* face.

'Jack and Sarah,' Fee went on, warming to her theme. 'Sarah just got a distinction in her grade four flute exam. You're obviously an involved parent.'

He had the nerve to look flattered.

'Listen to her scales and her arpeggios, do you?'

He nodded.

'C sharp minor's tricky, isn't it?'

'Fee, my home life's shit. Can we drop the subject?'

'*What* home life? You don't *do* C sharp minor for grade four – I know, I played flute in a youth orchestra.'

'Both sorts?'

'Sorry?' She was thrown off-balance.

'The silent flute, the pink oboe –'

'Oh for heaven's sake,' said Fee, her new-found confidence cutting him off in mid-sentence. 'You're not sidetracking me with sex this time. Yesterday it was grade three, and your kids were called John and Sandra. And I bet it was you that pranged Saul Slick's car in the car park of St Anne's Chapel.'

He looked at her sharply, as though he suddenly felt he might have made a big mistake about her. Then he said, 'OK. I think we need to talk. In my room, if you don't mind. I need to tell you a bit about myself.'

All right, thought Fee, let's hear what you've got to say. She followed him upstairs. When they reached his door he didn't open it straight away. Instead, he crouched down and peered at it. Then he gave a little nod of satisfaction, stood up again and put his key in the lock.

'What was that about?' asked Fee.

'Someone broke into my room earlier.'

Fee's eyes widened. 'So you stuck a hair across it to make sure it hadn't happened again?'

He gave her another sharp look. 'Yes.'

'And it's still there.'

'Yes.'

'Someone trying to filch your answers? Seems a bit extreme for a recreational treasure hunt.'

'There's a bit more to this treasure hunt than meets the eye.' He opened the door and they went inside.

Chapter Ten

*T*he laptop was on the table, along with some papers. 'Actually,' said Fee, 'you've got a bit of a nerve getting upset about someone else's underhand methods. You're using outside help. That's what your phone call from your imaginary wife was about.'

'I admit it all,' he said. 'A lot of these clues are beyond me. Fortunately, Grace is very good. I'm not a word buff; I read archaeology, not English.'

'Archaeology?' Fee was surprised.

'That's how I got into the salvage business. Chasing up dodgy antiques. And that is what all this is about. Drink?'

Fee nodded and he poured her a glass of wine. Then he went over to the table, and rummaged through the papers. He found what he was looking for and handed it to her.

It was a photocopy of a drawing of two statuettes. Eastern in origin, each statuette consisted of a woman with her legs wrapped round a god, who was fucking her and touching every orifice she possessed with a superfluity of hands. Underneath there was some handwriting: Solid gold, acquired 16.4.1979 from Sanjay Patel.

Fee looked at Graham Steel. 'Is this the treasure?'

He nodded. 'You could buy a house for what that pair of figures are worth.'

'And they're dodgy in some way?'

'This is a photocopy of a page from Alfred Hicks's catalogue of his collection of antiques. The original ledger was stolen at the same time as the figures – along with most of the other pieces. A very professional job; whoever it was got past two burglar alarms and blew the safe. Everything was insured and the pay-out Alfred got was substantial. So far unremarkable. I have some fairly unsavoury contacts – I have to, in my line of business. One of my informants gave me this photocopy and he said the Hicks robbery was an inside job. Hicks had sold most of his collection through an intermediary and the burglary was a fraud.'

'So he got the money for everything twice over?'

'Yes. Hicks had been told he'd only got a year to live, and he'd decided to live it to the full. His go-between managed to sell everything – everything except for one pair of figures. The figures were so recognisable – and so valuable – that the only way he could get rid of them quickly was have them melted down. And Hicks couldn't bear the idea of that. So he decided to make a bit of mischief – he devised this treasure hunt, with the figures as the pot of gold at the end of his rainbow. They belong to the insurance company really, of course, so whoever wins won't even be able to keep them – but there *is* a reward. And that's why I'm here. To recover the pieces for the insurance company.'

'I see.'

'The phone call yesterday – a colleague – confirmed a suspicion. Hicks's intermediary knew about the proposed treasure hunt and is here in person with the intention of winning at all costs. And as for my deception – it was *you* who asked if the caller was my wife. I couldn't think of anything else plausible to say on the spur of the moment, so I went along with it. It was really my informant, pretending to be a colleague with an emergency at work.'

'And *that's* why you were so pleased I'd teamed up with Summers again. So that you could pick his brains through me.'

He didn't say anything.

'That's the only reason you wanted me in the first place.'

'No, Fee. I fancy you like mad.' He ran his finger down the line of her jaw. 'You arouse so easily; I simply have to touch you in the right place and you respond without thinking.'

For a split second she felt slightly insulted: press the right buttons, get the right result. Automatic. She was a washing machine again. But his finger had crept round to the nape of her neck now, and it was stroking up and into her hair. Oh shit, thought Fee, I've got no self-control at all when it comes to this. She put her arms round him and he started to kiss her, which was fatal. He did it so well that she couldn't imagine breaking it off for any reason other than a fire or an earthquake. She rationalised it in a rather perfunctory way; he'd given reasonable explanations for everything, he wasn't married after all, and ... and ... Why the hell should she need another reason? She was enjoying it, dammit.

He undressed her as he kissed her, then he undressed himself. She was about to lie down on the bed when he said, 'Let's try something a bit different.'

Fee raised an eyebrow. Different? How different? She wasn't into S and M.

He grinned. 'I found a couple of things in the wardrobe.'

'What?'

He went over to it and opened the door. Inside was a collapsible cot, presumably for people staying there at other times who had youngsters. On the top shelf there was a pile of bedding to go with it. He pulled out a blue rubber sheet and spread it on the bed.

Haven't tried that, thought Fee. I wonder what it feels like?

'There's this as well. Colour co-ordinated, naturally.' He went back to the wardrobe and brought out a feather duster. It was shaped like a miniature witch's broomstick, with a white wooden handle and a fluff of pale blue feathers. 'Lie down. On your front to begin with.'

Intrigued, Fee lay down. He started to brush her gently with the duster, up and down her arms, across her shoulders, down her spine. Then down each leg to the soles of her feet, and right the way back up again to the nape of her neck. He concentrated on her neck for a while, knowing it was a particularly susceptible area. Every fluttering stroke made it more and more sensitive. She sighed, a long drawn-out murmur of contentment. She was beginning to get wet – and it wasn't just between her legs. The rubber was making her body perspire and things were getting slippery and strange.

'Lots of people get aroused by this,' said Graham softly. 'It's all to do with childhood memories of comforting sensations.' And the smell of the rubber did seem oddly evocative, reminiscent of warmth and security and pleasurable feelings.

He began to deal with the more erogenous zones – her armpits, the crooks of her elbows, the backs of her knees. Her buttocks, and the crease between them. She felt alive to his lightest touch, her skin was reaching out to him – and at the same time, she was powerfully aware of the alien texture beneath her.

'Turn over.'

She turned over. He wiped her dry with a towel and started to dust the front of her body in a fussy yet funny way, like an elderly cleaning lady. They both laughed, and he kissed her on the sole of her foot. Then he adopted a more seductive style, long sweeping strokes of the duster up and down her body. This was much more horny, as every so often he touched her nipples. The pleasure became more and more intense; her back started to sweat as well, and before long she was almost floating across the rubber on a film of perspiration.

'Open your legs.'

She opened her legs as wide as she could. He stroked up the inside of her thighs, getting closer and closer. Then he plucked one of the feathers from the duster, spread her pussy lips wide open and began to tickle her in the most sensitive places of all. It was exquisite. She wriggled against the slippery sheet, but her body couldn't get any real purchase. She wanted more pressure now, the duster wasn't enough; she wanted to come. She could see that he had quite an erection, and it seemed a waste just to leave it there. She reached out and touched it and it jerked.

'OK,' he said. 'But this time, *you* can fuck *me*.'

Hm, thought Fee, he wants a bit of the rubber action as well. She moved over, so that he could lie down on his back. Then she straddled him and slid herself down over his cock. He made a little noise of satisfaction. Fee began to fuck him, slipping up and down the length of him, making sure the angle was right for maximum stimulation. She watched his face. The hard regular features softened the longer she fucked him. He lay there, his eyes closed, his breathing getting more spasmodic. The more excited he became, the more excited she became. At the last minute he opened his eyes and looked at her, although she couldn't quite decode his expression; then he came. As he pumped his load into her she reached down and began rubbing herself furiously, abandoned to all else, but giving herself the climax she craved. After only a few seconds, she lost it, powerfully and noisily. Then they each just lay there for a while, not speaking.

'Grand slam,' said Fee eventually, remembering Beatrice's conversation about bridge.

'Sorry?'

'Rubber,' she elaborated, reflecting that Summers would have got it immediately.

After that, other attempts at conversation flagged, and she felt strangely flat. When they'd got their respective breaths back they went and had a shower together.

He made it quite clear that he neither expected nor wanted her to stay the night. He didn't do it in an unpleasant way; he just announced how tired he was and Fee took the hint and left. She pecked him on the cheek in the doorway – then she said, 'I never asked you who

Hicks's middleman is. You said your phone call confirmed your suspicions.'

He looked faintly annoyed that she'd raised the matter. 'Who is it?' demanded Fee, upset by both his reticence and his clear desire to spend the night on his own.

'William.'

It made complete and utter sense. 'I think I knew it anyway,' said Fee. 'Night.'

'Sweet dreams.'

On her way back to her room she bumped into Angus. 'Don't rush off,' he said, 'I haven't seen you for ages.'

Fee looked at him, wondering if he and William were in it together. They have to be, she thought, though William's the brains.

Angus tried the sexy smile. 'Fancy a nightcap?'

'Scarab turned you down, did she?'

'I don't fancy Scarab.'

'Like hell,' said Fee, suspecting that he fancied anything that was the right age and the right gender – and reasonably pretty. What was it Rachel had said, presentation over content? It was uncomfortable looking at it the other way round so she said, 'Incidentally, what's William's line of work?'

'Er . . . salvage. Why?'

'Any particular areas of interest? Jade? Porcelain? Solid gold Eastern figures, maybe?'

Angus stiffened.

Bull's-eye, thought Fee. 'I think one of the clues requires some knowledge of antiques,' she lied. 'You and William will be well away, won't you?'

He ran his finger up her arm. 'Tell me more.'

'No chance, sunshine,' said Fee. 'Night.'

The next morning there were two hours to kill before the appointment to see Rose. Summers and Fee spent part of it in the library, talking to Saul Slick and Joan. Saul Slick seemed a little uncomfortable in Fee's presence to start off with, but it soon wore off.

'I didn't have anything like as good a time at university

as my sons,' he said. 'They bring home these pneumatic girlfriends. They're good material for the soap I write, of course.'

'Don't they recognise themselves?' asked Fee.

'Oh, I disguise them,' said Saul.

Joan laughed. 'Not very well. Someone will sue you one of these days, Saul. It's a good job the last one you used had a sense of humour.'

Fee badly wanted to tell Summers what she'd learned about Graham Steel, and how she'd caught Angus out. After a while she said, 'Oh, that book, Eric. It's in my room.'

Summers stood up and excused himself. As they left the library, Fee glanced back and saw the expression on Saul Slick's face. He thinks I'm taking Summers off to fuck him, thought Fee. He thinks Rachel and I are both tarts.

They went up to her room and she told him everything she'd found out. He listened with interest. Then he said, 'I wouldn't be too sure Graham's telling the truth, even now.'

'What do you mean?'

'Why shouldn't Steel be the middleman, and William be the investigator?'

No, thought Fee. Graham's just become the good guy again, I can't get my head round this.

'You don't want to hear that, do you?' said Summers. He glanced at his watch. 'We ought to make a move if we're to get to Rose's in time for elevenses.'

They went out to his car, and drove to 14B Mount Pleasant Road.

'Eric. My favourite naughty boy,' said Rose, opening the door and ushering them in. She was wearing something hideous in puce silk that showed her cleavage in all its geological glory. Fee looked around her with interest and peeped into a couple of rooms as they walked past. The décor reminded her of a pub; a heavy dark-red wallpaper that looked like brocade, well-used leather furniture, patterned carpets. There were patterns everywhere – an Arabic design on the velvet cushions, a different one on the curtains. An Indian rug, a chenille tablecloth in dark greens and gold flung over the hall table. Rose led them upstairs. There were prints on the wall all the way up the stairwell – spanking scenes, mainly. They turned left at the top and Rose took them into a bedroom.

'You can get ready in here,' she said. 'Any sharp jewellery on pierced bits we can't see, Fee?'

Fee shook her head.

'I don't think I need to ask you the same thing, do I Eric?'

Summers laughed. 'No.'

'Right then. You're both to get undressed – unless you want your clothes covered in mud. No laundry service available here, I'm afraid; part of my contract. Then go into the room next door and I'll be waiting for you.' She left in a swirl of Rive Gauche, puce silk and flesh.

'That dress was unquestionably the most hideous thing I've ever seen,' said Summers, unbuttoning his shirt.

'I thought it was quite stylish,' teased Fee.

'It's not the style, it's the colour.' He made a face. 'Somewhere between red and purple. Revolting.'

Fee grinned. He took his own opinions so seriously, as though no one with an ounce of savvy could ever disagree with him.

'This is getting to be a familiar situation,' he added, removing his trousers.

He was being so businesslike that Fee didn't feel in the slightest bit self-conscious any more. She looked at him, unabashed, remembering the shape of his body. Compact, a little on the hairy side, but well proportioned. He could never have been called muscular – but he wasn't flabby either.

'Ready?'

'Mm hm.'

They went into the room next door. There was an inflatable pool in the middle of the floor, with some kitchen steps standing next to it. There was an en suite shower at the far end of the room, and the pool was filled with something grey and glutinous.

'The next clue is at the bottom of the pool,' said Rose. 'It's another one of those laminated cards. But the mud is too deep for you to bend down and feel around with your hands, so you're going to have to accomplish it with your feet. It's a fairly watery mixture – not the consistency most of my clients prefer, I might add. But it's quite opaque, so you won't be able to see below the surface. Shower's through there when you've finished. I'll leave you to it then. Call me if you need me – if you can't get out again, or one of you gets cramp. I've turned the heating up, so it ought to be quite pleasant. Good for the complexion, or so they say.' She left the room.

'After you,' said Summers.

Fee climbed up the kitchen steps and slithered into the pool. The mud had the consistency of a milk shake, and it was just about at blood-temperature; difficult to move through, but progress could be achieved slowly. Fee felt as though everything that happened in there would have to happen in slow motion. As Summers lowered himself into the mud she started to feel around on the bottom of the pool with her toes.

'We ought to be methodical about this,' said Summers. 'I'll start at one end, and you start at the other. We'll meet in the middle, and if we haven't found anything we'll try again.'

Fee swept the floor of the pool with her foot. She was fairly sure she wasn't missing any bits, but she couldn't be certain. It took much longer than she'd expected. She kept hoping she would hear Summers announce that he'd got it, but it didn't happen. They got closer and closer until eventually they met in the middle. She could feel his body against hers now and again; his thigh sliding past hers, his wrist slithering against her forearm. It was sensuous stuff. His face was splashed with mud – as was hers, presumably – and his hair was messed about and splattered with grey. It made him look very different. He was usually so neat and tidy, a quiet unobtrusive presence. Here he just looked like a man.

'I've got it,' he said. 'It's under my left foot.'

'Can you pick it up with your toes?'

'Yes, but I don't think I can necessarily hang on to it – it's very slippery. I need something to brace my foot against. I could use my other leg, but acrobatics aren't really my thing, and I have a horrible feeling I'd overbalance.'

'Use *my* leg then.'

'OK.' A look of intense concentration came over his face as he manoeuvred the card with his foot.

'You only need to work it far enough up my leg so your hand can reach it.'

'I know. But you're going to have to hold me at the same time so that I keep my balance.'

She put her arms round his waist, feeling the resistance of the mud slowing her down. It was hard to keep a grip on him, to stop him slipping through her fingers. She felt the edge of the card touch the side of her foot; then it started to move up her leg, very, very slowly, going off course now and again. They swayed dangerously a couple of times, but progress was steady, if snail-like. Then, just as he got to her knee, the card evaded him and scooted off somewhere, and they had to start all over again, feeling around for it with their feet until they found it. This time it was Fee who struck lucky. Summers put his arms round her in slow motion. It was a better arrangement, more stable, and progress was a little faster. Up the side of his calf to his knee; a little higher, a little higher – and then she'd got the card. He didn't loosen his arms straight away – he just smiled at her and said, 'Well done, stork.' They stayed like that for a little while. Moving was an effort, after all, and the slithery contact felt companionable and nice.

'How are you doing?' Rose's plump face appeared over the rim of the pool.

'Just found it,' said Summers.

'I'll turn on the shower,' said Rose. 'It takes a minute

or two to get to the right temperature. Do you like mud then, you little minxes?'

'It's surprisingly pleasant,' said Summers, letting go of Fee and slowly making his way towards the side. It took him three attempts to get out. Fee did it in one, and they went and had their shower.

'The mud was an improvement,' said Fee, as Summers shook the water out of his hair.

'Thanks a lot.'

'I only meant you didn't look so prissy.'

'*Prissy?*'

'Well you do. You don't dress casually – you don't wear a tie, but that's about all that can be said. Your hair's always tidy, and your room's as neat as a hotel advert.'

'The OED defines prissy as prim and prudish.'

'Well maybe you are.'

'After everything I revealed in that damn questionnaire?'

'Polygraphs are notoriously unreliable,' she replied, quoting him word for word.

For once, he looked really annoyed. Then he said, 'You've missed a bit,' and he ran his hand from her shoulder right the way across both her breasts, and washed off the last traces of mud, treating her nipples as though they were just another piece of skin. He remained quite expressionless, and so did she. Then he turned off the shower and threw her a towel. They dried themselves, got dressed again and went downstairs.

'That was quick,' said Rose.

'Are we the first ones to do this clue?' asked Fee.

'Can't tell you that,' said Rose. 'But I will tell you one thing. You've only got two more clues to do that have any connection with me.'

'We're getting near the end then?'

'I'd have thought that was a logical deduction. I'll need the laminated card back for the next couple by the way.'

Summers got out his notebook and copied down the

clue. When he'd finished he snapped it shut and said, 'Until we meet again then.'

'Looking forward to it, darling,' said Rose, and they left.

They sat in the car and read the clue. The first part was in verse and went as follows:

> O dive into that fountain, for
> Her temple's name. Then Babylon,
> And Egypt. You can swear by Zeus
> And see the tomb of Mausolus.
> The rest would give the phrase away –
> Just take one word, the room to play
> Is there; begin again, to free
> The Latin; then you'll say, I see.

The second part was another crossword clue:

This fellow loses his head, though not his genes, screwing with stamina almost to the end (6).

'Isn't the tomb of Mausolus one of the Seven Wonders of the World?' hazarded Fee.

'It is,' replied Summers. 'And there are references to most of the others. And seven is a plausible room number, if you think of the others we've had.'

'What about the rest of the verse? *Begin again* . . . begin what again?'

Summers began to list synonyms. 'Recommence . . . restart . . . restore . . .'

'How about begin the verse again?'

Summers laughed suddenly. 'Yes. You're right.'

'I am?' said Fee, who hadn't actually worked out the answer.

'*O dive* is an anagram.'

'Oh!' squeaked Fee. '*Video*. The Latin for *I see*.'

'You did Latin at school?'

'I wasn't any good at it.'

'You remembered it when you needed to.'

Fee suddenly wondered how much else she could remember if she needed to. There had never been a practical application for Latin before. 'So we need to head for Room 7 and watch a video,' she said. 'Let's go, partner.'

'Hold your horses. I want to solve the other part first. It won't be there for no reason.'

'Can't we just get going?'

'No.'

'Why can't we just head for Room 7? Then I can start going through the videos to save time while you solve the clue.'

He didn't say anything; he just sat there looking at the piece of paper, wearing his thinking expression.

'Is *this fellow* a similar device to *this chap*?' tried Fee, knowing it was pointless to try to get him to leave before he was ready. 'We had *this chap* in the first clue, and it meant the letter I.'

'I don't know,' he said.

'And does *loses his head* mean losing the first part of a word?'

'I don't know.' He looked annoyed with himself.

Fee glanced back towards Rose's house and saw Graham Steel walking up to the door. He's on his own, she thought, it's going to take him longer than it took us. But we do need to get to Room 7 before he does.

'All right,' said Summers, following her line of vision, 'we'll go back to the house and take a look.' He drove off rather faster than usual, and when they reached their destination he surprised her by doing a macho handbrake turn to park the car – although when it came to rest, it was positioned as precisely as ever. She heard him say 'Prissy, my foot,' under his breath.

'This wasn't the sort of establishment I had in mind when you said you'd take me shopping,' said Rachel to Peverall. 'I do think you were clever to get Adults Only out of Aunt Dolly's though.' They were standing in the queue, waiting to ask for something under the counter. Saul Slick was at the head of the queue, looking very uncomfortable indeed.

'Eighty *pounds*?' Rachel heard him say. 'I'm sure that can't be right.'

'Merinos cost,' said the assistant, very low-key but perfectly audible. 'Marines I can do you for forty.'

'A video of fucking *sheep*?' said Saul Slick in a stage whisper, a suggestion of hysteria creeping into his voice.

'Been surprisingly popular recently.'

'This is not my idea of a treasure hunt,' said Saul Slick to the floor, under his breath.

'Did you say treasure hunt just then?'

'Yes.'

'Oh, right, you'll be wanting this then.' The man behind the counter handed Saul a small brown envelope. 'No charge. Next.'

Saul Slick strode out of the shop, his face crimson. Peverall and Rachel grinned at each other.

'Seen anything you fancy?' asked Peverall.

'Standing right next to me,' said Rachel.

Peverall smiled and squeezed her hand.

Rachel looked round the shop as they waited their turn. There were some very fancy vibrators, and some nifty costumes. The French maid's outfit was particularly fetching – a little white lacy cap, a matching apron and a very short black dress.

Peverall saw her looking. 'Just tell me your size,' he said, 'and we'll get it.'

'I'll need stockings and suspenders. Black stilettos I already have.'

Peverall bought the lot, and refused any contribution from Rachel. He asked quite simply for the treasure hunt clue that was under the counter and got it without any problem. After that they went to a jeweller's for a silver teaset. They chose one with a fancy tray, a teapot, a sugar bowl and a cream jug.

'This is a bit over the top, Peverall,' said Rachel, although she was loving every minute of it.

'We have to have the right equipment,' said Peverall.

'And by the way, my French maid wears jewellery.' He pointed at a slim gold chain with an emerald pendant, and the assistant brought it out and laid it on the counter. It was simple but very classy.

'You can't,' said Rachel. 'It costs a fortune.'

'Rachel,' said Peverall, 'I have a house in London, a flat in Paris and a yacht in the Med. I'm not exactly hard up.'

'Oh,' said Rachel, and Peverall bought the pendant. Then they did a bit more shopping, and Rachel suggested a few sartorial changes to Peverall's wardrobe. He took it all in good part and bought what she advised. After that he took her to lunch at the swishest restaurant in the town, and they took the clue out of the little brown envelope and looked at it.

'Bam! Thud! Splattered in runny clay!' exclaimed Rachel, with appropriate expression. 'Three letters, then four.'

'Mud bath,' said Peverall.

Rachel smiled fondly at him. She realised that she was actually finding his clue-solving ability sexy; this was very curious, and no doubt she would analyse it later. She read out the second part: 'Ask for the above at the following location: Dearest Cornelia; Peace, Prosperity, Orangeade and Summer Sunshine Pour toi.'

'That's somewhat harder,' said Peverall.

'Wasn't Cornelia one of King Lear's daughters?'

'Cordelia, I'm afraid. I think we go back to the library and look up as many references as we can.'

'Right,' said Rachel.

Summers opened the door to Room 7 and he and Fee went inside. It was full of electrical apparatus of one sort or another. A computer, a television, a CD player, a tape machine, a record deck. Some things that looked like mobile phones, but weren't. In one corner, curiously, three spades, stacked against a pile of magazines. The walls were lined with shelves, and on the shelves were records, tapes, CDs, videos and computer games.

'Hm,' said Summers, 'now maybe you see why I

wanted to solve the second clue. You could get *Room 7* quite easily by solving part of the first clue – but you need the anagram of *O dive* to know it's a video.'

They both went over to the video shelf and scrutinised the titles. There were about forty of them – unless you knew what you were looking for, the task of pinpointing what you wanted was virtually impossible. Some were films, some were wildlife documentaries, some had merely a number for a label.

'There's something here called *The Seven Wonders of the World*,' said Fee, pulling it out and putting into the video machine. An ancient historian – in both senses of the word – started to talk about the pyramids, against a backdrop of camels.

Summers wasn't watching; he was still thinking. 'This fellow loses his head, though not his genes,' he recapped, 'screwing with stamina almost to the end.'

The ancient historian was standing in front of the opening to a tomb. 'The Egyptians were fond of puzzles,' he was saying. 'And they liked concealed rooms. A necessary deterrent against grave-robbers, as each pharaoh was buried with a king's ransom in treasure. Find the concealed room, and you've hit the jackpot . . .'

Fee stopped the tape, rewound it and played it again. Then she said, 'Maybe there's a secret passage somewhere.'

'It's possible.' He took out the map and looked at the enlarged area in the corner – the plan of the house itself. And there was that tiny pyramid, in the passageway between the kitchen and the games room.

'That's it, surely,' said Fee. 'A concealed room.'

'Or a red herring.'

'You're being difficult.'

Summers cast her a look that said: Me? Difficult? Never. 'This fellow loses his head, though not his genes . . .' he repeated.

'Charles I,' said Fee. 'He may have been beheaded – but his son certainly spread those royal genes about in great style. Nell Gwyn, Barbara Castlemaine . . .' She went back to the video shelf – and there, sure enough, was a documentary about Charles I. She put it in the machine.

'Charles has got seven letters, not six,' said Summers. 'Although I suppose *almost to the end* could mean chop off the final letter. I still don't like it though.'

The same ancient historian appeared, in front of a portrait of Charles I. 'Charles I was devoted to his wife, Henrietta Maria,' he intoned. 'He was a very different man from his son, Charles II, who was famous for his many liaisons. The answer to this conundrum is summed up in 1660, when Charles II spent the night of his triumphant arrival at Whitehall in the arms of . . .' Fee stopped the tape, and rewound it.

Summers was looking at the plan of the house again. 'Mm hm,' he said. 'Room 13. It's by the back door, and it's the changing room for the pool.'

'Room 13,' said Fee. '*Summed up in 1660*. One plus six, plus six, plus zero. Thirteen. Cool.'

'What are we looking for, though?' asked Summers. He pressed *play*, and they watched the rest of the video. The only thing that seemed relevant was a number of references to paintings.

'Maybe there's a painting on the wall,' suggested Fee.

'Mm.' He still didn't seem happy.

'Let's go and look,' said Fee.

'OK.' They went out into the corridor and made their way to the back of the house. Their route included the passageway between the kitchen and the games room.

'Where was that pyramid?' Fee asked.

'I really think that was a red –'

'Oh!' said Fee, stopping dead. In the corner of one of the oak panels, someone had scratched a tiny pyramid. She ran her finger over it. Then she pushed. There was a loud creak and the click of some mechanism. Then the panel opened inwards, and Fee could see steps disappearing down into the dark.

Chapter Eleven

'*T*he Tudor rose symbol on the plan,' said Rachel, twirling a lock of her flaming hair round her index finger. 'It was over the library.'

Peverall looked up from his encyclopaedia. 'Yes. To lead us to that book on the language of flowers.'

'There's something bugging me about that book.'

Peverall went over to the shelves, retrieved it and handed it to Rachel. Rachel started to flick through it, and before long the name *Summer Sunshine* caught her eye. *That* was what had been bugging her, the fact that she'd seen the name before. There was an illustration above it, of a rich yellow hybrid tea rose. She turned the rest of the pages. No more names leaped out at her. She ran through the clue again in her head: *Dearest Cornelia; Peace, Prosperity, Orangeade and Summer Sunshine Pour toi. Peace.* That was a rose, wasn't it? She replaced the book and found one on gardening. There was a section on roses ... and there they were, every single one of them. Even *Dearest* was the name of a rose.

'Look,' she said to Peverall, passing him the book.

He kissed her on the top of her head. 'Rose's. So Rose possesses a mud bath, does she?' he said. 'I think we'd better give her a ring.'

They went out to the payphone, but Rose couldn't give

them an appointment until the next morning. 'I'm very busy at the moment, darling,' she said to Peverall. 'But I can fit you in first thing tomorrow. Ten o'clock.' Both Rachel and Peverall could hear someone moaning faintly in the background. The sound of a slap was cut off mid-thwack as Rose hung up, presumably with her other hand.

'Oh well,' said Peverall, 'never mind. I think it's time for afternoon tea.'

Rachel remembered the maid's outfit and giggled.

'There's a kettle in the room and cups and saucers. I bought some leaf Assam, and some fresh milk. Oh, and some Viennese biscuits.'

'You think of everything,' said Rachel.

They went up to his room, and Rachel got changed in the bathroom. The clothes were very saucy – the dress hardly covered her backside. She pinned up her thick red hair and fitted the little white lace cap over the top. Then she rolled on the stockings – pure silk, of course – and fastened the suspenders. They showed beneath the dress, purple lace on bare flesh. She put on the apron and went back into the bedroom. She could see the top of Peverall's bald head above the back of the armchair, but nothing else of him. She boiled the kettle, warmed the silver teapot and made the tea. She arranged everything rather artistically on the silver tray and carried it across.

Peverall was wearing a Japanese silk dressing gown, a pair of slippers, and nothing else. He looked like someone from the thirties, used to being waited on. He waved his hand at the coffee table in front of him and Rachel placed the tray on it, bending over to do so. She wasn't wearing any knickers. She felt his hand stroke her buttock, just once, and she turned round.

'Zut alors,' she said.

'Callipygian,' he said, 'but not steatopygous.'

'Speak English, monsieur.'

'You have a beautiful posterior,' said Peverall. '*Les fesses incroyables*.'

'*Merci, monsieur*.' She poured him a cup of tea.

He took a couple of sips, then put it back on the table. After that he ate one of the biscuits, a long thin one. He licked off the sugar and consumed it very slowly and sensuously, looking at her all the while. Then he said, *'Viens-ici, je vais te montrer quelque chose.'*

Rachel moved closer. Peverall opened the front of the dressing gown, revealing an enthusiastic erection.

'Oh, là,' said Rachel.

'Mademoiselle,' he said, 'it is you who have brought me to this sad state of things, and only you can relieve it.'

'Monsieur?'

'I want you to kneel on the carpet in front of me, and suck my cock.'

'It cost extra, monsieur.'

Peverall brought out the emerald pendant, and hung it round her neck. She felt his fingers, cool and assured, fastening the clasp. Then he slid his hands down her back and cupped her buttocks with them, pulling her forward. She fell across him, then slithered on to her knees in front of the armchair. He moved her sideways on, so that she was at a right angle to him. As she bent her head over his cock, he started to caress her buttocks with his hands. She took him into her mouth, as far as she could, then slid back up the shaft again. He made a satisfied little sound, and his fingers started to explore beneath the straps of the suspender belt, moving from flesh to lace and back again. Then down to the stocking tops, as if to verify their existence, his finger circling her thigh. Up again, and over her protruding behind, glancing almost accidentally across the damp hairy place between her buttocks. She changed her approach and licked his cock from head to root in long rhythmical strokes. He ran his index finger from clitoris to anus, mirroring her actions. She fluttered her tongue across the sensitive underside of his cock; he inserted his finger a little way into her pussy, and fluttered it against her G-spot.

The arousal was building far too quickly to the point of no return. She lifted her head and said, 'Monsieur, for a mouthful of spunk, I prefer to be comfortable.' Her back was beginning to ache, and Peverall couldn't be all that comfortable either.

'*D'accord*,' said Peverall, and he leaned back in the chair.

Rachel straightened herself, then returned to Peverall's cock. It was very hard indeed, so she finished him off with some fancy tongue-work and swallowed the result.

He sighed deeply, ruffled her hair as though she were a favourite Labrador and said, 'I've spent half my life dreaming about someone doing that to me. Someone faceless, and nameless. But the fantasy was nothing compared to the reality.' He cupped her chin in his hand, looked deep into her eyes and said, 'I am head over heels in love with you, Rachel Carpenter.'

'Oh shit,' said Rachel. Then she felt dreadful and added, 'The bugger is, I seem to be getting rather fond of you as well.' And the bugger was, it was true. She'd thought about why she found his erudition so sexy – and it was the old alpha male thing. The way a man protected you in the modern world was by his ability to outthink the opposition, not flatten it. But she still couldn't make herself actually say she loved him. It was too scary.

'I wouldn't fight it, if I were you,' said Peverall.

William and Beatrice stood under the shower in Rose's house, washing off the mud. Rose had apologised profusely when they rang the bell, and asked them to wait in the car. The client before them had taken rather longer than she'd anticipated and she was behind schedule. Eventually Graham Steel had emerged, and William and Beatrice had their turn in the mud. William got dressed while Beatrice dried her hair, and he went downstairs before her.

'All hunky-dory then, sweetie?' said Rose, tucking something horrible in lime green over her ample bosom.

'You're a major player in this treasure hunt, aren't you?' said William.

Rose regarded him steadily. 'I'm being well paid.'

'You must have known about a lot of things in advance, so that you could set them up.'

'What are you driving at, William?'

'I don't know how many more clues concern you, but you're going to know which is the last one on your list. What's to stop you doing the treasure hunt yourself?'

Rose laughed. 'All the word-stuff is way beyond me,' she said. 'I failed English.'

'Maths?'

Her gaze sharpened.

William pulled his wallet out of his trouser pocket and thumbed through a wad of notes. 'How many of these would it take for you to give me the last clue you have?'

Rose smiled. 'Five should do it.'

William peeled off five tenners; Rose went over to the sideboard and pulled out another laminated card. William copied down the clue. By the time Beatrice came downstairs, he and Rose were sitting innocuously on the settee, drinking herbal tea.

They went back to the house, and William gave Beatrice the Seven Wonders of the World clue to work on. He left her in the library, poring over some books; then he got back into his car and drove off.

Once Beatrice had cracked the first clue she went to look for him – but she couldn't find him anywhere, so she decided to go through the videos in Room 7 on her own. She discarded the ancient historian's secret room immediately, as there was no reference to it in the second clue. But Charles I . . . he and Henrietta Maria had had several children . . . and they had been a devoted couple, right up to the end. She got out her copy of the map, looked for Room 13, and discovered it was the changing room for the pool. Excellent, thought Beatrice. William is going to be rather impressed when he comes back and finds me two clues further ahead.

She removed the Charles I video from the machine and put it back on the shelf exactly where she'd found it – between *The Seven Wonders of the World* and a wildlife documentary on insects. Then she made her way to Room 13.

She wasn't entirely sure what she was looking for – but changing rooms tended to be bare places, with slatted wooden seats and metal lockers. Whatever it was ought to be fairly obvious. She opened the door and stepped inside. The walls were sprayed a cold pale turquoise, and the floor was grey stone with sparkly bits. There were a couple of dryers on the wall, one at hand-height, one at head-height. Lockers, benches, a mop and bucket, a mirror. Beatrice caught a glimpse of herself – a furrowed brow, a tight little cap of dark brown hair, close-set dark eyes behind gold-rimmed specs. The pointed little chin that she hated. She was no beauty, but she had developed a certain vivacity since William had come into her life. Leaving the mirror, she went to the centre of the room and turned slowly round. There was nothing there that made any sense. She walked down to the end, investigating a few nooks and crannies.

And there, between two lockers, she found it. It was a painting of a fish. A red herring.

'I can't feel a light-switch anywhere,' said Summers.

'I've got a Maglite,' said Fee, feeling in her bag. She pulled out the thin metal torch and switched it on. A narrow but powerful beam of light swept down the steps in front of them. She felt pleased with herself. 'After you.'

Summers tackled the steps rather gingerly, waiting until she shone the light on each one before he put his foot on it. Fee heard voices from outside; she didn't want to give away what they were doing, so she pushed the panel shut. It made a faint click, and the light from outside disappeared instantly.

'Did you just shut the door?' Summers turned round to look at her and raised his hand to shield his eyes from the direct beam of the torch.

'I heard someone coming.'

'And is there a handle on the inside?'

Fee moved the beam over to the door. There was a

heavy lock of some sort on it, but no handle. She tried to get a purchase on the protrusion – but even when she did, nothing gave. A wave of panic swept through her.

He came back up the steps, took the torch from her and shone it on the lock. Then he put his ear to it. 'It's a time switch,' he said.

'You mean we're shut in here until it decides we can open it again?'

He was peering at the mechanism more closely now. After a moment or two he said, 'Two hours.'

She'd really let him down this time. Why wasn't he angry? 'Can't you alter it?'

'No.'

'That takes us up to curfew.'

'It might take us that long to solve the next clue. If we find it.'

'I suppose we'd better look for it then,' mumbled Fee, her face hot with embarrassment. She turned round and started to descend the steps. After a moment Summers followed her.

He didn't have a go at me, she thought. I did something really *stupid* and he didn't call me a dickhead, or shout at me, or go sarcastic. He didn't even give me a reproving look or a disappointed sigh. Why? I've just proved I'm the thickest person here.

When they got to the bottom of the steps they found themselves in a cellar, which had been split into rooms. There was a light switch down here – although the lamp proved to be just a bare bulb hanging from an ancient flex, and rather dim. The first room had a stack of old furniture in it, as had the second. The third room was empty, but a picture of a fish had been sprayed on to the brick wall.

It was a red herring.

'Oh shit,' said Fee, feeling gutted – which, she reflected, was undoubtedly the appropriate response.

'I knew there was something wrong with that last clue,' said Summers.

'We haven't tried the changing room yet,' Fee pointed out. 'Room 13.'

'I don't hold out much hope of that one bearing fruit either,' said Summers. 'We've got two hours to kill. We might as well make ourselves comfortable.'

They went into the one of the rooms with the furniture and found a chaise longue under some chairs. They stacked the chairs elsewhere, rummaged around for some cushions and sat down.

Fee took a deep breath. 'Why aren't you angry with me?'

'Because the next mistake could just as easily be mine,' said Summers. 'Right. Back to the beginning.' He opened his notebook and they studied the words once more. *This fellow loses his head, though not his genes, screwing with stamina almost to the end (6)*

'Louis the Sixteenth?' tried Fee. 'He went to the guillotine, didn't he?'

'Supposing *screwing* is an anagram indicator . . .' said Summers.

'Stamina has seven letters.'

'Let's take off the A at the end then. Matins . . .'

'Mantis!' squeaked Fee.

Summers looked surprised at her sudden enthusiasm. 'Are they wildly uninhibited? I know very little about insects.'

'Oh, it's much better than that,' said Fee. 'Usually, when the male impregnates the female, she decapitates him – and his body carries on copulating, even without the head. After that, she eats the rest of him. And there was a wildlife documentary on insects among those videos.'

'You see?' said Summers. 'You're not a waste of space at all. It's a sound answer in every respect.' He glanced at his watch. 'Well, that didn't take up much time. What shall we do now?'

'Talk,' said Fee.

'OK,' said Summers. 'Tell me what you're going to do about your mother, after this week is over.'

'God,' said Fee, 'I don't know. Try to stop caring what she thinks, I suppose.'

'No,' he said, 'that's not the answer. That would diminish *you*, in the end. You need to see things from her point of view.'

Fee stared at him.

'She could have been jealous of you.'

Fee snorted.

'It sounds as though you had a better relationship with your father than she did.'

'That was her fault.'

'You don't know that. What goes on in a marriage is rarely privy to the children of it. She sounds like a disappointed woman, in many respects. Maybe she didn't want you to be disappointed either.'

'Why are you taking her side?'

'I'm not,' he said. 'She sounds tactless and brittle. But tactless just means an inability to empathise, and brittle is a defence mechanism. Don't you have any good memories of her?'

Fee made a face. 'Yes, I suppose so.'

'Don't let the negative ones take over,' he said. 'It's a downward spiral. You start looking for the bad things and forget the good ones. Tell me about a good one.'

Fee sighed. 'She did play games with me; ones she'd made up, where I had to go looking for things. Names of rivers, kings and queens, capital cities.'

'Educational. What's wrong with that?'

'It was only to give her a bit of peace, so that she could do the crossword.'

'She can't be all bad then.'

Fee wanted to hit him.

'When did you last speak to her?'

'Eighteen months ago.'

He raised his eyebrows. 'Did you send her a Christmas card?'

'No.'

'That's just petty. Send her a postcard – you're on holiday.'

'Tell me some more about *your*self,' said Fee, anxious to change the subject. 'What went wrong with your marriage?'

He leaned back against the cushion, put his hands behind his head and closed his eyes. 'You know from the questionnaire I was twenty-four when I lost my virginity. On my wedding night, as it happens.'

Fee's eyes widened. 'I didn't have you down as religious.'

'I'm not,' he said. 'But Clara was. Still is; we see one another from time to time. It was a good match in some ways – she's a theoretical physicist; she plays the cello rather well, and it's an instrument I like. That and the flute.' He smiled. 'She was a technically proficient player rather than an interpretive one. Theoretical about everything, you see, no passion. No fire, just regularly tended coals. I hoped it would come, but it didn't. I seemed to like sex a lot more than she did. And no children either, which was a good thing in the end. Five years after we got married she was offered a two-year contract in the States, and it seemed like an ideal opportunity to go our separate ways. I suppose I pushed for it harder than she did – there was more missing in the marriage for me than there was for her.'

'What happened after that?'

'I went a bit mad. Sold the house and went off round the world on the proceeds. Found quite a bit of passion here and there. Came back to England, got a job, bought another house, wrote a very dry textbook, meandered from one relationship to another . . .'

'But no one special?'

'Some have lasted longer than others. What about you?'

'Long trail of false starts. I make snap judgements about people, and sometimes they're wrong. Quite often, actually. And then I discover I don't want to get close to whoever it is and it just peters out. My longest attempt was with Dan – he looked like a film star, and his virility made up for his lack of conversation – and he didn't make emotional demands on me.'

'Like fidelity?'

'Mm. We both screwed around.'

'You haven't had a proper relationship then.'

'And you have?'

'I've had more of a stab at it than you.'

'I've been faithful to one person.'

'For how long?'

'Six months,' said Fee, feeling like a tramp.

He laughed.

'I'd rather have six months of unbridled passion than five years of dead coals,' she snapped.

'So would I,' he said, suddenly serious again.

'Have you? Have you had six months of unbridled passion?'

'Oh yes.'

'Tell me about it.'

'Her name was Lillian. I met her a couple of years after I split up with Clara. She was . . .' He smiled, and his eyes twinkled suddenly. 'She was a trapeze artist.'

That was the last thing Fee had expected. 'Straight up?'

'Straight up. She travelled a lot, and I went to see her whenever I could. It used to scare the hell out of me, watching her up there – but it was exciting, as well. She was beautiful, athletic and very adventurous sexually. I learned more from Lillian than I learned from all the rest put together. She tired of me in the end; I just couldn't match her energy. But I was totally besotted for close to a year, couldn't think of anything else but the next time I'd be in bed with her. If it was a bed. It was a railway track once.' He laughed. 'Disused line, but it's the thought that counts.'

Fee shivered. It was cold in the cellar, a nasty damp chill that crept up on you when you weren't paying attention and attacked the backs of your arms and your shins. She sniffed one of the cushions. It smelt musty.

'Are you cold?' Summers asked.

'Yes.'

He slid along the chaise longue and put his arm round her. The side of her body that came into contact with his started to feel warmer very quickly. She snuggled a little closer and he tightened his grip. She was reminded of the time he'd held her hand, walking across the lawn at The Elms. On this occasion, too, the contact was just right – the right position to transmit the maximum warmth, his hold on her just firm enough to keep her in place. He felt soft and welcoming and she sank into him. It was a good, businesslike arrangement again.

'Why do you think passion is important?' he asked her suddenly. 'Lots of people manage without it.'

Fee thought for a moment. Then she said, 'Perhaps it's the urge to find something that sweeps us away, something that erases a sense of self. Some people get it in their work. I get it when I play the flute sometimes. But sex is the best escape ever.'

'I suppose that's one view,' he said.

'What's yours?'

'That it's the moment when you're most yourself.'

'I don't agree,' she said. 'What about acting out fantasies? What about pretending to be someone else? Don't you fantasise?'

'Of course I do.'

'What about?'

'Your fantasies are more exotic than mine,' he said.

'What on earth can you know about my fantasies?' She lifted her head to look at him, and saw that he was smiling.

'A sudden blow,' he said. 'The great wings beating still, above the staggering girl. Do you know it? It's a sonnet by Yeats. *Leda and the Swan.*'

'No,' said Fee in a tiny voice, remembering her reaction to the misericord, and the way that Summers had noticed it.

He recited the rest of the poem to her, and it was one of the most sensual things she had ever heard. She closed her eyes and laid her head on his shoulder. The hollow of his neck was soft and smooth and warm. She changed position slightly and felt the glasspaper roughness of his chin. He was someone who needed to shave twice a day.

The chin felt rather nice, like the sugar coating on a fruit pastille. He leaned his head towards hers and they stayed like that. Fee's mind started to fill with odd images; camels and swimming pools and Captain Cook. A dictionary that snapped at her heels – but this time it had lost its teeth, and gums don't draw blood. And then she was asleep.

Beatrice went back to Room 7 and looked at the selection of videos again, to see if any of them fitted the *losing his head* clue. She tried a couple of likely-looking ones, certain that Hicks would have put the clue somewhere near the beginning – it wasn't his style to make people wait if they'd actually solved something correctly.

When she couldn't find anything logically, she started trying videos at random. The documentary on insects looked singularly unpromising. She pressed *play*. A large green leggy thing turned its head towards her, and suddenly two large eyes were looking at her in a very predatory way. Magnified to this extent, the creature was terrifying. The two front legs looked more like arms, furnished with curving spines, and the triangular face had a sort of alien intelligence about it. When it moved, it moved quickly. The camera cut to another insect, similar but smaller. This one was hiding behind some twigs and peeping through them every so often. After a moment or two it decided to venture out, and it started to inch towards the other one.

'The male mantis is well advised to approach the female with caution,' said the voice-over. 'In many species of mantis, the female bites the head off the male while he is inseminating her; this releases a hormone that makes him copulate all the harder, though he is, technically, dead. The female then eats the rest of him.'

Beatrice clapped her hands with delight, finally getting the anagram. The male mantis climbed on to the female's back and their abdomens made contact. Then the female bit his head off; he pumped away like crazy, and the clip ended. Beatrice realised that she'd found the spectacle compulsive viewing. The idea of kamikaze sex was wick-edly exciting. The screen went blank for a moment, and then the following appeared:

> Make your deposit here, O man,
> And bring your partner, if you can.
> It's quicker as a joint account,
> This place won't query the amount,
> Lots or little, who's to know–
> Apart from Maurice Bigelow?
> Now, if you find Lacrosse, tick *Done*;
> Don't shop around, you're near this one.

Beatrice copied down the clue. Then she got out her map and looked for the banks. There were three. One of them was opposite the Marquis of Queensberry, the second was next door to a sports shop called Lacrosse. The third was a bit further along, next door to a place called the Maitland Clinic. Make your deposit here, *O man*, thought Beatrice. It's the man who needs to speak to Maurice Bigelow, I'm going to need William for this one. Where the hell has he got to?

She decided she'd better go and have a good look for him.

William had solved the clue he'd bought from Rose quite quickly – *Roasted Bert* had to be an anagram of *Broad Street*, and *ether* was an anagram of *three*. He found the address and rang the doorbell. There was a longish pause; then the door was opened by a young woman wearing a cheap scarlet kimono. She had sloe eyes and a golden skin, and her blue-black hair fell to her waist.

'I'm part of a treasure hunt,' said William.

'Ah so,' said the girl in a breathy voice.

'Do you have a clue for me?'

'Clue? Ah, clue. You treasure hunt man.' She opened the door and let him inside. The décor was not unlike the décor at Rose's, but it had oriental touches here and there. A hookah standing on a brass table, a Japanese print on the wall – quite an erotic one, too. The girl led him upstairs, and into a bedroom. This was hung with silk, so that it looked like the interior of a tent. In the middle of the floor stood a circular bed, with rumpled satin sheets. There was a sweet cloying perfume everywhere, and lots of boxes of tissues. The waste-paper basket in the corner was overflowing with used ones.

'Me Koko,' said the girl, undoing the sash round the kimono in a businesslike way. 'You?'

'William,' said William.

The sash tumbled to the floor, and the garment fell open. Koko had a beautiful body, neat and compact and honey-coloured all over.

'Look,' said William, 'is there something I have to do before I get the next clue?'

'You do me,' said Koko, dropping the kimono on the floor and flinging herself on to the bed. 'You do me, then I give Swedish massage.' The sight of her spread legs usually worked pretty quickly on most clients, which saved all that licky stuff.

William was no exception. For a moment it looked as though he might say something else – then he simply dropped his trousers and climbed on top of her. 'First you take off shirt,' said Koko, 'then you put on this.' She handed him a condom.

William did as instructed, and with some haste.

Koko guided him inside her, and he started to fuck her. Pity this one had to be the one, thought Koko, I'm not sure he's the sort that can take a joke. I'm just a thing to him, something he can empty himself into. I hope he doesn't have a quick temper, because I'd hate to have to knock him out. I don't think he'd like the humiliation. She looked into his eyes, and saw nothing there.

Perhaps he'd seen something in hers, however, because he withdrew, turned her over, pulled her on to all fours and entered her from behind. His hands were on her hips, holding her firmly in place, his nails digging into her skin. There was no tenderness in the contact, it was simply the most practical way to go about what he was doing. He said nothing, and neither did she. Men like him didn't frighten her; she was a black belt at karate, and she could very definitely take care of herself. A fly buzzed somewhere behind a curtain, accompanied by the occasional slap of flesh on flesh and the ticking of a clock. Somewhere in the distance a dog was barking, and a car alarm had started up.

William began to speed up, and to hold his breath every so often. The scent of his sweat started to mingle with the air freshener, producing an odd lavender musk-iness, the smell of cheap commercial sex. Koko decided it was time to make the appropriate noises of arousal, which was what her clients expected.

'Shut up,' said William.

Koko shut up, and started to compile a shopping list in her head. Tea-bags, KY jelly, bean sprouts, massage oil, onions . . . It passed the time.

William banged away relentlessly for several minutes – then he made a few short sharp thrusts and after that he came, in total silence. He withdrew straight after and lay back against the satin sheet, breathing hard.

Now for the good bit, thought Koko. She knelt down beside the bed and pulled a washing-up bowl from underneath it. 'Please to turn body over for massage,' she said.

William turned over. Koko removed the massage accessories from the washing-up bowl, and started to strike William with them. The room suddenly stopped smelling like a boudoir, and metamorphosed into a fish shop.

'What the hell?' William rolled over as though he'd been stung and sat up.

Koko hit him round the face with her accessories, first with the one in the right hand, then with the one in the left. William seized her by the wrists and stared in aston-ishment at what she was holding. Koko let out a hysteri-cal little laugh.

'*Fish?*' said William, his voice almost shrill with disbe-lief. '*Why?*'

'They're herrings, mate,' said Koko, her Japanese accent replaced by a London one. 'Rose said I had to paint them red, but I couldn't be arsed. Was it crucial? Like, a fetish?'

William went white with fury. His jaw clenched, his eyes narrowed, and for a moment it looked like he didn't quite know what to do with his hands. Koko mentally prepared herself to deliver a swift kick where it hurts. Then he got a grip on himself and started to get dressed.

'What's got your knickers in a twist?' demanded Koko. 'You got a free fuck. Rose said she'd give me fifty quid.'

'Fifty quid,' said William sourly. 'Bitch.'

'This was all set up ages ago,' said Koko. 'I've had the fish in the freezer for the last two weeks. Rose said I might get several punters, or none at all. You've been the only one, so far. She rang me to say you'd be coming. So to speak.'

Fee felt warm and safe. She snuggled against the source, dimly aware that it was another body. Then she realised that she was awake, and a little unsure as to where she was. Or who she was with, for that matter.

'Are you awake now?'

Summers. That's who she was with. She kept her eyes closed and stayed where she was.

'There's only another ten minutes to go before we can open the door.'

'Good.' She was thirsty, and she wanted to go to the loo.

'It'll be dinner time in half an hour.'

'Long enough to go and ferret out the mantis video,' said Fee. She opened her eyes. She felt his cheek against her forehead as he turned his face towards her.

Then he stiffened. 'What's that?'

'What?'

'Shh.'

They listened. It was the creak of the door. They looked at one another, but before they could make a concerted effort to stand up they heard footsteps coming down the steps – and then Graham Steel was standing in the

201

doorway, arms folded, looking at them. Summers made no attempt to remove his own arm from Fee's shoulders. He just said mildly, 'Did you leave the door ajar?'

'Why?'

'There's a time lock on it. If you've shut it we're down here for another two hours.'

'Good job I wasn't fool enough to close it then, isn't it?' He glanced round, checking things out.

'It's in the other room,' said Summers. 'On the wall.'

Steel went into the other room. Fee heard him say *shit* under his breath. He reappeared, smoothed out again. Then he said, 'Oh well. We're still all in the lead, I imagine. Maybe we should pool resources on the last clue.'

Summers shook his head.

They all went back up the steps and emerged into the corridor. Fee was first out, and she bumped straight into Beatrice. Beatrice was smiling. She looked strange when she smiled, as though it wasn't an expression ever intended for those intense dark eyes.

'How long have you been standing there?' asked Fee.

'Long enough to find out all about that red herring down there,' said Beatrice.

Fee made her excuses and dashed off to the loo. As she sat there, having a long-awaited pee, she reflected that some bodily functions could be almost as pleasurable as the big one. A long non-sexual cuddle on a damp chaise longue, for example, could be a surprisingly satisfying experience. It felt similar to soaking up the sun, after a long spell of cloud.

Chapter Twelve

Graham, Summers and Fee arrived at Room 7 together. Summers took out a coin and said, 'Toss you for first crack at it.'

'Heads,' said Graham, and it was. He smiled icily and disappeared inside, shutting the door firmly behind him.

'I bet he stays there until curfew,' said Fee.

Summers shook his head. 'If he solves the clue quickly, he'll want to capitalise on it before dinner.'

They sat down on the floor outside and waited. After a few minutes William appeared. He glanced at the closed door and said, 'Beatrice in there?'

Fee shook her head. 'Graham Steel.' There was a sudden smell of fish – but it didn't seem to be coming from the direction of the kitchen. Fee wrinkled her nose and looked up and down the corridor. Perhaps it was a delivery of some sort. William looked momentarily uncomfortable, then he went. The fishy smell went with him.

Ten minutes later Graham emerged, looking cheerful. 'All yours,' he said.

Fee and Summers went inside, found the mantis video immediately, watched it and copied down the clue.

'Presumably,' said Fee, 'we have to try to open a joint account at whichever bank has a Maurice Bigelow. Map, please.'

Summers handed her the map.

'Oh *look*,' said Fee, 'there's a shop here called Lacrosse.'

'Does the name Maitland figure anywhere?'

Fee's brow furrowed. 'Yes, there's something called the Maitland Clinic, quite near the Marquis of Queensberry – and all the banks, as it happens. How did you get that?'

'Look at the seventh line.'

Fee read it aloud. 'If you find Lacrosse, tick *Done*. Oh wow. *Acrostic's* hidden there, isn't it? A poem where the initial letter of each line spells out a word.'

He smiled.

She re-read the verse out loud.

> Make your deposit here, O man,
> And bring your partner, if you can.
> It's quicker as a joint account,
> This place won't query the amount,
> Lots or little, who's to know –
> Apart from Maurice Bigelow?
> Now, if you find Lacrosse, tick *Done*;
> Don't shop around, you're near this one.

'OK,' said Fee, 'but a clinic? You make a deposit at a bank – or a building society.'

'Mm,' said Summers. 'I'm getting a slight sinking feeling about this. Let's go and have dinner.'

When Beatrice hadn't been able to find William, she'd decided to investigate the banks on her own – but there was no Maurice Bigelow working at any of them. She went into the Marquis of Queensberry for a drink and sat looking at the clue again. When she isolated the word *acrostic*, she realised her mistake very quickly. She downed the rest of her gin and tonic in one and went outside. The Maitland Clinic wasn't very far away – fifty yards down the road, above a computer firm. It didn't look very salubrious – a frosted-glass door with a just a sheet of printed paper pasted on the inside, giving the name of the place. No indication as to what the clinic's speciality was. Beatrice rang the bell.

A small man with a gingery moustache opened it.

'Maurice Bigelow?'

'That's me.'

'I'm doing the treasure hunt.'

'Ah.' He had a face with an astonishing number of lines on it, although he wasn't an elderly man. 'You're on your own.'

'Temporarily lost touch with my partner.'

'I'm afraid you're going to need him. Come in a moment, and you'll see why.'

Beatrice followed him inside. There were several posters of babies on the wall. A paediatric clinic? The place looked very run-down, peeling wallpaper and threadbare carpets. He took her into a room the size of a cubicle, and her eyes widened. This had posters of naked women on the walls, and a pile of erotic magazines. There was a row of bottles on a shelf, each bearing a blank label, and in the corner there was a small washbasin and paper towels.

'Sperm donor clinic,' said Maurice Bigelow.

'I thought sperm donors had to be below a certain age? And that they had to be screened?'

'We're private,' said Bigelow. 'High IQs are the priority here.'

Beatrice wasn't convinced, although there was no doubt that the treasure hunt contestants fulfilled the necessary criteria. Perhaps the place had simply been rented for the week and done up like a film set. Not that it would have needed much doing up. Whether it was genuine or not was immaterial, really; all she had to do was get the next clue.

'So we're trading a test-tube of spunk for a clue here, are we?' she said.

'That's right.'

'Bit unfair on anyone who's impotent. There are a lot of elderly men on this treasure hunt. My partner, for instance. He's having a lie down at the moment. Has to be careful, with his heart problem.'

205

'I thought you said you'd lost touch with him?'

'He'd have to be dead to be more out of touch than when he's asleep.'

'Tricky one,' said Bigelow.

'Not necessarily,' said Beatrice, looking him up and down in a slow, appraising way, and lingering somewhere around his genitals.

'I'm married,' he said. 'The wife wouldn't like it.'

'The wife doesn't have to know. I can do a very efficient hand-job.'

He swallowed.

'Got a bit of oil?' She glanced round. And there on the shelf, sure enough, was a bottle of intimate massage oil. She lifted it down, unscrewed the lid and sniffed it.

'Rose petals,' she said. 'Very nice.' She poured a little of it on to her hands and rubbed them together. His eyes were fixed on her hands now, so she massaged the oil into her palms as suggestively as she could.

His face creased into a few more lines as he said, 'What would you tell your partner?'

'Nothing. I'll just tell the old boy I solved it, and give him the next clue.' Beatrice looked pointedly at Bigelow's crotch. Something was stirring. She lifted down one of the bottles, took a pen out of her bag and wrote *William Dacre* on the label.

'All right,' said Bigelow suddenly, and he unzipped his trousers. His cock stood proud immediately, rising like a young parasol mushroom from the ginger foliage between his legs, the end of it as smooth and sculptured as a bronze helmet. It was enormous. Beatrice's mouth dropped open. Bigelow smiled, his face resembling crazy paving. 'The wife likes it too,' he said. 'And she's something of an expert.'

Beatrice wondered what on earth he meant. Was his wife a doctor? 'She's a lucky woman,' said Beatrice, taking hold of it. The tips of her fingers only just met the tip of her thumb. She started to wank him, sliding her hand up and down the impressive shaft, pressing his foreskin as it slid over the tip. Then she dribbled some more of the oil

206

over him, until his prick was gleaming with it. She put the bottle back on the shelf, took hold of him again, and slid her palm round and round, using little up and down movements as well.

He shuddered slightly. He wasn't looking at her; he was looking at one of the posters on the wall. The woman in it was big and blonde and busty, and she looked vaguely familiar. Beatrice felt a momentary flash of annoyance – wasn't she sexy enough? She took off her glasses with her other hand, and when that didn't make any difference she unbuttoned her blouse. That did the trick. He was looking at her breasts with a real intensity now; they weren't very large, but they were nicely shaped. She wanked him a little faster, and his eyes glazed over. The rigidity of that huge cock was quite a turn-on on its own; Beatrice was getting high on the feeling of power. She was dominating him with her fingers, manipulating him into something he hadn't wanted to do.

She suddenly remembered the bottle – and it was as well that she did, for she had only just placed it in position when he came. Jets of milky liquid shot into the glass, spattering the sides and running slowly down them like jellied tears, collecting at the bottom. Beatrice handed him one of the paper towels and put the plastic stopper in the bottle. 'Thank you,' she said.

He rubbed his eyes with his hands, as though he rather regretted what he'd just done. Then he took the bottle from her and went into the other room. Beatrice followed him. He gave her the next clue and she copied it down.

'Not a word to anyone?' he said as she made to leave.

'I'm not going to confess to cheating now, am I?' said Beatrice.

'I suppose not. I just don't want the wife to know.'

'Don't worry,' said Beatrice, 'she won't.'

Hardly anyone was missing that evening, when Fee and Summers went into the games room. There were only two days of the treasure hunt left to go, and Saul Slick wanted to know if anyone was getting near the prize.

'I can't actually tell you that,' said Gavin Smythe. 'But I do know that Alfred Hicks reckoned he'd timed it out quite well, and that whoever won would win on the last day. He couldn't be certain, of course, but I have to keep his solicitor informed of the general progress, and we seem to be keeping more or less to schedule. There won't be a curfew tomorrow night, by the way – last night, and all that.'

William was sitting in a corner, next to Scarab. After a little while Scarab left him for Saul Slick. Angus went and sat next to William. Angus said something, and Fee heard William say, 'I've *had* a shower, dammit.' When she walked past them to refill her coffee cup, there was a faint but unmistakable smell of fish. Beatrice went over to him, looking like the cat that's got the cream. She stared pointedly at Angus until he got up, looking disgruntled, and moved elsewhere. Then she started to talk very quickly and quietly to William. William patted her on the head after a moment or two, and they both got up and went.

'Looks like Beatrice has just solved something,' said Fee to Summers.

Summers rang the bell at the Maitland Clinic the next morning at half past nine, and the door was opened by a small man with a gingery moustache. His face reminded Fee of Sid James – lines everywhere, like elephant hide. He was also sporting the most spectacular black eye.

'Treasure hunt,' said Summers. 'Are you Maurice Bigelow?'

'That's right,' said the man. 'Come in.'

Fee looked at the posters of babies in astonishment – it wasn't what she'd expected at all. Summers didn't look surprised, however, just vaguely depressed.

'Through here,' said Maurice, leading them into a room the size of a cubicle.

The pictures on the wall were a shock at first – then

Fee's eyes strayed to the bottles on the shelf, and the magazines on the table – and they all suddenly made sense. Oh my God, it's a sperm bank, she thought. Everything in the verse fits. *Make your deposit here, O man, and bring your partner, if you can. It's quicker as a joint account, this place won't query the amount . . .*

'Solo or double act?' asked Maurice, and when neither of them seemed able to say anything he added, 'I'll leave you to discuss it. Not at my best today, got a bit of a headache.'

'I'm not surprised,' said Fee. 'How did you get that shiner?'

'The wife took exception to something,' he said. 'She's bloody psychic sometimes. I'll leave you to it then.' And with that, he went.

Summers looked despondently at the posters on the wall, flicked through a magazine and looked even more fed up. Fee peered a little harder at the décor. There was something about one of the posters that seemed familiar. 'That looks uncannily like Rose,' she said. 'Twenty years ago, mind you.'

Summers glanced across at it. 'You're probably right,' he said despondently. He reminded Fee of a small boy waiting for a dentist's appointment.

'Would you like me to wait in the corridor?' she asked.

'Yes please,' said Summers.

Fee turned the handle of the door. It was locked. She felt a giggle rising unbidden, struggled with it, and failed to suppress it.

'I wonder how you'd feel if the positions were reversed?' said Summers peevishly. 'That *you* had to have a wank while *I* watched. Not quite so amusing, I suspect.' He flung one of the magazines against the wall, and it fluttered to the floor like an injured bird. It was the first demonstration of temper she'd ever seen in him.

'I could shut my eyes,' she said.

'But not your ears.'

'Oh, you're a noisy one, are you?'

'This is acutely embarrassing, Fee, and flippant remarks aren't going to help.'

'Oh for God's sake,' said Fee, 'it's a perfectly normal activity. Monkeys do it in front of everyone.' Then she suddenly thought, I'm being crassly insensitive here; maybe he can't get a hard-on. She bit her lip.

As if he'd read her mind he said, 'That's not the problem.'

'What then?'

He made a face.

We're not getting anywhere fast here, thought Fee. There are two alternatives open to me. Either I offer to toss him off, or I keep him company and do it as well.

He raised his eyebrows and waited. When she didn't say anything he said, 'Which alternative are you going to opt for?'

There was no point asking him what he meant. 'Which one would you prefer?'

'I think that's up to you,' he said.

Oh, great. 'Thanks a lot.'

He waited.

'Someone's got to make a decision,' said Fee.

He put his hand in his pocket and pulled out a coin. 'Toss you for it,' he said. 'Sounds appropriate.'

She smiled.

'Heads we both do it separately, tails . . . the other.'

It was heads.

We've seen each other naked on more than one occasion, thought Fee. Why is this so difficult? But she knew why. It was because they would both have to let go, and see one another naked in another way.

She started to undress. She thought briefly about only removing her trousers and knickers – then that seemed cheap, somehow, so she took off her blouse and her bra as well. Summers took everything off too. She felt absurdly grateful to him – he didn't have to, he could have simply unzipped his flies. But this was going to be share and share alike, awkwardness for awkwardness, and she relaxed a little.

'Last one to come's a custard,' said Summers.

And suddenly it was all right and the embarrassment just evaporated. He took his cock in his right hand and started to move the foreskin up and down. It was a bit mechanical, but you had to start somewhere. Fee lay down on the harshly carpeted floor, made a pillow of her clothes, opened her legs a little and began to rub. She could see Summers standing at her feet – there wasn't enough space for him to be any further away.

Why do I always think of him as Summers, thought Fee. Why can't I call him Eric, like everyone else? *Concentrate*, she reprimanded herself, you don't want this to take very long. She closed her eyes and nestled her finger next to her clit, with a fold of flesh between. As she massaged herself she tried to conjure up some favourite fantasies, but they didn't seem to have their usual impact. Mythological scenarios just seemed theatrical; the faceless stranger on the Tube tacky. She wasn't doing terribly well. She opened her eyes and saw Summers looking down at her. There was a softness about his expression she hadn't seen before. His forehead was smooth and relaxed, the corners of his lips slightly upturned. His eyes were smiling, and he seemed to be doing rather better than she was – his hand was moving up and down somewhat faster now. When he noticed her watching him he smiled properly, a *what the hell* smile, and she couldn't help smiling in return. Suddenly, the action of her own finger between her legs started to have an effect. Her breathing quickened. She saw her arousal register in his eyes; his cock jerked slightly and she heard him catch his breath. The feeling started to build, a delicious tingle inside that radiated further and further. She rubbed a little faster. His smile had completely gone now; his eyes were fixed on her face and she couldn't look away, he was willing her to come, and she him. And there was something she had to remember. Something important. The feeling was all over her now, every part of her crying out for the finale. Something important she had to remember.

'The bottle,' she said hoarsely, 'don't forget the bottle.'

He closed his eyes and an *oh shit* expression crossed his face. He let go of himself, stepped back a pace to the shelf, reached up and took down a bottle.

They started to masturbate again. She could see that he was holding back, waiting for her. The earlier urgency had been suppressed; he was very much in control now. She began to find his self-discipline a turn-on. Without even realising she was doing it, Fee started to synchronise her movements with his. She could see in his eyes that he was aware of it, and found it exciting. But he was determined to wait for her. She realised that she was enjoying it all far more than she'd expected; there was something very sexy about the lack of physical contact between them. It was as though they were making love in their heads. What he was doing mirrored what she was doing so closely that it might have been his finger touching her, and her hand around his cock. But they weren't looking at each other's genitals; their eyes were locked together. They weren't rushing at it, the way they had earlier. The *let's get this over with* atmosphere had gone – prolonging it seemed like an act of courtesy, one to the other. She wondered how he fucked; long and slow or hard and fast? Both, probably. She had a feeling he was rather good at it – nothing she could analyse, just a feeling. He seemed at home with his body, as though it didn't hold any surprises for him; it would do whatever his head instructed – his orgasm would be perfectly timed, perfectly aimed, and achieved with the minimum of fuss.

They carried on wanking. Fee had reached a plateau of arousal now, everything was waiting for the final push. He gave her a questioning look, and she moved her head fractionally in assent. She saw his body stiffen; he took a deep breath, and so did she. The approaching climax gathered within her, no going back now, this was going to be a big one . . . Summers threw back his head and started to ejaculate – and then she was coming too, and it was out of this world. She heard him cry out – he was far more uninhibited than she'd expected, not neat and tidy about it at all. For a few seconds, he really lost it.

Strangely, the embarrassment returned almost immediately. They got dressed very quickly and knocked on the door to be let out. Maurice Bigelow took the bottle of semen and gave Summers the next clue. Summers copied it down in his notebook, as always, with his fountain pen. There was something very decided about the way he put the lid back on the pen each time and secreted it in his top pocket.

They said their goodbyes and went out to the car.

'These clues are getting more and more outrageous,' said Summers. 'I didn't enjoy that last one at all.'

Could have fooled me, thought Fee.

Rachel and Peverall took rather longer in the mud bath than anyone else. When they went downstairs Rose was working at a computer. She closed the file as soon as she saw them and got to her feet.

Peverall smiled. 'Updating the treasure hunt records, Rose?'

'I'm very conscientious, Peverall.'

'I don't doubt it,' said Peverall, looking at the screen. The words *Licensed to Rose Bigelow* had appeared.

They said goodbye to Rose and left.

'Do you suppose that's her real name?' wondered Peverall, as he and Rachel walked back to the Mercedes.

'Probably,' said Rachel. 'It's not one you'd adopt by choice. I wonder if there's a Mister Bigelow?'

'Do women take the surname into account when they're deciding whether to marry a man or not?'

'I don't know,' said Rachel, 'the issue's never arisen.'

'Would Danby be a disincentive, do you think?'

'There's nothing wrong with Danby,' said Rachel. 'But I really don't wish to pursue this topic of conversation any further, Peverall.'

As they turned the corner, they saw William and Beatrice waiting in a car. They were talking rather heatedly;

the window was wound down, so Rachel could hear them quite clearly as she and Peverall approached them They didn't look up, as they were too engrossed in their conversation. Rachel hid behind a tree and signalled to Peverall to do the same. Then they both just stood there and listened.

'What have you got against Rose?' Beatrice was saying in her clipped, well-educated voice.

'She's a sadistic bitch, and I don't trust her. What's to stop her doing the treasure hunt herself?'

'She couldn't solve the clues.'

William sighed. 'Can't you do this one on your own, Beatrice?'

'When I made the appointment, she said she wanted both of us there. Oh come on, William, don't louse things up. We're in the lead, we have to be . . .'

Fee and Summers sat in the car, the way they had done so many times before, looking at the clue they'd just collected. 'Oh, this one's easy,' said Fee. 'Location: Peace may be found in prose (4). Request: Better than sex.'

'I'm impressed,' said Summers. 'Go on then.'

'Have you done it?'

'Only the crossword clue.'

Fee rubbed her hands together. 'Right. *Peace* – everyone ought to know that's a rose by now. And *rose* is in *prose*. So it's back to Rose's house again, and we request the one thing that's better than sex.'

'I can't think of anything that *is* better than sex,' said Summers.

'Chocolate!' squealed Fee.

'*You* can ring her,' said Summers. 'It's obviously a gender thing.'

They went back to the house and Fee rang Rose.

'I'm a bit tied up at the moment, darling,' said Rose. 'What was it you wanted?'

'Chocolate,' said Fee.

'One-thirty then.' Faintly, in the background, it

sounded as though someone was being sick. 'Oh bloody hell,' said Rose, and the line went dead.

Angus and Scarab sat on the chaise longue in the cellar, waiting for the time lock to open. Scarab was wearing a skimpy top and a very short skirt, and it rode up her leg with no difficulty whatsoever when he brushed his hand against her thigh.

'It's cold down here,' he said, putting his arm round her. 'What do you do for a living, Scarab?'

'I castrate things,' said Scarab, removing the arm as if it were a dead branch.

Angus stiffened – and then something started to vibrate against his leg. 'You've got a mobile,' he said, astonished. 'Why on earth didn't you tell me before?'

'It's for when I'm on call. Couldn't get cover for the whole week . . . Hello?' She listened attentively, then said, 'No, you don't shave its balls, you pluck them.'

Angus seem to shrink slightly.

'Yep, make an incision in the scrotum, then squeeze out the bollocks and suture them. You don't need me.' She listened for a moment, then said, 'Yeah, that's cool. Bye.'

Angus was staring at her with an incredulous expression.

'I'm a *vet*, Angus,' said Scarab. 'Gavin's okayed the mobile; he knows they'll only call me for advice – unless there's an exotic, of course.'

'Exotic?' Angus's voice had gone a bit squeaky.

'An African toad or a Tasmanian devil or a tarantula.'

Before Angus could react to this the door opened. They both leaped to their feet and made a dash for the stairs.

Scarab got there first, and collided with Saul Slick in the doorway. There was a muddle of bodies, then Saul side-stepped and Scarab pushed past him. Saul overbalanced, put out a hand to steady himself and found the door itself – which swung shut as he struggled to regain his balance. There was a loud metallic click.

'You *prat*!' yelled Angus.

Saul nearly jumped out of his skin.

'This is a red herring,' said Angus. 'You've just sentenced us to another two fucking hours down here.'

'I hate this game,' said Saul Slick, with feeling.

'Well why don't you pack it in and go home?' said Angus irritably.

'Because I'm collecting ideas for my sitcom. I've got five new characters so far – people no one could have invented in a million years – and two new plot-lines.'

Fee and Summers walked up to Rose's door for the third time that week, and rang the bell. 'Darlings!' exclaimed Rose. 'Come in.' She led the way inside, but this time they were taken to a downstairs room, which was a sort of overblown parlour, with ruched velvet curtains and an ornate gilt-edged mirror. She indicated to Summers to sit down. 'Fee and I have to do a little preparation, Eric. Help yourself to magazines and I'll give you a shout when we're ready.'

Summers eyed Rose cautiously. 'I've had a taxing morning,' he said.

Rose laughed and said reassuringly, 'Don't worry, Eric, your cock isn't required.' She ushered Fee upstairs and into the room next door to the mud bath. There was a brass bedstead in the middle of the floor, with just a bare mattress. There were sparkly pink metal chains attached to the four corner posts, and on the ends of them – handcuffs. A dressing table was covered with pots and jars and phials and bottles, and there were some things that looked like date-stamps, resting by an inked pad.

'You need to strip off for this one,' said Rose. 'Not shy about it, are you?'

'I wouldn't have got this far in the treasure hunt if I were,' said Fee, undressing. 'What do I have to do?'

'I'm afraid I'm going to have to chain you up and gag you,' said Rose.

'Hang on a minute . . .'

'Don't worry, dear, nothing nasty is going to happen. When you're ready, Summers will come in and find the clue. He's a bright boy, bless him, but it doesn't take a genius to work this one out. Right. Gag first.'

It was made of black latex, smooth and skin-like, and it wasn't nearly as unpleasant as she'd feared – in fact, it was rather sensual.

'Now then. On your back on the bed, please.'

Fee did as she was told. Rose secured first her wrists, then her ankles. She judged the tightness of the restraints very well; loose enough for comfort, but affording no opportunity for escape.

'Now then,' said Rose. 'I've got a couple of date-stamp thingummies here. I'm going to roll them over your tits, so that the clues are printed there. They'll wash off after a few days.'

She did it on the underside of Fee's left breast, quite close to the nipple. The rubber mould felt cool and strange. Even if Fee craned her neck, she couldn't quite see what was written there, so she just lay back and waited. Then Rose did the right one, with a different stamp.

'Now for Eric's dessert,' said Rose. She opened a jar of chocolate body paint, and set to work. When she'd finished, the front part of Fee's body was wearing a brown bikini. Rose hadn't plastered it on; the layer was almost transparent in a couple of places – there was a painterly quality to it, the way an artist might scumble one colour over another. 'No washbasin in here,' she said. 'No tissues, towels, or even sheets. Nothing to remove that chocolate except the one thing it was intended for – the human tongue. Right then. I think we're ready. I'll go and get Eric.'

Rose left the room. So, thought Fee, the last clue needed a male orgasm – this one's to pleasure the female half of the partnership. I hope Summers likes chocolate.

He entered the room rather diffidently, and Rose shut it and locked it behind him.

'She's so conscientious,' he said, in a charmingly sarcastic voice. He stood there for a moment or two, surveying Fee from head to toe. 'I see,' he said eventually. 'I thought it would be something like this – had to be, didn't it? The question is, where has she put the clue?' His eyes drifted over her body, then returned to her face. 'You're pretty well trussed up, aren't you? But I take it you can still blink.'

She blinked.

'One blink for yes then, and two blinks for no. Is the clue below the belt?'

Two blinks.

'Breasts?'

One blink.

'OK,' he said. He took off his clothes, and folded them neatly in a pile.

Either he's worried he'll get chocolate over them, thought Fee, or else it's another gesture of solidarity. Or possibly both at once.

'Left or right?'

Both thought Fee, and blinked three times.

'Both, then,' said Summers. He lay down on the bed next to her and tried an experimental lick at the outside edge of the chocolate bra. 'Mm,' he murmured, 'not bad.'

She saw him glance down her body.

'Consuming the whole lot might be a bit much to ask,' he said. 'Hence the blinking inquisition. Right then, here we go.'

He started to lick off the chocolate paste in a systematic fashion. The rhythm of his tongue was hypnotic to start with, and she closed her eyes and relaxed into it. As he got closer to her nipple, she began to feel little twinges of arousal. The twinges became more frequent and more pronounced, and then they started up a sympathetic reaction between her legs. She shivered. She knew her nipple was as erect as it ever had been, and she was scared he would by-pass it, find the clue and never lick it at all. Down the outside of her breast now, almost to her armpit. The sensation was divine, only a hairsbreadth away from a violent reaction to the tickle of it, but he seemed to know when to ease off. The underside of her breast now, the crease where it joined her ribcage, then up again, up towards the nipple once more. Her clit responded enthusiastically, and she writhed her hips against the mattress. His tongue wasn't being businesslike about this at all; he was licking where he'd already licked, concentrating on the places that made her squirm with pleasure. He's awfully good at this, thought Fee; he seems to be able to second guess me, to know what I'm going to want before I do myself. As if to prove it, he flicked his tongue across her nipple. Her whole body convulsed, and her wrists jerked quite painfully against the handcuffs.

'Sorry,' he said. She saw him peer at her breast. 'Aha,' he said. 'Here we are. *Curious? Tania's, 9.30.* Not a lot to go on. And there's more on the other side?'

One blink.

'Here we go then.' He started on her right breast, treating it exactly the same as he had the left. Fee knew what to expect now, which made her feel hornier than ever. The ghostly caress of his breath on her damp skin, the curl of his tongue, the softness of it, the tingling at the very tip of her nipple, wanting contact. When he finally licked her in the right place she nearly went through the roof again.

He did it again. She held her breath. Then he put his mouth right over her nipple and started to suck. He did it very gently to start with, but the rhythm of it was there from the beginning. After a while she could feel the pulse of her blood as he drew it towards him, then let it go again. She tried to clench her thighs, but she couldn't. She wanted to come, but she needed that little extra something to get there; she heard herself moan through the gag, and it sounded muffled and distant.

And then, gentleman that he was, Summers put his knee between her legs – although he wore his thinking face and looked politely at the ceiling. She rubbed herself against him, and it was enough. The orgasm was strange, a lyrical journey through her body, but she felt wonderful afterwards. She knew she was smiling, she really couldn't help it, she felt so weightless and happy and relaxed –

and she knew he couldn't see her smiling because of the gag.

'I've got the second bit of the clue,' he said. 'I'll call Rose and we can wash the rest of this stuff off in the shower next door.'

Chapter Thirteen

'Still an hour to go,' said Scarab, shivering on the chaise longue in the cellar.

'Here,' said Saul Slick gallantly, 'have my jacket.'

'How kind,' said Scarab, almost snatching it the moment he took it off. She put it on and hugged it to her. Angus hadn't offered.

A click, then the door opening. Angus did a good impression of a jack-in-the-box, and made a mad dash for the stairs. His despairing 'No!' coincided with the click of the door shutting again.

'Have I done something silly?' asked Arnold, nervously twiddling the ends of his moustache.

'You brain-dead old fool!' yelled Angus. 'You've just imprisoned us for another two fucking hours!'

'A fool I may be, but brain-dead I most certainly am not,' returned Arnold.

No one said anything further. The silence became oppressive. The musty smell was mixed with something sweeter, but unpleasant, and now and again the ticking of the time lock was just audible.

Eventually Arnold made a wry face and said, 'My brain may still be tickety-boo, but my bladder isn't.'

'There's a brass waste-bin in the other room,' said Scarab. 'We've been using that.'

* * *

'Are you feeling better now?' Beatrice asked William.

'Just about.' He had been very sick, having licked off all Beatrice's chocolate before he found the clues.

Beatrice had been quite annoyed – all he had had to do was ask her where they were, and she'd have indicated with a movement of her eyes. But it obviously hadn't occurred to him – he'd gone straight for the bikini bottoms, assuming the clue to be in the most delicate place. Beatrice had enjoyed it, certainly – but the throwing up afterwards had made her feel quite ill. She couldn't bear other people's infirmities.

William looked at what he'd copied down. 'Curious? Tania's, 9.30,' he read out. 'Bit concise.'

'Well it would be, wouldn't it?' said Beatrice. 'There wasn't enough room to write more than a few words.' She snapped her fingers at him. 'Map.'

William handed her the map and read out the second part of the clue. '*Make it to get the final clue.* Genuine, or red herring? What do you reckon?'

'Genuine,' said Beatrice. 'It's Saturday: we all go home tomorrow. We *have* to be near the end. Right. Curious is an anagram indicator.' She ran her finger across the map. 'Got it. There's a place here called *Anita's*. Doesn't say what it is – restaurant, maybe?'

'Let's go and take a look.'

'OK,' said Beatrice. 'But the 9.30 must be there for a reason – and there's no curfew tonight, remember? If this does lead to the final clue, it could be a sort of celebration. For the people who've got to the last puzzle.'

'People? I thought we were in the lead.'

'We are,' said Beatrice. 'We had first shot at the chocolate this morning. But there may be others who get there today too.'

They drove into town and went looking for Anita's. It turned out to be down a tiny cobbled sideroad, with no access to traffic apart from delivery vehicles. William parked the car in a nearby street and they walked from there, Beatrice's heels making sharp click-click noises on the stones. The buildings were a mixture of private houses and shuttered offices, interspersed with oddities such as a Korean supermarket and a rubber importing business. Eventually they found Anita's; several of the letters were missing, which made them think the place was called *nit's* at first glance. It too was shuttered – but there was a side door with a bell. William rang it. There was no reply.

'There's a passageway round the side,' said Beatrice. 'Let's go round the back and see if we can deduce anything from their dustbins.'

'You're a regular Poirot, you are,' said William.

'Yes,' said Beatrice, 'I am. Maybe you can explain how you came to have Alfred Hicks's catalogue?'

William stiffened.

'You turned down the page with the picture of the treasure on it, didn't you? The gold statues. Which makes you the person responsible for the robbery at Alfred Hicks's house, doesn't it? I've done a bit of digging. There was an article in the paper – the insurance company are suing the security firm.'

'Hang on –'

'Oh, don't worry,' said Beatrice, 'I'm not going to grass you up. I'm enjoying myself far too much. I'm discovering a nefarious side to my own personality – a side I never even suspected existed.'

They reached the end of the passageway and saw a row of industrial-sized dustbins. Each one was painted with the name of the premises to which it belonged.

'It's not what you think,' said William. 'Alfred Hicks *paid* me to stage the robbery, so that he could get the insurance. He'd already sold most of the pieces – through Angus; that's Angus's line of business – but these two statues were difficult to dispose of, though given enough time it would have been possible. He didn't *have* much time though, and he knew it. When I heard about this treasure hunt, I just knew that was what he'd done with them.'

'How did you find out about it?'

'There was a sheet of paper in the catalogue – he must

have put it there for safe keeping. Or maybe he'd forgotten he'd put it there. It was a rough for a flyer for this word-games week; his name was there as the treasure hunt author. Funny old boy, he was – weird sense of humour.'

'Yes. I met him once. He spent most of the time looking up my skirt. Are you and Angus going halves on the proceeds then?' And when William didn't answer immediately, Beatrice added, 'You're planning to double-cross him, aren't you? You must have a buyer lined up, otherwise you'd need Angus to help you fence them. I wonder where that leaves me. Nowhere, I suspect.'

'On the contrary,' said William. 'We've no idea how difficult the last clue might be. I need you. And you need me, don't you?' He grabbed hold of her by the hair, pulled her to him and kissed her with an easy brutality.

Beatrice felt a familiar surge of lust. After a moment, with a supreme effort of will, she pushed him away from her. 'Fifty-fifty?'

'Sixty-forty. That's still a fair old whack, Beatrice.'

'Done,' said Beatrice, completing the charade. She didn't trust him an inch.

'There's the dustbin for Anita's,' said William, looking over Beatrice's shoulder.

They started to rummage through it. There were a lot of empty bottles, bits of cardboard packaging, cellophane. Broken light-bulbs, plastic bags, ripped envelopes ... Beatrice pulled one out and looked at it. It was from a company that dealt in bondage tape and blindfolds. She slipped it into her pocket.

'Aha,' said William, extracting a bundle of photocopied lilac-coloured papers. He smoothed one out and they read it.

Saturday Night at Anita's – the night when everyone cums. Lap dancing, strippers, live sex. Be amazed by Anna and her anaconda, horrified by Hank and his Harley Davidson. Nine-thirty start, strictly members only.

'I see,' said Beatrice. 'Make it to get the final clue.'

'Make the nine-thirty start. There's no curfew tonight – it all fits.'

'*Make it* has another meaning as well, William.'

They made their way back to the road, and William rang the bell once again for good measure. There was still no reply.

'It won't open for hours yet,' said Beatrice. 'Let's go back and see if we can put a few spanners in other people's works.'

William looked at Beatrice with something close to admiration. 'Good thinking, Batman,' he said.

Rachel and Peverall were having a blinder of a day. Peverall got the mantis clue immediately – he seemed to know quite a lot about entomology. Without even realising it, they by-passed the red herrings and drove to the Maitland Clinic. Peverall produced his sample in record time, with some assistance from Rachel, and solved the new clues on the spot. Rachel was very impressed by his understanding of the importance of chocolate in a woman's life.

Peverall rang Rose from the clinic. He'd made a friend of Maurice Bigelow by suggesting a homeopathic remedy for his black eye.

'Darling,' said Rose, 'I can fit you in about four. I always try and fit my favourites in if I can.'

'Thank you, Rose,' said Peverall. 'Seeing you always brightens my day.'

'That Rachel doesn't know when she's on to a good thing,' said Rose. 'Put her on the line.'

Rachel took the receiver.

'If you don't marry that man you'll regret it for the rest of your life.'

The line went dead. Rachel glanced at Peverall, to see if he'd heard. He gave no sign that he had.

'I honestly think,' said Grace to Graham Steel, as they sat in Rose's parlour, 'that expecting me to cover myself with chocolate at *my* age is going one step too far.'

'There can only be two or three more clues left,' said Graham. 'We're nearly there. And I did do the Maitland Clinic one on my own.'

'Sorry,' said Grace. 'I'm drawing the line at this one. It's probably carob anyway – really decent chocolate is so expensive. There must be some way round it though. Hicks was always fair.'

Rose stuck her head round the door. 'Ready?'

'I'm afraid not,' said Grace, with dignity. 'I'm seventy-three, and there are limits.'

'Well, you did take the trouble to turn up and tell me in person,' said Rose. 'So you shan't be penalised. Come along, Graham, you can have Inga instead.'

Inga turned out to be an inflatable blonde. It took Graham half an hour to strip the bikini off her and find the clues. He only looked at her face once; the combination of baby-doll blue eyes and pouting red lips, growing out of her face like a bracket fungus, beggared belief. By the time he'd finished, the taste-combination of chocolate and plastic had reached retch-making proportions. He retched. But he didn't stop thinking, and by the time he joined Grace in the parlour, he had solved the puzzles printed on Inga's salmon-pink chest. He did a detour to Anita's on the way home, leaving Grace sitting in the car while he went to have a look.

He rang the bell. No answer. No letter box to peer through either. He walked down the side passage and came to a row of dustbins. On the ground was a lilac piece of paper. He picked it up, read what was written and went back to his car.

'So what sort of place is it?' asked Grace.

'Strip joint,' said Graham.

'I might have guessed. I think you can count me out this evening.'

'That's all right,' said Graham. 'I quite understand.' He started the car and they drove back to the house.

'Nit's?' said Fee.

'Two of the As are missing,' Summers pointed out.

'Oh yes. Ring the bell then.'

Summers rang the bell.

After a long pause, they heard the sound of shuffling feet approaching. Two bolts were drawn back, then a key turned, and then another key. Eventually the door opened and a tall thin man with snow-white hair stood there, looking surprised. 'I thought you were the vet,' he said.

'Vet?' Fee's voice squeaked with surprise.

'Vet,' repeated the man.

'Why? What do you keep here?'

'The snake's having trouble shedding its skin,' he said. 'I told her to get a python. An anaconda's semi-aquatic. A bath is no substitute for the Amazon, even if she does have a jacuzzi.'

Fee tried to keep a straight face, failed, and covered it up with a coughing fit.

'Anna and her anaconda are a big draw,' said the man, annoyed. 'It's no laughing matter. Strippers are ten a penny, but a snake with a truly professional attitude and a flair for performance is hard to find.'

'What else is do you have lined up tonight?' asked Summers.

'You a reporter?' asked the man suspiciously.

'No,' said Summers. 'I'm chasing clues in a treasure hunt.'

'Oh, *right*,' replied the man. 'Come back at nine-thirty then. Tell them Little Trevor says to let you in.'

Little Trevor? thought Fee. He's six foot four if he's an inch.

'Membership rules are dead strict, see,' he went on. 'We've got a couple of very enthusiastic bouncers who enforce the said rules very enthusiastically.'

'And is there much ... er ... audience participation in the show?'

'Oh, that's rich. Free entry into the best sex club this side of Amsterdam, and you want to know what you're getting for the money you didn't have to pay?'

'I'd just like to know what I'm letting myself in for,' said Summers.

'It's going to have to be a surprise, isn't it?' said the man, moving past Summers and looking up and down the road. 'Where the hell's that sodding vet got to?'

Beatrice told William all about how she'd eavesdropped at the top of the cellar steps.

William found the idea of the time lock highly amusing. 'I wonder if there's anyone stuck in there at the moment?'

'Surely you're not suggesting we let them out?'

'Of course not. But we could point a few other people in the same direction – and tell them to make sure they shut the door the moment they get inside.'

They went into the library and saw Elsie and Joan. The two women looked up and Elsie said, 'You haven't seen Arnold anywhere, have you? He's been missing for an hour.'

'So has Saul,' said Joan.

'I think I know exactly where to find them,' said William, and he told them. They thanked him profusely and both of them strolled off in the direction of the passageway that led to the kitchen.

William and Beatrice grinned at one another.

'I'll be sorry to say goodbye to you two,' said Rose, as she ushered Peverall and Rachel down the hallway. 'Enjoyed the chocolate, didn't you?'

'Smooth creamy texture, with just a hint of armagnac,' said Peverall. 'Belgian?'

'You're a man of the world, Peverall Danby. If I were twenty years younger, I'd have you.'

Peverall grinned. As he opened the door, Rose looked questioningly at Rachel, and then at the third finger of Rachel's left hand.

'I haven't ruled it out,' said Rachel.

They got into the Mercedes and Peverall pulled out the map. Then he studied the clues he'd copied from the stamps on Rachel's bottom (Rose had varied where she'd put the stamp depending on the person) and said, 'Anita's. Let's go and take a look.'

They parked the car more or less where Summers had parked his and walked down the little cobbled street. When they got to the shuttered shopfront, Peverall rang the bell. It was answered quite quickly.

'Oh bloody hell,' said a tall thin man with white hair. 'How many more times?'

Peverall's brows drew together. 'I'm sorry?'

'I thought you were the vet.'

'What's the problem?'

'It's Sammy. He's only a baby.'

'A baby what?'

'Anaconda. He's having trouble shedding his skin.'

'Let's take a look,' said Peverall, and before Rachel could really take it in they had gone up some stairs and were standing by a tank, and Peverall was talking knowledgeably about thermoreceptors and Jacobson's organs and ecdysis to Anna. She had big tits and a tattoo of a snake on her forearm. And then, amazingly, he'd sorted out the problem, and Sammy was getting on with shedding the ghostly shroud that had been his previous overcoat.

Then Scarab arrived.

'I didn't expect to see *you*,' said Peverall.

'Nor I you,' said Scarab. 'What are you doing here? Chasing a clue?'

'Aren't you?'

'No,' said Scarab. 'I'm the vet.' She went over to Sammy and examined him. Sammy didn't like it, and he tied himself into several intricate knots trying to get back to Anna. 'You're such a coward,' said Scarab to the snake. 'One injection six months ago, and you've never forgiven me.'

'Nine-thirty,' said Little Trevor to Peverall, 'that's when you need to come back. And you're the second lot from that treasure hunt.'

'The second lot?' said Peverall. 'What was the first lot like?'

'Pretty girl, black hair, pale skin. And some fairly

nondescript bloke – oh, that's right, wanted to know what he was letting himself in for tonight.' He laughed.

'Eric,' said Peverall. 'What did you tell him?'

'Nothing,' said Little Trevor. He glanced at the clock on the wall. The pivot for the hands was the head and body of a naked woman; the hands themselves were her legs. She looked fairly normal at the moment, for it was twenty to six, but she would become a contortionist by midnight. 'I'd go back and have a kip if I were you,' said Little Trevor. 'We close at four-thirty in the morning. It's going to be a long night, and you're going to need . . .' He stopped. 'I'm not meant to say anything, really.'

'I don't think you need to,' said Scarab. 'See you at nine-thirty. Serendipity or what?'

Yeah, lucky old Scarab, thought Rachel, getting the penultimate clue by sheer chance. I suppose that means we'll see Angus there too. Oh well.

At six o'clock Gavin Smythe opened the door to the cellar. There was a flurry of activity, and Angus reached the foot of the steps first.

'Don't worry, I'm not going to lock you in again,' said Gavin. 'Dinner's in half an hour.' He stood back and watched as the captives emerged, one after the other. Angus was followed by Saul Slick and Joan – then Jennifer, Martin, Heather, Patrick, Rodney, Arnold and Elsie.

Elsie disappeared in the direction of the Ladies as fast as she could go, muttering darkly about brass rubbish bins and last straws.

'There's no lock-up tonight,' said Gavin. 'And all the rooms stay open as well.'

Arnold headed off for Room 7 again and watched the mantis video. When he came out, Angus, Rodney and Jennifer were all waiting outside.

Dinner was a lively affair, with everyone present. Eric and Fee sat next to Rachel and Peverall, laughing every so often about the week's exploits.

'I'm meant to be writing this up for a puzzle magazine,'

said Summers. 'But I don't think I'm going to be able to, do you?'

Peverall looked thoughtful. 'A cruciverbal cornucopia of cataglottism, cunnilingus and calorific carnality?'

'I love it when he talks dirty,' said Rachel.

'What's cataglottism?' asked Fee, realising to her astonishment that it was now the only word she didn't know.

'French kissing,' said Summers.

Rachel glanced at Summers's plain white shirt. 'Are you two going to get tarted up for tonight? I think one ought to get into the spirit of the thing.'

Fee glanced at Peverall, then at Rachel. Peverall's clothes sense left a lot to be desired – practically everything he possessed seemed to be in shades of mustard.

'We went shopping,' said Rachel. 'He hasn't worn anything we bought yet, but he will tonight. He's going to look like a million dollars.'

'So are you,' said Peverall.

Rachel grinned. 'He bought me a rather special dress. I shall surprise you all.'

Fee was going to have to improvise. Most of her clothes came from charity shops; she was good at spotting designer labels and she had an interesting selection of items – but it was a hit-and-miss method as far as matching things up went. She'd never been able to afford to go out and buy precisely the right accessories. But she did want to get dressed up – she would have to be inventive. She glanced at Summers.

He smiled. 'I shall wear what I usually wear – a designer suit by Mr Anonymity.'

'I could lend you a shirt,' said Fee. 'I've got a nice loose turquoise one that ought to fit.'

'I couldn't possibly wear turquoise,' said Summers.

'Why not?'

'It's a tertiary colour,' he said. 'I don't wear tertiaries.'

'Why on earth not?'

'Tangerine, plum, lime green?' He shuddered.

'What's wrong with them?'

He just looked at her as though it were self-evident that tertiary colours were *de trop*.

'Come on, Peverall,' said Rachel, standing up and kissing him on the top of his bald head. 'Let me transform you.'

'Oh,' said Peverall. 'I can feel my batrachian characeristics melting away like snow. I shall be a prince among men.'

'I can always turn you back into a frog.'

'I might croak with the disappointment of it.'

'Upstairs,' said Rachel severely, and they went.

'I've got other shirts as well,' said Fee to Summers.

'All right,' he said unexpectedly.

'You'll dress up?'

'As long as you don't expect me to wear vermilion. Or violet.'

'I'll see what I can manage,' said Fee.

Peverall had a shower, and Rachel joined him. They stood under the water, soaping one another's bodies in provocative ways. Rachel knew him so well now – she had never learned anyone's body so fast; she knew exactly what it took to get him from nought to sixty in fifteen seconds. And he knew her too. For someone so inexperienced he had learned at a phenomenal rate, and he could turn her on with just a look – the *I know I can make you come* look. He never forgot the things that she'd responded to, and he continually fitted them together in ever more ingenious combinations.

At the moment he was stroking the back of her knee with his foot, holding on to the wall with one hand and shampooing her cunt with the other. He was also kissing her neck. This three-pronged attack was having a powerful effect, and Rachel closed her eyes and let it carry her away. The shivery little things he was doing just below her left ear, the way he rotated his fingers as he soaped her, varying the direction, catching her unawares with a new twist of arousal time and time again. She could feel his erection brushing past her, slippery with suds, big and warm and hard. He turned his attention to her breasts and washed them very carefully, as though they were made of crystal. She felt his tongue touch the tip of the left one, and her body jerked with the thrill of it. He nibbled at the nipple for a while, using just his lips; then he sucked gently and rhythmically – and all the while the warm water poured over them, and all she could hear was the white noise of it.

He's virile, imaginative, considerate, thought Rachel. Why am I hesitating? If I told him I loved him, he would propose immediately. With wine and roses and on bended knee, in all likelihood. Or he might be a bit more self-controlled and take me to the top of the Eiffel Tower, or the Taj Mahal, or Venice. I can't see myself tiring of him, that's the strange thing. He's like a treasure trove all on his own. He's the nicest man I've ever known, though I never used to rate niceness overmuch. Preferred the dark brooding type. Brooding. Is that it? Am I getting broody all of a sudden and looking for a prime piece of DNA? I wonder what colour Peverall's hair used to be?

He ran his finger down the side of her face. 'What are you thinking?'

'What colour did your hair used to be? Your eyelashes are blond. And so are your eyebrows. You're more of a chestnut elsewhere . . .' She ran her hand down his cock and into the bush of hair at its base.

'Same colour as yours,' he said. 'Red.' He didn't have to add that any children they might have would, in all probability, be red-haired too. He just smiled. Then he kissed her. The kiss was the most tender kiss she had ever had. It went on and on, an emotional pillow of sensation, and she lost herself completely in it. It was only when he moved slightly, and she felt his cock between her legs, that she realised she wanted more.

'I'm a lot taller than you,' he said. 'A stasivalent approach is impractical. I think this calls for a canine moment.'

There was sufficient room for Rachel to get on all fours, and for Peverall to mount her doggie-style. He fucked her like that, with the water still pouring over them, and he slipped his hand round the front and massaged her clit at the same time. The combined assault couldn't be withstood for long; Rachel screwed her eyes shut and concentrated on the sensations until she felt herself start to come, and then Peverall came too.

He dried her with the towel, then himself. Then they went into the bedroom and Rachel blow-dried her hair while Peverall selected the clothes they'd decided to wear.

She put on the purple lace suspender belt first, then the silk stockings. Peverall sat in a chair and watched her, dressed only in his boxer shorts. The bra that matched the suspender belt came next. It plunged in the middle and gave her more of a cleavage than usual. Then she put on the purple high-leg knickers, and the purple silk camisole. She looked like an advert for lingerie, her red hair tumbling over her shoulders, her legs smooth and waxed, her lips naturally full and red.

Peverall sighed appreciatively, and Rachel felt warm right the way through. Pleasing him was so pleasing in itself. She picked up the dress. It was silver, a long straight shift with a deep V-neck that glittered and sparkled when she moved. It slunk over her body as she dropped it on; it was lined with oyster silk and was heavy, though not unpleasantly so. There was a slit to the thigh up one side, and just occasionally there was a flash of stocking-top. It needed no jewellery; it was a complete adornment in itself, simple and classy and very sexy.

'Now you,' said Rachel. She dressed Peverall in some tight black jeans and a black designer T-shirt. She added a black jacket and a pair of shades. The dark colours drew attention to his bald head – but it looked hard now; you wouldn't want to meet him in a dark alley. He had a straight nose and a firm jaw; there was something very solid about him. The whole illusion fell apart when he smiled, of course, because he smiled like a small boy, and she always wanted to hug him.

* * *

Fee rummaged through the contents of her wardrobe and felt depressed. Nothing leaped out and said, 'Wear me.'

Mind you, there was that red velvet top ... that was bosom-hugging. She tried it on. Then she suddenly remembered the tight black trousers she hadn't worn, so she fished them out and pulled those on too. With high heels the outfit was quite passable.

There was a tap at the door. Summers for the shirt, thought Fee, and she opened it, smiling. It was Graham Steel.

'We haven't seen each other for quite a while,' he said.

'No,' said Fee.

'Can I come in?'

Fee waved a hand vaguely, meaning if you must.

He looked at her get-up with appreciation and said, 'Going out somewhere?'

She shrugged.

'Come on,' he said, 'I know where you're going. Anita's, like me. Nine-thirty.' He glanced at his watch. 'Time's getting on. Listen, Grace is leaving – her taxi should arrive in a minute. I have a feeling that, whatever we have to do to get the clue tonight, it's going to take two. Two people who know they can get it together. We've had everything else – nudity, masturbation, oral sex. There's only one major activity left – and do you want to do it with *Summers*?'

Fee stiffened. She realised she hadn't thought through the forthcoming evening at Anita's. 'What are you suggesting?'

'That you ditch Summers, and team up with me.'

There was another tap at the door, and this time it *was* Summers. 'My partner,' said Fee charmingly to Graham. 'If you don't mind, we've got a few things to sort out ...'

Graham gave her a filthy look, and went.

Fee gave Summers a blue shirt. It was a bit more exotic than what he normally wore, but not by much. 'I know,' she said suddenly, 'a waistcoat. I've got one.' She pulled out a black velvet garment with a silky back.

235

'I'll look like a mole,' he said petulantly, but he put it on. It fitted him, as long as he didn't try to do it up.

'Eric,' said Fee. 'What do you reckon we're going to have to do this evening?' Something felt skew-whiff all of a sudden. Then she realised; she'd just called him Eric.

'No idea,' said Summers.

'Graham's going to be there. He's at the same stage as us.'

'And presumably he wanted you to partner him? I saw Grace leaving in a taxi. She had her suitcase with her.'

'Yes.'

'And?'

'Not interested.'

He smiled. 'I think it's time we went.'

They made their way downstairs. Fee realised she was noticing everything, the way a condemned man might. She'd never stayed anywhere as luxurious as this before; perhaps she never would again. The oil paintings on the walls, the deep-pile carpet underfoot, the tasteful vases of flowers in the alcoves. 'It's weird, isn't it?' she said. 'Tomorrow evening all this will seem like a dream; I'll be back home.'

'Where is home?'

'A one-bedroom flat over a flower shop in Reading. Wonky bookshelves and vermilion woodchip wallpaper.' She grinned at his expression of horror and said, 'Only joking about the vermilion. What about you?'

'A townhouse in suburbia, built by the same Mr Anonymity who designs my suits. Too many bookshelves to even *see* the wallpaper.'

They drove into town and parked the car where they'd parked it before. The noise level increased as they walked towards the club. Other premises were open now and there were lots of neon lights and people and thumpy bass music. There was a smell of curry, so strong you could almost taste it. Anita's had rows of fading photographs outside, and a little kiosk inside. Two stony-faced bouncers stood at the entrance.

Summers cleared his throat. 'We're people from the treasure hunt. Little Trevor says we're to be let in.'

'You and five million others. Where's your membership card?'

'We're not members,' said Summers.

'Well you'd better bugger off then, hadn't you?'

'Can we speak to Trevor?'

'Little Trevor to you, mate,' said one of the bouncers threateningly.

'And Little Trevor says we're to be let in,' said Peverall, arriving behind them.

'And you ain't got no membership card neither, am I right?'

'Well, strictly, with that number of double negatives . . .' said Peverall.

'Are you taking the piss?'

'Oh for God's sake, Ronnie,' said Anna's voice, 'let them in. He's the man who made my Sammy better.'

'Oh, right,' said Ronnie, and the four of them walked through without any further problem.

Chapter Fourteen

*A*nita's got very crowded very quickly. They sat down at a table in the corner and Fee decided to try a few of the cocktails. There were names she'd seen before – *Sex on the Beach*, and *A Long Slow Screw* – and ones she hadn't, like *Three in a Bed*, and *Sixty-nine*. Rachel looked absolutely gorgeous, sparkling in every possible way, and Peverall looked surprisingly presentable – a suave and sophisticated gangster. Until he smiled, that was.

Summers nudged Fee on the arm. Fee looked towards the entrance and saw Graham Steel come in. He scanned the clientele, acknowledged the four of them briefly as soon as he spotted them, and went and sat at the bar. A woman in a black basque homed in on him immediately, and a five-piece band made their way on stage, tuned up, and started on some soft background schmaltz.

'Come on,' said Rachel, 'let's dance.'

Peverall looked alarmed – but Rachel grabbed him by the hand, pulled him to his feet and put her arms round his neck. They smooched off as though they'd been doing it for years, perfectly in time, hips moving in a stylishly well-synchronised fashion.

Then William, Beatrice, Angus and Scarab appeared. William scanned the crowd and acknowledged the rest of the treasure hunt contingent with a nod.

'So,' said Summers, 'there's quite a few of us.'

The lights dimmed and the compère came on and introduced the first act. The music went into the age-old stripper theme and a woman wearing an evening dress and a feather boa sashayed onstage. She did the standard routine, tossing her garments into the audience. When she was down to her underwear, she began to move the feather boa between her legs, and to do a very passable performance of serious arousal. Bit by bit she broke off the end of the boa, tossing each segment to the men closest to her. Then she took off the last of her clothes, rubbed herself to a very convincing simulated orgasm, and strolled offstage.

The compère reappeared and told a few blue jokes. Then he said, 'Let's have a big round of applause for Hank.'

The audience clapped, and nothing happened. After a while the applause petered out and people began to talk among themselves.

Five minutes later there was a sudden roar and a whiff of exhaust fumes. Hank and his Harley Davidson made their entrance and pulled up to a halt. Hank took off his helmet. A beautiful black girl dressed in thigh-length red boots sauntered on; she was crimped into a red leather corset that left her breasts free, and she was carrying some rope. Hank took off his motorcycle gear. All he had on underneath was a black leather codpiece and some spiky silver wrist-bands. The girl tied him to the motorbike, with his legs spread wide. He behaved like an obedient slave, doing everything necessary with his head slightly bowed in submission. Then she slid her hand across the codpiece and it quickly became evident that he had a genuine erection.

Fee watched, fascinated. The girl was rubbing herself against the motorbike as she caressed him; then she undid the thong holding the codpiece in place and his prick bounced free. Hank had obviously been selected with care. The girl spat on her hand and massaged his strapping cock for a little while, and then the music began to rise to a frenetic crescendo. Hank was straining against the ropes, his back arching as he tried to thrust himself harder against the girl's hand. Then the girl bent right over, so that the audience could see she was wearing a pair of panties with a hole cut in the crotch. A few glistening black hairs were just visible through it. She lifted her leg and climbed across him, positioned herself, and moved down so that she impaled herself on his member. Then she rode him the way the music dictated: one long, deep penetration, as the band played an extended chord – then a very slow withdrawal, until his hips were writhing from his need for more. Another deep thrust of her hips – all the way down the shaft, until her arse was touching his balls.

Fee felt a tingle of arousal, imagining what it felt like – that sudden brush of scrotum against an equally sensitive place of her own.

The long, slow, sensuous withdrawal again. Hank's face was rigid with tension, the sinews on his neck taut, his hands balled into fists. The girl smiled the smile of someone totally in charge and poised herself for the kill. Hank groaned and strained a little more at the ropes. As the notes of the chord died away, it seemed as though the whole club was holding its breath.

A final shattering chord and a long drawn-out descent into chaos. The girl pushed her body down Hank's cock with more force than before; Hank let out a roar not unlike that of his motorbike. Then the girl withdrew so that everyone could see, and Hank came in a series of violent shudders.

The stage lights went out, the main lights came on, and the band was replaced by piped music.

'End of part one,' said Summers. 'Classier than I expected.' There was the sound from the darkened stage like an exhaust falling off, and someone swore. Summers laughed.

During the interval that followed, Angus caught Fee's eye and waved at her. Scarab didn't appear to be speaking to him. Fee didn't wave back. She finished her cocktail and ordered another, and then it was time for the second half.

Anna and her anaconda got a massive round of applause. She was obviously a long-time favourite, although her act wasn't anything like as explicit as the one that had gone before. It consisted mainly of walking round the tables, semi-clad, swivelling her hips to some Indian pipe music, with Sammy draped across her more exciting bits. If a customer agreed to hold Sammy, he got to see the bit of Anna the anaconda had been concealing. As soon as Anna spotted Peverall she headed towards him, smiling at him as though she was re-acquainting herself with a long-lost friend. Peverall held out his arms for Sammy and made a fuss of him. He didn't look at Anna's tits once. Anna retrieved her snake, patted Peverall on his bald head, and moved on to Summers.

Summers stiffened slightly – but he took Sammy, and scratched him lightly under his chin, the way he'd seen Peverall do it.

Anna carried on moving round the tables. When she got to William and Beatrice, William shook his head violently and shuddered. Beatrice laughed and held out her arms for the snake. There was a chalk-on-blackboard noise as William's chair scraped across the floor in his effort to put more distance between himself and Beatrice. The snake hissed obligingly and waved its head in William's direction. Beatrice smiled maliciously. Then Sammy noticed Scarab. He unravelled himself at full speed, made a bee-line back to Anna and tied himself in a knot around her.

Anna moved on and gave a few more men a thrill. She finally left to a chorus of whistles and applause, which seemed rather out of proportion to her act. A moment later, Fee wondered whether they were just pleased to see her go, for the next entrance caused a real explosion of applause. Six scantily clad women came on to the stage and did a brief but provocative dance to get the rhythm going, then they left the stage and started to mingle among the guests.

Fee looked at them askance. 'What now?'

'Lap-dancing,' said Summers. 'The women choose a man, sit on his lap and gyrate to the music until he either comes, or wishes he had.'

Fee finished her third cocktail. She knew she was a bit drunk – nothing incapacitating, just enough to make her feel relaxed and happy. She was enjoying herself – she'd never been anywhere quite like this and she'd often wondered what it was like. A girl with blonde hair and fishnet stockings shimmied over and smiled at Summers.

It seemed to take Summers by surprise. One moment he was looking blankly at her, as though he was wondering where she'd sprung from and the next moment she was on his lap, pressing her breasts against his face, and his arms automatically went round her to stop her sliding off him. The blonde started to slide her bottom across his lap in a circular fashion, singing along with the track that was playing. Fee glanced round the room. It was in semi-darkness, and the music was too loud to hear any grunts or groans. She glanced back at Summers. She could see his profile quite clearly against the lights at the back of the bar. The straight nose, the high brow, the serious mouth. He was sitting there with his eyes closed – but after a while the girl obviously saw him as a lost cause and moved on, and he opened his eyes.

'Saving myself for the real performance,' he said. 'Rehearsals tend to detract from it, rather than add to it.' And before she could reply he added, 'I'm talking about karaoke, naturally. I have to look after my voice.' He cleared his throat theatrically, and Fee laughed.

She suddenly realised that he'd had more to drink than usual. 'You're driving,' she said, looking at his empty glass.

'I think I'll stop now, then,' he replied. 'I've still got a few hours to sober up.' He followed her eyes to the glass. 'Dutch courage,' he said, as though he'd been a bit of a disappointment to himself. He glanced round. 'It's an odd atmosphere in here. It's so good-natured and there's so little embarrassment. Maybe it's because there isn't much passing trade in a backwater like this – the people here are regulars.'

The lap-dancers eventually departed, and a couple of men scurried off to the Gents. Fee decided to head for the Ladies. As she entered the washroom, she saw a woman drying her hands. The woman looked round, smiled and said, 'Hello, Fee.'

The voice was decidedly familiar, although the tastefully attired Rubenesque figure was not immediately so. Fee squinted into the light – and the woman laughed. There was only one laugh like that. Rose. 'Hello,' said Fee. 'What are you doing here?'

'That would be telling,' said Rose.

Fee studied her. In the harsh white neon light she looked different, somehow. Not so blowsy. You'd have expected it to be the other way round, thought Fee. I ought to be able to see the skin imperfections, the hard edges of the make-up, the dark roots to her hair. But she's a natural blonde, I'd swear it; her eye shadow isn't so garish, her clothes are more tasteful.

Rose glanced at her and a flicker of amusement crossed her face. 'You're no fool, are you Fee?' And suddenly her accent was different too – pure drama school.

'Rose,' said Fee, 'who are you really?'

The noise of the dryer ceased, and Rose reapplied some lipstick – not her usual harsh red, but a subtle upmarket pink. 'I was Alfred Hicks's lover for the last five years of his life,' she said. 'No one knew, apart from Maurice. Maurice was his chauffeur. I married him very recently – I was lonely after Alfred died. And I'm fond of the old fool, known him for years; he does have hidden depths. Mind you, they're not that well hidden if he's wearing swimming trunks.'

'You're an actress, aren't you? You're not a hooker at all.'

'I was a porn starlet, darling, let's be honest about this – but you have to make a living. I did a good Mistress Quickly in my youth, but I was a bit too busty to make a convincing Ophelia.'

'But what about your other customers? Was that all part of the charade?'

'What other customers?' said Rose. 'Did you see any?'

'No.'

Rose smiled. 'It's easy to give an impression of something, if that's what the person's expecting.'

Fee laughed. 'A lot of things make sense now. You were too involved with it all – you really seemed to care that everything was done by the book.'

'Alfred compiled the clues; I checked them. That's why he put all the roses in. I'm not bad at crosswords myself, you see. Nowhere near Peverall or Eric's standard, of course – or Alfred's, for that matter – but competent enough to be useful. It was his last wish, that this be carried through, and I'm determined to fulfil my promise to him. And yes, there is a contract with the solicitor – that was for my protection not to ensure I got my payment at the end of it. You see, Alfred left me very comfortable. Sold a lot of his collection, and gave me the proceeds. No tax, no trace. A strange man – liked beating systems, whatever they happened to be. So, I'm here to ensure there's fair play, among other things. And that the people who irritated him – like Saul Slick – get a bit of aggro. Pity Saul didn't make it tonight, but you can't win them all.'

'Why are you telling me all this?'

'I like you. And I know you won't blab to Graham or Angus or William. They're the ones who might turn nasty, if they thought I could point them straight at the prize.'

'How nasty?'

'Nasty enough. I've got my Maurice to look after me, of course. He may look like a wimp, but he's very handy with a knife.'

Rose smoothed back her hair and put on a wine-coloured silk turban. It matched the loose dress she was wearing, which gave her more of the air of a diva than a whore. That's why I didn't notice her, thought Fee. With-

244

out the tacky clothes and the tarty make-up, she's a different person.

'See you later then,' said Rose, and she wafted out of the Ladies in a cloud of Chanel No. 5.

Fee joined the others again and pointed out Rose and Maurice as surreptitiously as she could. Even Maurice looked less like a petty gangster and more like an ordinary human being.

'None of these revelations surprises me,' said Summers. 'Rose is too quick for the role she seemed to have been allocated. It means she knows where the treasure is, of course.'

Then the compère reappeared and asked for a round of applause for Sandra and Simon. This time it was Simon who was black and Sandra who was white. They did a witty little number about dreaming up a dessert with both black and white chocolate in it – then Sandra turned to the audience and said, 'It's no good without cream, is it?'

'No!' the audience yelled back.

'But has he got it in him?'

'You'd better believe it,' said Simon, running his hand suggestively across the front of his leather trousers.

'Give him a blow-job!'

'Suck him off!'

'Go down on him!'

There was something of *The Rocky Horror Show* about the gleeful audience participation. A steady thump-thump-thump began to build up, as people stamped their feet and clapped their hands in unison.

Sandra unzipped him and pulled off the tight black trousers. He wasn't wearing any underpants. The room went quiet again. His cock was a beautiful dusky colour, thick and straight and as stiff as an aubergine. Sandra knelt down in front of him and licked it ostentatiously, running her tongue from the base to the head and back again. Simon's muscles tensed. Sandra took him all the way into her mouth and he groaned with pleasure. She trailed her long red fingernails across his balls and he shivered with delight. Then she started to fuck him with her mouth – slowly at first, then faster – until he was alternately holding his breath and letting it out in a quick rasp. She finished him off to the last few bars of Ravel's *Bolero*, using her hand at the last moment so that he could come all over her face. He did it flamboyantly and enthusiastically – and kissed her affectionately on the top of her head when he'd finished. It was an odd little touch and suggested that they had an offstage relationship as well as an onstage one.

The compère came back, told a few more jokes, and glanced at the clock on the wall. There's only a couple of hours to go, thought Fee, and no signs of the treasure hunt clue.

'And now,' said the compère, 'the moment you've been waiting for. The masked ball. We select twelve members of the audience, take them backstage and dress them up. Then we start the ball rolling, folks, and when the music stops . . .'

Whistles from the audience, some of whom had obviously witnessed this before.

The compère smiled. 'When the music stops, the couple who find themselves at the end of the row have to entertain us. And there's a prize for the best performance, as always.'

Shouts of 'What's the prize?'

'That would be telling.'

'Who's the judge?'

A spotlight came on, traversed the audience, and stopped on Rose. Rose stood up and gave a bow. Angus did a double-take, Graham went tight-lipped, William looked thunderous and Scarab laughed.

'If you'd like to select the lucky twelve, Rose,' said the compère. The room was now completely silent.

Rose started to walk between the tables, tapping people on the shoulder. William and Beatrice first, though not Angus or Scarab; then a man with dark hair. Graham Steel, the woman in the black basque. Another woman, who was quite simply beautiful. Then Rachel. Peverall looked really upset – then Rose tapped him on the shoulder as well. Summers was next. Then a woman who could have been one of the lap-dancers, and a man who looked familiar – Hank, of the Harley Davidson. Makes sense, thought Fee, you need to plant a few performers to make sure there's some suitably improper action.

And then she felt Rose's hand on her own shoulder. She'd expected it, really. The prize for the best perform-ance had to be the last clue. She stood up and followed the rest of the chosen backstage.

The women all went into one dressingroom and the men to another. There were a lot of costumes hanging on a rail, in a variety of sizes. The variety was mind-boggling – everything from Little Red Riding Hood to a pantomime goose. Or was it a swan? Fee tried on a nun's habit and a cat costume but they were both very hot, so she found herself a pale-blue off-the-shoulder crinoline dress, a white wig and a black butterfly mask. Then she helped herself to make-up and painted her face as white as she dared. Rouge, red lipstick, a beauty spot – and hey presto. She was an eighteenth-century woman.

The woman in the black basque was ready first – she seemed to know where everything was and she quickly transformed herself into a Barbarella-type spacewoman. The lap-dancer wasn't far behind; she had turned herself into a nurse, her identity concealed behind a theatre mask. Fee slipped her shoes back on and stood up. It was time for the grand finale.

Beatrice had chosen a skintight black latex catsuit that laced up the back and a black mask that covered her whole head. She then selected some stiletto-heeled boots and a soft red-leather whip, which she tucked into a spiky belt. She looked very intimidating, for she had a natural military posture. The girl with the beautiful face looked utterly gorgeous as a flower fairy in bright magenta, and she couldn't stop giggling. Rachel had opted for the veiled Eastern look. They all went out on to the stage, to a round of deafening applause.

The men came on. The bearded monk, the executioner

and the gorilla were all equally tall – William, Peverall and Hank then. The dragon and the werewolf were shorter: the man with dark hair and Summers. Pierrot was the only one of medium height, so that had to be Graham Steel. The compère explained the steps of the dance. It wasn't particularly difficult – but everyone changed places, so there was no knowing who you might be with when the music stopped.

As soon as the dance started, Fee was pretty certain she'd identified Summers – surely he was the one with the two left feet who partnered her first, wearing the turquoise dragon mask. She glanced across at the next couple. The werewolf was dancing competently enough, though not gracefully.

Pierrot danced economically but well, and he gave her a little bow as he moved on to his next partner. The bow said it all: I'm here, you're here, we can win this if we want. He'd known who *she* was straight away.

The music stopped. The Barbarella-clone was at the head of the line; the gorilla was next to her. Rachel caught Fee's eye – then she shook her head slightly. Rachel knows which one Peverall is, thought Fee, and it isn't him. The gorilla's probably Hank. That would make sense: start with the professionals.

The spotlight lit up a mattress at the front of the stage. The gorilla dragged Barbarella across the floor and threw her down on to it. The suit obviously had a zip in the appropriate place, because it was clear that Hank had got his second wind. The cock that rose to the occasion was shockingly pink against the dark fur of the costume, and it lent a strange authenticity to the disguise. Barbarella wriggled and made unconvincing sounds of distress. The ape unzipped her spacesuit with thick clumsy fingers and pulled it off her. Then he cupped her breasts in his leathery hands and licked the nipples in turn. Fee found the juxtaposition of black fur and pale skin disgracefully erotic: bestiality without the beast, deviance without danger. Pure lust, with no messy human emotions in the way. Was that why she had found Leda and the swan such a turn-on? The swan had really been Zeus in disguise, true – but Zeus wasn't human either.

The gorilla grunted a few times and explored her all over with his tongue. Barbarella made the transition from reluctance to enthusiasm and grabbed hold of him so hard that a tuft of shoulder-hair came away in her fingers. He roared and beat his chest, and then he entered her. He fucked her very energetically and she moaned and writhed and dug her hands into his fur. When he came she arched her back and cried out, and there was a round of applause. Both performers were then allowed to leave the stage.

The dance resumed. Fee was hoping that Rose had set it up so that the treasure hunt people were correctly partnered – but she couldn't be sure. There was only one non-contestant left now among the men – the man with dark hair. She was pretty sure he was wearing the werewolf mask.

The music stopped. This time Rachel was at the head of the line, and the bearded monk was standing next to her. Wouldn't it be ghastly if it were William, thought Fee. But Rachel didn't look in the slightest bit apprehensive; in fact, she winked at Fee. Her partner laid her down on the bed as though she were made of porcelain, and if that wasn't enough to identify Peverall, his hood slipped sideways and a flash of pink skull completed the job. He made love to her with what looked like telepathic skill, but it was performance for two, not for an audience. As they made their way back to their seats Rachel passed by close to Fee and whispered, 'It's quite exciting, really. Though I don't think Peverall could have done it if he hadn't had a beard to hide behind.'

Fee was getting nervous. They were down to eight now. The music started again and the dance resumed its stately progress. As she took the dragon's fingers in hers to execute a half-turn, she felt him squeeze slightly. It *is* Summers, she thought, and her heart was in her mouth as they made their way to the head of the line. The music will stop now, she thought, but it didn't. They kept their fingers in contact to the very last second. The moment they broke apart, the music *did* stop. Fee found herself between two partners – the dragon and the werewolf.

She looked from one to the other, the panic rising. The werewolf took a step towards her. Fee looked helplessly at the compère. He wasn't paying attention. She scanned the audience for Rose, but the audience was in darkness. She couldn't just stand there indefinitely. The dragon took a step towards her, his turquoise face alien and unreal, his eyes shaded by the mask – and she realised she had to choose.

As she reached out her hand for the dragon, the word *turquoise* rang a bell. *I couldn't possibly wear turquoise. It's a tertiary colour. I don't wear tertiaries.*

She drew back her arm, as though something had stung her. There was the sound of an exhaled breath, which could have expressed either annoyance or disappointment. She took the werewolf by the hand instead, and led him over to the bed. His hand wasn't cold or clammy or fleshy; it was dry and slightly warmer than hers. His grip was neither too tight, nor too loose, and she knew she'd made the right choice.

He undressed her, leaving just the wig and the mask in place. Then she undressed him, leaving the wolfmask and the hat. It had a feather in it, and it looked rather dashing. She knew he had a hairy body – it fitted the werewolf persona rather well. He had an erection as well. There were condoms by the side of the bed, so she put one on him. It was the first time she had intentionally touched his cock, and the contact was a significant one. He reacted immediately, though he tried to disguise it, and she wondered if it was the prospect of fucking *her*, or just the certainty of a fuck. Any fuck. She remembered his remark in the linen cupboard at *The Elms* – 'An erection's a knee-jerk reaction, Fee, nothing more. Automatic.'

'We need to turn in the performance of our lives here,' he said, *sotto voce*.

She seemed to have lost her voice.

'I suggest a spot of pretend rape,' he said. 'You sit on

the side of the bed, take off the wig, and brush out your hair. I'll lurk, and pounce at the appropriate juncture. There's a mirror on the wall over there; you can watch what I'm doing.'

Fee sat on the edge of the bed, feeling oddly weak, and took off the wig. Then she began to brush her hair, although her arm felt like rubber and she didn't seem to be able to judge the distance of the brush from her head very well. She wondered whether it was the effect of the alcohol, but somewhere deep down she knew it wasn't. It was the lull before the storm, the interval before the last act, the two-bar rest before the final note. She was going to have sex with Summers. And what was more – it was going to be one of her favourite fantasies. Sex with a not-quite-human. A mythological being. A werewolf.

He vanished into the gloom behind the spotlight, and after a few moments she saw him prowling up and down, watching her. He was doing it rather well – there was a looseness to his movements that suggested an animal physique rather than a human one. She heard him growl, and that was eerily convincing too.

She looked behind her, then put her hand to her mouth in a theatrical gesture of alarm. Summers rushed her then and knocked her back on to the bed. She felt his body on top of hers, familiar yet unfamiliar, softly reassuring and powerfully masculine at the same time. She was unable to see his face through the mask, unable to gauge his expression.

She suddenly remembered that she was meant to be acting, so she let out a few little screams and struggled. He put his hand over her mouth and snarled. She let herself go limp. She felt as though she were in a silent movie; everything in black and white, hardly any sound, all actions exaggerated for effect. He pawed her, his hands raking up and down her body, his fingers curved into blunt claws. Whenever he touched her she felt the urge to press against him, and sometimes she just couldn't stop herself.

She heard a man in the front row say, 'This is a good one.'

Summers leaned over and whispered in her ear, 'What's a wolf to do without a tongue?'

'Move the mask up,' said Fee.

He moved it up, wrinkling the nose in a sudden snarl and freeing his mouth. It was like looking at an ink-blot; wolf one moment, man the next. He took off the hat and threw it debonairly into the audience. Then he began to lick. He kept in character – the movements were made with long, deliberate strokes of his tongue, starting at her neck and moving slowly but inexorably down. One breast, then the other, then down to her navel. Back and forth across her abdomen, then a sudden excursion to the backs of her knees, from where he inched up to the inside of her thighs. It was Summers, and yet it wasn't Summers. He was playing a part, and so was she, and if she wanted she could let it take her over. The hairy head was weird, the pointed ears; he'd managed to keep the eye-slits over his eyes, but she wasn't able to see his eyebrows, or the skin around his eyes. There were no little creases to give clues to his expression.

She remembered to struggle a bit, and he pinned her down with his arms. After he'd subdued her with his hands and his tongue he suddenly pulled her to the edge of the bed and knelt down beside it on the stage floor. He pushed her legs up in the air and bent her knees so that she made Z-shape and her bottom was visible to every-one. All of it, from clit to cunt to anus. She couldn't see the audience at all, however, just the tips of her toes and the stage lighting far above them. After a moment she felt his fingers spread her open. The audience can see right inside me, she thought, and the thought was wildly exciting. She hadn't realised she was such an exhibitionist. Rachel was right, she thought, the mask makes anything possible. I can be whoever I like, as long as my face is hidden. His tongue started to lick round the entrance to her pussy. The slight rustles and occasional coughs of the audience faded away, as her mind focused on sensation alone. The position was absolutely incredible; he had access to every bit of her, and plenty of room to manoeuvre himself and find new angles. He seemed to be reading her mind, moving where she wanted him to move, pressing the way she wanted him to press. Inside a little way, then out again, then in between the folds, then round her clit – though he hadn't actually touched it yet. All her concentration was focused on that small area and nothing else existed. It was almost as though she were conducting the whole thing, telling him what to do. And then he started to surprise her every so often, darting from place to place, sensitising new areas and then returning to them when she least expected it. She was tingling all over with arousal, from the crown of her head to the tips of her toes. She pushed against him.

He changed his tactics immediately, and she felt his tongue move to her clit. He teased it with delicate little touches, licked it, pressed it, took it between his lips and gently sucked at it. A whoosh of excitement swept through her and she felt her body collect itself for orgasm. She took a deep breath – and then someone in the audience coughed, and he stopped for a moment.

She tumbled back into the real world and remembered where she was. It all suddenly seemed quite bizarre.

He slid on to the bed beside her, and his face came level with hers. She could see his hazel eyes looking at her, narrow and slitty behind the mask. The wolf's nose below them, scrunched up, the way a dog's nose crinkles when it's angry. His mouth and his chin, wet from cunnilingus. Everything took on a more menacing feel. She felt the muscles of her face tense, as though rigor mortis had set in.

'Do you want me to stop?'

The voice was low and expressionless, much as she'd have expected a wolf's voice to sound. His long grey whiskers were just touching her forehead; they felt like the bristles on a paintbrush. She could see the glint of a white canine tooth, and the dark lip curled above it.

'I'm not sure who you are any more,' she said.

'I'm still Eric, Fee. Say stop, and I'll stop. We'll go. We'll say sod the treasure hunt, it wasn't worth it. Or . . .'

'Or?'

'We can fuck.'

'Let's fuck then.'

Chapter Fifteen

Someone scraped a chair across the floor. The sound dislocated her mentally for a moment – then Summers turned her face towards him and took off the mask. His regular features looked suddenly familiar and reassuring; she felt safe. After that, he took off *her* mask. She'd forgotten she was still wearing it – had he been as unable to read her face as she had his?

He ran his finger lightly across her top lip, then the bottom one; it was as though he were asking permission to kiss her. She touched his finger with her tongue, and then his lips replaced it, very soft, very gentle. He pulled back slightly and looked at her. She could see the red imprint of her lipstick on his mouth. He kissed her again, and this time she responded. The detachment vanished and the contact between them became very personal indeed – there was a sudden closeness that seemed a lot more powerful than a week's friendship. He explored her mouth the same way he had done her cunt, seeming to know what she wanted and surprising her as and when he felt like it. His hands travelled over her body, stroking her, smoothing her out, emptying her of everything except a very particular sort of wanting.

When he did enter her, it was slow and gradual and perfectly timed, and she had the odd sensation of coming home. It felt absurdly right. He pushed himself in as far as he could go and stayed there for a moment, just looking at her. She slid her arms round his back and held him there. It suddenly seemed as though the week had been building to this moment, and not the prize at all. He withdrew just as slowly, and then moved in again. The feeling was exquisite; she was very wet. He slid in and out with delicious ease, slowly increasing the tempo, his eyes fixed on her face.

After a while he raised himself on to his arms to increase the leverage. The build-up carried on, persistent, assured, a little bit at a time. He was very controlled, completely in command. She wanted to make him lose it again, the way he had at the clinic. In out, in out, as regular as an oarsman. She slid her hands on to his buttocks, pulling him against her with every thrust, forcing him to go as deep as possible. She snaked her hand down between their bodies and began to frantically rub herself. She wanted them both to come now, the tension was getting unbearable, a non-stop ache for release. A little smile crossed his face. He began to thrust much harder; then he speeded up until she felt everything inside her contract. His reaction was immediate, and it was clear that this time he couldn't contain it; his face blanked, his head jerked back, and they both came together. It went on for what seemed like a long, long time.

She was vaguely aware of some background noise going on, like the roar of a gale. The sounds gradually came into focus and she realised that it was applause. Eric kissed her briefly on the forehead, climbed off her, turned to face the audience and bowed. There was an explosion of laughter and the clapping redoubled. He walked back to the bed, took Fee by the hand, led her to the front of the stage and got her to bow as well. The clapping went on; someone whistled, then someone else, and a few feet started to stamp in unison. Eric grinned, picked up their clothes and shepherded Fee to the exit at the back of the stage.

They went back to the dressing rooms and put on their own clothes. Fee washed off the make-up and they returned to their seats.

'Hot stuff,' said Rachel.

The dance on the stage had resumed; there were only six participants left. When the music stopped it was Graham Steel's turn. He was opposite the flower fairy. Although Fee watched them fuck, she couldn't concentrate, and it was over before she'd had a chance to evaluate it.

Then it was the dragon and the lap-dancer nurse, and after that only William and Beatrice were left. Beatrice went over to the band and said something. The guitarist nodded and pointed to an electric violin, and after a moment Fee heard the tortuous opening notes of *Venus in Furs* by the Velvet Underground.

Beatrice stroked her thigh-length boots with long crimson nails.

'Shiny shiny, shiny boots of leather . . .' sang the vocalist. He was making a good job of it, sly and suggestive and sexy. Beatrice took off the catsuit. She was wearing black leather underwear with a hole in the crotch. She flicked the whip at William.

'Whiplash girlchild, in the dark . . .' the vocalist crooned. The bass thumped along underneath, dark and menacing.

'Strip,' said Beatrice.

William stripped off the executioner's gear.

'On your knees.'

William knelt.

'Lick my boots.'

William licked the boots. After another couple of bars Beatrice ordered him to move up, and then to finger-fuck her. He did everything with a bowed head, acting the slave to perfection.

When the vocalist got to 'Strike, dear mistress,' Beatrice lashed him for the first time with the whip. William started with surprise; she'd obviously done it harder than he'd anticipated.

'Bend over,' snapped Beatrice.

William bent over. Beatrice lashed him with the whip again, first one buttock, then the other. They turned pink and a few criss-cross marks appeared. William moaned, and it sounded very genuine. Beatrice smiled a really evil smile and lashed him one last time with all her strength. His body jerked in response and he screamed.

'Now fuck me,' said Beatrice, her voice cold and imperious.

William looked happier and obliged. Beatrice raked her nails across his back, leaving long red weals, and William fucked her like a lunatic. It was hard to tell whether his urgency came from lust or a sudden desire for it to be over.

The applause when he came was deafening.

'I think I'd give that a six for technical merit,' said Eric, 'and a five point five for artistic impression. Slick, but not original.'

The spotlight crossed the audience and came to rest on Rose. Rose stood up. 'Some pretty impressive performances,' she said. There was a muttering of general agreement. 'It was very hard to choose the winner,' Rose went on. 'So hard that in the end I decided to tie two couples for first place. William and Beatrice . . .' She waved a hand in their direction. 'And Eric and Fee.' Everyone clapped. 'Prizes then.' Rose had two envelopes in her hand. She gave one to Beatrice and the other to Fee. She patted Fee on the shoulder and said, 'Good luck, darling.' The band struck up something smoochy and people started to leave.

Fee opened the envelope. It was the final clue.

'Need any help?' asked Peverall. 'We're not about to usurp your position or anything, we just want to see you beat William and Beatrice.'

Fee glanced at Eric and he nodded. She laid the clue on the table and they all read the following:

The gaps in your knowledge can all be resolved –
If you leave out an A, your procedure is solved;

You'll find one of these in the room with a view,
The figures below won't disorient you.
Play your hand wisely, and don't miss a trick;
Leave the club, shed your diamonds – lose heart?
   No, be quick –
Equip yourself wisely, it's no load of bull
That the answer will win, and your cup will be full.

'What are those figures at the bottom?' asked Rachel.

'Latitude and longitude,' said Peverall. 'Oh, I see. Take the A out of gaps . . . GPS.'

'What's GPS?' asked Rachel.

'Global Positioning System,' said Eric. 'The thing looks like a mobile phone – keypad and a small screen. I tested one a few years back. It's linked up to lots of satellites and gives your position to within half a metre.'

'A room with a view,' said Peverall. 'Room 7, where we watched the video.'

'Let's go,' said Fee.

'Hang on . . .' Eric was looking at the second half of the clue.

Fee realised that William and Beatrice had gone already.

'Leave the club, shed the diamonds, lose heart . . .' he said. Then he smiled. 'But take a spade. We're going to have to dig, I think.'

They said goodbye to Rachel and Peverall, walked back to the car and drove back to the house. Everything was now in darkness, but Room 7 was still unlocked. They found what they were looking for quite quickly – there were several GPSs, so there was no knowing whether William had already taken one. And there were the spades, stacked in one corner, beside some metal detectors. Eric glanced at Fee's trousers and high heels and said, 'I'd change my shoes if I were you.'

Fee dashed upstairs, put on some trainers and ran back down. They went outside. Eric punched in a few things on the keypad. 'We're not far away,' he said. 'A mile or so to the south-east, I reckon.' He passed her the GPS.

'See the little arrow? Shows us the direction we take. Still got your dinky little torch?'

'I'll have you know these dinky little torches are used by the LA police.'

He looked at it with distaste.

They drove off, checking their position every so often. When they got within a few hundred metres, he stopped the car in a lay-by and lined it up neatly behind the three other vehicles parked there – a lorry, a Range Rover and a BMW.

'That's not Graham Steel's car, is it?' asked Fee.

Eric looked at it. 'Could be. I'm not sure.'

'You mean you haven't memorised everyone's registration number?'

He looked annoyed. 'I'm not infallible, Fee. Now then. Our goal's beyond that field somewhere. We can't get any closer by car, so it's Shanks's pony from now on.'

Carrying the spade, the GPS and the metal detector they climbed over a stile and made their way across a field of sheep. There was another stile into the next field, which appeared to be just grass, nothing else, and a big oak tree in the middle, its shadow very black against the moonlight. There was small pond to one side of it. They walked across the field towards the middle, sweeping the metal detector in front of them as they approached the right area. When they got to the foot of the oak tree the metal detector started to beep softly. Eric took off his jacket and started to dig.

Fee shone her torch where he dug, and the hole developed nicely. She wasn't surprised when the spade hit something metal – but a shiver went through her. We've almost won, she thought: is this going to change my life? The top of a metal box was just visible, a dull grey rectangle. Eric carried on digging. She could see one side of the box now, and something that looked like a handle. Eric put down the spade and turned to Fee. 'There's a metal band that goes right round; the catch must be underneath. You take one handle, I'll take the other. When I say heave, we heave.'

Fee took hold of the metal handle and braced her back against the wall of mud. Eric did likewise and they both pulled. Nothing. He kicked it, which surprised her. He glanced at her and smiled. 'Trying to loosen it,' he said. They tried again. This time, the box lifted. They dragged it out and put it on the grass; Eric undid the catch and lifted the lid. There was a lot of polystyrene packing. He rummaged around inside and after a moment or two he said, 'Got them.'

Very carefully, he lifted out the statues. The gold glinted in the torchlight and the figures seemed almost alive. There were hands everywhere, doing erotic things; the eyes were made of emeralds, and the woman's nipples of rubies.

'Very pretty,' said William, from behind them. 'Hand them over.'

Fee turned round. William had a gun.

Fee just stared as Eric handed the statues over. She couldn't believe the firearm was real. William and Beatrice must have approached them from the other side of the tree-trunk. Then she remembered looking at William's briefcase earlier in the week, and seeing something metal . . .

'Well,' said William, 'it's been nice knowing you all. Now I've got a plane to catch, so if you'll just climb the oak tree – nice and high – you'll give me the head start I need. You first.' He waved the gun at Beatrice.

Even in the moonlight, Fee could see that Beatrice had gone white.

'Get on with it, Beatrice,' said William. 'You know I'll use this if I have to. I wouldn't kill you, of course – I'd just give you a nice dose of pain to remember me by.'

Beatrice swung herself up on to the lowest branch and started to climb.

'Now you.' William waved the gun at Fee.

'Fee . . .' The call came from the other side of the field, thin and faint. They all turned to look. A ghostly white shape . . . no, silver . . . it was Rachel, still wearing the long evening dress. She was standing on the other side of a stile, Peverall beside her.

There was a thud and a grunt. Fee spun round, just in time to see the gun fly through the air and fall into the pond with a resounding splash. Her mouth dropped open in astonishment. Summers had actually *kicked* the weapon out of William's hand while William's attention had been distracted. He looked mildly surprised with himself. William lifted one of the statues as though he were about to retaliate with it – then he seemed to change his mind.

'Eric!' It was Peverall calling this time. 'There's a bull in the field! There's a warning sign here!'

Fee felt something inside her turn to ice. They all scanned the field. Beatrice stayed where she was, halfway up the tree.

'Christ,' said William.

Fee followed his line of vision, and then she saw it. A big blunt shape, only just visible in the shadow of the tree. The animal wasn't very far away. She could see its flank rising and falling as it breathed. If it decided to charge, there was no way she could shin up the tree in time. She looked at Eric, but the new man of action had retreated behind his thinking expression.

William started to back away, circling the pond. The bull raised his head and stepped out of the shadow. He was huge; he had a dark body, with a few pale markings. Hard to ascertain the colour by moonlight; everything looked so monochromatic. The bull just stood there, watching William and breathing. There was a ring through his nose; he had a pronounced dewlap and his horns were curved.

'Dairy Shorthorn,' said Eric. 'Shit.'

He and Fee edged away, in Peverall and Rachel's direction.

'Why's a Dairy Shorthorn particularly bad news?'

'Filthy temperament. Scarab got gored by one last year.'

William was on the other side of the pond now, backing away across the field, the statues clutched to his chest.

The bull took a pace forward. Fee and Eric were a third of the way from the tree to the stile.

William stumbled; there were some large tussocks of grass. For some reason this seemed to irritate the bull no end; he lowered his head, pawed the ground and snorted. William steadied himself, turned and ran. The bull went straight through the pond as though it were a puddle, spray sheeting out and fragmenting into silver droplets in the moonlight. Then, fortunately for William, the bull slipped on the mud and stopped as he tried to recover his footing.

Eric seized Fee by the hand and started to run. There were squeals of encouragement from Rachel, who was leaning over the bit of fencing at the side of the stile. The bull staggered to his feet and looked round. William had realised that the only certain exit was the stile, and he had veered towards it. The bull snorted again and turned in a little circle. William was sprinting flat out and it looked as though he'd make the stile shortly after Eric and Fee.

Eric practically threw Fee over it, then scrambled over it himself. The bull spotted William and broke into a run. As William reached the stile he stumbled again. His hand went out automatically to grab hold of something – and the something it found was Rachel's dress. Most other fabrics would have ripped, but the metallic dress was made of sterner stuff. Rachel was already leaning over the fence; William's hold made her completely lose her balance and she tipped right over, and down on to the grass on the other side. William got to his feet and hauled himself over the stile, and the bull stopped and looked confused.

Then he saw Rachel. He lowered his head and snorted.

Peverall vaulted into the field and took off his jacket. It was lined with red silk, which looked very dark in the moonlight. The bull looked even more annoyed and he pawed the ground again. Fee heard Rachel say, 'I've sprained my ankle.'

'Hop,' instructed Peverall, facing the bull. He moved

263

out into the field, and the bull followed him with his angry little eyes. Eric and Fee manhandled Rachel over the stile.

Then, all of a sudden, the bull charged. Peverall swung his jacket with the precision of someone who had once fenced for Trinity, and the bull passed him harmlessly by.

'I'm OK now!' Rachel called out.

Peverall started to move back towards the stile. The bull charged him once more, hooking the end of the makeshift cloak and ripping it. Peverall held on to it, flared it out with a flick of his wrist, pivoted, put a hand on his hip, clicked his heels Spanish-style and shouted '*Olé!*'

'Idiot!' yelled Eric. 'Just get out of there!'

Rachel made a funny little noise. She seemed to have turned to stone, and her eyes were white-rimmed with fright. The bull made two more passes and Peverall played matador again, though not quite so flamboyantly as before. Rachel looked as though she wasn't even breathing. Then all of a sudden the bull got fed up and trotted away. Peverall walked back to the stile and climbed over it. Rachel flung her arms round him and burst into hysterical tears.

Fee looked round. 'Where's William?'

Eric looked round as well. 'Buggered off, treasure and all. Mind you, if that *was* his car in the lay-by, we can catch him if we're quick.'

'And then what?'

'Don't know. Come on.'

When they got back to the car, William was sitting on the bonnet.

'Just thought you'd like to know,' said William, 'that the bloody things are fakes.' He upended one of them and showed them a scratch on the base. A dull silver metal was showing through. 'Lead.' He laughed. 'What a fiasco, eh?'

Fee couldn't tear her eyes away from the evidence.

After everything they'd been through.

Fakes.

'Why did you bother to wait and tell us?'

'I just wanted someone else to feel they'd wasted a whole bloody week, like me.' He hesitated. Then he said, 'Was Rachel OK?'

'Yes,' said Fee shortly. 'But I imagine Beatrice is still up the oak tree.'

He laughed again. 'Best place for her.'

'You've been horrible to her.'

'She likes it.' He registered the disapproval in Fee's eyes and added, 'Oh come on, you know Peverall is far too much of a gentleman to leave even a Black Widow in distress. He'll get the fire brigade or something.' He suddenly stiffened and started to tap his fingers, staring into the middle distance. It was the classic posture of someone who has just had a very good idea. Then he smiled, slid off the bonnet and simply walked away.

Fee got into the Saab and Eric just stood there for a moment, thinking. Then he got into the driver's seat and said, 'He's going to see Rose. He thinks Rose got there before the hunt even started and substituted fakes. And I don't think he'll be very polite about asking her where the real ones are.' He started the engine.

'We ought to call the police.'

'Where from? We'd have to find a phone box. No, come on, it's not that far.'

He put the car in gear and accelerated away.

'Supposing he's got another gun?'

'I don't think that's very likely. Always assuming the previous one was a real one, of course.'

It took them longer than they'd anticipated – a few hundred metres down the road there was a loose cow standing on the white line and they had to shoo it out of the way. When they got to Rose's door it was, alarmingly, open. They looked at one another.

'I think you should wait in the car, Fee.'

'No way.'

'Please.'

She shook her head and pushed past him. People were

talking in the parlour. The door was open. Most of the furniture had gone.

William was sitting in a chair, and Maurice had a knife at his throat. Rose was lying down on the sofa. She saw Eric and Fee in the doorway and sat up.

'Take it easy, Rosie,' said Maurice. He looked across and saw them as well. 'This bastard threatened to cut her up a bit, so I'm just giving him a taste of what it feels like.' There was a thin red line on William's cheek; it looked as though Maurice had given him a small slice rather than a taste.

'Well, this is cosy,' said Graham Steel from behind them.

'Full house,' said Rose.

'There are six of us,' Eric pointed out.

Rose laughed. 'Pedantic as ever, eh, Eric? Though, as you can see, this slightly overfull house was only a temporary abode. I've got a very nice place in Surrey that I can't wait to get back to. This treasure hunt has brought back a lot of memories about what I used to do for a living, and to be perfectly frank, I'm glad it's over. Though I did have a bit of fun from time to time.'

'How did you get here?' Fee asked Graham.

'I bugged William's car,' said Graham. 'I was ahead of you all, in the end. Things didn't go to plan, however, and I watched your little adventure from a hedge. I phoned the farmer, by the way, and told him about Beatrice. He wasn't very pleased – Peverall had just done the same thing – but he'll go and rescue her. I got something in the clue none of you did, you see – the load of bull. You forgot about Hicks's sex angle to each clue – what you had to do was let a cow into the field. Unfortunately, the cow I chose had other ideas.'

Fee laughed. 'The cow in the lane.'

'Mind of her own, that one,' said Graham. 'Now then – whatever you may think of my methods, I am on the side of the law. Those statues belong to the insurance company, Rose.'

'I sold them,' said Rose. 'To a client from overseas. There won't be any trace of the transaction.'

'I thought you might have. Ah well.'

William seemed to slump.

'So the whole thing was a con,' said Fee.

'No,' said Rose, 'Hicks was always fair. I thought burying the statues was too risky – so I turned them into cash.' She turned to Graham. 'Who were the real winners of the treasure hunt, Graham?'

'Eric and Fee.'

Maurice put his knife away and said, 'You can sod off now, William. And if I ever see you again, I'll give you a bit more than a decorated cheek.'

William didn't need telling twice. He went.

Rose made out three cheques; one to Eric Summers, one to Fiona Ferris, and a smaller one to Graham Steel. 'That's what you would have got as reward money,' she said. 'Will you let the whole thing drop now?'

Graham smiled. 'Yes.'

Fee looked at the row of noughts and felt a bit light-headed.

'I've done my duty to Alfred Hicks, may he rest in peace,' said Rose. 'And now – it's been a long night, and I'd like to get some sleep.'

Graham, Eric and Fee said goodbye to Rose and Maurice and went back to their cars. 'I think I'll head off home,' said Graham. 'You two were worthy opponents, much as it pains me to admit it. I'm satisfied with the outcome.' He got into his car and drove away. Eric and Fee drove back to the house.

'What are you going to do with your share?' asked Eric.

'Not sure,' said Fee. 'A degree, maybe. But I wouldn't mind a bloody good holiday first. This was the only one I've had in years, and it was damned hard work. I fancy a bit of lounging on a beach somewhere. Rarotonga, maybe. It looked idyllic.'

They got out of the car and made their way upstairs. Peverall and Rachel were sitting in Fee's room. Rachel's ankle was bandaged.

Eric told them what had happened. Peverall looked pleased – the money was nothing to him, but he knew it meant rather more to both Eric and Fee. Eric was comfortable, but not wealthy.

'*We'd* been considering Rarotonga, but we've opted for the Taj Mahal,' said Peverall. 'For our honeymoon.'

Eric's face broke into a broad grin. 'Congratulations,' he said.

Fee hugged Rachel, and Rachel got slightly weepy. 'I'm not used to being this happy,' she said. 'There's always been a catch somewhere, in the past.'

'You *are* the catch, darling,' said Peverall. He opened a bottle of champagne and they all toasted each other. It was beginning to get light. 'Bed, I think,' said Peverall. 'See you at lunchtime, maybe.' When Rachel tried to stand on her dodgy ankle Peverall swept her up into his arms and carried her off down the corridor.

Fee looked at Eric, and Eric looked at Fee. She wanted to say, stay here. As the silence lengthened she wondered whether *he* would suggest it. Then the moment passed, and they said goodnight.

Gavin Smythe announced the treasure hunt winners over lunch, and Eric and Fee took a bow and waved their cheques in the air. As far as everyone else was concerned, a sum of money had been the prize all along – although there were gasps at the amount. Angus looked pissed off and kept glancing round the room, presumably for William. Beatrice came in late, looking thunderous. There was a long scratch down her arm. She helped herself to what remained of the roast beef, slicing into as though it were Dairy Shorthorn.

'Strange sort of week,' said Saul Slick to Eric. 'Well done though.'

'Did you enjoy it?'

Saul made a face. 'Good and bad in parts, like the curate's egg. I haven't wasted my time though.' He glanced towards Beatrice.

'Another new face for the sitcom?' queried Scarab.

Saul gave her a sharp look and ran a hand through his mad hair.

'You've used Beatrice before, Saul,' said Eric. 'We all recognise your characters, you don't disguise them very well.'

'Not the new Beatrice,' said Saul darkly.

'I'd be careful of the new Beatrice if I were you,' said Eric. 'She's turned into the sort that might exact revenge.'

Arnold came over and congratulated them in person. 'Extraordinary week,' he said, twirling the ends of his moustache. 'Haven't enjoyed myself so much for years.' He suddenly started to whistle 'She'll be Coming Round the Mountain When She Comes' between his teeth. He stopped just as suddenly, and smiled. 'See you next time then,' he said. 'Though I doubt it will be anything like as exciting.'

Everyone went upstairs to pack. Fee flung her clothes into her suitcase in a temper, sat on the bed and sulked. Summers hadn't asked for her address, hadn't said anything about seeing her again.

She had a shower, slipped on her robe and packed her toiletries. Talcum powder – that had been Angus. A packet of condoms. That had been Graham, by the statue of Pan. The lipstick she'd used the previous night. That had been Eric. She glanced at her watch. She had come with Rachel, and she would leave with Rachel – but she wasn't going to interrupt Rachel and Peverall's goodbye. They didn't have to be out of their rooms for another two hours; it seemed a long time just to sit on the bed and wait.

And then there was a knock at the door. Fee felt a sudden rush of adrenaline that sent goose-pimples up her arms and gave her a funny sort of ache at the base of her neck. She got up and opened it.

'Hello,' said Eric. 'May I come in for a little while?' He was carrying a very large holdall.

She sat on the bed, still wearing just her white satin

robe, and he sat on the chair. They were opposite one another, several yards apart.

'I've enjoyed this week,' he said, as though he were talking about a church outing.

'Me too.'

They talked about inconsequentialities for a while. Eventually Fee said, 'I really ought to get dressed and see whether Rachel is waiting for me in the library.'

'There's something I want to say before you do.'

She waited.

'It would have been very easy for me to make a pass at you during the treasure hunt.'

'Why didn't you?' The space between them had become so sexually charged that she almost felt an incursion would cause a shower of sparks.

'Because I didn't know whether everything was ... well, just part of the game.'

'Oh.' She couldn't think of anything else to say.

'I like games, of course. Perhaps we could finish with one.' He glanced at the holdall.

She didn't like the word *finish*, but she was intrigued nonetheless. 'What do you have in mind?'

'A bit of role-play.' He unzipped the bag and she caught a glimpse of white feathers. 'I persuaded Little Trevor to sell it to me,' he said. 'If you're game, I'll go and change.'

She nodded. He took the holdall into the bathroom and emerged a couple of minutes later as a pantomime goose. Or was it a swan? Her first reaction was laughter; he was having difficulty with the webbed feet – it was like trying to walk in flippers – and the curved breast of the bird had given him a beer belly. It was clever costume though – the S of the neck had been compressed to accommodate mammalian anatomy, and it looked surprisingly authentic. It had obviously been designed for a man, as there were flies in the appropriate place. He had left these unzipped.

'Nice one,' she said, and had hysterics again.

He said something in a foreign language, and she shook her head with incomprehension.

'That was Greek for I'm going to wipe that smile off your face, Leda.'

And suddenly the swan didn't look quite as comic. The beak had a sardonic leer, and the feet were tipped with sharp little claws. The sheer scale of the creature was intimidating in itself; she felt small and pathetically human by contrast. His arms were inside the wings; he flapped them experimentally a couple of times and a rush of air blew open her robe. She could see him watching her, his eyes dark against the white of the feathers, the rest of his face hidden. The bill opened, and then closed again. He could, presumably, operate it with his mouth. He took a couple of steps towards her – and suddenly the awkwardness had gone, he had mastered the intricacies of swanhood and the fantasy was up and running.

With a blow from his wing he knocked her sideways across the bed. She hadn't expected it to be so hard and she was momentarily winded. The robe slipped off her shoulders. Before she had time to recover he was kneeling above her, his leathery feet resting against her thighs, his wings beating as if to retain his balance. The claws were just as sharp as she'd imagined, and the feathers just as soft. He bent towards her and caught hold of the hair at the nape of her neck with his beak. She pushed at him with terrified vague fingers, exactly as Yeats's poem had dictated, and he straddled her, his weight holding her in position. She felt his knee force her legs apart, and then she felt the warmth of his feathery belly against hers. He began to move back and forth, and the feathers tickled and caressed her as intimately as his fingers once had. She closed her eyes and let the fantasy envelope her. It really felt as though she were being ravished by a swan – the brute strength beneath the down, the strange dusty smell when the feathers covered her face, the way her breath came back at her still warm. She fought against him, but her lack of success only increased her feeling of helplessness. The one time she did nearly manage to

271

wriggle free he hissed at her so aggressively that she stopped.

The feathers were damp now, where they'd trailed between her legs. The robe had fallen off altogether and her breasts were being subjected to the same sort of treatment as her clit. He kept the distance between them exactly right – it was like being seduced with dandelion clocks: breast, nipple, solar plexus, other breast, other nipple, then back again. She had dreamed of this, but never thought for a moment that anyone could make it a reality. Her skin was becoming more and more sensitive as he titillated it with his plumage; the pinpricks of his claws on her legs made the feathers seem even softer. The contrast heightened everything.

She felt his cock brush against her. The touch of real skin was like an electric shock. He changed position so that he could enter her. When he did it was fast, hard and accurate. The sudden friction inside her elevated her to a plane of arousal that felt positively Olympian. He whispered something else in Greek, but she was too far gone to ask him what he'd said. The orgasm overtook her like a tidal wave, and everything clenched into ecstasy over and over again.

When it was finished she felt oddly bereft. She didn't want a swan embracing her any longer, she wanted Eric. Wanted the warm soft furriness of his chest, the pleasantly abrasive touch of his chin, the muscular security of his arms.

Without saying a word he withdrew, stripped off the costume, yanked her by the ankles and pulled her down the bed. There was a real urgency to his expression now; serious, deliberate, purposeful. Then he entered her again, and she knew that he'd lost it already this time. His sudden and overwhelming need turned her on more rapidly than she could ever remember being turned on before. When the pleasure enveloped her it was once more white-hot in its intensity, and it left both of them exhausted.

They seemed to lie there for a long time, not saying anything, just stroking one another.

'We're not going to lose touch, are we?' said Fee eventually. He still hadn't verbalised anything about the future.

'I'm not very good at long-term relationships,' said Eric. 'Too self-centred. But I could handle the occasional wining and dining.'

'And holidays?'

'And holidays.'

Actually, thought Fee, that would suit me rather well. We're too different to make a permanent go of it. His pickiness would drive me round the bend eventually. But he's given me the confidence to look for the right sort of man. And until that happens –

'Roar, O gnat,' said Eric unexpectedly. 'Nine letters.'

Fee thought for a moment. Then she laughed and said, 'Rarotonga.'

Rarotonga? Whatever are you thinking of? Fee's mother's voice had been absent for so long that it took her quite by surprise. She stiffened slightly.

'But just you and me,' Eric said, smiling. 'We'll leave your mother behind. You could send her a postcard though.'

Visit the *Black Lace* website at

www.blacklace-books.co.uk

Find out the latest information and take advantage of our fantastic **free** book offer! Also visit the site for . . .

- All *Black Lace* titles currently available and how to order online
- Great new offers
- Writers' guidelines
- Author interviews
- An erotica newsletter
- Features
- Cool links

Black Lace – the leading imprint of women's sexy fiction.

Taking your erotic reading pleasure to new horizons

BLACK
lace

BLACK LACE NEW BOOKS

Published in August

MINX
Megan Blythe
£6.99

Spoilt Amy Pringle arrives at Lancaster Hall to pursue her engagement to Lord Fitzroy, eldest son of the Earl and heir to a fortune. The Earl is not impressed, and sets out to break her spirit. But the trouble for him is that she enjoys every one of his 'punishments' and creates havoc, provoking the stuffy Earl at every opportunity. The young Lord remains aloof, however, and, in order to win his affections, Amy sets about seducing his well-endowed but dim brother, Bubb. When she is discovered in bed with Bubb and a servant girl, how will father and son react?

**Immensely funny and well-written tale of lust among
decadent aristocrats.**

ISBN 0 352 33638 2

FULL STEAM AHEAD
Tabitha Flyte
£6.99

Sophie wants money, big money. After twelve years working as a croupier on the Caribbean cruise ships, she has devised a scheme that is her ticket to Freedomsville. But she can't do it alone; she has to encourage her colleagues to help her. Persuasion turns to seduction, which turns to blackmail. Then there are prying passengers, tropical storms and an angry, jealous girlfriend to contend with. And what happens when the lascivious Captain decides to stick his oar in, too?

**Full of gold-digging women, well-built men in uniform
and Machiavellian antics.**

ISBN 0 352 33637 4

A SECRET PLACE
Ella Broussard
£6.99

Maddie is a busy girl with a dream job: location scout for a film company. When she's double-booked to work on two features at once, she needs to manage her time very carefully. Luckily, there's no shortage of fit young men, in both film crews, who are willing to help. She also makes friends with the locals, including a horny young farmer and a particularly handy mechanic. The only person she's not getting on with is Hugh, the director of one of the movies. Is that because sexual tension between them has reached breaking point?

This story of lust during a long hot English summer is another Black Lace special reprint.

ISBN 0 352 33307 3

Published in September

GAME FOR ANYTHING
Lyn Wood
£6.99

Fiona finds herself on a word-games holidays with her best pal. At first it seems like a boring way to spend a week away. Then she realises it's a treasure hunt with a difference. Solving the riddles embroils her in a series of erotic situations as the clues get ever more outrageous.

Another fun sexy story from the author of Intense Blue.

ISBN 0 352 33??? ?

CHEAP TRICK
Astrid Fox
£6.99

Tesser Roget is a girl who takes no prisoners. An American slacker, living in London, she dresses in funky charity-shop clothes and wears blue fishnets. She looks hot and she knows it. She likes to have sex, and she frequently does. Life on the fringe is very good indeed, but when she meets artist Jamie Desmond things take a sudden swerve into the weird.

Hold on for one hot, horny, jet-propelled ride through contemporary London.

ISBN 0 352 33??? ?

FORBIDDEN FRUIT
Susie Raymond
£6.99

When thirty-something divorcee Beth realises someone is spying on her in the work changing room, she is both shocked and excited. When she finds out it's sixteen-year-old shop assistant Jonathan she cannot believe her eyes. Try as she might, she cannot get the thought of his fit young body out of her mind. Although she knows she shouldn't encourage him, the temptation is irresistible.

This story of forbidden lusts is a Black Lace special reprint.

ISBN 0 352 33??? ?

Published in October

ALL THE TRIMMINGS
Tesni Morgan
£6.99

Cheryl and Laura, two fast friends, have recently become divorced. When the women find out that each secretly harbours a desire to be a whorehouse madam, there's nothing to stop them. On the surface their establishment is a five-star hotel, but to a select clientele it's a bawdy fun house for both sexes, where fantasies – from the mild to the increasingly perverse – are indulged.

Humorous and sexy, this is a fabulour yarn of women behaving badly and loving it!

ISBN 0 352 33641 2

WICKED WORDS 5
A Black Lace short story collection
£6.99

Black Lace short story collections are a showcase of the finest contemporary women's erotica anywhere in the world. With contributions from the UK, USA and Australia, the settings and stories are deliciously daring. Fresh, cheeky and upbeat, only the most arousing fiction makes it into a *Wicked Words* anthology.

By popular demand, another cutting-edge Black Lace anthology.

ISBN 0 352 33642 0

PLEASURE'S DAUGHTER
Sedalia Johnson
£6.99

It's 1750. Orphaned Amelia, headstrong and voluptuous, goes to live
with wealthy relatives. During the journey she meets the exciting,
untrustworthy Marquis of Beechwood. She manages to escape his
clutches only to find he is a good friend of her aunt and uncle.
Although aroused by him, she flees his relentless pursuit, taking up
residence in a Covent Garden establishment dedicated to pleasure.
When the marquis catches up with her, Amelia is only too happy to
demonstrate her new-found disciplinary skills.

**Find out what our naughty ancestors got up to in this
Black Lace special reprint.**

ISBN 0 352 33237 9

To find out the latest information about Black Lace titles,
check out the website: www.blacklace-books.co.uk or
send a stamped addressed envelope to:

Black Lace, Thames Wharf Studios,
Rainville Road, London W6 9HA

Please note only British stamps are valid.

BLACK LACE BOOKLIST

Information is correct at time of printing. To avoid disappointment check availability before ordering. Go to www.blacklace-books.co.uk

All books are priced £5.99 unless another price is given.

Black Lace books with a contemporary setting

THE TOP OF HER GAME	Emma Holly ISBN 0 352 33337 5	☐
IN THE FLESH	Emma Holly ISBN 0 352 33498 3	☐
SHAMELESS	Stella Black ISBN 0 352 33485 1	☐
TONGUE IN CHEEK	Tabitha Flyte ISBN 0 352 33484 3	☐
SAUCE FOR THE GOOSE	Mary Rose Maxwell ISBN 0 352 33492 4	☐
INTENSE BLUE	Lyn Wood ISBN 0 352 33496 7	☐
THE NAKED TRUTH	Natasha Rostova ISBN 0 352 33497 5	☐
A SPORTING CHANCE	Susie Raymond ISBN 0 352 33501 7	☐
TAKING LIBERTIES	Susie Raymond ISBN 0 352 33357 X	☐
A SCANDALOUS AFFAIR	Holly Graham ISBN 0 352 33523 8	☐
THE NAKED FLAME	Crystalle Valentino ISBN 0 352 33528 9	☐
CRASH COURSE	Juliet Hastings ISBN 0 352 33018 X	☐
ON THE EDGE	Laura Hamilton ISBN 0 352 33534 3	☐
LURED BY LUST	Tania Picarda ISBN 0 352 33533 5	☐
LEARNING TO LOVE IT	Alison Tyler ISBN 0 352 33535 1	☐

-------✂-------------------

Please send me the books I have ticked above.

Name ....

Address ....

....

....

.... Post Code ....

Send to: **Cash Sales, Black Lace Books, Thames Wharf Studios, Rainville Road, London W6 9HA.**

US customers: for prices and details of how to order books for delivery by mail, call 1-800-805-1083.

Please enclose a cheque or postal order, made payable to **Virgin Publishing Ltd**, to the value of the books you have ordered plus postage and packing costs as follows:
    UK and BFPO – £1.00 for the first book, 50p for each subsequent book.
    Overseas (including Republic of Ireland) – £2.00 for the first book, £1.00 for each subsequent book.

If you would prefer to pay by VISA, ACCESS/MASTER-CARD, DINERS CLUB, AMEX or SWITCH, please write your card number and expiry date here:

....

Please allow up to 28 days for delivery.

Signature ....

-------✂-------------------